# Journey of a Fugitive

by

Raymond Graff and Jayne Dionisiou

Acknowledgements

We would like to thank everyone who encouraged and helped with the publication of this book.
For their dedication and support, we are especially grateful to Abdul, Alex, Charlie, Georgia, Hannah, Isabella, Katherine, Louise, Nadia, and Tim.

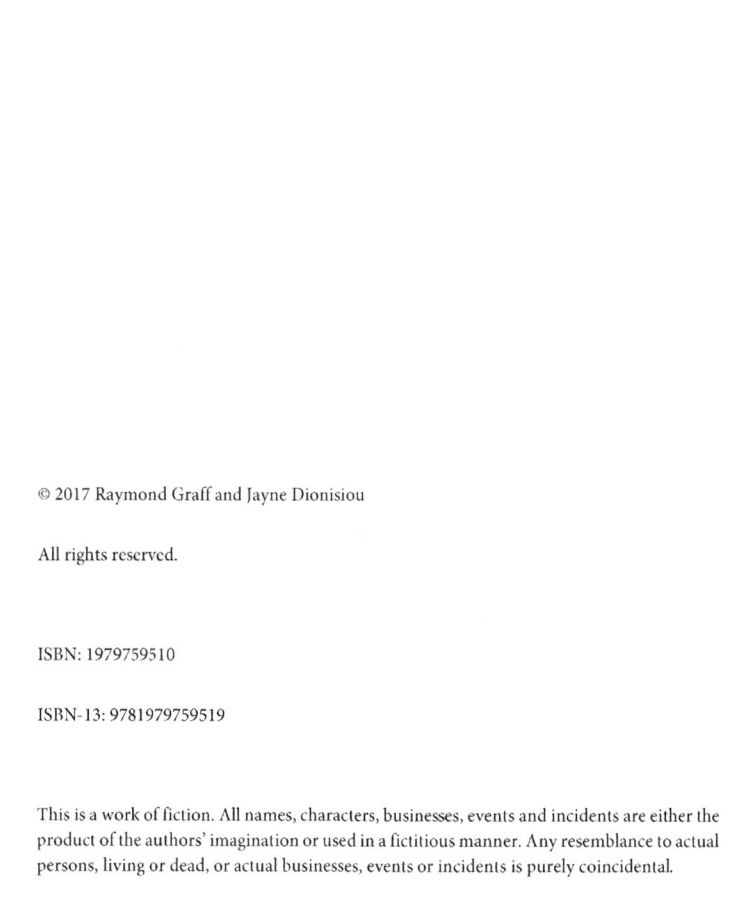

© 2017 Raymond Graff and Jayne Dionisiou

All rights reserved.

ISBN: 1979759510

ISBN-13: 9781979759519

This is a work of fiction. All names, characters, businesses, events and incidents are either the product of the authors' imagination or used in a fictitious manner. Any resemblance to actual persons, living or dead, or actual businesses, events or incidents is purely coincidental.

In loving memory of Shirley Irene Chubb, cherished mother of Jayne, who passed away during the writing of this novel. She will be forever missed.

8th March 1932 – 23rd October 2014

# Chapter One

As they soared through the dark skies, Ruth and her new husband, Javier, held each other's hand tightly. Ruth had been dreaming of their honeymoon, visiting a part of the world she had only read about in books. The lights of Heathrow glistened below as they climbed higher and higher, leaving the twinkling city of London behind them.

Who would have thought that Ruth, a twenty-one-year-old student, would now be married to the sophisticated, suave Spanish artist who had wooed her from the moment they met only eight months earlier?

The night they first saw each other, Ruth had popped into the Rosewood Hotel with her tutor from UCL where she was studying classics. A quick drink to discuss the day's lectures and then home—that was the plan until she felt eyes watching her intently. As she looked toward him, she melted. She had never seen such a beautiful face, and as she stared into his ebony eyes, she knew her life was about to change forever.

Nothing her family said would convince her. She was not able to slow down, consider the future, check out Javier's credentials. She was madly and passionately in love. This headiness was out of control, and Ruth loved it. The marriage took place in July 2013, just three weeks after their first meeting. The Marylebone registry office had a cancellation, and Javier had insisted they take the slot. Ruth willingly agreed, and with nobody else present apart from two young passers-by who had agreed to witness the unusual joining of the young girl to the rugged dark-haired artist, Ruth and Javier were pronounced man and wife.

Ruth had turned her back on her family and their concerns, and with heavy hearts, her parents had no choice but to let her go. They prayed she would see the folly of her ways and come home, back to the strong Jewish family that had cared so well for her for the last twenty-one years. But she was married now, and both her mother and father knew there was little they could do but wait and see as their little girl became the wife of Javier Manuel, an artist from Santiago de Compostela, twenty-five years her senior.

Javier had by all accounts travelled the world and was taking his bride on an exotic cruise to the Far East. He was excited to show her the world and to show the world his wife, the daughter of Moishe Cohen, the biggest dealer in ancient artefacts the world had ever known.

The seat-belt signs were switched off, and Ruth relaxed. She closed her eyes and imagined Javier's rugged features and artistic hands. She saw the perspiration that collected on his top lip and the dark sweep of hair that framed his olive skin, and she knew he was all she wanted.

The plane levelled, and Hong Kong was only hours away.

# Chapter Two

David had grown up in the oil-rich state of Texas. Always different, he struggled as a young boy. His mother drank too much, and his father was not often home. At the age of twelve, he was sent to special schools.

He never wanted for anything, but relationships were so very difficult for him. By his early twenties, he found himself alone, awkward, and wealthy. Both his mother and father had passed away, and David spent his days in the rambling family home with his only relative, Auntie Wilma, who wore too much makeup, drank too much whiskey, and never had a good word to say about anybody, except for David, who reminded her of her only brother, David's father, whom she had adored.

As the years passed, David's wealth increased, just because the oil continued to pump from the earth, and by the time he entered his sixtieth year, he was once again flying to Hong Kong to board the *Dream of the Seas* to embark on his tenth world cruise.

David felt safe in the bosom of his adopted family. Auntie Wilma had died, and he now found comfort with his fellow world cruisers. They understood he suffered with severe autism, and as the world had moved on, they made him feel secure and loved. He never felt alone as he cruised the world. He enjoyed meeting the small number of people who joined the ship for short journeys. They broke up the monotony of seeing the same faces day after day. He sipped his seventh—or was it his eighth large whiskey and wondered who he might meet on this adventure. He felt tired and closed his eyes. The hum of the aircraft sent him to sleep quickly. As he snored he was covered with a blanket, and the plane headed to Hong Kong.

# Chapter Three

It was a cold, rainy evening, quite typical of London. Karmen Zimmerman put the finishing touches to her lipstick, checked her slim figure in the tight-fitting rust dress she had bought that day, and left her bedroom. She walked elegantly down the sweeping marble staircase, her shoes clicking as she gracefully approached the bar that was situated in the gorgeous sunken living room of the apartment she shared with her husband, the famous diamond dealer Richard Zimmerman.

Her guests were due to arrive in an hour, and that gave Karmen time to visit the kitchen, make sure everything was in order, and check that the canapés were ready to go. Karmen was one of those natural beauties, a strawberry blonde with eyes that melted the hearts of most who met her. That was what Richard had noticed almost thirty years ago—the softest blue eyes he'd ever seen.

The kitchen was running smoothly with Jennifer at the helm, so Karmen felt able to relax, sit at the bar, and have a well-deserved vodka and tonic while waiting for Richard to come home and soon after greet their guests. She hoped Josephine and James would arrive first. They could have a minute to discuss their trip that began tomorrow evening: leaving Heathrow at 9:00 p.m. and flying to Hong Kong to join the *Dream of the Seas* cruise liner to explore the Far

East. It would have been rude to talk about their pending trip in too much detail in front of their friends; it would sound too show-offy. One thing Karmen knew was never to make anybody feel uncomfortable. This was another quality that Richard had fallen madly in love with—her caring nature to include everyone and make them feel special.

Yes, Richard had found a gem in Karmen, and as he parked his Ferrari in the underground carpark, said hello to the night porter, and took the lift directly into the apartment, he admired his wife's elegance and beauty. She sat at the bar, surveying their magnificent home with love and excitement. She appreciated her life as a child would when Christmas-time came, and he loved her for that too.

Richard was learning to enjoy life as his wife had always done. His business had grown from very humble beginnings. Back in those days, there were no expectations, just a hard-graft-and-pay-the-bills attitude toward life, and as luck would have it, he had created an empire that spanned the world. His diamonds were second to none, and he was the expert who had never forgotten his roots.

Josephine and James did arrive first, and Karmen swept them into the kitchen to discuss what lay ahead for all four of them tomorrow.

Josephine was entering into a new stage of her life. At fifty-four, she had recently placed her mother into a nursing home, and her only child had moved into a small flat in Maida Vale. Luckily, both she and James had a zest for life, and together they embraced the change that was coming their way. Karmen and Richard had loved these two from the first time they met, and tonight, years later, at the

Zimmermans' dinner party, Karmen, Josephine, James, and Richard spent a few moments in the kitchen discussing the journey ahead of them. Their excitement was etched all over their faces, and even though their ages added up to more than two hundred years, they felt like teenagers, full of expectations. They went through the final checklist, arranged to meet in the first-class lounge at Heathrow the following evening, and made their way to the front door as the other guests began to arrive.

Dinner was a success as usual at the Zimmermans'. Everyone had a wonderful evening, and in separate homes, Karmen and Richard and Josephine and James closed their eyes, thinking about the journey ahead.

First stop, Hong Kong.

# Chapter Four

Sven Larson had been the captain of numerous cruise liners. His career spanned thirty years, and at fifty-seven, he was delighted to be offered the head position on the world-renowned *Dream of the Seas*. His dear friend Antonio Cadiz had secured the placement some time ago, and Sven would be eternally grateful to him. After all, Sven needed calm and a stress-free working environment at his age. Gone were the days of boozy cruisers and the chaos that brought. An elderly, more sophisticated clientele was what he wanted, and with his colleague Sebastian Greco as the cruise director, he felt confident life would be slower and calmer, giving him time to concentrate on his well-being.

After all, the vast majority of the *Dream of the Seas* clientele were world cruisers, which meant they didn't want or need to cram fun and madness into a short two-week vacation. They had months. Routine was paramount to surviving so much time aboard a cruise liner circumnavigating the world, with all the wonderful food that could be eaten, not to mention the drink to be drunk.

Yes, Sven was embarking on his new position at the helm with an incredible sense of well-being.

Sebastian returned to sit next to his friend after chatting with the young stewardess. He really couldn't resist. He often thought he should go to Sex Addicts Anonymous so that perhaps he could learn to control the thing that he loved so much. Sex! It filled his every breathing moment. He had four gorgeous women scattered around the world, waiting desperately for his visits, and he juggled them well. His wife was content with the financial side of their marriage and never really questioned him. After all, he was away for months on end. She had become used to it and bringing up their three children aged from seven to thirteen kept her busy. The tennis coach who gave her lessons weekly kept her feeling like a woman, and as long as Sebastian never found out, she saw no reason to change the status quo.

Sebastian couldn't have cared less. He had already set his sights on the yoga teacher who was coming to join the ship for the season. She looked fit, and the thought of having her on the high seas made his body surge with a blood rush. Now that was what Sebastian lived for. Everything else—family, career, friends—all paled into insignificance. He thought of one thing and one thing only: sex.

The pretty stewardess passed by and smiled at him. She had always found men with silver hair attractive, and Sebastian was grey beyond his forty years. He decided to try his chances; it had been some time since he'd enjoyed pleasuring a fellow passenger at thirty-five thousand feet, and as he remembered it, she had been rather old and desperate. Now this fresh pretty thing excited him, and he knew the chase would be worthwhile. Life couldn't get better.

Hong Kong was getting nearer by the hour.

# Chapter Five

Richard, Karmen, Josephine and James were collected at the airport and whisked away with all their luggage, to begin their dream holiday - first stop, two nights at the Intercontinental Hong Kong, before they boarded the ship.

The first evening they ate seafood at a wonderful restaurant on the river. The food was fabulous and later that evening they sat in their hotel lobby having a night cap watching the skyline ablaze with lights and colours. Boats of varying shapes and sizes glided up and down the River which stretched majestically before them.

It was a spectacular setting.

They'd planned to explore the district of Kowloon the next day, so Richard could visit one of his many state of the art offices. He'd check on things and they'd grab some lunch in a Vegas style hotel that adorned the area. As they had to be up early, they decided to retire for the night to be fresh for the next morning.

Richard was pleased with his office, it was very impressive. The staff showed incredible expertise and enthusiasm. In the workshop the diamonds were displayed perfectly in magnificent cabinets, lighted to show the items in their full glory.

Richard quite rightly felt a sense of pride. He was, after all, a leader in the business of exquisite gems. His building oozed opulence, from the hand woven carpets, to the vases of magnificent flowers that covered the spare areas, nothing had been missed.

After a long lunch , it was time to go back to the mainland. The return ferry journey was extremely rough and both Karmen and Josephine felt terribly unwell. Nothing however that a late afternoon rest wouldn't put right and typically both ladies looked stunning as they met in the lobby to have their last meal together in Hong Kong.

The two couples sipped cocktails on the 130th floor of the Ritz Carlton. Dinner was booked for 9.00pm fifty floors below. The lights and bustle of the city were spectacular from both heights and the four friends laughed and chatted as they always did when they were together.

James lifted his glass and toasted them all…"Here's to a journey of a lifetime!"

"A journey of a lifetime!" came the response from the others.

February $22^{nd}$…The day had arrived. As they approached the ship they were full of expectations.

The six star 'Dream of the Seas' awaited their arrival at the port in Hong Kong. It was a beautiful day and as their luggage was taken away the four friends made their way up the gang plank. The liner was magnificent and the embarkation system simple.

As Richard looked around he observed a mixture of passengers boarding the ship. Some were so old they could hardly walk and others seemed far more energetic and lively. Suddenly his eye caught sight of a very odd looking woman. She looked like a freak. He wasn't sure if he should laugh or be frightened.

The woman had the body of a ninety-year-old with a hideously ugly face of a young girl. He'd never seen such a strange sight. She held an enormous umbrella over her head, shading herself from the sun. She looked as if she'd melt, should the rays touch her skin. It was as if she was made from plastic. He hoped he wouldn't dream of her tonight, one thing he knew for sure it wouldn't be a sexy dream, it would be a ghastly nightmare. Hopefully her disturbing image would leave his mind before he slept.

Everyone had now boarded, unpacked and were beginning to relax. Richard laid out on a sun lounger tanning and admiring his wonderful body, he had a very confident self-image!

Karmen and Josephine were chatting happily, sipping a cold glass of wine.

James, as always, thinking of his health and body shape, drank only water. He hardly ever had alcohol in the day.

Louis Armstrong's "What a wonderful world " echoed around the deck as the sail away began. Everyone was in a great mood. A large group of Brazilians, holidaying together, were the first to dance, once the band began to play. The ship slowly began to set sail and as the warm breeze blew gently, the place began swinging, the music creating a holiday spirit for all those on deck for the sail away.

Suddenly Richard heard his name being called from the other side of the deck. Looking up, the sun making it impossible to see, he knew he recognised the voice, but he couldn't see the face. A cloud interrupted the sunlight and the person became visible. Richard could focus and realised it was Oscar from Birmingham. Oscar had met Karmen and Richard on a previous cruise and the Zimmermans had tried to avoid him then. He had to be the loudest man in the world. Full of well-meaning but also full of annoying chit chat. Richard couldn't believe he was on this cruise too.

"Hi Oscar, how are you? I never saw you board."

"Come on Richard, you know I'm a world cruiser. I boarded in LA. We had the conversation the last time we met."

Richard changed the subject quickly " Oscar, these are very good friends of mine, Josephine and James and of course you remember my wife Karmen."

"Of course I do!" He gave Karmen a big, big hug. Anyone who'd met him, knew what he was like. He loved the ladies and as he hugged her, he pushed his body into her buxom bosom. He probably wasn't much different to most of the male species, just a little more obvious!

Then he turned to the others.

"Nice to meet you Josephine... James, hope we can have dinner. I'm on board for the world cruise so if you need anything, I'm your man."

Suddenly Captain Larson made an announcement. There had been a plane crash in the South China Seas, not far from where they were heading. He asked the passengers if anyone one had seen anything and to look out for any wreckage and let the crew know immediately if anything was sighted. The whole ship went into over drive. Crew members were everywhere. Oscar created a frenzy by saying he thought he'd seen something, but when questioned further, it was found to be nothing more than a pod of dolphins jumping out of the Ocean!!!! Typical of Oscar, he was always looking to be centre of attention, to be famous. Maybe one day he'd achieve his dreams.

He was married to a lady called Sadie. She let him get on with things, mostly. On previous cruises she'd put him in his place, from time to time, and then go off to play bridge, leaving Oscar free, to roam and annoy…

As nothing was sighted, things began to calm down and passengers began returning to their cabins.

Sadie had met a fellow bridge player, he was a handsome man in his late sixties.

A Mr. Playboy type, All the women seemed to be besotted by him. Maybe it was his salt and pepper suaveness or maybe it was because he had an immense amount of wealth.

On this cruise he occupied the largest penthouse.

He was the kind of man who thought every woman wanted to get into his pants.

He was somewhat delusional, even though he was extremely attractive.

Most of the ladies on board were interested in him and his athletic look, but there was an underlying intrigue, mainly due to his accommodation and, when the news spread that he had travelled with his personal Japanese chef and butler, his appeal grew!

As the ship left land behind, the two couples had a long lunch, sitting outside, watching the azure waters being carved in half by the enormous vessel that carried them.

Richard felt tired and as soon as he laid his head down on the sun lounger he went off to dream land.

As he slept, he heard someone call his name…slowly he opened his eyes and was blinded by the strong sunlight. He reached for his sunglasses and saw it was the Freak.

"What do you want?"

She smiled, her face contorting. "I know all about you, Mr. Zimmerman. You're a diamond dealer. The world's largest. You're going to be of great help to me, if you're interested."

Richard was frightened. How did this woman know about him? What was her agenda?

"I've a business deal for you. We need to discuss it. This could make you a billionaire, cash rich. I need you to come to my suite in an hour. My cabin number is eight eighty eight, a very lucky Chinese number."

In a flash she was gone…

Doris otherwise known as agent 739 had worked from the moment she breathed, it seemed. Her father was a secret agent with the CIA, the FBI and the SAS. She knew no other life.

She'd been educated at academies around the Western world. Lecture after lecture, attending drugging programmes that had started when she was fourteen years old, after her hormones had settled down. She was one of the most powerful agents the West had ever created. And yes created was the word. Due to years of experimental programmes, Doris was an enigma. She followed instructions like no other human being could, spoke ten languages fluently, had knowledge only a computer could access and made love to both men and women with such ability that those who were touched by her were never the same again. She did admit women were her preference. Those who worked with her thought she was the ultimate professional and over looked her strangeness.

Richard woke. Was he dreaming? He had a glass of water and got his thoughts together. Was the Freak there talking to him and if so, what was she talking about and how did she know so much about him? He'd never set eyes on her before boarding the ship. Maybe she'd checked him out on the Internet, after all, people's lives were out there for the world to access, if they wanted to.

He was worried, this woman was playing on his mind, things weren't stacking up.

James, Josephine and Karmen were still not back from lunch, probably getting pissed, as usual, he thought to himself.

What should he do? He checked his watch, five minutes to go... He decided he'd go to cabin 888.

He rang the bell, tentatively…

It opened…

There in front of him stood the most beautiful woman he'd ever seen, dressed only in her underwear. She was so incredibly sexy. Firm legs that were long, hips that held her panties gently, a waist that gorgeously showed her womanly figure to its fullest.....and large, full breasts that stood pert, temptingly. Her face was perfection, everything was symmetrically beautiful.

"Is this cabin eight eighty eight?" he spluttered.

"Come in Richard, you don't recognise me, do you? Rumours tell me you've nicknamed me 'The Freak'.....Looks can definitely be deceiving…Never judge a book by its cover, my mother always told me that and it's so very true, come inside."

Richard began to tremble, he felt out of his depth. He was confused, who was she? Surely it wasn't the same woman? This magnificent creature couldn't possibly be 'The Freak'?

As he walked into her suite she beckoned him to sit down and he did what he was told.

"I need to explain myself to you. I'm an ex CIA agent, now working with the Mafia underworld. The Brazilian and Russian Mafia are a powerful team. My real name is Doris. The plane that supposedly crashed into the ocean, didn't.

It was full of ex CIA agents, who, like me defected to the other side.... The plane was able to land and a submarine collected all our agents. They're below the ocean waiting for further information from our spies aboard ' Dream of the Seas'.

There's a South American drug dealer, probably the biggest in the world, on this ship. He's smuggled diamonds on board. He's concealed them in red, green and yellow peppers, all plastic replicas of the real thing. When he tries to get them off of the ship, our intention is to intercept and take them. This is a massive operation, probably amounting to 2.5 billion dollars."

Richard was flabbergasted. He was desperately trying to digest what he's ears were hearing.

"I know my darling Richard, it's a lot for you to take in. Please, my love, don't discuss our conversation with anyone"

With that she approached him and weaved her body around him. He became immediately aroused, she was so very sexy.

Suddenly he felt a sharp pain in his arm.

"What the hell was that?"

Doris smiled, "My darling Richard, I've put a pellet into your arm, one of the CIA's best. I can hear everything you do and I can make you do things you don't won't to. It's amazing how today's technology works. I'm not called agent seven thirty-nine for no reason, I've a reputation to uphold. As long as you have an iPhone on, I'm in complete control."

Richard left Doris's cabin in shock. He needed to absorb everything he'd heard and seen. Under his breath all he managed to say was " Fuck me." And with that he took a very deep breath…

The next morning, he woke in a cold sweat. His head was spinning. Karmen had gone down for breakfast and he laid wondering what he should do. Suddenly the phone rang. On answering, he heard her voice at the other end.

"Morning Richard. Have you had time to digest yesterday's conversation and work out how we move forward?"

Richard was in such a bad way that no words came from his mouth. His whole body was shaking.

Slowly, he managed, with a high pitched voice, to tell her he wanted nothing to do with her plan.

"The sea Richard, is a very dark and cold place at night. The sharks will swallow you up, never to be seen again. Are you completely sure you're not interested in being involved in joining me and my compatriots? You are, after all, an expert in diamonds and your knowledge is highly interesting to us all."

Richard put the phone down shaking…

As Richard was having breakfast and slowly getting his thoughts together, Doris's voice echoed in his ear.

"Enjoy your breakfast honey."

Richard almost jumped out of his skin. This woman was controlling him and he didn't like it. He hated to be controlled by anyone, especially by a woman. She was messing with his mind. He wondered if she knew he was a Scorpio, with a sting in his tail. She'd better watch out he thought to himself, he was one step ahead...or so he hoped.

Someone had dropped a piece of smoked salmon on the floor and as Richard went to refill his coffee he slipped on it, stumbling. The remains of his last cup went into the air and spilt all over a young lady who was quietly having breakfast with her husband.

Richard apologised profusely and just at that point, luckily, Karman arrived. She lightened the situation. Pouring tonic water on a cloth she managed to magically remove the stains.

The four of them started to chat and laugh and a new friendship was forged.

The breakfast buffet was due to close, so Richard left Karmen chatting, to refill his coffee and snatch a croissant with some butter and jam. As he made his way back to the others, he saw Mr. Playboy, who smiled and in a very friendly way asked Richard to come and join him. Richard, being Richard agreed. He loved to get to know people, and this guy was definitely worth getting to know.

"Please remind me of your name again, it's clear gone out of my mind."

Richard didn't think this guy had ever known his name, but courteously introduced himself.

"Nice to meet you Richard. My name's Antonio Cadiz."

The men shook hands and began talking.

"So Richard, how long are you on this cruise?"

"Sixteen nights, just to Singapore."

"Why so quick? you'll be off before you've settled."

"Some of us, my friend, have to work! How long are you on?"

"The whole world cruise, unless my circumstances change. Almost 4 months, I needed to get out of South America."

"Which part?" Richard knew the answer, but pretended he didn't.

"Brazil.... I've a supplying business that spans the Americas and beyond. You?"

A fucking drug dealer is more like it, Richard thought to himself. He turned his iPhone off... He didn't want Doris to be involved in any of this conversation.

"I'm in the diamond business Antonio."

"I love diamonds. The more you look at them, the more in love you are with them. Just like a woman, if she's the perfect one, of course. We must get together, I'm sure we could do business."

I bet we can, thought Richard. If you've as many diamonds as Doris says you've got hidden on this ship, I certainly could be your man. Approximately two point five billion dollars' worth, that sounds like a very, very good proposition.

"That would be fantastic Antonio, just call me and we'll have dinner and talk further."

As Richard took a sip of his coffee, he nearly choked as he saw Doris approaching. She had a habit of just appearing from nowhere. She wasn't in disguise. She looked fantastic.

Antonio's blue eyes nearly popped out of his head as she came up to them. He smiled at her, his teeth looking like piano keys against the tan of his skin. What a smoothie, Richard thought to himself...

"I haven't seen you before. Where have you been hiding, my gorgeous lady?" Antonio spoke with a velvety tone to his voice.

You have seen her before, thought Richard. She was dressed as a freak and you took no notice of her. I certainly can't blame you for that he chuckled to himself.

"This is a big ship; you can't always see everyone." Doris purred.

Antonio touched her hand. "You're so beautiful. Tell me something are you here with a partner, a husband?"

Doris leaned over and whispered loudly enough for Richard to hear. "You want to get into my knickers, I can see it in your eyes, your undressing me as we speak."

"What's all the whispering about? I'm feeling jealous and left out here." As soon as Richard spoke, Doris leaned towards him and kissed him on the lips, forcing her tongue slowly into his mouth. He was flabbergasted by her sudden action, but wanted it to last forever.

She broke away and left both men in a state of shock. They both knew she was trouble, but both desired her.

As she disappeared Karmen arrived. " Is everything OK, you look flustered?"

Richard was sure she had eyes in the back, front and sides of her head. Composing himself he replied, " I'm fine darling."

# Chapter Six

The dream of the Seas docked in Ho Chi Minh City and the four friends excitedly were taken to go on their pedicab tour that they'd booked on board.

Each person had a seat, behind a cyclist, who would take them around the whole of the city. As the trip began and the cycles left, Josephine and Karmen realised this was going to be one hell of an experience. Motor bikes tore around, weaving their way in and out of the individual cycles.

With more than three million bikes in the city, they all felt their lives were in danger and the further in to the heart of the place they went, the more chaotic it became.

Whole families travelled at speed, with no helmets. Children cuddling tight to the person in front of them. It seemed incredible that they didn't see anyone be killed.

The tour was exhilarating and the friends realised that Ho Chi Minh was a bustling, fast moving city, with great infrastructure, full of success.

Later that evening the foursome went for a local meal in a restaurant named Lemon Grass. They were all starving and typically ordered way too much. The food was delicious, if not a little filling.

While they were coping with reflux and wishing they had some Gaviscon to stop the acid from repeating, Richard's mind started to wander. What was Doris planning regarding the two point five-billion-dollar diamond heist?

He needed to talk to Antonio, Mr. Playboy himself and sideline Doris. The shit would hit the fan once they cut her out completely.

The plot was thickening and Richard felt great excitement and immense fear.

The ship left very late in the evening and arrived into Ko Samui the following morning.

They were taken by private transfer, arranged by Oscar, to a beach resort to have lunch and enjoy the one day they had on the beautiful Island.

After a short journey they arrived. The sea was turquoise and warm like bath water, the sand white and burning hot.

The friends took their positions on the beach and ordered some drinks.

Oscar seemed only interested in finding out where he could have a massage from a young Thai girl and disappeared off.

The others took little notice and let him carry on!

Suddenly Richard heard his name being called. When he turned around, he saw it was Mr. Smoothie himself, Antonio.

"Hi Antonio, what a great resort."

"Sure is Richard, come let's take a dip in the water."

As they strolled together Antonio spoke "I've been thinking, you have contacts I have gems. Together we can make a killing."

"OK Antonio, let's cut to the chase. How much are we talking about and where are the diamonds?"

Antonio looked at him seriously. " This is big Richard, we're talking about two-point-seven-five billion dollars. The diamonds are hidden safely on the ship. I can cut you in for twenty-five percent of the profit, which could make you a nice few million dollars. How does that grab you?"

Richard was speechless, but knew he had to act cool. Antonio obviously thought he could handle this.

He calmly replied, "OK, I'll give it some thought and let you know if I want to be involved."

If only Antonio knew Richard would have bitten his hand off to get a cut of this deal, but he remained calm and in control. The two men strolled back to the others as if nothing had happened.

Richard's head was spinning. How was this deal going to be crystallised? It wasn't going to be easy, but nothing was in this league.

Oscar came back with a smile on his face. No one asked him about his disappearance for the last hour.

Richard asked him if lunch needed to be arranged and Oscars reply was typical.

"Richard my boy, I've arranged everything, we've got the best table in the whole resort. Leave it all to me."

After lunch Richard had to hand it to Oscar. The lunch and setting were fantastic, although he couldn't remember much about what he ate, his mind was on bigger things. Much, much bigger things.

# Chapter Seven

The next morning, Jason, the butler, who was part of the package when you paid for a small penthouse, gave Richard a note. It read *AC is waiting for you*. Richard couldn't think what it meant, and then he twigged—of course, Antonio Cadiz.

His penthouse on the eleventh floor had bright crystal lights on either side of the enormous oak door. This denoted the wealth of the person inside. Antonio was spending four months behind these doors, cruising the world. Richard rang the bell. Antonio answered in a pure-silk dressing gown. The colour matched his vivid blue eyes, and with his piano-key teeth and bronzed skin, he really looked the part.

As Richard walked in Antonio asked what he'd like for breakfast ,reminding him that his chef was fully trained,

Richard said he was OK, but Antonio insisted he have what he was having. Richard agreed, even though he was not at all in the mood for food of any kind. He remembered to turn the receiver off because he was worried that Doris would pick up their conversation. She really frightened him and was always at the back of his mind.

"Well, Richard, do you have some good news for me on this beautiful morning?" The sun was beating down on his sundeck. It was large enough to host a party for at least a hundred people.

"Well, Antonio, I've given your proposal a great deal of thought. I need you to agree to something before we continue."

"What is it you want, Richard?"

"I don't know where to start."

"The beginning would be a good idea," Antonio replied as he poured them a drink.

Suddenly, Richard blurted out, "I need protection. My life's in danger!

Antonio was shocked, "What do you mean?"

"Just guarantee me that I will be OK."

"I'll give you protection. I'll fly in one of my top bodyguards. Then nobody will mess with you."

"Do I have your word?" Richard asked.

"When I give my word, that's my bond."

The men shook hands.

Richard continued, "I've been offered a deal to heist your diamonds. Listen, and do not interrupt; otherwise, I'll lose my train of thought. I've got some big surprises for you. The woman I call 'the Freak' is dangerous. You have no idea how crazy she is. Doris is the Freak when she's in disguise. Bet you can't believe that, can you? Doris knows all about your diamonds. She told me they are hidden in red, green, and yellow peppers. Someone is leaking information. She's working with the Mafia, she's an ex-CIA agent, and there's a submarine circling us with ex-CIA agents waiting on standby, ready to take the diamonds. She's asked me to be part of her team because I understand gems and have contacts. She's already threatened me if I pull out. Now you've offered me a deal and I've thought this through all night long and decided it would be better to do the deal with you, as you own the goods already. All I'd need to do is move them, which won't be an easy task, but if you give me protection and we dispose of Doris and her team, I think we can pull it off."

Antonio looked at Richard. "I can't believe that bitch was stringing me along. She'll suffer big time."

"Please, Antonio, be careful how you go about it because she'll know the information came from me."

"Let's leave things for now and think about our next move," Antonio sounded serious.

"Before I can commit to you, I want to see your bodyguard, as my life's at stake here. How will you get him on board the ship? He'll have to be with me twenty-four seven."

"Leave it to me," Antonio replied. "It'll be done."

That afternoon, Karmen and Richard spent time relaxing in the sun. Then about four o'clock, they went back to the penthouse to get ready for dinner. Luckily, Richard walks faster than Karmen, so he arrived at the room first. As he opened the door, he saw a note under it. *AC sorted B* was all it said. He understood it very well. Now they could dump

Doris and her threats. He loved it when a deal came together, but there was still a long way to go. Things were heating up and getting exciting. Tomorrow, Antonio and he would need to discuss how Mr. Tough Guy was going to board the ship.

# Chapter Eight

At breakfast in Antonio's penthouse, things were becoming clearer.

"Richard, your minder will be here tomorrow; all's been arranged. His name is Bruno Cortijo. He's gay, but don't underestimate him; he is one of my best. I trust him with my life. When you see him, you'll see what I mean. He likes to be called Brick because his body is as hard as one. I've arranged everything with the captain. It's cost me a roll of dollars, but it'll be a good investment, I'm sure. Brick's cabin will be on the eleventh floor, close to both of us, and you'll be safe.

We'll need to get that chip in your arm deactivated and removed. The doctor in the hospital on board will do it. The captain has arranged this procedure, so don't worry."

"Antonio, I'd like us to start planning how we're going to deal with Doris and her team because they'll be a thorn in our side, and as they're highly trained, we have to be careful. We also need to identify the informant."

"You're right, Richard, we'll have to dispose of them all quietly and quickly before we can move on. Be patient."

That night, Karmen and Richard were having a quiet dinner together in their cabin on the sundeck terrace.

"Darling," Karmen spoke softly, "I must tell you something really strange. I saw a really attractive woman today who reminded me of the ugly, freak woman who boarded the ship with us… Do you remember her?"

The thought of it sent shivers up Richard's spine. He knew he had to fill her in.

"Karmen, I want you to know that it was her. When we saw her as a freak, she was in disguise. She's actually very beautiful and very dangerous. Her name is Doris, she's a CIA agent."

Karmen made history – her mouth was open but nothing came out.

The relief that came over Richard, speaking to his wife, was like a weight being lifted from his shoulders. He told Karmen all about the plan with Antonio Cadiz, how they were going to make a new friend called Brick. He told her Brick was a minder, a hunk, but gay, so not to get any ideas.

"Don't question me yet, as we haven't worked anything out, but we are going to be very, very rich."

Karmen made history again. Richard was enjoying this. How many more times could he get Karmen to make history?

"Please be careful. This is very dangerous," Karmen replied after the longest silence he'd ever witnessed from her. He didn't let on that Doris would be living in the land of the fairies, either dead or brain dead once Antonio was finished with her. He just hoped the Brazilian drug lord knew what he was taking on. Doris, after all, was one of the best the West had created, and now she worked for the biggest criminal organization in the world. She was a frightening woman, to say the least.

# Chapter Nine

James and Josephine had taken a dislike to Sebastian Greco, the cruise director. There was an arrogance about him. He spent most of his time flirting in public areas with the yoga teacher, Sophia, and seemed little interested in his passengers. He had someone different by his side each night, whether crew or cruiser, and somehow the ladies seemed to swoon over him.

On one particular evening, when everyone was dancing in the bar and Sebastian was drinking red wine with Sophia, the music stopped, to everyone's disappointment. James approached him and asked him to sort things out. After all, he was the person in charge of the guests' enjoyment, and they were having a wonderful time. With a smirk on his face, Sebastian said that the night was over and left the bar with his hands tightly gripped around Sophia. James was furious, and the passengers had no choice but to go to bed. Sebastian couldn't give a damn. Sophia was putty in his hands now; his perseverance was paying off, and his night was just beginning.

James and Richard decided they would try and fix Sebastian up with a transvestite from one of the acts, put a hidden camera in the cabin, and show the action on one of the channels broadcast in all the staterooms on board. That would put an end to Sebastian's arrogant ways; he would have no self-respect left at all. And seeing as Antonio Cadiz had the captain in his pocket, anything was possible. What a bastard that Sven Larson had turned out to be; money could buy anyone. "Let's have some fun and watch Sebastian's downfall," Richard said.

The following day, Richard went to see Antonio, he didn't want to talk on the phone. On his way he saw Oscar, or rather Oscar's belly first. He was getting fatter by the day. Poor Oscar.

"Hi, Oscar, how you doing?"

"Great. I'm just on my way to have breakfast with the Captain. As I'm a world cruiser I have special treatment you know." Oscar winked and sauntered off.

Under his breath Richard muttered "Get a life, Oscar, and fuck off. Hope you get food poisoning. At least then you'd lose some weight."

Richard got to Antonio's cabin, stopped, and looked at the entrance. You're so flash, he thought to himself, but good luck to you, even though you're making the world into cokeheads. But if it hadn't been Antonio, it would have been someone else, he reckoned. Richard wondered if Antonio ever felt guilty. He decided he didn't.

He knocked on the door. Antonio opened the it in his silk dressing gown. "I knew it was you because everybody else rings the bell. When will you learn?"

Richard thought Antonio must have a mental illness because small things drove him nuts. He wondered if he was indulging himself with his own product.

"Hi, Antonio. I've some news for you. I've told Karmen about our plans, she can be trusted"

"How do you know for sure?"

"Please, Antonio, trust me."

"Richard, I don't trust my own shadow."

"Well, this time trust me."

"OK, but if you knock on my door again and don't ring the bell, I'll kick you so hard that your balls will end up in your mouth."

Richard was convinced Antonio had lost the plot, but would make sure he rang the fucking bell next time. A definite cokehead, he thought.

"When will Brick be on board?"

"He's here now. You're booked to go to the ship's hospital to have the chip removed from your arm at two thirty p.m. Brick will go with you to make sure the job's carried out correctly. We'll discuss how we're going to deal with Doris later."

Suddenly Richard heard a noise in the bedroom. "Who's that?"

"One of the showgirls." Just as he spoke, a beautiful girl came out from the room, wearing a G-string and a bra two or three sizes too small for her. Her legs went on forever. How Antonio could stand the pace with this amazing woman Richard couldn't fathom, but he would've liked a try. His head was running away with him. What chance did he have to compete with this man? Why would a woman like this let him near her, when Antonio could give her the world and more?

The doorbell rang, and Antonio said, "Open it, Richard."

"What am I now? Your messenger?" Richard moaned under his breath, but opened the door anyway. My God he thought to himself. Standing in the doorway was something so big it looked like the Incredible Hulk when it turns green and wild, but this apparition was black and extremely relaxed.

"Hello, darling," he said in a seductive voice.

Richard nearly wet himself as he held in his laughter.

"My name's Brick. Who are you?"

Antonio saw Brick at the door and shouted, "Come in. This is Richard, the guy you're going to protect with your life."

Brick took Richard's hand and shook it. Richard thought his arm was going to come out of its socket. "Looking forward to taking care of you, darling."

Suddenly, Richard started to get worried.

"Brick, don't start with him. He's not your sort. If you feel randy, I'll arrange something, but don't mix work with pleasure." Antonio sounded mad.

Hang on, Richard thought, don't I have a say here? Then a wonderful idea came to him. What about getting Sebastian and Brick together? What a scream that would be.

The time had arrived for Richard's operation to remove all control from Doris. Brick turned up at 2:25 p.m. and escorted him down into the ship's medical quarters. The doctor gave Richard a jab in his arm, and the next thing he knew, he was back in his cabin. All done, but his arm was killing him.

Antonio called. "All went well, I understand."

"You should see my arm. It's really hurting," replied Richard.

Antonio growled, "Grow up, or I'll send Brick in to give you something to really think about."

"Maybe I can cope with the pain after all" Richard whimpered.

"Thought you might say that, you big girl's blouse."

The phone rang again. This time it was Doris. "I've lost contact with you. Is there something wrong?"

"No, there's nothing wrong. The chip is out of my arm, and I think you should lie low because your days are numbered," Richard stammered.

With that he hung up the phone, and their connection was lost.

# Chapter Ten

Bruno, aka Brick, knocked on the door of Richard's cabin. Karmen opened it. Standing there was an enormous frame, a giant of a man.

Karmen gasped. "Can I help you?"

"Yes," he said. "I have come to see Richard. He's expecting me. You must be Karmen. I've heard a lot about you."

Richard came out of the bathroom with a towel wrapped around his waist. "Hi, Brick, you're early. Would you like some coffee?"

"No, thanks. You get ready. I'll wait for you outside. This cabin is too small for the three of us. Take your time. I'll go through today's agenda with you when you're dressed." With that he left.

Karmen looked at her husband. "Who the hell was that?" She looked totally bewildered.

"He's our minder. We can't trust Doris. When she finds out that I'm not part of her plans anymore, she could be extremely dangerous. We need protection. Antonio has provided us with his best, this guy will protect us with his life."

They both got dressed quickly. Karmen left, and Richard invited Brick back in. As Brick strode through the cabin, Richard knew no one would mess with him.

"I just love your fashion sense, darling," he purred.

"Whose? Mine or Karmen's?"

His reply took Richard by surprise. "Come on darling, your's of course."

Richard started to worry. Was this guy hitting on him, he wondered. He needed to stay focused and forget about this possible attraction. There were far more important things to concentrate on at the moment.

Richard's thoughts were interrupted as Brick spoke. He'd been with Antonio earlier that morning and had the agenda that needed to be discussed.

1. How to snuff out Doris and her team, including those in the submarine below the water. Captain Larson had located their whereabouts and was tracking every movement they made.

2. Deciding when they would make their move. Timing would be crucial.

3. Getting the diamonds off the ship, bearing in mind that they wanted to create little or no fuss. It needed to be an unnoticed operation, very casual, creating absolutely no suspicion.

4. Finding out who Doris's informant was. Someone, they knew, was feeding her information.

5. Deciding who would transport the gems and how many people should be involved.

6. Choosing who they wanted and needed to create the perfect team for the operation. They would have to be reliable and totally trustworthy.

7. Coming up with a plan to deal with Sebastian Greco because he was an absolute ass, and they all wanted to take him down.

In answer to the points raised, Richard quite rightly suggested that Doris was the one they needed to focus on, as the gems could be stolen by her and her team at any time. Then there would be a huge problem.

He agreed the informant needed to be identified, the sooner the better.

Brick nodded. He was in total agreeance. Doris, her team, and the insider needed to be priorities. Everything else could wait. After all, they were on a world cruise.

Richard suggested that the goods be moved to Singapore or South Africa as the customs agents there were notoriously laid back. They were more interested in stopping drugs from entering their country than anything else. It might be a good idea to split the haul into a number of batches. That way, they had better odds of getting them through. By splitting the gems and having a number of runners involved, along with a few decoys, they might get lucky and get them through customs with only minimal collateral damage. Perhaps, if all worked well, no one would be stopped, and they could be home and dry, $2.75 billion richer!

"Brick, I think we should consider a few people who could potentially be part of a trustworthy team," said Richard.

"Leave it with me. I'll talk to Antonio and fill him in on our conversation. By then it should be clearer what our next move will be. It 'll also give you and your friends time to relax a bit and enjoy yourselves. After all, this is a holiday, even though it's turned into something quite different."

Richard agreed and Brick left.

Karmen was in the Spa. James was in the gym pumping iron, and Josephine sipped a cocktail on her balcony, looking out to sea as the sun began to set. This evening, the couples were meeting for dinner, taking in a show, and then potentially heading for the club, where karaoke was on the agenda.

Only Richard knew fully what was going on under the facade of the calm, beautiful cruise. Perhaps he needed to discuss things with them, he thought. Karmen knew some of it but definitely not everything. He just wanted to decide when. After all, he had two days until he met with Brick again. Maybe he should just enjoy the cruise for a moment. He knew his back was being covered, so he could relax.

# Chapter Eleven

Antonio sat in his penthouse. It was time to bring everyone together and reveal his master plan. He called Brick and arranged a meeting for midnight. He told Brick that from now on, all participants were to use the code name SMEG when communicating with one another. Simple to remember and obviously *gems* spelled backward.

Brick felt the adrenaline rush through his enormous frame. Tonight, he thought, the show goes on the road! Richard was the first person to be contacted. He was, after all, vital to the whole operation. The knowledge and expertise he had with diamonds could not be surpassed, and how to distribute them was paramount. Richard obviously had contacts around the world, and this was going to be so very important to the success of the operation that was about to begin.

Everyone else subsequently received calls, inviting them to drinks in Antonio's penthouse. Just prior to midnight, the group gathered. When everyone was seated, Brick filled them in on Antonio's grand plan and how each of them had a role to play.

As the clock struck midnight and drinks were being served, Antonio arrived. An air of power surrounded his every move, and everyone watched as he took his seat.

"Good evening, everyone. I 've called this meeting to discuss the plan I've been creating. From now on, we have to be professional, aware at all times of our security, and watch out for one another. This operation will be referred to as SMEG, is that clear?"

"Yes, boss" was the immediate reply.

Antonio looked around at his team members. He took a moment to look directly into each and every one of their eyes, starting with Brick, to his left and then Richard, Josephine, James, Karmen, Captain Larson, Javier, Ruth, and lastly Oscar. No one flinched. They returned his gaze, and they all felt an immediate respect inside the walls of the luxurious room where they were all seated.

"I've been checking the seven of you out over the last few weeks, and I believe I can put my trust in all of you. Brick, as some of you already know, has worked by my side for years, and I would trust him with my life. Captain Larson has been known to me for some time now. I think I am a very good judge of character, but should I be proven wrong and anyone tries to double-cross me, you'll be dead meat. If, however, you remain part of this operation, trustworthy and loyal to me, and SMEG runs smoothly, you'll all end up wealthier than you could ever have dreamed. Is that clear?"

Once again, Antonio held everyone's gaze, and then in unison, the reply came again: "Yes, boss!"

The respect in the room was palpable.

"You're probably wondering how I got you all here. Well, I've been planning an operation called SMEG for some time now, and I've been studying each and every one of you closely. I decided you were going to be part of my team long ago. I'll give you the details as to why I chose you later. First, let me tell you how I got you all here.

"Please cast your minds back to when you originally booked your cruise of a lifetime. Remember the amazing discounts your travel agents offered you? Prices none of you could refuse?"

There was an uncomfortable silence, Ruth looked at Javier, and he felt the heat rise around his collar. Perspiration gathered on his top lip. He remembered well, his travel agent offering a whopping fifty percent discount. He couldn't believe his luck and decided to mention nothing to his new wife. She had seen the brochure price, and he wasn't going to say a word.

Richard and James had used the same travel agent, and both now remembered the joy they felt when he had surprised them with their invoices—almost half the price that they were anticipating. Both men shared the news with their wives and ordered an extra-expensive bottle of red the evening they celebrated the final payment on their pending holiday. Since then, they hadn't given it any more thought.

"Well," continued Antonio, "it was I who approached your travel agents. I paid the balance of your fares directly to them, plus a very nice bonus, to make it worth their while and to keep their mouths shut. And here you all are, just as I had hoped. You should realise that in life, you never get anything for nothing without strings attached."

He spoke with a smirk on his face, and a shiver went down everyone's spine.

"We have a problem that we have to deal with before we can move on. The lady we have seen, the hideous-looking one with the umbrella—you know who I'm talking about?"

Everyone nodded.

"She was named 'the Freak' by Richard, who has had dealings with her." Eyes turned toward Richard, but Antonio continued. "Her real name is Doris. She's extremely dangerous. We need to examine her closely. Someone on board this ship has been informing her of my intentions. She's working with the CIA, and under the waters, agents are lying in wait in a submarine. They think we're unaware of them. But we've been watching them, and with our captain's help, we've them tracked."

Captain Larson smiled and nodded.

"This penthouse has been debugged, so their ability to listen to us has been reduced, but always be careful. By tomorrow all our staterooms will be cleared of their listening devices. We'll be able to close in on them all shortly. Once we've dealt with them, SMEG moves into the next stage of its operation—removing two-point-seven-five billion dollars' worth of diamonds from the ship. We need to do this in a casual way, bringing little attention to ourselves, mixing with fellow cruisers and acting normally throughout. We need to get the diamonds abroad, sell them, and launder the proceeds carefully so nothing can be traced back to me."

Those who had never heard any of this before were dumbfounded, their brains trying hard to digest what they'd been told. Brick and Richard were composed. Karmen was slightly calmer. The others were in shock, and when Antonio spoke again, they couldn't believe what he said.

"You may all be surprised to know that two-point-seven-five billion dollars' worth of top-quality diamonds is not really a very large quantity, although their value is vast. Our haul is hiding in a locked deep-freeze cabinet. I've arranged for us to go and view the diamonds tomorrow, in the early hours of the morning when the kitchens are free of staff. Brick will contact you when the coast is completely clear. They're magnificent. I think we should refill our glasses and toast the future."

Moments later, the champagne was flowing. "To SMEG, to our futures. Let the journey begin."

"To SMEG," repeated the others.

The stars twinkled in the clear skies as the *Dream of the Seas* moved quietly through the ocean. Below the waters CIA agents were listening in but heard nothing. Antonio was one step ahead of them.

# Chapter Twelve

The next morning, with heavy heads, team SMEG was rising. The evening had continued into the early hours, and a bond was forming amongst them all. Excitement, nerves, fear, and anticipation were emotions everyone was feeling.

Karmen and Richard showered and arranged to meet Josephine and James for breakfast. Javier and Ruth decided to have coffee in their room. Captain Larson, being the ultimate professional, was at the helm of his ship alongside his cruise director, Sebastian, who unsurprisingly looked worse for wear. Sven assumed, quite rightly, that the yoga teacher had kept him extremely busy the night before. If it wasn't for SMEG, Captain Larson would have taken his second-in-command to task; he was definitely behaving badly, considering his position. But Sven had too much else on his mind, so he turned a blind eye to the appalling behaviour his colleague was demonstrating.

Oscar and Sadie were busy talking to their children and grandchildren on the phone. After all, as world cruisers, they saw no family for months on end, so a catch-up every now and again was to be expected. Somehow, though, Oscar's mind was elsewhere. He was thinking of the money and fame he might one day have. Sadie didn't even notice; with her grandkids on the mobile and bridge to follow, Oscar was the last person she was thinking about.

The day was beautiful, the seas calm, and as no one had anywhere important to go to until they heard from Brick, they carried on like all the other passengers having a wonderful time.

After a great evening meal, the eight members of SMEG returned to their penthouses and staterooms, not sure whether to retire or wait to receive the anticipated call. It wasn't long before they heard that clearance had been given, and they made their way down to the rendezvous point on deck eight.

Luckily for Oscar, Sadie was sleeping soundly when the call came through, so he slipped quietly out of his room. He did, however, have a slightly heavy heart. He knew that even if Sadie had been awake, she really wouldn't have cared a less if he disappeared in the early hours of the morning, as long as he didn't bother her.

What, he wondered, had happened to them? It hadn't always been like this, or had it? He decided to stop thinking. SMEG needed his full and undivided attention.

After the ten of them quietly collected outside the coffee shop on deck eight, Antonio led the way. It was funny to see the ship so empty and still. They went down to the lowest deck that the guest lift had access to, and from there they followed Antonio deep into the bowels of the ship. They went through door after door, corridor after corridor, and climbed down metal staircases that took them lower and lower, until they could hear the massive ship being enveloped in cold, dark, endless waters.

Josephine suddenly felt aware of the enormity of the ship and even more, the enormity of the ocean in which they surged through. So far down, everything seemed louder, colder, and more frightening. The metal around them creaked and groaned with every movement. Gone was the decor, the furnishings, the gold, and the glamour. Here, only rusty pipes that went on for miles, connecting one end of an enormous metal casing to another. They reached the very deepest part of the *Dream of the Seas*. Somehow, it now seemed more like the nightmare of the seas.

Suddenly, Antonio's voice interrupted the hollow whine that surrounded them. "You need to wrap yourselves up now; the temperature will change dramatically as we pass through the next few doors. Don't be deceived by the heat and humidity you're feeling at the moment."

The door ahead was smaller than the one before, and as they passed through it, there was a dramatic decrease in warmth. Another corridor, another staircase and then suddenly approaching the third metal door ahead of them, they felt the coldness embrace them. As they walked through, it became freezing. Then they all realised they were getting closer to the diamonds.

The cold store was minus twenty-five degrees; luckily Brick had warned them to wear warm layers. However, no one had anticipated such freezing conditions. Josephine, Karmen, and Ruth felt as if their noses were about to fall off, and even with sweatshirts wrapped around their heads, their ears were numb beyond anything they had ever experienced.

"Antonio, why the hell didn't you tell us to pack some woolly scarves and woolly hats? It's bloody freezing," Josephine said through chattering teeth. Antonio shot her one look, and that was it; he just ignored her as if she had never spoken. Josephine pushed her freezing fingers deeper into the pockets of her sweater and bowed her head.

"Are you ready to see the most magnificent collection of gemstones ever to be in one place at one time? This collection has taken over ten years to bring together. Some lives were lost in the process, but those who fell have never been forgotten. Without them SMEG would never have existed."

Antonio looked toward Brick and nodded. Together, they walked to the huge door that faced them and began turning the enormous handle situated right in the middle. They seemed to be struggling. Antonio suggested that the hinges were perhaps frozen; Brick agreed. He stepped back, took a deep breath, and with one foot on the side of the door, turned and pulled. His face grew darker, the veins in his biceps enlarged and protruded massively from his muscles. Suddenly, with an almighty cry that sounded like a dying animal, the door opened.

Inside, they could all see trays of green, red, and yellow peppers, perfectly wrapped in cling film, sitting side by side on metal trays.

"This is it!" shouted Oscar, rubbing his frozen hands together in glee.

"What's going on here?" snapped Antonio. "Shut it, Oscar. If you want to be involved, don't be a dickhead. Have a day off and act like a grown man." Oscar stood there, mouth open, feeling very embarrassed.

Slowly, Antonio opened a pepper. Inside, the diamonds were sparkling. As he removed a single gem from its casing, it frosted over from the freezing conditions. And when it was returned to its hiding place inside the pepper and placed back behind the door, they all took turns looking at it as it returned to its sparkling splendour.

Antonio showed them a number of diamonds in varying sizes and colours, some as large as eggs, in shades of blue, pink, yellow, brown, and the whitest of white. They all looked in amazement. Never had any of them seen such beauty. Nobody spoke; they were all in awe of the diamonds' magnificence and their immense value.

Antonio explained that with diamonds, you had to be incredibly careful not to let them touch each other. Because they were the hardest material known to man, if one should rub against another, it could cause lasting damage—chipping, fracturing—and seriously reduce their value. So at all times, they had to remember to use cotton wool when handling them.

Javier was the first to speak; he asked if the trays behind the door contained all the diamonds in operation SMEG. He was extremely surprised to be told that, yes, what they saw was the sum total of $2.75 billion worth of gems. Javier's reply made them all giggle slightly: "This is going to be a piece of cake!"

Antonio told them they were docking in Singapore the day after tomorrow. The ship would be there for three days, so the time had come to move one step nearer to D-day. Each one of them took five trays from the storage unit, and Brick closed the door tightly behind them.

No one spoke. They held on to the trays, aware of their immense value. The cold was no longer noticeable. Slowly, they retraced their footsteps, and before they knew it, they were back outside Antonio's penthouse. No one had seen them; the security cameras had been turned off from the bridge. They entered carrying $2.75 billion worth of diamonds and placed them on the dining-room table. Five high, ten in total. No one could believe that fifty metal trays could be worth such an incredible sum of money. As champagne was poured, the group began talking about life and families. It was as if the future was something everyone was reluctant to talk about. Bonds were being forged, and for a moment, SMEG was not being considered.

Javier was leaving the guest bathroom as Antonio passed by, and he took advantage of their time alone. He asked the question that others had no doubt been thinking: Why, if Antonio owned these wonderful diamonds, did he have to hide and smuggle them in such an elaborate way?

Antonio liked Javier's directness and realised he had a very bright and inquisitive person on his team. He told Javier to meet him in the study, just along the corridor to the left, in ten minutes. He would explain everything then. The others were laughing and joking in the main sitting area. They were unaware that the two men were missing. Brick was getting to know everyone and had an immense feeling of pride that he was responsible for these wonderful people Antonio had introduced him to. He was a good man and a bloody incredible minder. He would protect them all with his life.

As Javier entered the beautiful oak-panelled study, Antonio was seated in a comfortable worn chair. He beckoned Javier to sit, pouring them each a brandy, and as the two men sat opposite each other, he began to explain.

"I've a large bounty on my head. The Brazilian government has been searching for me for some time. I'm on the run from my country. When police found a large haul of cocaine along with other hard drugs and cash linked to me, they knew they had cracked my lifetime operation. I was the king, the drug baron who ran Rio's streets. I'd done it for years and years, as had my father before me.

They started to blackmail me, and after a while, they began squeezing me, not happy with a fair cut of the take. They wanted more and more, until I felt like I was fucking working for them. And Antonio Cadiz works for no one!

I stopped my payments to them, and then I heard that government officials were very upset, as their backhanders had stopped as well. They were planning to incarcerate me in Rio's most notorious hard-labour prison and take over my operation.

I managed to get out of Brazil, taking a small fortune with me. I've worked all my life. It's been hard rising to the top and taking my inherited operation to levels beyond my father's wildest dreams. In the drug world, there are murders more violent than you could ever imagine. I've seen it all.

I ran the biggest sex cartel in South America, importing women and men from every corner of the globe. I controlled everything, even the scumbag pimps. I never felt proud of what I did, but I grew up with it. I had an obligation, and the power felt good. I always looked out for the underdog, and Christ, there were plenty of those. When the police and the Brazilian government started to squeeze the life out of me, I knew the time was right to exit."

Javier was mesmerised. "So how did you get involved with diamonds?"

"I met some people in Bombay. When I escaped from Brazil, I went to India to spend some time with an old school friend. We were both in England at boarding school years earlier. He was from the United States. Came from an oil-rich family in Texas. He was a good guy and unlike anyone I'd ever met before. He had a simplicity about him that touched me.

We never saw each other after our school years, but kept in contact, letter writing, that sort of thing, and when I needed to get away, I called him. I wanted to be free of confusion and heaviness. I remembered how easy things were when I was around David, he and I alone, just enjoying calm and quiet. Such a far cry from the family I left behind in Brazil. Those boarding-school days always remained close to my heart.

He invited me to join him in Bombay. He had recently lost his last family member, a rich old eccentric aunt. I'd never been to India, so I decided to join him. When we met up all those years later, David was still the odd American boy I remembered from Burridge boarding school in Berkshire, England. We spent two wonderful weeks together. David would walk the streets, caring for every child, adult, and animal he came across. He gave away a small fortune to those he met, and as worried as I was that he would find himself in trouble, he came back every day, safe and sound, filled with the innocent joy of giving and helping those less fortunate than himself. He made me feel good for the second time in my life.

It was there I met a friend of David's family, the son of one of the largest diamond dealers in the world. He and David had known each other from birth, and I immediately knew Vickran cared deeply for him. Vickran Hirani was a Hindu and had a spirituality about him that matched David's. I felt at ease with them both and could happily leave Brazil and the corruption behind for a while.

Vickran had offices around the world, selling the most magnificent diamonds. I was introduced at a cocktail party to an Arab customer of Vickran's called Ali, who was part of the Saudi royal family, and an elderly man called Raj, who was part of an old maharaja family. I found out rather quickly that Raj was desperately in need of money.

I had the cash, he had the jewels. Within a few days, I had bought the family's collection. We were both happy. I wanted to get rid of the heavy, ornate gold jewellery. Ali Musan thought his wives might like them to add to their never-ending collections, so we struck a deal.

Then I bought diamonds from Vickran, who gave me good prices. After all, we had a dear friend in common, David, and as I said good-bye to my old school buddy, I felt sad. I wasn't sure when or if we would meet again, but I'd managed to transform my blood money into exquisite diamonds—light, transportable, and extremely beautiful.

The Brazilian government is still searching for me, but I managed to find someone who could be my twin. He has flown to Japan to take them off the trail for a while. By the time they realise they have been following the wrong guy, I hope to have had plastic surgery to change my appearance, change my identity, and live a quiet life on a remote island somewhere. So now all I need to do is get these diamonds off the ship in Singapore and sell them, realise the cash, pay you guys your share, and get on with living my life."

There was silence for a while, and then Javier thanked Antonio for being so honest.

"You screw me," added Antonio, "Brick will deal with you. Don't underestimate him; he can be vicious. I've seen grown men cry when he gets his hands on them."

"You have nothing to worry about with me or the others, Antonio. We will all do you proud."

The two men shook hands and made their way back to the lounge to join the others. As they mingled, it was clear they hadn't been missed. Antonio clapped his hands and cleared his throat. Everyone stopped what they were doing and turned toward him. He oozed power, and the respect in the room for him was enormous.

"Now let's look at our merchandise!"

Slowly and very carefully, the diamonds were taken out of their hiding places and laid gently on the felt cloth that covered the enormous table. There were a few gasps as the whole of the collection sparkled before them.

"Which ones can we have?" Josephine and Karmen said in unison.

"Are they exciting you?" came Antonio's reply. He smiled at them both in a flirtatious way and said nothing to answer their question. He continued, "Later on, Javier will fill you in as to how and why this operation came about. These beautiful gems before you are our passport to freedom and new and exciting lives. But first, we need to concentrate all our attention on Doris and her team. She is highly trained, as are her colleagues. They believe they are tracking my every move, but I am one step ahead. With Captain Larson's help, we are now tracking *them*!

"It's nearly time to dispose of them all. I'll leave you for a while so Brick can outline how we're planning to do this, and Javier can update you on the history that has brought me here. We've also managed to identify the person who's been leaking information to Doris. It came as quite a shock, but now that we know, we can deal with him."

"Who is it?" shouted everyone, pretty much at the same time.

"Brick, you take over. I have a pressing engagement. Goodbye, ladies and gentlemen. I look forward to seeing you all later." And with that Antonio left.

All eyes darted to Brick.

"I'm saddened to tell you that our informant is none other than our cruise director, Sebastian Greco. We all know what a scumbag he is, but finding out he's an informant for Doris's organization has come as a mighty shock. We must make him suffer; no one stands for a grass."

Sven looked genuinely upset; he knew Sebastian was a bad egg, but this? James looked at Richard and smiled. That bastard will get all he deserves, he thought.

Meanwhile, as plans were discussed, Antonio was watching Eva undressing. God, she was something, he thought. Skin the colour of milk chocolate, legs that went on forever, and a body that took his breath away. She stood before him, wearing only her heels. She gave him that very, very naughty smile that he loved so much, and he let all thoughts of Doris, her team, Sebastian, and the diamonds escape his mind. There was plenty of time later to put the final touches to operation SMEG.

After about an hour, Eva was slipping out of Antonio's penthouse and very quickly slipping out of Antonio's mind. She was a great lay, that was sure, but like all the women in Antonio's life, she had never taken his heart.

After a shower Antonio rejoined his team in the living room. Brick noticed him immediately. The others were busily chatting about all they had learned and only became silent when Antonio asked Brick to tell him how much everyone knew. Brick relayed everything of importance to his boss, and Antonio looked pleased. He loved having reliable people around him to do the nitty-gritty things, allowing him to have fun and be free to focus on the important issues.

"OK, guys, now that you're all up to speed with things, I want to move on. How are we going to deal with Sebastian Greco?"

No one spoke, and Antonio enjoyed watching them furiously thinking of ideas. He chuckled to himself. He knew exactly what was going to happen to that scumbag.

"Well," he continued, after nothing was forthcoming from his team, "I have an idea."

Antonio was a born leader and had learned from a very young age that if you surround yourself with loyal people and make them believe they are an integral part of decision making, you ultimately can make all the decisions yourself with no one even realising. They hadn't called him the King of Rio for nothing.

"Well," he continued, "I'm hosting a party here in the penthouse tomorrow evening for around fifty people. I've invited a mixture of other world cruisers, a handful of crew, and a few of the entertainment team. It should be a spectacular evening. Jonathan, our resident singer, has agreed to share his magical voice with us, and a fireworks display will light up the night sky as we make our way to Singapore. This is where the fun begins. Captain Larson, we need your help."

Antonio always referred to Sven as "Captain" out of respect.

"We're going to drug our cruise director, get him onto a tender as the party is in full swing. Then, using two of your strongest Eastern European deckhands, take him out to sea and leave him with a decent supply of class A drugs. Then the two men will come back in the tender before the party has ended. We'll call the coastguards and report a tender stolen. Mr. Greco will be doused in whiskey so when he's found he'll appear to be a drunken fool, and that of course will be when the drugs are found.

The Singaporean government does not tolerate drug abuse in any shape or form. He'll be incarcerated for life, and by the time he gets to appeal, our mission will have been accomplished, and we'll be miles away, enjoying the fruits of our labour. What do you think?"

James was first to answer. "An amazing plan, but can we set him up even further? I'd really like to think of something bad that we could do to him before he gets taken off the ship."

"Sure thing, James, do whatever you want. I leave that to you," replied Antonio.

Richard and James smiled at each other; they had a lot to discuss before tomorrow evening.

Everyone started to make their way back to their rooms. Tomorrow was going to be a big day. With Sebastian dealt with, it only left Doris and her team to be considered, and everyone had complete faith that Antonio would come up with something very soon to leave the path clear for them to exit the ship with the diamonds.

As Antonio loosened his collar, ready to retire for the night, his telephone rang. It was approaching 4:00 a.m., and he couldn't imagine who would be calling. Perhaps one of his team had left something behind. As he picked up the phone by his bedside, he heard a familiar purring voice.

"Antonio, darling, I've been thinking about you. I'd love to see you and have your company. My bed is very warm but lonely."

It was Doris.

Antonio arrived at cabin 888 a few minutes later. Why have I come here? he thought as he rang the bell. I must be out of my fucking mind. Talk about your brain being ruled by your dick. Too late now, though.

Doris opened the door in an extremely sexy outfit. For the second time in one evening, Antonio felt himself become overwhelmingly aroused.

"Hello, Antonio. I knew you wouldn't let me down." And with that, she threw her arms around him and wrapped her legs tightly around the back of his. She pulled him close and kissed him passionately. Their breathing became heavy, and he felt himself getting lost in her. Suddenly, she looked into his eyes, and for a moment, as he stared back into hers, he felt a surge of love for her. This was new to him, and he felt wonderfully good.

Doris led him to her bed. She ripped at his clothes, and as they lost themselves in passion, they stared deeply into each other's eyes. It seemed as if they had touched the other's soul. When they both reached climax, it was like nothing either of them had ever experienced before.

After a while Antonio felt tears fall onto his shoulder, and as he looked down, he saw Doris gently crying. She smiled at him, and at that moment, he knew he had fallen hopelessly, madly in love with her.

Quietly, Doris whispered, "I won't carry on this charade any more. I can't continue being part of an organization that's ready to steal everything you've spent your life building. I think I love you, Antonio, and these people I work with terrify me. I fear for my life daily."

As he listened to her, he looked at her beautiful face. She was not dissimilar to him. They had both killed, they had both fought tooth and nail to survive, and tonight, they had both bared their souls to each other. What am I getting myself into? he thought.

# Chapter Thirteen

The morning sunlight streamed through the window into the cabin where Doris and Antonio lay, still in each other's arms. They had made love and talked into the early hours. Neither one of them had felt such happiness before, and they agreed to tell team SMEG about their sudden relationship that very morning. Antonio was convinced that Doris had no agendas and every word she spoke was the truth. He had, however, made it perfectly clear that if she ever tried to double-cross him, he would personally take revenge and destroy her.

He needed to make sure that everyone was clear about Doris and him being an item. After all, she was going to be on his arm tonight at the party, and he wouldn't accept any negative comments. He was the boss, and if he trusted Doris, then his team had to as well. This was real, and he loved how he was feeling.

The two of them got ready, and as Doris walked out of her dressing room, Antonio could not believe how beautiful she looked. Everything about her was impeccable. He wanted this woman by his side forever, to share the life he'd planned, once he'd disposed of the diamonds.

They'd decided to have breakfast together in Antonio's penthouse, and as they walked in, his Japanese chef, Koi, was laying the table with the most beautiful tableware. Roses stood proudly in a crystal vase, and champagne was chilling in the ice bucket. Antonio had told Koi someone special was coming, and as Koi had worked for Antonio for years, he knew the man, perhaps better than the man knew himself. He had no doubt this "someone" was very special to his boss.

He had seen women come and go over the years; he knew Antonio had never requested that he prepare a romantic meal before, let alone a breakfast. This had to be the real deal. And Koi was happy for him.

Antonio and Doris sat on the terrace with the breeze interrupting the heat of the morning and talked and laughed as Koi busied himself serving a wonderful breakfast. Suddenly, Doris's telephone rang. After saying very little, she turned to Antonio and told him her guys down in the submarine were apparently dropping like flies with a terrible virus, and they wanted her to get some medical supplies from the ship's hospital.

Antonio couldn't believe his luck. A quick call to Captain Larson, and the medicines were being boxed. All Doris needed to do was take the pills to them and let them poison themselves. Apparently, it would be over within twenty-four hours, and then the submarine would just remain at the bottom of the ocean, its crew sleeping the long sleep.

Just as they were taking their first sip of champagne, Brick walked into the room.

Shit, thought Antonio. He'd completely forgotten that he had told Brick to stay in one of the guest suites to keep his eye on the diamonds. Although they were in the safe,

Antonio wanted Brick to be around just in case. After all, they were worth a small fortune.

"Boss, what's she doing here?"

Antonio took Brick aside, and it took a while to persuade him that Doris was no threat to them and, in fact, would be a great help. He told him about the guys in the submarine, and finally, he told him of their feelings for each other. "I've told her if she ever double-crosses me, I'll kill her with my bare hands, and if I can't, you can do the honours. OK, Brick?" Antonio gave Brick a jesting wink. "Now go tell team SMEG everything. I want no comments from anyone. I'm in charge. I make the decisions, and I want total and absolute respect from everyone for both me and my lady. Is that perfectly clear?"

"Sure thing, boss."

Just as Brick was leaving, Antonio called out, "And tell Richard I want him to come over earlier than everyone else. He needs to have a good look at the diamonds. I want him to give me a professional valuation. Tell him to be here at five. The party begins at seven."

Brick gave the thumbs-up sign without turning and closed the door behind him.

Antonio and Doris continued their breakfast. As Koi filled their champagne flutes, they looked at each other and smiled. Things were working out wonderfully.

At lunch on deck eleven, the team sat together, digesting everything they'd learned from Brick. Richard couldn't believe that the Freak was now Antonio's love interest. Ruth understood his frustration, but in her logical and intelligent way, she convinced him that it was better to have Doris in the team than outside it, and everyone seemed to agree.

"We'll keep a wide birth, say little, and hope Antonio has indeed made a wise choice," added Karmen.

"Thank God we've gotten rid of the guys in the submarine. I honestly had no idea what Antonio intended to do with them," said James.

"I'm sure he would have had a plan in the making," replied Josephine. "He always seems to pull something out of the hat."

Richard told everyone he would be inspecting the diamonds more closely at 5:00 p.m. and that he'd see the rest of them later at the party. He had a massage booked, so he left his friends chatting.

Oscar seemed pleased that Sadie was joining him this evening; he had decided to ask Antonio later if it was OK to share operation SMEG with his wife. He really hated sneaking around, even though he knew she couldn't have cared less. Maybe once the diamonds were gone and the money made, he and Sadie could rekindle their relationship. He hoped so, more than anything. For all his faults, he was a loyal, honest man, and family did mean everything to him.

James and Javier were gossiping about how they could cause maximum damage to Sebastian later that evening, and the three girls sat with their drinks, letting the sun warm their bodies before they had to go to their staterooms and start getting ready for tonight's party.

Richard rang the doorbell of Antonio's penthouse dead-on five o'clock. He was a stickler for keeping time. Koi answered and showed him directly into the study. Richard heard a commotion coming from the lounge that led out onto the terrace and correctly gathered it was coming from the staff, who were putting the finishing touches on what promised to be a lavish, wonderful affair.

Antonio was waiting, seated in his favourite worn armchair, and as Richard came in, he stood up to greet him. Brick was there too. All three men looked dashing in their dress suits.

"Follow me." Antonio beckoned to Richard, and they walked into an adjoining room. There laid out in rows were the diamonds, some the size of buttons, others the size of eggs. Brick stood by the table, his massive bulk casting a shadow over the gems.

"Please, Brick, can you move? I need to inspect these diamonds closely, with full light."

Brick looked toward his boss, Antonio nodded, and it was only then that Brick moved away. Richard examined each exquisite stone. He held them gently in one hand, with his eye glass in the other, and took them to the window so he could see them clearly. Using the magnifying glass provided, he began to document each gem carefully.

"Brick, I'm going to need some help. Can you ask James and Javier to come here as quickly as possible?"

After a few minutes, Brick returned, bringing the other two with him.

"Hi, guys, thanks for coming. I need your help. Can you match these stones to their appropriate certificates?"

Richard weighed the stones, colour-coded them, and slowly moved along the length of the table, removing each stone gently to observe it. Antonio watched him closely. He knew this guy was an expert, and he got great pleasure when he heard the occasional gasp as Richard picked up the next magnificent piece.

An hour later, the diamonds were being carefully put away, not to be touched again until they arrived in Singapore.

Richard had done his job well, and the two men discussed values together calmly. Richard had seen some of the world's finest gems, but it had to be said that these were something else. Once they were safely disposed of, they would all be fabulously wealthy, more so than any of them had anticipated. Richard was ecstatic, and when Antonio asked him to have a drink with him and Doris before the other guests arrived, he quite happily agreed. He had to forget the past and think of the future.

The terrace looked stunning. Sweeping yards of white fabric created a sense of being in a beautiful Moroccan palace. Flower displays, adding colour and fragrance, were positioned for maximum effect. Candlelight gave just the desired result—not too bright but allowing everything to be seen. A buffet was spread out in the far corner. Magnificent ice carvings housed seafood of all kinds. Salads of every description were displayed in large crystal bowls, with sushi and sashimi delicately placed on enormous trays with orchids in various colours adding to what already looked like a work of art. There were curries and pasta stations for those who required hot food, and a chef was waiting by the grill for anyone who wanted fish or meat simply prepared.

Waiters and waitresses with trays of champagne were ready for the guests to arrive, and the bar had two of the best cocktail mixologists ready to shake up a storm. The band played gently, and Jonathan sang along, his voice as smooth as velvet.

As Antonio and Richard stood looking at the ocean, Doris walked out to join them. She looked incredible. She wore a white gown that caressed her slim bronzed body, her legs were long and shapely, and as she walked toward the men, they could be seen very elegantly through the slits that ran from the ankle to the thigh on both sides. Her hair was up, and she wore strings of pearls with earrings to match, which complemented her outfit perfectly. My God, thought Richard, she really is something. Antonio felt a pride he'd never felt before. And as she kissed him gently on the cheek, his heart melted.

"Richard, so very nice to see you again." Her voice was as sexy as he remembered.

"You too, Doris. I have to admit I was taken by surprise when I found out about you and Antonio, but now having time to digest the information, I wish the two of you the very best. Let's forget about the past."

With that Doris smiled, kissed Richard very gently on the cheek, and whispered "Thank you." The three of them stood together and toasted the future and waited for the others to arrive.

An hour or so had passed since the guests had collected in the penthouse. Everyone was mingling and chatting. The music was jazzy and seductive. Drinks were flowing, and stars twinkled brightly in the skies above. Captain Larson moved from person to person, making sure he missed no one. Karmen and Josephine were flirting awfully with Sebastian. James had asked the two of them to use their charms on him, while he concentrated on bringing cocktail after cocktail to the arrogant cruise director.

Sebastian assumed that both Karmen and Josephine could be his if he wanted, and the thought crossed his mind that it might be fun to have them both together. He really did think highly of himself. He also assumed that Doris was setting Antonio up and that she had a plan to screw him over. He would talk to her later; for now, he didn't want anyone to see them together. Theirs was a secretive relationship, in which information was passed, and not a soul knew. Sebastian grinned to himself. He loved being so incredibly clever.

Ruth and Javier were deep in conversation with two elderly world cruisers. Their joint knowledge of art and artefacts kept the American couple mesmerised; there seemed nothing these newlyweds didn't know. Just as James brought over another drink for Sebastian and the girls, Captain Larson interrupted the music to make an announcement.

"Ladies and gentleman, you're probably not aware, but today is, in fact, our host's birthday."

Everyone turned to catch sight of Antonio, and then the clapping began.

"We have a surprise for him," continued Sven.

The room went silent. Antonio began to feel uncomfortable; he didn't like surprises very much.

"There is a person here this evening who wouldn't have missed this gathering for the world. It has been extremely difficult to keep him out of your way, Antonio, but we managed. David, come and join us."

David was looking very much older than Antonio remembered, and it came as a shock to see him being pushed in a wheelchair by a nurse, but as soon as David said, "Hi, there, buddy, been too long" in his Texan drawl, it was as if the friends had never been apart. David was introduced to those people he didn't already know, and the music went up a notch.

Sebastian was getting louder by the second and began making improper suggestions to Karmen and Josephine. Of course, the girls said nothing yet. James continued bringing the cocktails. It wouldn't be too much longer before Sebastian could be removed from the party in disgrace, and then Antonio could put his plan into action.

Sophia was getting annoyed at the amount of time Sebastian was spending away from her. And seeing those two women giggling girlishly around her man was starting to really piss her off. It was times like this that she hated being "staff." If she was a cruiser like these two rich bitches, she'd be able to give them a mouthful. Actually, if they carried on like this much longer, she thought, she just might have to say something. With that she grabbed another glass of champagne from a passing waitress.

Josephine and Karmen were completely aware that the yoga teacher was watching them, and as Sebastian started to tell Karmen how magnificent her breasts were, Josephine whispered something in his ear and looked straight at Sophia.

All hell broke loose! Sophia rushed over and grabbed Josephine's arm, wildly shouting, "Keep your hands off my man!" Everyone looked around.

Both Josephine and Karmen kept their composure. Sebastian staggered and tried to get Sophia away from Josephine. Karmen very cleverly managed to trip and spill red wine down the front of Sophia's dress, adding in an extremely disingenuous voice, "Oh, I'm so very sorry."

Sophia launched herself toward Karmen, but Josephine saw her coming and pulled her friend out of harm's way. Instead, Sebastian took the full force of the wild yoga move, which sent him crashing into a table full of drinks.

Brick was called and both Sebastian and Sophia were forcefully removed, Sebastian swearing and shouting all the way to the front door. James went and found Antonio. "Mission accomplished. Now it's your turn to finish him off."

Back on the terrace, James and Richard found their wives. What a team those two girls made, both looking calm, composed, and beautiful. Yes, both men had found very special women in Karmen and Josephine.

"Shall we eat?" James asked. "After all that excitement, I'm starving." As they walked toward the buffet, he teasingly pinched his wife on the bottom.

The party was jumping. The food had been cleared away, and the whole terrace became a dance floor. Everyone was having a ball. Even David and his loyal nurse, Nora, were moving to the beat. Antonio had been occupied for a while, and when he joined the others, he had a smile on his face. Everything had gone according to plan. Sebastian was no longer their problem. He took Doris in his arms, and together they danced around the floor. Team SMEG were having the time of their lives, and knowing that Singapore was getting closer made each and every one of them tingle with nervous anticipation.

Five miles out to sea, the tender swayed from left to right; Sebastian lay slumped in a corner. He was out for the count. As the night sky came alive with the sound and colour of fireworks, he snored deeply. Nothing was going to wake him until the morning. By then, the coast guard would have found him and his drugs.

All the guests watched in amazement as the fireworks continued to light up the clear night sky, each one more beautiful than the last, shapes cascading full of colour downward toward the horizon. As the evening drew to a close, team SMEG huddled together to watch the finale. As they looked up, they saw diamonds of all shapes and sizes fluttering majestically above them. The time was coming very soon.

# Chapter Fourteen

Karmen noticed that Richard had a stressed look on his face, as if he knew something the others didn't. After the party ended and everyone had said their good-byes, only Antonio and David remained. They had so much to catch up on. Doris retired to her cabin and Nora to hers, giving Antonio instructions to call when he needed her to come back and take David to his cabin. She had grown so very fond of David in the time that she had become his carer.

When Auntie Wilma passed away, David had felt very lost and lonely, finding refuge in whiskey. Unfortunately, one evening he took a tumble. After a stay in the hospital and a successful operation, he returned to his rambling family ranch and had no choice but to look for someone to care for him. Nora had responded to his advert, and ever since her arrival, David had companionship, and their relationship was forged.

When Karmen and Richard were getting ready for bed in their cabin, Karmen asked her husband what was bothering him. Richard told her that he had inspected the diamonds closely, along with their appropriate certificates, and his valuation was quite a lot less than Antonio had originally suggested. He knew Antonio would be furious once he was given this news.

The next morning Richard left early and made his way to Antonio's penthouse. He took a deep breath and rang the doorbell. To his surprise Brick answered. "Well, hello, Richard. What are you doing here so early?"

"I've come to see the boss."

"You must be joking. Didn't you know he runs up and down the ship first thing in the morning, training, and then he meets James in the gym so the two of them can keep their bodies looking gorgeous?"

"Why are you here so early?" asked Richard.

"I've been on duty for two days, guarding the diamonds, and I don't mind telling you that I'm missing my training. I'll end up a gay man with an out of shape body, and nobody will want me. Darling, please tell me I still look great."

"Brick, listen, you're not my type; I'm not gay, but I do admit you have an exquisite body."

With that Brick smiled happily and said, "Oh, darling, I could kiss you!"

"Not today, Brick," came Richard's response, in a light-hearted, joking way.

As Richard sat waiting for Antonio's return, he felt edgy. How was he going to break the news that the diamonds were not worth as much as Antonio thought, and how would Antonio react? When Brick came back and informed him that his boss was having breakfast with Doris and wouldn't be back for an hour, Richard took the opportunity to go for a walk around the decks and clear his head.

As he breathed the fresh air, Richard started to feel a little calmer. He passed the pool and saw Karmen having breakfast with James and Josephine. He made his way over to them.

"Hi, Richard," said James. "What's wrong? You look absolutely terrible."

"My valuation of the diamonds falls way short of two-point-seven-five billion dollars, and I'm meeting Antonio in an hour to tell him."

"Shit," came James's response. "By how much?"

"Many millions of dollars. The haul is still worth a fortune, but to be told there's such a shortfall will be a hard pill to swallow. I feel sick to my stomach."

Karmen jumped in and quite rightly told Richard that he hadn't done the original deal, so none of this was his fault. "All you did, Richard, was value the diamonds honestly, based on your expertise."

"She's right," said James. "Although I don't envy you the task of telling Antonio. He was in a great mood when I left him at the gym. I think he was off to meet Doris for breakfast."

"Bet breakfast wasn't all he was getting," giggled Josephine.

The friends chatted, and by the time Richard headed back to Antonio's penthouse, he was feeling a whole lot better. Antonio was sitting on his terrace, and he smiled as Richard came to sit with him. Being an incredibly intuitive man, he immediately noticed something was not quite right with Richard.

"What's up, Richard? Nothing to do with the diamonds, I hope."

Richard took a deep breath. "First," he began, "I want you to know that the diamonds are simply incredible. No one has such an impressive collection that I am aware of anywhere in the world. They are old stones, from mines that were closed maybe fifty or sixty years ago because they were not yielding enough rough diamonds, and costs were too high for little or no return. Therefore, these stones are extremely rare."

"That's great news, isn't it?" asked Antonio.

"Yes, but please let me finish. James and Javier were a great help to me yesterday. We matched the gems to their GIA certificates."

Antonio gave Richard a lost look.

"GIA stands for Gemological Institute of America. It is an American company that is independent of buyer and seller, so you get a true and honest description of a stone that is recognised worldwide. Therefore, with that information, it is not too difficult to calculate values.

"Yesterday, I split the goods into groups and colours. So looking at my spread sheets"—Richard handed them to Antonio— "you can see how I made my valuations."

Antonio was deep in thought, and for the first time, Richard could see he was totally interested in what he was being taught. Richard explained, with the spreadsheets laid out on the table so Antonio could see his calculations clearly, that the most valuable diamonds were the red, blue, and pink ones. There were ten stones with a total weight of 250 carats at three million dollars a carat, for a total value of $750 million.

He explained that with coloured diamonds, there was no specific chart to follow; therefore, their value could vary depending on the buyer. They were extremely rare and very collectable, and if an individual wanted to get his or her hands on one, then values could skyrocket.

Next, Richard continued, were white diamonds. These were valued by colour, with D being the best. All their white diamonds were D, E, F, and G, which were the best colours. Then, he explained, after colour you had to look at clarity. This ranged from flawless and internal flawless to VVS1, VVS2, VS1, and VS2. He pointed to his spreadsheets, so Antonio could see that the certificates showed a chart. There were sixty stones with a total weight of 369 carats at just over $2.3 million a carat, for a total value of $850 million.

Next, he told Antonio, there were thirty stones of mixed qualities that he had valued at $650 million. "So you see, we have a hundred stones valued at two-point-two-five billion dollars. Therefore, we have a shortfall of approximately five hundred million from your purchase price. But please remember, Antonio, there may be some collectors out there who will pay a lot more for the coloured diamonds. And after all, we still have a magnificent haul of exquisite gems worth a fortune."

Antonio was digesting all the information. His eyes began bulging, and he quietly said, "I will get even with that Indian bastard, Vickran Hirani. And to think I believed he was a good man, a Hindu, whose heart was as kind as my friend David's. I was a fool. I needed to get my blood money out of Brazil fast, and I took my eye off the ball. But Richard, thank you for your expert help. I hope once these diamonds are off the ship, we will continue to work closely together as a team."

"Of course, and Antonio, it's been my pleasure to help, but there is one thing. You know how much I love these gems?" Antonio looked perplexed. "Well," continued Richard, "I was wondering, when it comes to my cut, can I have a diamond instead of money?"

Antonio seemed not to hear Richard and said, "I want a meeting with team SMEG sometime today to discuss our final plans. Call me and let me know what time suits everyone. And once again, Richard, thanks for everything." With that he was gone.

Four hours later, the group was gathered. Antonio took his place at the head of the table. "I'd like to update you all on what's been happening. First, I want to reiterate that Doris and I are now an item. Whatever your thoughts were before, forget them. She is one hundred percent with me. She has managed, with the help of Captain Larson, to dispose of the team that was targeting us from the submarine below the waters. We have no worries about them anymore. Sebastian is in prison, awaiting his trial. So we've dealt with our informant. However, it's not all plain sailing.

"The Brazilian police arrested my double in Japan and have now put out a worldwide search for me. I believe he may even have told them, after a number of brutal beatings, that I was cruising in the Far East, so I have to be extremely careful. The team that Doris was connected to is desperately chasing my investment. They want to get their hands on our money, and having lost contact with the submarine and Doris, they are now frantically trying to track her down and get to me.

"Our haul consists of one hundred stones. Richard has valued each and every piece, and even though they are worth slightly less than I originally anticipated, we are still talking two-point-two-five billion dollars' worth of fabulous diamonds. I will deal with the man who cheated me at a later stage. My plan is to split up the diamonds. Fifty percent of them will stay with me until I get off the ship in South Africa. The seven of you will disembark in Singapore taking seven diamonds each, with one of you taking eight. You decide among yourselves who will be responsible for the extra stone, bearing in mind the immense value involved.

"You will then fly to Botswana, where you can relax and perhaps go on a safari before I arrive with Doris via Cape Town. Brick is remaining with me, so he can watch our backs until we leave the ship in South Africa. Now, Oscar, will you have a problem explaining to Sadie why you are getting off in Singapore and leaving her to continue on to Southampton?"

"As long as she can play bridge and sunbathe, boss, she'll be pleased to get me out of her hair," came Oscar's reply.

"Good. And now, Captain Larson, without your help none of this would have been possible. So I want to thank you and allow you to get back to focusing on being captain of this wonderful ship. You will receive the balance of your money in due course."

Everyone said good-bye to Sven, and as he left the group, he turned and, with genuine warmth in his voice, wished them all good luck. The room was charged with anticipation and fear. Tomorrow, the liner would dock in Singapore, and the seven friends had to leave with more than a billion dollars' worth of diamonds on them. None of them would get much sleep tonight.

# Chapter Fifteen

In the morning, after a restless night, everyone met in Antonio's penthouse for the last time. Each of the seven wore appropriate clothing to conceal the merchandise they were to carry off the ship. Brick handed every person a long pouch with pockets and zips. In each were the diamonds, carefully wrapped and stored. He showed them how to attach the pouches to their ankles using Velcro strips to secure them safely. Once their trousers were over their shoes, no one would guess that these seven cruisers were in possession of such incredible valuables.

The group had been versed the night before by Antonio as to how they would leave the ship in Singapore. The three ladies would be collected at the dock by someone who would recognise them; the only word he would say would be "SMEG" to which they were to answer, "What a sparkling day it is." Then they would be transported to the airport to take their flight to Botswana. The pouches were made of fabric and plastic, so there were no worries going through the metal detectors. They just had to be calm and casual.

The men had the same instructions, except they would be taken to an airstrip a few hours earlier, and a private jet would take them to Botswana. On their arrival, both groups would be met by other contacts of Antonio's and, using the same greeting, would be taken to a lodge deep in the bush, where they could relax for a while until Antonio, Brick, and Doris joined them.

At six in the morning, the call came through to tell Antonio the ship would be clearing customs by six thirty. The time had at last arrived for the SMEG team of seven to leave. James had been put in charge, and after their farewells, the two groups made their way separately to deck five to disembark. Within minutes of their walking down the gangplank, Antonio watched from his terrace and saw both groups being approached and led away to waiting minivans. He prayed they would get to their destination with their merchandise safely. As he walked inside, he turned his attention to keeping Doris and himself out of harm's way. There were many people after them, and he needed to keep one step ahead.

James and his team had boarded their private plane and were sitting back sipping champagne, delighted that everything had gone smoothly. Oscar was awestruck. He had never seen such a beautiful aircraft, and the hostess serving the champagne was simply stunning. Her legs went on forever, and she had the most luscious lips he'd ever seen.

"This is the way to travel, boys," he said, accepting a top-up from Kelly as the engines started.

Javier and Richard were busy discussing the menu, which boasted lobster, caviar, and an array of other fantastic dishes. James was looking pensively out of the window.

"What's up with you, James?" shouted Oscar. The other two stopped what they were doing and looked over in his direction.

"This is the easy part, guys. I don't think everything is going to be plain sailing. I foresee a number of problems ahead. The Brazilian government is on Antonio's trail; they want his blood and money. The organization that Doris was involved with is after her, wanting to find out what happened to their team down in the submarine. I don't think we are home free yet."

"Well, I intend to enjoy myself on this flight," answered Oscar, giving Kelly a little wink.

Just at that moment, the pilot came over the intercom. He wished the four men a very good morning, welcomed them on board, and asked them to fasten their seat belts. Within minutes, they were airborne, flying above the white, fluffy clouds. James continued to look out of the window, lost in thought. He hoped this was going to work out OK and that Josephine and the girls were safe.

Meanwhile, the ladies were sitting in the first-class lounge waiting for their flight, which had been delayed two hours. Josephine was drinking her usual vodka and Diet Coke, and both Karmen and Ruth were having vodka and tonic light. They had passed through security easily and were feeling elated and nervous in the knowledge that they had diamonds hidden on them worth more than half a billion dollars.

As they chatted, an announcement came through telling them that Singapore Airlines flight 732 to Johannesburg connecting with South African Airways to Botswana was now ready to board. The girls calmly collected their belongings and walked out of the lounge, heads held high. As they sat in their seats, they thought of the men and hoped all was going well for them. They were offered champagne, and then the captain came over the intercom system, apologizing for the delay. There had been an engine problem that was now rectified, and he asked them to fasten their seat belts as they were about to taxi down the runway, taking off to the east. He wished them all a good flight and said he would speak to them as they neared Johannesburg.

Karmen, Josephine, and Ruth settled back in their comfortable seats, and within ten minutes, they were into the clouds and relaxing.

Two days went by very quickly in Singapore. Antonio and Doris walked the streets like every other tourist, except in the shadows, Brick was following them, watching their backs. He would lay down his life to protect his boss.

At 6:00 p.m. the ship was ready to sail, and everyone was on board. Antonio stood with Doris on deck twelve and felt a great sense of relief. They had survived the stopover with no incidents, and South Africa lay ahead. Suddenly, as the foghorn sounded, the band started to play and the ship left dockside, Antonio noticed a waiter he had never seen before. He was staring at Doris in a very odd way.

Quickly Antonio grabbed her arms, and as she began to protest, he looked at her in a way that immediately stopped her from saying anything more. She left deck twelve with him very quickly.

Back in the safety of the penthouse, Antonio was telling Brick about the unknown waiter. He described him as a man of about six feet one, medium build, shaved head, fit looking, and wearing a ring with a red stone in its centre on his little finger. He looked as if he could be South American. Brick told his boss that he would go and make some enquiries, but he questioned Antonio about how any intruder could possibly slip through security at the boarding point. Antonio was furious at Brick's stupidity and screamed, "You fucking idiot, I thought you had a brain. How difficult would it be for a few fellow passengers to be bumped off while in Singapore and their passes stolen? There could be all sorts of problems awaiting us. Now get the fuck out of here and find this guy."

By the afternoon, Brick had to report back that there was no sign of the guy Antonio had seen, and according to the staff, no new faces had boarded the ship since Singapore. Antonio had to accept that he might have been a little paranoid, but he told Brick to be vigilant, just in case there were any unwanted intruders lurking around.

Antonio decided to have dinner in his penthouse that evening. He felt under the circumstances it would be wise, just in case. He told Brick to continue watching and instructed Koi to come up with a wonderful meal for him and Doris. He put his finest champagne on ice, took a shower, and let the stresses leave him. Wrapped in his silk dressing gown, his thoughts turned to Doris and her beautiful body. He began smiling to himself. Tonight was going to be a good night, he thought.

Antonio was lying awake, breathing heavily, with Doris curled up asleep in his arms. What a wonderful night, he thought. Doris was so incredibly sexy; he'd never met anyone quite like her. As he was reliving the evening's events, he felt his eyes suddenly becoming extremely heavy.

He smelt a strange smell, and his body felt oddly limp. He managed to look toward the air-conditioning unit and saw a thin blue haze circling above them. They were being gassed!

He called Doris's name. Nothing—she was out for the count, breaths coming in short gasps. Antonio mustered all his energy and got to his feet; he grabbed Doris's lifeless body and stumbled out onto the terrace. The fresh air engulfed them, and Antonio began to feel his limbs again. Doris still lay motionless, but her breathing was less erratic. Soon enough, her eyes were opening, and together they sat on the floor of the terrace, taking in the night air. They knew they had big problems ahead that needed to be sorted out, the prospect of which was terrifying.

James and his team had arrived in Botswana after a very comfortable eleven-hour-and-twenty-minute flight. They would have slept extremely well if it hadn't been for Oscar's snoring and continuous muttering in his sleep. The views from the jet windows were amazing. Miles of untouched land stretched beyond them, trees of varying colours, shapes, and sizes breaking the flat landscape. The sky was the bluest of blues, with not a cloud to be seen anywhere. A haze shuddered from the tarmac runway, indicating the heat that awaited them.

The captain came over the intercom. "Good morning, gentlemen. I hope you all had a good rest and enjoyed the breakfast our lovely hostess prepared for you. We need you to wait here until customs comes onto the plane to clear us for immigration purposes. Then you will be able to leave. I believe you have transportation arranged, so I will radio through to get your jeep to come directly to the aircraft as soon as I can."

"This is the way to travel," Richard chuckled.

"The only thing I'd change," piped in Oscar, "is next time, I'd like to be alone with Kelly. Then I could join the mile-high club."

"Oscar, you couldn't manage it, even if it was handed to you on a plate," came Richard's reply.

Javier and James agreed, and they all started to laugh. Even Oscar joined in. He knew he was all mouth and no trousers, but it was fun to dream.

Back on the ship, Antonio was tightening up security. Someone was definitely trying to end his or Doris's life, or both. The gassing attempt confirmed that. As he spoke to Brick and the ship's head of security, Koi came into the room and handed him an envelope.

"What's this?" he asked.

"It was just slipped under the door," said Koi. "Thought it might be important."

Antonio ripped open the envelope and removed the handwritten note. It said *I can help you; your lives are in danger. I will be in touch soon.*

Antonio reddened. "Find this guy, Brick, and kick the shit out of him. I want to know what he knows, and who he works for. Who the fuck does he think he is, telling me to wait for him to get in touch. I'm the boss. I'm Antonio Cadiz! Go get him. *Now!*"

Brick stood up. He knew he had to find this guy. Someone was after his boss, no question, after last night's attempted gassing plot. He left the penthouse in search of information.

Slowly, Antonio calmed down and carried on with his conversation, discussing continuing security support until they reached Cape Town.

The girls' flight was nearing its destination. They had slept well on the first leg of their journey, which wasn't too hard after all the champagne and vodka they had consumed. But in true style, they emerged from the bathroom of the South African Airways flight looking as fresh as when they had first boarded their flight in Singapore.

The pilot informed them they were starting their descent into Botswana and they needed to return to their seats and fasten their seat belts. Land came into view. Karmen, Josephine, and Ruth looked down in amazement. Below them they saw animals walking in groups freely through the bush—elephants, giraffes, and other species too small to identify from the aircraft.

As long as they got through passport control, they felt they would pretty much be home and dry. Then they could look forward to a couple of days relaxing, perhaps going on a safari while waiting for the other three to arrive.

The plane landed with a gentle thud. All mobiles were immediately turned on. Josephine received the first message, telling her that James and the guys had successfully reached the lodge. The valuables were safely stored away, and they were now sitting around a campfire with drinks, waiting to hear from the girls to confirm they had arrived. After passing the message to the other two,

Josephine replied, telling James, *So far, so good. Only passport control to deal with, and then we'll be on our way.*

Josephine was the first to leave the aircraft. And as she took her first few steps, the heat hit her. She breathed the hot, arid air, and her lungs hurt. But there was something magical about being in such natural surroundings, and excitement whelmed up inside her.

The three girls walked toward passport control, trembling inside, but outside, looking as if they didn't have a care in the world. Karmen took the lead and, holding her papers in front of her, gave the guard one of her drop-dead gorgeous smiles. He instantly melted. Never having seen eyes the colour of hers, he just stared in amazement. Josephine and Ruth sidled up behind her and began fluttering their eyelashes. The guard cast his eyes from one to the other as he stamped all their passports, adding, "Welcome, beautiful ladies, to my beautiful country." The three of them swaggered out, turned, and gave him a flirtatious wave as he sat, still staring at them.

After collecting their luggage, they walked through the "nothing to declare" channel, hearts beating fast, and suddenly arrived outside to a hive of activity: women in colourful outfits with babies hanging from their necks and children holding tightly to their skirts; men talking loudly in groups, smoking and whistling; dogs roaming in between everyone's legs. It was chaos. The girls stood startled for a minute, and then they heard the word *SMEG*. They turned to see a man almost twice their height and as thin as a rake. He beamed at them and said nothing more. Karmen replied, "What a sparkling day."

"Follow me, ladies," he beckoned, and he led them to a large open-topped jeep with their luggage in tow.

En route, Josephine called James and told him everything had gone without a hitch and they should be at the camp within the hour. Karmen and Ruth asked what he'd said, and Josephine giggled. "He said they have our drinks ready and waiting."

The three of them sat back and looked up at the night sky, full of stars that seemed to go deeper and deeper into the universe and beyond. The temperature had cooled, but still the warmth enveloped them, and as the three girls headed toward their husbands, they felt they had truly arrived in Africa.

# Chapter Sixteen

Brick got wind of who was messing with Antonio. He was someone who had worked alongside Sebastian. As dusk fell, Brick hung around the staff quarters and found the guy he was looking for. As he came through the staff door, Brick grabbed him by the scruff of his neck.

"Hello, mate. I think you and me need to have a little chat." With that Brick lifted his knee and whacked it in the middle of the guy's stomach with such force that he immediately collapsed on the floor. "Get up, you piece of shit," screamed Brick. "You're coming with me—now."

The guy scurried to his feet, eyes wide, like a rabbit caught in headlights. "Please leave me alone. I've done nothing."

"Shut the fuck up, or I'll throw you overboard, but for good measure, I'll break your arms and legs first. Do you understand me?"

"What have I done to you?" he whimpered.

Brick dragged him by his hair back to his room. He threw him like a rag doll on the floor. Brick stood towering above the guy, who was shaking uncontrollably, and asked him who he worked for. "No one," came the reply. With that Brick put his fists straight into his face. His nose exploded, and blood poured from his mouth, where his front teeth had been knocked out.

"Now you can see I mean business, so tell me, who do you work for? And don't fuck me around, or else I'll pull your arms out of their sockets, very slowly. Get me?"

Gasping for breath and trembling with fear, the guy proceeded to tell Brick that some people had boarded the ship. They had approached him, knowing he had worked closely with Sebastian, and had told him how Antonio Cadiz had set his friend up by planting drugs on him. They wanted revenge, and there was something they wanted to relieve Antonio of. Also, there was an employee of theirs called Doris, who they needed to sort out. They had asked him to just scare Antonio, send him a note, and they'd do the rest. As he told his story, blood covered his whole face, and his blue eyes looked wild against all the red.

"I promise that's the truth. They told me if I delivered the note, they'd give me a thousand dollars for my time. And because Sebastian was my mate, I decided to go for it."

"For a thousand dollars? You piece of scum. A thousand dollars? Do you think it's been worth it?" With that, he launched his foot directly into the guy's cheekbone, which shattered on impact. "Now tell me, where do I find this guy?"

Hardly able to speak, the man answered softly. "Cabin six-eleven. He's about six foot two, slim but well built, has a bald head, from South America, I think." With that Brick put a gag around his bloody, misshapen mouth, put him on the bed, and told him to shut up or he'd end up being meat for the sharks.

In Antonio's penthouse, Brick relayed everything. He told Antonio that the guy was a nobody and that he'd been promised a measly thousand bucks to frighten him and do some snooping.

"So, Antonio, I'm going to give this guy the biggest surprise of his life. Do you want to come with me and question him too?"

"Brick, I think that's a very good idea."

Brick and Antonio made their way silently down to deck six. Cabin 611 was the first door after they turned into the passageway. The ship was quiet; most passengers had retired for the night. Brick knocked and called out, "Room service." As the door opened slightly, Brick put his foot into the gap and with unbelievable strength, forced it wide open. The occupant tumbled backward, landing heavily on the floor. As the two men closed the door behind them, the South American shouted, "Who the fuck are you?"

Brick replied, "More to the point, who the fuck are you?"

Antonio interrupted. "Antonio Cadiz is my name." As he spoke, he pushed Brick to one side. "I believe you've been sent to look for me?"

"Who told you that?"

"The piece of shit who works on this ship who's been hiding you. Now tell me, how many of you are there?" Antonio stared directly at the man while Brick questioned him.

"My name is Jose, and I was asked to find out about one of our agents who has suddenly disappeared. Her name is

Doris, and she is very important to the agency." Antonio gave a nod, and Brick pinned Jose up against the wall.

"Let me tell you something," boomed Antonio. "You've messed with the wrong person. How many of you are there?"

"I'm working alone at the moment, but I can get reinforcements at any time."

Brick tightened the pressure around Jose's neck, and slowly, his face turned blue. As Antonio gave the signal to continue, Brick head-butted him, and Jose slid unconscious down the wall, leaving a streak of blood behind him. His arms lay listlessly at his sides.

"Tie him up and gag him until we decide what to do with him. I want you to bring that ring on his little finger to me." With that, Antonio exited the small room, leaving the smell of sweat and blood behind him.

Back in the penthouse, Antonio had poured himself a brandy and was deep in thought. Moments later, a cool, calm Brick arrived. He passed an envelope to his boss and said, "The ring you wanted."

Antonio looked inside and saw the gold ring with a ruby centre, glistening. It was attached to a little finger that twitched, as if it still belonged to a body. "I want you to go and get our snitch and take him to cabin six-eleven. Then we can dispose of the two of them together."

Brick left immediately and easily brought the lifeless, bloody body back to cabin 611. After about an hour, Antonio walked quietly into the cabin. Brick was sitting silently, watching for any signs of movement. Suddenly, they heard a whimpering noise, and Antonio immediately kicked the larger man in the ribs. Silence resumed.

Together, they stripped the men. They had decided that they were going to wrap both bodies up in large heavy nets, which they had located on deck nine, just next to the tenders. It was hard work; Brick treated it like a heavy workout, and once both men were totally encased in the netting, he felt the adrenaline rush through his veins.

After they carried the men to deck twelve, Antonio removed a knife from his pocket and sliced through their skin, as if he were cutting into a steak. Then Brick picked the men up one at a time and effortlessly threw them overboard. The gushing blood would attract sharks within minutes, and the heaviness of the nets would make sure everything would sink into the depths of the ocean before dawn.

As Brick was washing down the deck, Antonio showered and then enjoyed a large whiskey back in his penthouse. They had managed to dispose of their immediate problems, but he knew this was just the beginning. He had to make some decisions and fast. Time was running out.

# Chapter Seventeen

The seven members of SMEG were sitting under the immense blanket of stars, quietly staring at the stillness that surrounded them. They were all feeling slightly light headed. They had been drinking cold champagne and eating canapés that had been provided for them by Paddy, the lodge manager. They lay on loungers around the kidney-shaped pool that led from the sitting area of their tented suites and listened to the occasional sound of an animal interrupting the quietness.

Suddenly, James's mobile rang. He moved away from the group so he could take the call more privately. Immediately, he recognised Antonio's voice.

"We have big problems." Antonio began filling James in. "I think you need to beef up the security, James. There's a possibility that you'll have some of Doris's team hunting you down for the gems, and the Brazilian government is at this very moment looking to find me. They're closing in. I must get off this ship before Cape Town. There's talk that Doris's team is going to land a helicopter on the ship and try and take her and I hostage.

I've a plan, but can't discuss it with you now. I don't know who could be listening or who could be leaking information, so I have to be vigilant. Just make sure you keep your wits about you at all times. Remember, you're in charge, and you need to keep the team and—more importantly—the diamonds safe."

With that the phone went dead. James replayed the information in his mind before joining the others. For the moment, he chose to say nothing. He began thinking how much he hated the fact that Antonio always hung up first. It really, really pissed him off.

Antonio was working hard on his strategy. He discussed it with no one. Doris was lying, bored and idle, on her bed. Brick paced the penthouse, always alert, but becoming more and more frustrated by the hour, missing his workouts at the gym. Even though he knew that right now his focus had to be the protection of his boss, his body was nevertheless missing the buzz of hard-core exercise.

Antonio had some very good friends in Cape Town, and one in particular owed him big time. Now, he thought, he was going to call in the favour. Dominic answered immediately, as usual, slightly high on something. No doubt a joint made from the best grass the township had to offer.

"Hi, Dom. It's me. Antonio Cadiz."

Dom, who never had a care in the world, a true black happy South African, answered full of enthusiasm. "Hey, man, how are you? Great to hear from you, man. Are you chilling in Brazil?"

"No, Dom, I'm on a cruise liner, not far from Cape Town."

"Man, that's not your scene."

"Long story, Dom, but I need to call in a favour. I need your help. Are you alone and able to talk?"

"Sure thing, man, no problem. The ladies aren't coming over till later." He laughed loudly and then paused so Antonio could continue.

"The ship I'm on is called the *Dream of the Seas*. Can you find us on your navigation system and then arrange a high-powered speedboat that can reach the ship in the dark so I can get off before arriving in Cape Town? My life is in danger. I'll fill you in when I see you. This is all top secret, so Dom, I'm putting my trust in you. And by the way, when I jump ship, I'll have a woman with me. She's used to danger, so we have no worriers there."

"Leave things with me, man. I'll get back to you soon." And with that, Dom was gone.

Later that evening, as Doris and Antonio were having dinner, Antonio's mobile started to vibrate. Looking at the screen, he saw it was Dom. Antonio motioned to Doris, letting her know he needed to take the call, and left the room.

Dom informed Antonio that the *Dream of the Seas* was due to dock in Cape Town at 4:00 p.m. two days later. He had located a Riva speedboat, adding that there was nothing faster on the water and that he would personally come to the cruise ship and take Antonio and his friend to wherever they needed to go. Just before the conversation ended, Dom added, "Can't wait to meet up with you again, man." Antonio told Dom he'd get back to him with the final details the next morning and returned to finish his dinner with Doris.

Doris was patiently waiting, sipping her champagne. Koi had made sure the food was returned piping hot, so his boss would have no complaints, and the two of them started to eat. "Who was that, darling?" asked Doris.

"A great friend of mine. I'm arranging for us to escape from this ship before we get to Cape Town. There are too many people potentially looking to get us, and I've decided we need to exit quietly, before anyone notices we're gone. Leave it to me. Don't give it a thought. I'll sort everything out."

Doris looked into his eyes. "Of course you will, darling. I know I can rely on you, and with you I will be safe. That's why I love you so much." Antonio smiled. He enjoyed taking care of Doris, more than anyone else he'd ever known, and he knew for the first time in her troubled life, she was happy to relax and be looked after. They just needed to escape, get rid of the diamonds, and spend the rest of their lives together, somewhere hot and beautiful.

Antonio put a call into Captain Larson, who was surprised to hear from him so late in the evening. When Antonio finished explaining his situation, he sensed a little hesitation coming from the captain.

"Antonio, I thought we had severed our business relationship to allow me to concentrate on being captain of this ship."

Antonio took a deep breath. "I need to get myself and Doris off the ship before we arrive in Cape Town. I've received some information, and there could potentially be a helicopter landing on board, looking to either kill Doris and myself or take us hostage. They want to get to the diamonds."

"Antonio, I've helped you enough. This has got to stop. You're turning this situation into gang warfare. This is my ship, and my concern is for the safety of my passengers. Helicopters landing, it's madness. I really have to call it a day. You haven't stolen the diamonds, as you explained in the beginning; it was just a means to an end, to get your drug money out of Brazil. So you really have to leave me out of this."

Antonio felt the rage bubble inside of him. "Are you mad, Larson? While you were on the payroll, everything was fine; you couldn't have given a flying fuck about your passengers! You've had more out of me these last few months than you'd have made working on this ship in ten fucking years. So don't you mess with me. Do I make myself clear?"

"Why can't you inform the marine police? Tell them you're being targeted and get them to keep you and my ship safe?"

"How can I get the police involved? Are you a complete idiot? When they start digging deep, they'll find out why, where, and how I obtained these gems. Then I'd be deported back to Brazil, and the government would throw the book at me, lock me up for life. And I promise you, if that happens, I'll make sure you go down with me. You've been involved from the beginning; you took the bait, so you are well and truly part of this."

Larson started to shake, and Antonio sensed his anxiety, beginning to see him in a very different light from the strong man he remembered. "Fuck you, Sven, we've come this far. Now I'm at the final stage, getting off your fucking ship. Are you going to help me? I swear if you don't, I won't be responsible for what I'll do to you."

Captain Larson took a moment to compose himself and then asked Antonio what was needed, making it clear it was to be the last time. "I'm leaving this ship in the early hours of tomorrow morning, from deck five. I've got a speedboat coming alongside the disembarkation exit at approximately four a.m. I need you to make sure your navigation officer is taking a long break so Doris and I can quietly disappear and get out of your life forever. Oh, and before I forget, I will make sure your final payment gets to you as soon as I arrive at my next port of call. For security purposes, I'm not telling you where that is. But Captain, you know I'm a man of my word."

Sven finally agreed, telling Antonio he would speak to him in the morning and let him know how he was going to deal with his navigation officer.

Antonio decided he would fill Dom in before he retired for the night, so he put in a call and immediately Dom answered. In the background Antonio heard giggles and realised Dom was entertaining and sounded completely stoned out of his mind. "I'm going to make this short. You need to be here at four a.m. I want you to bring me an Uzi automatic machine gun. We may need it. And you need to be clear headed, so no fucking around. Is that understood?"

"Sure, man. I've got big connections in the township, so getting an Uzi should be no problem. Just so you know, my suppliers will want a large wedge for the gun."

"Whatever it takes, Dom. You pay it, and I'll sort you out very well. I'll call you early in the morning to make sure everything's in order."

Dom knew Antonio would never double-cross him, so he was happy. Besides that, this would give him great street cred in the township. As Antonio ended the call, Dom smiled. He put down the receiver and turned his attention to the two naked women lying on either side of him. Man, they were hot, he thought. He was going to enjoy himself tonight. Tomorrow he had to be calm, controlled, and not stoned.

James woke up with a start. He heard shouting and glass breaking. He jumped out of bed, ran to the sitting area, and saw Oscar being bundled into a black van by two large men. He opened the patio doors and ran toward the van without thinking.

Richard and Javier had heard the commotion and were running in the same direction. Suddenly, the van sped off, dust rising from the ground. Shots were fired, and one hit James in the leg. He fell to the floor, and the other two guys took cover. With that the van disappeared out of sight with Oscar inside.

When Richard and Javier reached James, they realised that luckily, the bullet had only grazed James's leg. "What the fuck was that about?" shouted Javier.

"I think these guys are after our diamonds. Antonio warned me things could get nasty. And now they've got Oscar," replied James. "I need to get hold of Antonio quickly."

The three men went back to their suite. All the girls were huddled in the main sitting area, desperately wanting to know what had happened. Richard and Javier began telling them what they'd just witnessed while James made his call to Antonio.

"Antonio, James here. We just had a visit from your friends. They kidnapped Oscar. What the fuck is going on? I don't like it. Guns are being used."

"Shit," came Antonio's reply. "Stay cool. I should be there in a couple of days. Take this number down. This guy will be able to make enquiries and find out who's involved. They want money, not Oscar, so keep calm, James. His name is Dominic—Dom to his friends—and he'll sort you out. Let me know of any more developments." And with that the phone clicked, and Antonio was gone.

I wish he wouldn't do that—just put the phone down in mid conversation, thought James. What a prick, he muttered as he dialed the number he'd just been given.

Early the next morning, Captain Larson told Antonio that all arrangements had been made. He explained that his navigations officer was having an affair with a guest who was a world cruiser. She had to be extremely careful as her husband was an elderly man with great connections, and he would kill his young wife if he found out.

Sven had arranged to give them a suite for three hours, between two and five a.m. "I told him it was a bonus for his hard work. He jumped at the chance. And the husband will be sound asleep, so she can easily disappear."

Antonio was delighted. Sven told him that two guys would be on deck five at 4:00 a.m., ready to assist them in leaving the ship.

"I can't wait to see the back of you," added Captain Larson with a smile. He wished Antonio good luck, and the two men shook hands and went their separate ways.

Antonio called Dom to make the final arrangements and was told that James had been in touch. Dom's guys from the township were organizing themselves to find out who had Oscar and where, and what it was they wanted. Antonio thanked him and told him he'd see him at 4:00am, adding, "Don't be late, and don't be stoned."

Doris came into Antonio's study. "What am I going to pack?" she asked.

"You are leaving with what's on your back, and that's all. There will be plenty of time to buy you a whole new wardrobe later, my love. Get some rest; we have to be up very early. It's going to be a long day."

In the middle of the night, Antonio and Doris quietly said good-bye to their dear friend and minder, Brick. He knew he would be by their side shortly, but he was extremely pleased to be able to hit the gym later and work on the muscles that were so desperately in need of stimulation. Funny, he thought, how some people needed booze, others needed sex, and some needed acquisitions to make them feel good. He just needed exercise. It made him feel good and in control.

The fog was lifting. Doris and Antonio were dressed in black, wearing balaclavas, standing on deck five. They felt anxious. Just before 4:00 a.m., they could make out the arrival of a speedboat through the fog, hurtling toward the enormous frame of the cruise liner. As Dom moved closer to the side of the ship, Doris and Antonio knew they had to leap. With a deep breath, the two of them closed their eyes, held hands, and jumped.

They landed awkwardly on the deck of the Riva but managed to stand up and find a seat where they could huddle together. Holding on to each other, they felt the power of the boat take them away into the darkness. The enormous door on deck five closed, and the *Dream of the Seas* silently slipped out of their view.

At first Antonio didn't recognise Dom. He was dressed in black all over. All you could see was his brilliant white teeth. "Stay down low," Dom said. "We should be inland in half an hour. I have a car waiting. It'll take you to a private airstrip where you'll board a plane to Botswana."

"Dom, man, I've missed you," shouted Antonio over the noise of the engines.

Dom put the speedboat into full throttle, and they sped away. It was cold. Doris started to shake. Nerves and coldness suddenly took over, and all you could hear was the chattering of her teeth.

Within half an hour, Antonio and Doris were climbing out of the speedboat and heading toward a waiting van. The headlights shone occasionally to let them know where it was positioned in the darkness.

Suddenly shots were fired, interrupting the quiet, still night.

"Take cover," yelled Dom, as he ran between some trees. He started firing his Uzi automatic rifle. Screams were heard, and as the headlights of the van came on, two guys could be seen rolling on the ground in agony, both having been shot in the leg. "Run for the van!" screeched Dom. "Now!"

Doris and Antonio ran as fast as they could. As soon as they were inside, the people carrier sped off, leaving Dom to deal with the two injured men. A motorbike had been left by the car for Dom to catch them up later.

Doris and Antonio held tightly to each other. They heard two loud shots pierce through the stillness of the night. They looked at each other wondering the same thing: Was Dom all right?

Their driver told them they would be at the airstrip within minutes. Out of the darkness, they saw lights, and ahead of them, they could see the plane waiting, engines fired and ready to go.

"Get out quickly, and board your plane," screamed the driver with a heavy African accent.

The pilot was waiting for them at the bottom of the steps. "Hurry up. Let's go!" he shouted.

Doris ran up first; Antonio followed. As soon as the pilot had closed the door and taken his seat, the plane was racing down the runway, picking up speed. Within minutes they were airborne, on their way to Botswana, the diamonds securely attached to their legs, ankles, arms, and wrists. Doris had the largest gem stuffed in her bra.

"That was a close call," Antonio muttered, his voice sounding full of relief. Doris took his hand, and the two of them settled back into their seats, hearts calming down and breathing getting back to normal.

Antonio called James to let him know they were on their way. "Have you heard from Dom? He was supposed to catch us up, but he didn't make it. What's the update on Oscar?"

"Antonio, calm down," came James's reply. "No, haven't heard from Dom, but I know his guys are working on finding out what's happened to Oscar, and they seem extremely professional. If anybody is going to sort this mess out, it will be them! Please God, Dom's all right."

"Please God," repeated Antonio, and with that the phone went dead. James had managed to hang up first.

Let's see how you like it, Mr. Antonio, James thought to himself, smiling as he went to wake the others up.

An hour later Doris and Antonio were standing in the tented suite that the seven members of SMEG shared. But this morning, there were only six there to greet them.

# Chapter Eighteen

Oscar woke up. His head and body hurt terribly. He realised he'd been drugged. He tried to move his legs, but they were extremely heavy. They seemed not to be listening to the instructions his brain was giving them. As his mind started to function, he saw that his legs were chained; however, they were loose enough to give him walking space. Very slowly, Oscar stumbled to his feet.

The room was in darkness. There were no windows, the walls were wooden, and a definite smell of damp encased him. He remembered vaguely being bundled into a van before he lost total consciousness.

One hell of a noise shattered the otherwise quiet night, and the door opened. Chains clattered, padlocks were unbolted, and then a torch shone directly into his eyes, blinding him.

"You're awake then?" A voice cut through the silence.

"Where am I? Who are you? Why am I here?" stammered Oscar, holding his arm in front of his eyes to block the glare from the torch. There was no answer for some time, and then a big burly guy became visible as Oscar's eyes adjusted to the light. He walked outside and came back with a coffee, some water, and a sandwich in a carrier bag.

"You must be hungry and thirsty; have this. My boss will be here shortly." With that he left, closed the door behind him, and locked the padlocks and chains. Silence resumed.

Oscar screamed, "Don't leave me here! I want to know why you're keeping me captive!"

Nothing. Only darkness and silence answered him. Oscar shuffled toward the bag and fumbled to retrieve the food, coffee, and water. He sat huddled in the corner and ate and drank for the first time in hours. He wondered what lay ahead for him. His thoughts turned to Sadie, his children, and his grandchildren, and he whimpered quietly to himself. What the hell had he done, jeopardizing everything he held dear for the lure of money? What a fucking idiot, he thought.

Time was passing slowly; it seemed he'd been waiting for hours by the time he heard the door being unchained and unlocked again. Slowly, the door opened, and in walked an extremely tall, well-groomed man.

"Hello, Oscar. You don't know me, but I know you. Why did you get involved with Antonio Cadiz? Is it that you're a man who can organise the impossible, and that's why Antonio made you an offer you couldn't refuse? Well, Oscar, this one is too big even for you."

"Why am I here?" mumbled Oscar.

"You are going to be my bargaining power. Stop messing around; you are fully aware of what I want."

"No, I'm not. Tell me."

"Oscar, if you start playing games with me, you'll get hurt. But if you do as I instruct, no harm will come to you. After all, it's not you I want. You've been an idiot; money has always ruled your head. You've sailed too close to the wind this time; you're messing with the big players of the world now. So do as I tell you, and you'll be fine."

With that two large men entered the room. They were instructed to remove the chains from Oscar's legs and to blindfold him.

"Bring him through to the other room; we are going to contact Antonio Cadiz. Oscar, you will speak to him and only say to him what you're told. One false move and you'll never be able to walk again. Do you understand? Oscar, do you understand?"

Oscar nodded, and then he was pushed to the floor. His legs were unchained and a blindfold was put tightly over his eyes.

Back at the lodge, James was filling Antonio in. The other team members sat around the sparking campfire and listened. James explained that everything had gone according to plan; the gems had been securely hidden in the large underground safe as soon as they arrived, and nothing out of the ordinary happened until the previous night, when Oscar had been kidnapped. "I should have been quicker. Perhaps I could have prevented them taking him."

"James, stop berating yourself. Had you gotten there any quicker, you and Oscar would probably be dead. At least this way, we stand a chance of getting Oscar back. Has Dom got any news from his guys in the township about who took him?"

"Nothing so far, Antonio, but he's still on it. With a bit of luck, we'll have some news soon."

"OK, thanks, James. Now I need to get hold of Brick. The ship has arrived in Cape Town. So if you'll excuse me, I'm going to make some calls. Enjoy the sun; get some rest. We've got a lot of work still ahead of us." With that, Antonio left the others and made his way back to his suite.

Inside the cool of his room, Antonio poured himself a large whiskey on the rocks and picked up the phone. Doris was coming out of the shower, her hair wrapped in a towel, her body completely naked and glistening with water. Antonio gave her a little wink, and she knew exactly what was on his mind. She also knew she would have to wait until after he'd made his call. She blew him a sexy kiss and closed the door behind her, leaving Antonio alone.

"Brick, it's Antonio. Can you hear me? Where are you? It sounds extremely lively."

"Hi, boss. I'm in a great new bar with a crowd of gorgeous guys. I'm hoping to get lucky tonight. It's been a long time."

"Sorry to ruin your fun, but I need you to get my friend David from the ship and fly with him to Botswana tonight."

"Don't do that to me, boss. Can't it be tomorrow? There's this guy, and he's such a hunk, and—"

"Get David and get a fucking flight tonight. Do I make myself clear?"

"Sure thing, boss." The phone went dead.

Antonio drained his glass and walked into the sitting room. Doris lay naked on the sofa, waiting for him. Her wet hair fell around her shoulders, and the look of desire on her face aroused him immediately. Business could wait, thought Antonio, as he walked slowly toward her beautiful, tanned, lean body.

Meanwhile, Brick had sadly made his excuses and left the bar, but not before getting Simon's mobile number. God, he was beautiful; damn Antonio, thought Brick as he made his way to the airport to meet up with David.

At Air Botswana check-in, David was waiting, Nora by his side. Brick saw them from afar, not hard considering David was in his wheelchair with his sweep of white hair caressing his head, and Nora, only inches taller than the wheelchair, was dressed in a white clinical uniform that identified her quite clearly as someone's nurse.

On board, David and Brick sat together, Nora quite happy to be behind them in the small business-class section of the Air Botswana 737 aircraft that was flying them from Cape Town up to Botswana. Nora slept, knowing she would be woken when and if David needed any help. Besides, she had no idea why they were flying north to a place she had never visited.

David and Brick were deep in conversation. They both knew they were forever indebted to Antonio. When Brick had met Antonio, he was jobless, homeless, and living rough on the streets of San Paulo. Life had thrown many bad cards in Brick's direction, and like a guardian angel, Antonio had miraculously walked through the alleyway that Brick called home and seen him. His incredible strong frame was the first thing that had caught Antonio's eye and then, after a few minutes of conversation, Antonio realised that Brick had a heart of gold. He was one of those unique human beings: more strength and power than most other men could dream of, more kindness than most women would ever know, and loyalty, all mixed together to make one hell of an individual. From that night on, Brick and Antonio had forged a relationship that would never be broken. Antonio the boss, Brick his minder, with true, deep love for each other never far from the surface.

David had experienced Antonio's decency many times through their long relationship, even if David had been the first person to give calmness to Antonio's otherwise chaotic life in those formative years. As he explained to Brick, Antonio had taken control of the massive oil empire that had become his completely after Aunt Wilma had passed away. At that time of his life, David was in no state to run anything. His drinking was out of control, his confidence at such a low ebb that his only chance was to go into rehab. Antonio had cared for the business, had run it as if it was his own, and had given it back to David when he was well and able to take the reins again.

No surprise the business was in better shape than it had been before. And for that, David would always be indebted to his school buddy Antonio. Both men knew they would always be loyal to their mutual friend. They would never, ever let him down, and as the flight started to descend into Botswana, they knew they would lay their lives on the line for Antonio Cadiz.

Antonio took the call. He was told that one of his team was being held captive and that no harm would come to him if he followed all instructions. The phone was passed to Oscar. "Do as they say, please. There's a gun pressed to my head. One wrong move and they'll blow my fucking brains out." With that the line went dead.

Antonio turned to James and told him to get hold of Dom as quickly as possible. "Tell him we need equipment to trace the calls coming in from Oscar's captors and armed manpower to deal with them."

Just as Antonio finished speaking, there was a sound outside the suite that sounded very much like a motorbike. As they went to see, it was speeding away. A package had been thrown by the front door. Antonio ripped it open. Inside, a dead bird, its eyes gouged out, lay lifeless. There was a note at its side. All it said was that contact would be made again later that evening, and if instructions weren't followed exactly, the next package would contain the right arm of the hostage.

James had heard from Dom, who had some limited information about Oscar's captors. He was making his way down now to meet them, bringing with him the equipment needed to locate where the calls were coming from and ammunition enough to deal with the kidnappers, if need be.

# Chapter Nineteen

Brick, David, and Nora had landed and were staying overnight in a local hotel. They would make their way to the lodge to meet up with Antonio and the other team members first thing in the morning, when the light would make for an easier journey.

Dom arrived. He was high as a kite. Antonio pulled him to one side. "Listen, Dom, we have serious shit happening here. I need you clearheaded and functioning. We're expecting another call tonight. I need you to hack in and locate where these bastards are, and being stoned isn't going to help."

"Chill out, man. I work better under the influence. I've been smoking the ganja since I was a kid. Have I ever let you down?"

Antonio had to agree. Somehow, Dom managed to get things done and done well, no matter how stoned he was. "OK, Dom, I'm putting my trust in you. Don't fuck up." And with that Antonio patted his friend lovingly on the back, and they went to join the others.

The girls were dining alone. They had all agreed that, under the circumstances, it was wise to keep them out of the kidnapping situation. They were going to watch a girlie film, leaving the men to get down to business.

Dom asked if Antonio thought the kidnappers were South African. Antonio said he doubted it from the telephone conversation he had just finished. "I think they're Brazilians. And if I'm right, man, Brazilians are ruthless!"

Oscar was chained up again. He had no idea what was going on. He began shouting. Soon enough, there was a voice outside the door. "Shut the fuck up. You're giving me a headache. If you don't, I'm gonna come in and put a towel so far into your fucking mouth that you won't be able to breathe."

Oscar was silent. Shit, this is bad, he thought. "Listen, mate, I need to take a crap. Please help me."

"There's a bucket in the corner. Use that," came the reply. And then silence.

The men sat waiting while Dom set up the equipment. Eventually, everything was ready. All they needed now was to receive the next call. Antonio had to try and keep the conversation going as long as possible so Dom could make a good trace. Easy for a pro like Antonio. He had no qualms about the pending telephone call. While the others waited anxiously, Antonio poured himself a large whiskey, put his feet up, and relaxed. Dom rolled himself a spliff, and both men looked up to the sky and enjoyed the stillness that surrounded them. A thousand stars were twinkling in the darkness. Javier, James, and Richard looked at each other; they couldn't believe the laid-back way in which Antonio and Dom were dealing with things.

Suddenly, the phone rang.

Dom flew into action. He switched the equipment on and gave Antonio the signal when it was appropriate to answer. Antonio was as cool as a cucumber. No one knew what was said; all they heard was Antonio pretending that the signal was weak. He walked casually around the room and waited for Dom to signal that he'd made a decent connection. After the thumbs-up sign from Dom, Antonio said the line was now clearer, and he listened to the caller's requests.

All of a sudden, they heard Antonio shout, "No way, you can do what you want with Oscar. You must be insane thinking we can do a deal like that!" A few minutes later, the conversation ended.

Sadly, there wasn't a definite trace on the call.

Antonio spoke first. "They asked for half the two-point-two-five billion to free Oscar. I sold them inferior drugs some years ago, and they have been watching me ever since. When they got intelligence of the diamond haul, they waited their time, and they're now using Oscar as a bargaining tool. They want half the gems by midnight, or Oscar will suffer the consequences."

"What are we going to do?" asked Richard.

"Nothing," was Antonio's reply. "They want diamonds, not Oscar's blood. We wait, and if we lose Oscar, so be it. We'll hear from them again, and then we'll know exactly where they are. Until then, have any of you killed?" Silence followed, and it became clear that no one there had ever handled a gun, let alone taken a life.

"OK. Dom, take these men outside; train them as best you can in what short time we have. Call your guys from the township. Get them here with extra weapons. Once we get an absolute trace on the next call, we'll take action. These bastards have to be taken out. If we can get Oscar back, that's a bonus. But they can fuck themselves if they think they can get half of our magnificent diamonds. We've worked too hard to get to where we are to give them away."

By midnight the men had learned the basics of handling a gun. Dom's guys from the township had arrived, full of testosterone and weed. Javier was having a cigarette outside when a motorbike sped past, and another package was flung to the ground. He took it immediately to Antonio, who ripped it open.

Inside, there was a photograph of Oscar, chained and blindfolded, with a noose around his neck. His right side was covered in blood. There was a large wad of cotton wool inside a Ziploc bag. It was soaked in blood, so much so that it was dripping through into the plastic. A note read, *You have one last chance to accept our terms, or next time your friend's heart will be sent to you, still beating. Expect our call later.*

Everyone was silent.

# Chapter Twenty

Oscar sat shivering in his room. Christ, he thought, the team is leaving me for dead. He stank. The tomato ketchup that had been poured over him before the photograph was taken had dried. His finger throbbed where they had cut him. Thank God it was only a finger. Next time, Oscar knew it would be the real thing. He was terrified.

His door was unlocked; the big guy who brought him food and drink earlier stood before him.

"Come with me. The boss is allowing you a shower. You reek. Let's hope your friends don't desert you because next time, you'll be sliced in pieces."

Oscar timidly followed him. Could this be my last ever shower? he wondered.

The team waited. Dom's guys paced outside. They knew the call was coming. Everyone was ready to go, but they needed a definite trace to identify Oscar's exact whereabouts. The last call had given them a rough area, about twenty minutes from where they were. But that wasn't enough. This next call was imperative.

At precisely 2:00 a.m., the phone rang. Dom gave the thumbs up, and Antonio answered. All the others heard was Antonio agreeing to deliver the diamonds personally tomorrow at 8:00 a.m. He said he would be alone and insisted on speaking to Oscar to confirm he wasn't dead. As they were talking, Dom signalled that an exact trace had been made, and Antonio finished the conversation: "Glad to hear you're OK, mate. We'll have you with us tomorrow."

The relief in knowing Oscar was alive was immense.

"OK, guys, time to take action. Girls, you pack. Once we have Oscar, we are going to a secret place, deep in the bush. Dom's guys are preparing the place with food, water, and camp beds as we speak. We'll leave the diamonds here, hidden safely underground, until we're ready to move on. Brick, David, and Nora will be joining us tomorrow. We'll have plenty of time to calmly plan our next move. So, gentlemen, are you ready to go and rescue Oscar?"

Richard, Javier, and James nervously held their rifles and said they were ready to go. Outside, Dom and his guys sat in a jeep, firearms loaded, all excited to do some killing. The others climbed in, and they sped away into the darkness.

"How'd you enjoy your shower, Grandad?" asked the big guy.

"The shower was good. A bit cold, and I didn't like the soap," came Oscar's reply.

"Suppose you didn't like the loo paper either, eh?" the man joked.

"Well, as you brought it up—"

"Shut the fuck up before I put a gun up your arse. No wonder your friends haven't rushed to do a deal for your return. I bet they were glad to get rid of you."

With that Oscar was thrown back into his dark, damp room. The chains and padlocks were bolted. He huddled up against the wall and wondered if it was true. Could his friends be pleased to have gotten rid of him? Did they dislike him that much? He knew he was a pain in the arse at times, trying to organise everyone's life, but he truly didn't mean any harm. Anyway, Antonio was coming for him in the morning, so Oscar closed his eyes and tried to sleep.

The team positioned themselves quietly around the camp. They knew where Oscar was; they had seen him be thrown into the hut a little while ago. Dom's guys cut the electricity and they rushed forward, shooting into the air, making as much noise as possible. James, Richard, and Javier pulled the triggers of their firearms with very little idea where they were aiming. Adrenaline pumped through their veins. It all happened so quickly. The Brazilians came running out of two huts, and one by one, they were shot to the ground.

Oscar heard the commotion and was frightened. He pushed himself up into a corner of the room, shivering. Suddenly, shots were blasting at the door, and it fell inward. Dom entered and fired his gun directly at the chains around Oscar's legs. They came apart immediately. Oscar was in a ball, fearful for his life. "Get up, man," screamed Dom. "Antonio has arranged for your escape. Quick! Come with me now!"

As they clambered through the door, Oscar heard a gunshot. He turned and saw one of Dom's guys standing over a lifeless body. As Oscar watched, the guy aimed his gun and, without any hesitation, shot directly into the man's head.

"What's he doing?" mumbled Oscar.

"Blowing their brains out, man! Making sure there's no life left in any of those bastards," came Dom's reply.

Oscar shuddered as another gunshot echoed through the night. This time, he heard a small cry of pain, followed by another shot. And then silence. No one was going to survive tonight's massacre; that was obvious.

They approached the jeep, and Oscar was pushed inside. He saw James, Richard, and Javier, all holding their firearms, surrounded by a group of locals who smiled widely at him. Tears welled up in his eyes; he couldn't believe he was free! The four guys hugged one another, and within an hour, they were nearly at the secret camp where the girls and Antonio were waiting patiently for them. Stars filled the night sky, and as Oscar looked up in amazement at their beauty, he had never felt so happy. These guys had risked their lives for him. He owed them all, big time.

Back at the secret camp, the girls were busying themselves with organizing their individual tents. Things were extremely basic. Outside each tent, a makeshift wooden structure created a screen for showering. Behind the screen a rope was attached to a metal bucket that was more like a large watering can. This could be hoisted up to a wooden platform and, using a second rope, could be tipped to create a flow of water. Showers were going to have to be quick, thought Karmen. The Jo Malone products would have to be put on hold for a while—too much lather and not enough water to rinse was probably not the wisest way to go. Just a basic bar of soap would have to do from now on, she figured.

The tents fared little better. Enough room in each for two roll-down camp beds and a little wooden box, upon which stood two gas lamps. Outside each tent, an awning covered two foldaway chairs and a table. The toilets were some way off and consisted of removable metal buckets that sat inside holes in the ground. Each had been dug and prepared in advance by Dom's guys, who had created an element of privacy by surrounding each with an open-top wooden screen, much like those around the showers. Every person had been allocated his or her own individual toilet, with names carved into the wood. There was plenty of space between each, which was something to be pleased about. The girls had been told that Dom's guys would be responsible for the removal of waste and the maintenance of each cubicle. The women's and men's areas were separated by a lot of foliage.

"I can't believe this is how we've got to live. The thought of those men having to empty these buckets makes me feel sick. And Christ, how the hell do we wash our hair in those pathetic showers?" Ruth wailed.

"Surely we won't be here for longer than a couple of nights," Josephine responded, trying to make a statement but actually asking a question.

"Look, we have to be positive," interrupted Karmen. "Once this is over, we'll have the rest of our lives to lavish ourselves with luxury. And then we'll look back on this and smile."

"I don't know about smile," grumbled Josephine, "but Karmen's right. Positive thinking. Truth be told, we really don't have much choice…I wonder when the boys will be back. I saw Doris a while ago, and she said they were safe and on their way here."

"She's an odd one. Never mixes with us, always by Antonio's side. Sometimes I really wonder if she's as genuine as Antonio seems to believe," murmured Karmen.

"Well, that's his problem," came Josephine's reply. "I just want James back here safe and to get through the next few days."

With that the three girls decided to open a bottle of white wine. "Thank God there are provisions," said Josephine, to which the ladies all toasted. In the distance they smelled food cooking. Dom's guys were preparing something over a campfire. It smelled good, although none of them wanted to think too much about what it was or how it had been foraged, especially Karmen. She doubted if there had been time for any of Dom's guys to go fishing, and she assumed the Okavango River was probably miles from wherever they were anyway. Oh well, she thought, at least she'd lose a few kilos.

Antonio passed by Josephine's tent where the three girls were busy chatting underneath a blanket of stars. He took them by surprise as he called out to tell them the jeep would be arriving at any minute.

When Oscar got out, each girl hugged him; even Doris came forward and awkwardly put her arms around him. Oscar felt like a hero coming home from war.

"Suppose you all thought that was the end of me, but I showed those thugs I'm not a lightweight. They were lucky they tied me up. Otherwise, I would have taken them out one by one with my bare hands."

"Oh, poor Oscar. You're back with us now," whispered Josephine.

"If I hadn't been blindfolded most of the time, they would have seen in my eyes I wasn't someone to mess with," he continued.

"OK, Oscar, enough of the dramatics," piped up Richard.

"Yeah, Oscar. Anyone would think you got yourself out of there singlehandedly," James said jokingly.

"I could have dealt with the lot of them if I wasn't carrying around tons of chains."

"Yeah, yeah," Javier, James, and Richard said together.

This guy lives in a fantasy world, they all thought to themselves but said nothing. Antonio sneaked in alongside them. At first nobody noticed him.

"Hi, Oscar. Good to have you back safe and well."

Everyone jumped. Oscar walked toward him, hand outstretched, ready to shake, and then his emotions got the better of him. He bear-hugged Antonio while whispering, "Thanks for getting me out of there. I owe you my life."

"Anytime, Oscar, anytime," came the reply.

The group decided to have a look at their new accommodation.

"How long do we have to stay here, Antonio?" Josephine asked as they headed off.

"We have enough supplies to last us a maximum of ten days. Once David, Brick, and Nora arrive, we can arrange a meeting and discuss our strategy then."

Ten days, thought Josephine. How the hell were they going to manage? But she smiled politely and said, "Thanks, Antonio. I'll let the others know. See you at dinner."

As Antonio made his way to his tent, his cell phone rang. It was Dom. He wanted to check that everyone was settled and safe in the new camp. Antonio confirmed that all was good, although the girls seemed to be struggling with the limited facilities.

"Dom, what are you going to do with the bodies? We don't want anyone to come across them."

"All taken care of, boss. They've been taken to the bush where a pride of hungry lions live. Once they've had their fill, the vultures will finish them off. And then in a couple of days, the boys from the township will go in and bury the bones." With that Dom went into fits of hysterical laughter and was gone.

He's as high as a kite, Antonio thought as he made his way back to his tent.

Doris was taking a shower, and Antonio decided to join her. He removed his clothes and stepped in. They stood naked in the wooden shack; the opening above them showed the darkness, interrupted only by a thousand sparkling stars. They smiled and began slowly lathering each other's bodies.

Antonio was strong and able to easily release some water from the overhead bucket. They seemed to be oblivious to the world around them and certainly weren't bothered by the basic conditions. In fact, they were both enjoying their surroundings and being together.

While their excitement grew, the other couples and Oscar were seated outside Karmen's tent, sharing some wine and complaining quietly to one another about the conditions they found themselves in.

"I just can't imagine showering in those disgusting wooden shacks," moaned Ruth.

"Forget that," interrupted Josephine. "Have any of you used the loos yet?"

"Thank God for baby wipes. I've got packets of them, and I'm more than happy to share them with you. Just let's try and stop complaining, guys. This time will pass. Let's have another drink." And with that, Karmen filled everyone's glass.

"What's that?" asked James. Everyone was still and listened.

"I don't believe it," came Ruth's answer. "Those two are actually at it in their shower."

"Oh, believe it," giggled Josephine. "She's like a fucking bunny rabbit."

"Lucky bastard," muttered Richard under his breath.

"I heard that," came Karmen's reply.

"Told you," piped in James. "Karmen's got ears like antennae."

"Shut up, you!" Karmen giggled as she threw her serviette at him.

Doris and Antonio were back in their tent getting dressed to meet the others for dinner. Dom's guys were setting up a large trellis table outside in a clearing, passing a joint around as they busied themselves. Dinner wouldn't be too long. Antonio's mobile began vibrating on the wooden box by the camp bed. He managed to answer it before the call went to voice mail.

"I don't believe it! Carl, I haven't heard from you in ages. How are things?" Antonio sounded animated. Doris looked at him, wondering who could possibly be so exciting to Antonio. He put his finger to his mouth, and she knew he would fill her in later. Quietly, Doris left the tent.

Carl Finkelstein was one of the world's largest diamond dealers. He dealt in both rough and polished diamonds. A Jewish man who had grown up in Johannesburg, he had moved his operation to Botswana a few years ago, after having robbery after robbery until the insurance company refused to insure him anymore. The diamond centre in Botswana had the best security there could possibly be and allowed dealers like him to go about their business unhindered.

He suffered from "little man" syndrome. At only five feet two, weighing about fifteen stone, he cut a very unattractive figure. He had a sweep of wiry black hair that grew around the sides and at the very base of the back of his head. The rest of his scalp was as bald as a baby's bottom. Antonio often thought his hair looked as if he had recently received an electric shock, the way it grew wildly outward. But he was a great guy with the best, funniest personality you could wish for. And of course, he was the toughest businessman you would ever meet and knew diamonds like the back of his hand.

"I hear you're in Botswana," said Carl.

"Yes, I only arrived a few days ago, but it seems like months. So much has happened. So how are things with you, Carl?"

"Good. Botswana is a great place for me. There's a strong demand for diamonds, and business is good. I still wish I could have surgery to be four inches taller. I'd pay anything. As you know, Antonio, I've always had a thing for girls who are at least six feet tall, and wearing shoes with platforms is starting to cause me back problems. They tell me they love me just the way I am, but they think I'm stupid. Take away their credit cards, and if my bank balance was zero, I'd not see their little arses for dust.

"Talking about arses, the one I have at the moment I really want to hold on to. She's a stunner. Can you imagine? Six foot one, legs that go on forever, blonde, lean, and never says no to sex. When I'm on top of her, she tells me she loves my wiry hair touching her boobs. She's a diamond. Excuse the pun."

"Sounds great, Carl. Good luck to you. But getting back to business, I have a haul of superb diamonds I want you to see. I can bring all the certificates with me for you to photocopy, and I want to bring a friend along as well."

"Male or female?"

"Male, Carl. His name is Richard. Richard Zimmerman."

"I'd rather a Brazilian beauty, but yeah, sure, bring the guy along. Give me a couple of days, and I'll get back to you to make arrangements."

"Sure thing, Carl. Take it easy." And with that the conversation ended. Antonio felt things were at last coming together. He adjusted his collar and walked out of his tent.

# Chapter Twenty-One

They had a fine meal, prepared well, consisting of kudu for the meat eaters and whitefish for the vegetarians. Jason, Dom's right-hand man, told Karmen that he had caught the fish from the Okavango Delta that morning. Apparently, the river was only fifteen minutes away. He told her he would be happy to take them there and show them his method of fishing, which had been handed down through generations of his family. Karmen was delighted and suggested the next day. Jason smiled enthusiastically.

They all drank plenty of wine, and as they tottered to the makeshift toilets, somehow the basic conditions surrounding them seemed less daunting. Each couple settled into their tents and slipped into their camp beds, extinguishing their gas lamps. Sleep came quickly, and neither the noises of the bush nor the noises of Dom's guys clearing away after the dinner woke any of them.

Oscar, however, left his gas lamp burning. Alone in his tent, he thought of Sadie, his children, and his grandchildren. He heard every noise outside and wondered if sleep was going to come to him tonight.

Early the next morning, David, Nora, and Brick arrived. Antonio was up earlier than the others and greeted his two oldest friends with absolute affection. He had a special tent arranged for David and Nora. It allowed them separate sleeping spaces but enough closeness for Nora to take care of David's needs. Antonio had organised ramps to be strategically placed around the camp, so David could be manoeuvred easily.

Josephine commented that the accessibility created was better than that of most London streets. There anyone with a disability or a pram seemed to be totally disregarded, unless they chose to spend their lives in shopping malls. She felt lucky she and James had been given a chance to eventually leave that city far behind them. Where they would end up was anyone's guess. But the journey was incredibly exciting.

Brick had his own tent next to Antonio and Doris.

After David and Nora were settled, Antonio excused himself. He told them he would be back later and arranged to meet them at dinner. Carl had made contact earlier than expected, so Antonio needed to wake Richard and get him ready for a trip into town.

At 10:00 a.m. a car arrived to collect the two men. The driver saw them and immediately jumped out and opened the car door. "Good morning, sirs. I believe you are going into the town centre. Is that correct?"

The car was nice and cool. It seemed the air-conditioning was the only thing that didn't shake. The suspension was completely wrecked, and it felt as if it had been used like a rally car for years. Nevertheless, it was doing its job and transporting the two men to the town centre some forty-five minutes away.

At one point, Antonio shouted, "Slow down, man! My back is killing me. Can you try and avoid the potholes?"

The driver found this immensely amusing and dissolved into fits of laughter. "This is Botswana," he chortled. "Our roads are not highways, you know."

They passed a few small villages where women balanced water buckets on their heads. The babies hanging around their necks were swathed in colourful fabric, cleverly wrapped around their mothers' bodies, matching the dresses they wore. This seemed not to bother either mother or child. Each woman had the most amazing posture: tall, upright, and very proud looking. Not an ounce of water was spilled, and the babies nestled closely to their mothers' bosoms. As the women walked, the rhythm created a repetitiveness that was conducive to sleep.

Little children ran and played along the dusty paths, keeping close to the women. Richard noticed the beautiful faces of these children, their smiles and laughter full of happy innocence. He wondered for a moment when he had last seen such happiness in children's faces back home in London. They seemed to be kept indoors there out of fear of abduction, and when they were out, they were attached to machines to keep them entertained. When had he last seen a group of children run, skip, and laugh?

A little girl, her hair braided tightly to her head, waved at the car, and Richard smiled. Her eyes were bright, her smile was wide, and she seemed so very happy with so very little.

Suddenly, his thoughts were interrupted. They had arrived at the bustling town centre in Botswana. Antonio had called Carl in advance, and a black limo with blackened windows was waiting for them. They said good-bye to their driver and happily left his car and entered into the limo. The new driver was dressed in a chauffeur's uniform. He was incredibly handsome— his skin was dark in colour and his eyes were an incredible green. Antonio and Richard looked at one another in amazement and thought, good job Brick wasn't with them.

"Mr. Antonio, Mr. Richard, would you like some iced water? There are bottles in the fridge at the rear of the limousine. Be our guests; take what you want. We have nuts, olives, and champagne if you wish. It's about an hour's drive to the diamond centre, so sit back, relax, and listen to some music." With that the screen went up, and Antonio and Richard relaxed into their comfortable seats, pleased that the horrific drive into the town centre was over.

After a very smooth and pleasant journey, they arrived at the security gates of the diamond centre. Passports were examined, fingerprints taken, photographs of their irises snapped. Nothing was left to chance. Security was taken to the limits. Each man was given an identity card to wear around his neck. A uniformed guard beckoned them to follow. As they walked with him, they were informed that they would be passing through a series of security doors. Their cards needed to be swiped to give them access to the deepest parts of the diamond vaults. Once there, they would have to use an in-house telephone that would immediately contact Mr. Finkelstein. All they had to do was press the red button.

Antonio and Richard assumed that different-coloured buttons would no doubt direct the call to others at this incredible diamond factory, set deep in remote Botswana, a country with two million inhabitants and yet the size of France.

Once down at their final destination, they picked up the phone and pressed the red button. An automated voice told them Mr. Finkelstein would be with them immediately.

In seconds they heard shouts coming from the corridor ahead of them. Carl was waving his hands frantically, and in the true fashion of little man syndrome, his voice boomed. He approached them, hair flapping around his ears, taking little steps at an incredible speed. Suddenly, he stood in front of them, all five feet two inches of him, craning his head to look up at them both.

"Carl, this is Richard Zimmerman; he is an expert in diamonds."

"Is he?" came Carl's response. "In your expertise, what would you value a D flawless twenty-five carat at, Richard?"

"I would need the GIA certificate before I would even consider giving a valuation, Carl," answered Richard.

"I like you. Let's go to my office."

With that, the little man turned around and sped off like a rocket. Antonio and Richard had to run to try and keep up with him. At the lift they swiped their cards, entered, and then were told to swipe again to close the door behind them. This time, they were on their way up. Carl pressed the button for the thirty-fifth floor, and in seconds they came to a stomach-churning stop.

"Can I go back to collect my insides?" Richard said, still feeling light headed.

"This is one hell of a high-tech building, eh?" Carl admitted. "I built it after getting fed up with the robberies I endured back in Johannesburg. In the end the insurance companies wouldn't insure me. But now it's a different story. Everyone wants to insure me, but they can all get stuffed. We are self-insuring. Nothing better than being free of all those money-sucking bastards."

"Carl loves to win," interrupted Antonio. "He may be small, but he's very powerful."

Carl grinned happily. The three men walked through enormous oak doors. In front of them, Carl's office sprawled.

"I've never seen offices as magnificent," Richard muttered.

"Wait till you see some of my stock," Carl said excitedly.

"With offices like this, I'd never want to go home," Richard joked.

"I have news for you Richard." Carl gave him a wink. "Sometimes I don't. Wait till you see my personal assistant. She is a very sexy lady, and she's a great diamond sorter, among other things. Get my drift?" Carl gave Richard another wink.

"How about we start talking business? Time for fun later," Antonio interrupted. He always knew how to bring situations straight back to where they needed to be.

# Chapter Twenty-Two

Back at the camp, Jason had arrived to take everyone to the Okavango Delta. He brought his younger brother Joe with him. He felt incredibly proud to be showing Karmen and her friends how they had been fishing in his family for generations. Joe was also excited at the prospect. Never having seen a white person before, he had only managed a couple of hours' sleep the previous night and couldn't wait to show off his fishing talents.

The group was equally excited to be getting away from the camp for a while and eagerly clambered into Dom's jeep, taking care to place David in his wheelchair in the specially adapted area at the back. Brick had declined the invitation, as Antonio insisted he be constantly on call and available, so he waved everyone off and watched the dust spew into the air as they sped away.

They drove through the bush in silence, watching the arid landscape pass them by. Suddenly, in the blazing sunlight they caught sight of glistening blue waters in the distance, shimmering like a thousand stars.

"That's where your meal came from last night, Miss Karmen," Jason said proudly.

Joe beamed as the jeep got nearer to their final destination, the Okavango Delta, lifeline to families throughout Botswana. Jason informed them that there were seventy-one species of fish to be found in the sparkling waters that ran for miles and miles. Sand rather than mud lay at its bottom, filtering the water to keep it crystal clear.

"You ate tilapia, Miss Karmen, but we could catch tiger fish and catfish today and give you a special treat for supper," he boasted.

He pointed to groups of grazing animals on the lush banks of the river and told them they were lechwe antelope. "There are more than sixty thousand of them along the delta. They are larger than impala and have a water-repellent substance on their legs to allow them rapid movement through knee-deep waters. Only the males have horns," he added. Everyone was amazed at Jason's obvious knowledge and slightly ashamed of their ignorance.

He continued, telling them there were 450 different bird species to be found, and passed everyone a small pair of binoculars with a list of some of the most unusual birds to look out for. He told them his family was part of the Bugakhwe tribe, Bushmen who for generations had traditionally practised both hunting and fishing. When he finished, there was a slow clap that got louder and faster as everyone began cheering. Jason took a bow, and Joe beamed.

"Come on, let's go fishing!"

David, at his request, was placed in the shade of a tree, with his small picnic basket and binoculars around his neck. Nora laid a blanket down by his side and sat with him. They watched as the others walked along the bank, moving far off into the distance, where Jason had said the fish were abundant.

The sun lay low in the sky, radiating immense heat. Birdsong could be heard from every corner of the delta. Everyone collected in the shade of a large Acacia tree. The picnic baskets were put down, and water was eagerly drunk. Jason and Joe put bone hooks on their lines, which were attached to bamboo sticks. They then dug into the ground and expertly removed earthworms. Within minutes the little tin box they had carried with them was filled with wriggling fat worms, perfect to catch tonight's dinner.

Karmen retched as Joe attached a worm to his hook and wondered if she would ever be able to eat fish again. Buying them from the fishmonger—or better still from Marks and Spencer, where they were fully filleted—seemed a far cry from this. Fat little worms being pierced almost to death and then being drowned while no doubt still alive to finally be eaten by the fish that adorned her dinner plate most evenings suddenly seemed very unappealing.

Joe and Jason swung their lines far out into the water, and within no time at all, the lines were buckling under the pressure of hungry fish. The brothers quickly used their homemade nets to collect their prey. The fish were placed in a large cooler to keep them fresh for the evening's supper.

Everyone watched in amazement at how fast the two men worked, and before long the cooler was full to the brim. Then the picnic baskets were opened. They shared sandwiches and wine, and before long, even Karmen relaxed. They lay and listened to the flowing water, the birdsong, and the calls from the lechwe antelope as they grazed along the banks of the beautiful Okavango Delta. Life surely couldn't get much better than this, they agreed.

\*\*\*

Carl, Antonio, and Richard were deep in general conversation, sitting comfortably in low sofas at the far end of Carl's enormous suite of offices. When it was time to look at the certificates to identify the diamonds, he suggested they move over to his desk.

The men made their way toward the large floor-to-ceiling glass windows that looked over miles of arid land. Antonio and Richard sat themselves in upright leather chairs on one side of the mahogany desk. Carl walked around to the other side. He sat down in an enormous chair and faced the two men. He suddenly appeared much larger than his five-foot-two-inch frame. Antonio realised that the desk and chair had been expertly made to give the illusion that Carl was twice the size he really was. The floor had been elevated on one side, and Carl sat beaming with a confidence that previously had been missing. Little-man syndrome had been bypassed with this cleverly designed office area.

"Now down to business," he boomed. "Show me the certificates."

Antonio passed the file over, and Carl went through them one by one without making any comments. His brow was furrowed deep in concentration. When he reached the certificates that related to the coloured diamonds, he caught his breath and looked up at Richard and Antonio. "Now these are stones I've not seen for many, many years." He continued going through the documentation, and after half an hour, he sat back in his chair and smiled. "Do you have a value in mind?"

Richard looked at Antonio, who nodded his approval, and then replied. "I've looked at each diamond very carefully, and my estimation is that the one hundred stones are worth in total two-point-two-five billion dollars."

Carl whistled through his teeth. "And who do you think has that amount of liquid funds to hand, Richard?

Richard smiled and replied, "You, of course, Carl."

The three men sat looking at one another, and then Carl began chuckling. The tension eased, and all three of them broke out into peals of laughter.

"What we want, Carl, is to sell part of our stock so we have liquidity and then make an investment in an asset. Any ideas?" Antonio looked directly at Carl and awaited his response.

"I may be able to come up with something. I know a Russian contact who is looking to dispose of one of his many magnificent yachts. It won't be cheap, but from what I've been told, it is probably one of the most beautiful yachts in the world. It was designed by Versace, and although some say it's slightly over the top, it apparently boasts every mod con known to man. I can make contact and arrange a viewing, if you like. Then you would have an asset that would, at the same time, give you flexibility of movement. I'll need to do my calculations as to the value of these diamonds over the next twenty-four hours, and then we can see if we're in the same ballpark. How does that sound, gentlemen? Let me add, these stones are some of the best I have seen, and I'm sure we can come to an amicable arrangement."

"I'm sure we can," Antonio replied. "But I am telling you, don't try to pull the wool over my eyes because Richard knows his business. I want you to earn, but don't be greedy because we already have other contacts who are interested, and I'll have no qualms about taking these diamonds elsewhere."

"Antonio, we go back a long way; I would never try to pull one over on you. I'm absolutely interested. I see a good earner coming my way, and I've always liked to make a buck or two. I have three top people on my team. They will value the diamonds separately, and then I'll take all three valuations and come up with a figure that will work for us all. We then need to decide how we cut our deal. Either we sell on and split the profit fifty-fifty, or I pay a price for all the diamonds and any profit I can achieve is mine. Whichever suits you two is fine by me, but I think we need to agree before we take things to the next level."

Richard and Antonio asked for a moment alone and left Carl sitting at his desk. When they returned, it was Antonio who spoke. "Carl, we've decided that once we agree on the valuation, we'll split any profit with you fifty-fifty, but you need to find the buyer. As far as the yacht is concerned, if we like it and the price suits us, we'll shake hands, and then should you be able to purchase it for less, you're welcome to anything you can make. How does that sound?"

"Sounds good to me."

All three men shook hands, and then Carl pressed a button on his desk. Immediately, a husky-sounding female voice responded, "What can I do for you, Mr. Finkelstein?"

"Darling, lots!" Carl looked at Richard and Antonio and winked. "But at the moment, coffee and sandwiches will do."

"Leave it to me. Any preference in sandwiches?"

"Surprise me; you know how I like surprises." Carl sat back in his chair and smiled.

Within minutes, coffee and a selection of sandwiches arrived, brought in by the most gorgeous blonde Richard or Antonio had ever seen. She wore a skirt that just about covered her exquisite bottom; her legs were slender and shapely. Her body was magnificent. As she placed the tray down on the desk, she leaned forward, showing her ample cleavage, and ran her fingers enticingly through her mop of thick hair.

"Are these to your liking?" she purred, looking at all three men.

"Wonderful, Stephanie, as always," came Carl's response. With that she smiled and slowly sauntered away, her five-inch heels clicking on the wooden floor.

"Isn't she something? I've got a few like her. Makes life very exciting."

Suddenly, Antonio's phone started to vibrate. When he looked at the screen, he saw it was James and knew it had to be urgent. James would never interrupt an important meeting for nothing.

"Do you mind?" Antonio asked. Carl motioned for him to take the call, and Antonio walked away from the other two.

"What do you mean he fell from his wheelchair? Where was the fucking nurse? He's what? Dead?" Antonio's face grew ashen as he continued to listen to James's account of what had happened to David. Apparently, his wheelchair had rolled down a slope and landed in the water, and by the time Nora had come back from the toilet, David was face down, showing no signs of life. Jason had heard her screams and rushed to help. Dominic had been called, and he in turn had arranged for a local medical team to rush to them. Unfortunately, there was nothing to be done. David had broken his back and drowned.

"I'm so sorry to give you this terrible news, Antonio," said James.

Antonio felt his knees buckle beneath him. He threw his phone to the floor and screamed. "Why do these things happen to great people? Poor David. He deserved so much more. Why did that woman leave him alone?"

Richard and Carl rushed to Antonio's side. Together, they pulled him to his feet. They sat him on the sofa, and Carl poured him a very large brandy. Antonio knocked it back and held the glass out for a refill. Slowly, the alcohol took effect, and Antonio composed himself. He repeated the full story. Richard needed a drink himself as he thought about the tragic end that dear David had met.

Carl arranged for his driver to take the men back to their camp. As they sped away, they both sat in silence, deep in sad thought. When they got back, everyone was waiting, all except Nora. David's body had been taken away to the local morgue, and a stillness enveloped them all.

"Where's that bloody nurse? Go and get her. I want to wring her fucking neck. How could she have let this happen?" Antonio began shaking. The others hung their heads, and Brick went to get Nora.

Nora arrived in floods of tears. "Stop the fucking waterworks. Where were you when this happened? You were supposed to be taking care of David, not fucking abandoning him. I can't believe he's dead. And it's all down to you!"

"Mr. Antonio, I have had a very bad stomach and desperately needed to go to the toilet. I made sure David's wheelchair had its brakes on. The last time I left him, I double-checked that he was in the shade, that the brakes were on, and that he had water by his side. He told me not to fret so much over him and that he was fine and wanted to nap. I, I…"

With that Nora broke down into shudderingly violent sobs. Her whole body shook. Antonio softened slightly and moved toward her.

"I loved David, Mr. Antonio. He became my life. I have cared for him for fifteen years. I want my life to be over. I never got to say good-bye." She buried her face in her hands and wailed. Antonio put his arms around her, and together, they cried.

Exhausted, Antonio went to his tent, leaving Nora alone with no more tears left to cry. There was so much for him to think about. Carl's suggestions were not far from his mind. The organization of David's funeral. Where should he be buried? he wondered. He needed to contact any distant relatives who might still be around. And what about friends—did David have any? Antonio suddenly realised he knew very little about the best friend he had ever had.

Nora would have to help him. She, after all, knew more about David than anyone. Oh God, how cruel I was to Nora earlier, he thought. Surely she felt worse than anyone, full of guilt and now she had nothing, nothing at all, just sad memories of the man she loved. Antonio's head was banging. He needed to rest, but he knew sleep wouldn't come. He needed a sleeping pill. Where had he put them? He rummaged through his bedside drawer. Nothing. Then he opened the drawer on the other side. Inside staring up at him was an envelope, his name clearly written on it. As he started opening it, he began to shake. It was from David.

> *Dear Antonio,*
>
> *I am so sorry to place this burden upon your shoulders, but I know your shoulders are wide. I cannot carry on my life like this anymore. My condition is getting slowly worse. I am in constant pain. I depend on everyone. I can't even go to the toilet without help. Nora has been the most wonderful woman. I have no idea what I would have done without her. I have been in love with her for almost fifteen years, and my heart breaks daily. I want to tell her, but what can I offer her in a romantic way? Nothing. Please take care of my finances and businesses. I want my darling Nora to*

*have nothing to worry about financially for the rest of her life. I want her to be free to care for her family back in the Philippines and to go home if she chooses and take a husband to grow old with, if that's what she wants. Please tell her not to blame herself for anything. Make sure she knows I took my own life and will be at peace and out of this constant pain. You are the best friend I have ever had, in fact better than any brother could have been. I have been planning to end my life for some time now and decided to take the opportunity while you and Richard were away for the day.*

*I will be gone by the time you read this letter, hopefully, but please know, I intend to have no pain. I will take a handful of sleeping pills, drink three or four large vodkas, and when Nora leaves to go to the toilet, I will wheel myself to the edge of the slope. As the drugs and alcohol begin to numb all my cares away, I will pray for forgiveness and hope I achieve my ultimate goal—eternal rest.*

*Please forgive me, understand me, and remember I love you.*

*Always and forever,*

*David. X.*

Antonio lay on his bed and sobbed into his pillow. "Oh my God, David—why, why in heaven's name have you done this? How am I going to break this news to Nora? I hate you. My day started off so well, and now it's ending so tragically. How could you do this to me?" Antonio lost himself in thought and slowly drifted off into a deep sleep.

When he opened his eyes many hours later, Doris was kissing him on the cheek. "Hello, lazy head. How do you feel?"

"What time is it?"

"It's ten thirty a.m., my darling. You slept all through the afternoon and the night. I slept in Oscar's tent to let you rest."

Antonio reached for David's letter, which lay by his side. He passed it to Doris. She read in silence, tears welling up in her eyes.

"Why didn't he tell me that he was in so much pain, mentally and physically? I might have been able to help. I could have gotten the best doctors money could buy; I could have made it better, Doris. I could have done something!" exclaimed Antonio.

"Darling, stop. You're beating yourself up. There's nothing you could have done. All you can do now is follow David's wishes. He's free from all his torment. Just do what you can to make sure everything he's asked for is fulfilled now that he's gone," Doris said reassuringly.

Antonio knew Doris was right, and as he looked into her eyes, she smiled and told him she loved him.

"I'll go and get Nora so you can break the news to her." With that she left.

Antonio was sitting silently outside his tent when an exhausted-looking Nora arrived, eyes bloodshot and pained.

"Mr. Antonio, please don't blame me again. I can't bear the guilt I'm feeling. I'm going to have to learn to live with this pain for the rest of my life, and I don't think I could take any more of your anger. In fact, I really don't know that I'll be able to carry on knowing what I've allowed to happen." Her eyes looked pleadingly at Antonio.

"Nora, please read this letter. I think it may just make you feel slightly less guilty." Antonio pressed the envelope into her hand and watched silently as she began to read. Tears started to spill from her eyes, and the occasional sob could be heard as she tried to hold herself together. By the time she finished reading, Nora was wailing uncontrollably. Antonio took her in his arms and held her tightly. "So you see, it wasn't your fault. He had been planning this for some time."

"Yes, but I shouldn't have left him alone and given him the chance to end his life," Nora sobbed.

"My dear girl, he would have found a way. This is what he wanted, and now we have to be strong, knowing David's at last at peace, and make sure we fulfil his wishes." Nora nodded her head and wiped her eyes. She knew Antonio was right.

Later that evening, the whole group gathered, and Antonio told them about what had really happened to David. Nora sat, her head lowered, wringing her hands. Everyone's heart broke for her, but they knew her suffering had to be less acute than when she was blaming herself for his death.

Antonio had been busy. He'd made arrangements with David's attorneys back in Houston for distant relatives, work colleagues, and friends to gather at the family's small

Lutheran church so David could have a good send-off. Everyone invited was to stay at the Hyatt Regency for the weekend, in the finest suites on offer. Caterers had been arranged, and nothing had been left to chance.

Nora was flying home with David's body the next day so she would be ready to greet the guests. Antonio had even arranged to bring Nora's sister from the Philippines to be with her so she didn't have to face everything on her own.

"Dom will take you to a small airstrip tomorrow, where you will fly on a private jet to Johannesburg. There you will be met and transferred quickly to take your flight to Houston. Arrangements have already been put in place for David to be on the flight in a special compartment, so you have nothing to worry about. The funeral directors will take over completely when you arrive at the other end. You are flying first class, so you should be able to get a bit of rest.

"When you get there, your sister will be at the hotel waiting for you. Then you can spend a few days preparing for the funeral. A girl by the name of Charlotte will be at your service throughout, and she is totally able to deal with everything and anything. Once the funeral is over, you and your sister will fly back to the Philippines to spend as long as you want with your family. David's attorney, Michael Land, will be in touch with you, so you can let him know how and where you intend to spend your time. Money will never be a problem for you, Nora, and I will honour my commitment to David and look after his interests as if they were my own. You can always contact me—always.

"And Nora, I just want you to know how much it breaks my heart that I can't attend David's funeral, but it's just impossible. I want you to understand, if I could, I would be there, but I can't." Antonio's eyes began to fill up, and now it was Nora's turn to go and put her arms around him.

"I know you would, Antonio. I think you loved that man nearly as much as I did. Thank you for doing all this and so quickly. I will never forget what you've done."

That evening everyone sat together. They managed to eat and drink and remember David with smiles and many tears. The following morning, Dominic arrived in the jeep as planned. Everyone was there to say good-bye. Nora was overwhelmed by the send-off she was receiving—hugs and kisses from them all.

Suddenly, she noticed Javier and Ruth were being hugged too, and they had suitcases by their sides. Nora looked from person to person, showing her confusion.

"Oh, come on, Antonio, tell her," chortled Karmen.

"OK, OK. Unfortunately for Ruth, her father has taken ill in New York. It's nothing serious, but she and Javier want to be with him. So they will be travelling with you to Houston. They'll have a night at the Hyatt and then make their way on to New York. So, dear Nora, you won't be travelling alone."

Nora was delighted. She hadn't admitted it, but the prospect of taking David home to a strange country by herself had filled her with dread. Now that she had Javier and Ruth by her side, she felt an immense weight off her shoulders.

Antonio said his good-byes and turned to Javier. Quietly, he reassured him that once they were home and dry with the money, Javier's cut would be transferred immediately. As Javier climbed up into the jeep, Antonio placed a small diamond into his hand. It weighed about five carats. "A gift for your services. Look after that lovely young bride." He gave Javier a wink, and then the two men hugged. The jeep started to pull away. Richard, Karmen, James, Josephine, Doris, Antonio, Oscar, and Brick waved until the jeep was out of sight.

Brick excused himself; he wanted to text Simon. They had been in contact since the night they had met at the club in Cape Town when Brick had taken his number before having to leave suddenly. Brick hoped a relationship was in the making. It had, after all, been years since he'd had someone special in his life.

Karmen turned to the others and said, "I think we deserve a nice glass of champagne to celebrate the fact that there are only eight of us left. There's a wonderful bottle in the cooler, and Brick's not joining us, so that'll give the rest of us a small glass each."

"We could open up two," giggled Josephine. "After all, we can afford it." They all began to laugh, and the seven of them walked off to where breakfast was being laid.

# Chapter Twenty-Three

The next morning, after a relatively good night's sleep, Antonio, Richard, and James were busily talking. They had decided it was time to get Carl to fix up a meeting with his Russian contacts.

They agreed that at the right price, a yacht could serve them well. They would try and keep the crew, as long as there were good references to support each member. They would offer a large bonus, on the proviso that team SMEG was taken safely to their final destination. This, however, had yet to be decided upon.

Richard had created a spreadsheet clearly documenting each diamond, with its corresponding identification code and the minimum price they would accept listed clearly. They discussed Carl's character at length and agreed they should play their cards close to their chests. He was a slippery customer, to say the least, and they had to keep one step ahead.

Antonio made the call. Carl said his contact was very interested in doing a deal. If the yacht was suitable, he wanted to act quickly as the Russian authorities were hot on his tail. Antonio chuckled to himself; he knew exactly how that felt. Not for a moment had he forgotten about the Brazilian police who were desperately trying to catch up with him. That reminded him: he would soon require a top plastic surgeon. He needed to transform himself before he arrived in paradise, wherever that might be.

The three men agreed to view the yacht the following day. It was moored in Cape Town, just outside the main harbour. Its size prohibited entry, but tenders would, of course, be available. They were to stay overnight to truly get a feel for her, and then a decision had to be made.

They were due to get to Carl's offices at 7:30 a.m. The four men would be taken to a small airstrip from where they would fly to Carl's Gulfstream jet that would be waiting to take them into Cape Town. Antonio was in two minds about taking Brick with them. He wanted the Russians to see he had clout and security, but he decided the girls needed looking after more.

So when Antonio told the women about the plans, Brick joked with them. "When the men have gone, we can watch girlie videos and get cosy. Oh, I'm so excited!"

Richard, James, and Antonio knew Karmen, Josephine, and Doris would be fine under Brick's watchful eye and would probably have a wonderful couple of days without them. So with light hearts, they went to their tents to pack and prepare for their imminent trip.

By 8:00 a.m., the temperature was already soaring. Carl's air-conditioned Mercedes glided into his office forecourt and there waiting was the little man himself, flapping about as usual.

"I've been racking my brains trying to figure out who Carl reminds me of."

"Who's that then, James?" questioned Richard.

"Danny DeVito. You know, from *Taxi*?"

"You are so right. Don't tell him, for God's sake. We need him to sell our diamonds."

The three men had done a lot of preparation in the cool air-conditioned car as they made their way to meet Carl. They were clear about their bottom-line figure for the diamonds. They agreed that they would not budge. Anything Carl could get above and beyond this amount would be split equally. Should the yacht prove desirable and be priced right, they would make an offer and use the diamonds for its purchase. They decided Carl could keep the difference if he managed to undercut their price but only after the deal had been finalised.

They all felt comfortable with their decisions and smiled as they saw Carl walking toward them with the most beautiful black girl any of them had ever seen. Her thighs reached Carl's shoulders. He had one arm tightly thrown around her bottom, the other swinging wildly by his side. His mop of wiry black hair framed his smiling face. He looked like a cat that had just gotten the cream. Somehow, the other three men guessed he had no idea how stupid he looked. Poor Carl, they all thought.

Carl patted the woman's backside as he got to the window of the car so his friends could see and shouted, "Keep my side warm, baby; I'll be back in two days." She blew him a kiss, swung around, and walked seductively away.

"Carl, where do you find all these amazing women?" Richard asked.

"I have a policy; pretty girls don't want to earn more money, so why employ ugly ones? Now, let me pour you a drink before we get to the airstrip."

They all smiled at him as he got into the car but inwardly thought what a foolish little man he was, especially when it came to his views about women.

"Now, let's talk turkey about your gems. You want two-point-two-five billion dollars. My team agree the price is accurate, so let's go see this yacht. If you like it, decide what it's worth to you, and we'll shake, deal done. Then I will continue the negotiations with the Russians alone over a couple of days and try and make a small turn for myself. Agreed?"

"Agreed," replied Antonio. "But I'm not prepared to use the best stones to buy this yacht. Richard will choose the diamonds we use in the transaction. Is that understood? I want to be left with the best to give me my liquidity. Have you got that?"

"Sure thing, Antonio. And just to let you know, I have a lot of interest from some of the biggest players around the world. Your diamonds are wanted!"

Just at that moment, Antonio's mobile rang. He answered, listened, and only said, "Of course I understand, Oscar. You'll get your fair share as soon as I have the funds. Good luck. Love to the family and wish that grandson of yours a speedy recovery."

The others looked at him. "Nothing major, guys. Oscar's grandson has fallen and broken his leg and Sadie needs him back in the UK. He was in a right panic, but what's new? We all know Oscar. Life will be calmer without him."

The Mercedes drew up to a small, dusty airstrip.

"Christ, Carl, we won't all fit into that. It's tiny," muttered Richard.

"I told you, the runway is so short, it's the only size that can take off from here, but you'll like what awaits us."

The four men clambered up the flimsy stairs, ducked, and very uncomfortably secured their seat belts. Luckily no one suffered from claustrophobia. They skidded along the dusty airstrip and very ungracefully took to the skies.

Very soon they were making their descent, and everyone rushed to get out. The heat was unbearable.

"There she is," crowed Carl.

The others turned to look. The Gulfstream sat elegantly, glistening in the bright sunshine. A sapphire-blue line ran from its tail all the way along its brilliant white body. The engines were purring.

"Wow, that's a bit better," Richard exclaimed.

"Yep, she sure is a beauty. Wait till you get in," Carl said excitedly.

As they climbed the sturdy metal stairs, two stunning women stood on either side of the cabin door, dressed in matching uniforms, which complemented their bodies wonderfully. One woman was black with dark hair and the other white with blonde hair. They held trays of champagne and gave the men enormous smiles as they reached the top step.

"Sirs, would you please remove your shoes?" asked the blonde hostess.

"I apologise in advance," stuttered Carl, huffing and puffing from behind them. "I think I have OCD. It drives me nuts but not much I can do. What do you think of the carpet?" As the others struggled to remove their shoes, Carl bypassed them and waddled through to the cockpit, arms flying in all directions.

The interior of the plane was luxurious and smelled of cleanliness. The carpet was white and dense; another sapphire blue line ran all the way along the middle. Each of the oversize seats were made of white leather trimmed with blue. They were set in rich mahogany casings.

James, Richard, and Antonio had just been given a drink and a seat so there was little chance of spillage when Carl appeared. "Meet Jessica, your pilot, and Tanya, your co pilot."

"Jeez," whistled James under his breath. Jessica was a redheaded beauty and Tanya a brunette with the greenest eyes he'd ever seen. Both wore matching uniforms: tight navy trousers with fitted white blouses, open, showing just a little of their cleavage. The stripes on their shoulders denoted their status.

"Hello, gentlemen. I have the pleasure of flying you down to Cape Town today, with the help of my co-pilot, Tanya.

So please relax; let Abbey and Carla look after you. See you later, Mr. Finkelstein. Enjoy the ride."

With that, the cockpit door closed behind them.

"Bloody hell, Carl. What are you like?" Richard exclaimed.

"Women are as beautiful as diamonds. All very different, and I love them all. My motto is if you can afford them, then have them. Don't you agree, gentlemen?"

Soft music was playing as the plane began to pick up speed. Soon enough, they were gliding above the clouds. The pilot announced that they were flying at thirty-five thousand feet at a speed of six hundred miles per hour. Their journey should take them just over two hours. The weather conditions were favourable, although she recommended that they keep their seat belts fastened in case of unexpected turbulence.

Soon after takeoff their tables were laid with the finest crystal and silverware, and all four men tucked into exquisite food, accompanied by fine South African wine. Carl informed them that his vineyard produced some of the best wine the country had to offer, and today's were chosen by him personally. Sleep followed shortly, and before long, they were awoken to be told that landing was about to commence. They would be on the ground in fifteen minutes.

"You've got to buy a plane like this once you've got your money, Antonio. In fact, I might buy a plane like this once I've got your money," Richard chuckled. "It's fantastic. Don't you want one?"

"You obviously don't know me that well, Richard; I'm not a flashy person."

"Antonio, you only live once," came Richard's reply, and in his head, he remembered the penthouse on board the cruise liner and thought, not much you're not flashy.

The landing was incredibly smooth. Very quickly, the engines were turned off, and both pilot and co pilot emerged from the cockpit.

"How was the flight?" enquired Jessica.

"Marvellous as usual, darling," responded Carl. "Don't you agree, gents?"

The others nodded in agreement as their eyes darted among the four beauties who stood before them.

"Are you freelance?" asked Richard. "Because I'd like to employ you when I buy one of these."

"Sorry, Mr. Zimmerman, we are permanently employed by Mr. Finkelstein, but we do have colleagues who might be interested."

"As long as they look like you, we could be on to something," came Richard's jesting answer. Although deep down, he loved the idea, and he knew Karmen would be in her element flying around the world in a private jet like this, he wasn't too sure how she'd take to an all-female crew.

Jessica asked Carl if they should stop over in Cape Town and wait to fly them back or return to Botswana and fly back in two days. She told him there was little difference in cost, taking landing charges and fuel consumption into consideration. So Carl told them to stay in Cape Town and added that he might even arrange for them all to visit him on the Russians' yacht, depending on the itinerary that had been planned by them, of course.

"As you wish, Mr. Finkelstein. We're at your disposal, as usual."

Lucky bastard, thought Richard.

The men were told they had customs clearance, and after each girl kissed them good-bye, they left the aircraft and walked toward the waiting stretch limousine.

"Well, Carl, that's definitely the way to travel," James said.

"We'll be doing more of that soon" added Richard. "Come on," interrupted Antonio. "We've got a lot of work ahead of us." As usual, Antonio got everyone to focus on the job in hand.

From the airport it took about half an hour to reach the stunning marina at Cape Town, known as The Victoria and Albert Waterfront. Restaurants, bars, and hotels surrounded the pretty harbour where boats of all sizes were moored. As the men got out of the limousine and stretched their legs, a handsome, bronzed young man in a uniform approached them.

"Mr. Finkelstein, welcome. And a warm welcome to your guests. My name is Patrick; please follow me." He spoke with a strong South African accent. He had an earpiece discreetly placed behind his left ear, and as he led the way, he was very subtly communicating to other people.

Shortly, the four men were standing at the dock. Two other uniformed, bronzed young men delivered their bags and introduced themselves with a handshake. One was Lance, the other, Tom. Both had Australian accents and looked incredibly fit and handsome.

A tender was waiting. Another healthy-looking young man greeted them; he was dressed in the same uniform and introduced himself as Toby. He sounded English. All four men were helped into the tender, luggage followed, and then the three young crew members gracefully jumped aboard. Everyone spread out, with plenty of room to spare, and Toby steered the tender out of the marina. They passed larger and larger yachts as they neared the open waters, and once they passed through the harbour walls, they picked up speed.

The nearer they got to the yacht, the bigger it became. Richard could see half a dozen crew members, dressed in the same crisp white uniforms, looking rather small in an enormous opening at the side of the boat. This yacht was more like a small cruise liner.

Toby must have read Richard's mind. "Welcome, gents, to the *Golden Eagle*. She is one of the finest superyachts around. She was given her name because when she moves through the sea, her sleek elegance makes her look like she's flying over the water just like an eagle. And when the sun catches her, the twenty-four-carat gold that runs through her bow lights up, and she truly looks golden."

As Toby came alongside the *Golden Eagle*, all four men looked up and realised her size. "Wow," was all James managed to say. Richard whistled quietly through his teeth, Antonio said nothing, and Carl began fussing. His arms flapped, and his little body positioned itself to be first off the tender. Patrick, Lance, and Tom made easy work of removing bags, and one by one, the men climbed onto the platform. Carl, of course, led the way.

The six crew members waiting to greet their arrivals were the captain, the first officer, the chief engineer, and three of the head stewards. All the men looked immaculate and introduced themselves personally. Toby, Patrick, Lance, and Tom sped away, the tender twisting at a ninety-degree angle, and then they were out of sight.

"Gentlemen, please follow me." The captain led the men to a staircase. The carpet was cream and soft, with a small border running on either side along the length of the stairs, which spiralled upward. Discreet floor lighting followed the twist of the staircase, and beautiful artwork adorned the walls. "This is one of six staircases that connect five levels of the *Golden Eagle* to one another. She really is quite amazing. It will take a while to get your bearings, but we have crew members on all levels. They will never be too far away to assist you. My colleagues and I will leave you in the capable hands of your main hostess, Natasha. We must get back to work. It's been a pleasure to meet you." All four men turned to see a beautiful mix raced girl approach them, smiling. She was holding a tray of cocktails. The captain and his team shook hands with the men and quietly slipped away.

"These cocktails are favourites of my boss, Mr. Strillian Kasparovsky. He has asked me to welcome you and make you comfortable while your luggage is being put into your suites. Please come this way."

They walked over to a sitting area where an array of canapés were laid out on the rectangular table. "Please take a seat." Natasha beckoned the men toward the comfortable sofas that were positioned around the table. She passed a cocktail to each of them. "Mr. Kasparovsky will join you shortly, along with his two younger brothers, Albert and Mical. Please enjoy your drinks and help yourselves to food. Should you require anything else, just press this bell and I will be straight back." With that, Natasha left the four men alone.

The room they were in was simply magnificent, with panoramic views of the ocean from all angles.

"Be careful of these cocktails," remarked Antonio after he took a sip. "A couple of these, and we'll be on the floor. I wonder where our host and his brothers are Carl?"

"Probably watching us on one of the monitors to see our reactions. He is one smooth operator, is Strillian. I've never met the two brothers, but I know they're a tight-knit family."

"This yacht is really something else. I've been on a few in my time, but this takes the biscuit, don't you think Carl?" asked Richard.

"Story has it that Versace took over the designing after the first guy, some dude from Russia, ripped them off big time. Strillian had to call in the heavies to sort him out, if you know what I mean, and then Donatella took over and voilà!" Carl's little arms fluttered about wildly.

"I've had enough agro in my life, thanks, Carl," responded Antonio. "I don't need any more, especially if these guys are the sort who call in the heavies when the going gets tough."

"Don't you worry yourself. Be straight with him. He'll try and make you feel like you've been friends for years; that's his way. He's always looking for the best deal, but who isn't, eh, my friend? Just don't try and pull the wool over his eyes, and then you'll have nothing to worry about. Oh look. Here they come. Strillian, my dearest friend, how wonderful to see you." Carl waddled up to the enormous Russian, his arms flying above his head, looking more like Danny DeVito by the second. He grabbed Strillian around the waist, hugging him as if they'd been friends all their lives.

What a fake, thought Richard, James, and Antonio simultaneously.

He then did the same to Albert and Mical before turning to introduce the others. Each brother took the men in their arms and planted a kiss on both checks. Richard and James felt totally uncomfortable. Antonio seemed to be taking things in his stride. Placing his arm around Strillian's broad shoulder, he said, "OK, my friend, show me this wonderful yacht."

Natasha and another attractive girl arrived, trays in hand, and as Strillian led Antonio away, Albert said, "Gentlemen, here's to a good couple of days. Lots of good food and even more good vodka. Nostrovia!"

James and Richard raised their glasses and slowly sipped; this was business, after all. Carl threw his down the back of his throat as if it were water and shook his head as the burn began, his mop of hair shaking like a Saint Bernard. "Nostrovia!" he shouted as he banged his glass down.

Albert and Mical burst out laughing. This was going to be a long couple of days, thought Richard and James as they gazed knowingly at one another.

"So, Antonio, I hear you are from Brazil. Are the girls as pretty as I've heard they are? In Russia they are beautiful and naturally lean. Cosmetics give them bosoms, something to grab hold of, you know what I mean? They have sharp features and take wonderful photographs, blonde and stunning. Very little emotion.

"But I believe Brazilian women have natural roundness in all the right places. I want to meet a dark Latina. I want to fight, love, and dance and really get lost in a woman's plumpness."

"Strillian, I think I might have the perfect woman for you. But let's talk about that later. I want to see this magnificent yacht of yours."

"I like you, Antonio. I think we could be very good friends. Come, let me show you around."

They walked into a lounge area. Flowers were placed everywhere in beautiful vases, and the room smelled exquisite. The decor was simply stunning. Fabrics and furnishings oozed opulence. The lounge led onto an elaborate dining room.

"Under this floor there is an Olympic-size pool. After our evening meal, the crew will rearrange things and open the electric floor. Tomorrow, you can see how fabulous it is."

The two men walked through room after room, each as beautiful as the last, each with breathtaking vistas.

"We have ten suites, each totally soundproofed and private. They all have panoramic views. The bedrooms are massive, each leading into an even larger lounge area. They all boast his-and-her bathrooms. Here, my friend, let me show you the Du Barry suite."

Strillian opened a large door in front of them. The thick pile of the carpet gave some resistance, but with a little push, the men were standing in the entrance of a magnificent lounge area. Strillian showed Antonio the fantastic lighting system, controlled by a single remote. Colours could be chosen; star, moon, and sun effects could all be created with a touch of a button. Even the painted wall behind the enormous dining table could be changed to another work of art, depending on what mood was wanted. It was remarkable.

The bedroom didn't disappoint either. A round bed sat on a raised platform in the centre of the room. There were no walls, just floor-to-ceiling glass, giving views of the ocean from wherever you were.

"Watch this Antonio. Depending on where the sun is rising or setting, you never need to miss out." He pressed a button at the side of the bed, and the platform silently began to move. "A complete three-hundred-sixty-degree view! Wonderful, don't you agree?"

Antonio had to admit he was impressed. "If the other nine suites are anything like this, I have to tell you, I am absolutely bowled over."

"Oh, they are, except the master suite. This I must show you before we join the others."

They walked along corridor after corridor, each displaying remarkable works of art. Ahead of them at the very end of one corridor were enormous double doors. As they entered, the room was in darkness. Strillian took a remote and pressed one of the many buttons. The expanse of white carpet lit up. Sewn into the carpet were hundreds of little lights that changed colour at the press of a button. It was almost as if they were standing on the floor of a disco, except for the softness of the plush pile underfoot.

"Don't you just love it? Some people think it's way over the top, but I think it's just incredible," said Strillian proudly.

Antonio smiled. Somehow, this suite did appear to be taking things just a little further than necessary, but each to his own, he thought. Perhaps he and Doris would take one of the other nine suites as their own. Strillian continued his tour enthusiastically, showing off his pride and joy.

Ninety-inch plasma screens were concealed cleverly in every room, including the enormous his-and-her bathrooms. Each of them were kitted out the same, except for the difference in colours. Hers had a pink circular bath, sparkly, with all matching accessories. His was gold and silver, but sparkly too.

"What do you think, Antonio? Could you see yourself here?"

Not wanting to upset him, Antonio said he thought this master suite was incredible, but he would possibly choose another for himself and Doris, simply based on size.

"Is there a Mrs. Kasparovsky?" Antonio politely enquired as the two men slowly made their way out of the master suite.

"Yes, in Moscow, but this has been my play pad for the last three years. Girlfriends are better than wives."

"Not if you find the right one, Strillian," Antonio muttered, thinking of Doris.

# Chapter Twenty-Four

As the men arrived back to the large deck, the others were fully in the swing of things, consuming frozen vodkas and the finest caviar money could buy. Platters of food arrived, served by the sexiest of women. Carl sat surrounded by cushions that almost drowned him. His black mop of hair and waving little arms were all they could see.

"Let's make a toast to the Kasparovsky family," Carl crowed as he negotiated his way through the cushions to stand up.

"The Kasparovsky family," came the response from everyone else.

"And here's to a good business relationship," added Antonio.

Antonio agreed that he was interested in purchasing the yacht after getting an independent valuation. They also agreed that he could use diamonds for its purchase. Strillian and his brothers needed to have movable assets; the Russian authorities were snooping around the family, and diamonds suited.

"What do you intend to do with all the other gems?" Albert asked.

"A few more investments perhaps. Selling some at the best price and keeping the cream of the crop for myself," came Antonio's reply.

The three brothers stood and raised their glasses.

"Now it's time to stop the business talk. Who wants a massage? We have some very beautiful and expertly trained therapists, male and female, your choice." A bottle of champagne popped, and all seven men knew it was going to be a long, long afternoon.

The three brothers arrived back to the top deck smiling. A few hours had passed, and the heat of the day was fading.

"Did you four manage to get a massage?" enquired Strillian.

"Sure did," came Carl's response. "I had a stunner."

Antonio raised himself from the sun lounger, showing off his buff, bronzed body, which was in amazing shape for his years. "My girl was a slight bony thing. She had fingers like steel. I'm sure my back is bruised all over; Christ she hurt me." With that he turned to show the others.

Mical responded quickly. "My God, did she do that to you, Antonio?" As he spoke he winked at the others. Mical was the joker of the family.

"What the fuck has she done to my back?" screamed Antonio. "Doris will never believe it was just a massage!"

The other men began to laugh.

"Don't panic, Antonio; your back hasn't got a mark on it. Tomorrow you'll feel great, that I guarantee you. And what about you, Richard?" asked Mical.

"I chose the Malaysian guy. I love a deep-tissue massage. I find most women too gentle, and he was so strong, just what I needed. I feel a million dollars."

"And you, James?"

"I was very tempted by the busty South American girl, I have to admit, but like Richard, I prefer strong massages. So, sadly, I opted for the other Malaysian chap, and I have to say it was wonderful."

"I told you guys; I have a spectacular team. Now, let's talk," Strillian interrupted.

He pressed a button, and minutes later, a leggy, beautiful girl arrived with a tray of cocktails.

"Let's take our drinks inside and sit around the table, where it will be easier to negotiate. I'll take this seat; the rest of you sit wherever you choose." With that Strillian sat. His two younger brothers positioned themselves on either side of him. Antonio, Richard, James, and Carl took the four remaining chairs in no particular order.

The seven men talked for more than an hour, replenishing their drinks a number of times. Carl was the only one who got distracted each time another beauty came in carrying cocktails on a large silver tray.

The brothers agreed that they were very interested in trading their yacht, even though it was absolutely their pride and joy. After lots of banter, it was decided that the two sides trusted each other enough to accept the valuations each brought to the table.

In private talks, Antonio, Richard, James, and Carl believed that business relationships with the Kasparovsky brothers could go beyond this initial deal, and for that reason and that reason alone, they were comfortable in agreeing the way forward to purchase the *Golden Eagle*. But before shaking hands, Antonio needed to know which of his gems would be used for the $225 million that was the agreed-upon price for the yacht. There were some diamonds that he was absolutely not willing to part with; he needed to discuss things further with Richard. So it was crucial that, if things were to proceed to the next stage, everyone was happy.

Carl was to receive his commission directly from the Russians. Both parties would retain lawyers to draw up all the paperwork and set up shell companies to avoid using any names in the transactions. The brothers agreed to give Antonio another $250 million for the diamonds, so he had a decent cash flow to sustain him when he finally disappeared. They would transfer the funds into five separate bank accounts around the world. They discussed the continued employment of the ship's captain and crew and agreed to inform everyone involved of the changes as soon as the deal was finalised.

With that the meeting concluded.

Strillian, Albert, and Mical embraced the four men in their normal bear-hug fashion and then called for frozen vodkas.

"Nostrovia!" they toasted, and they downed their drinks, slamming the glasses hard on the table.

"Nostrovia!" repeated Antonio, Richard, James, and Carl, trying to follow suit. But somehow, their glasses sounded far less noisy as they hit the table. They had a long way to go to keep up with the Kasparovsky brothers. Their ability to drink was second to none. Inwardly, however, all four men knew the deal was nearly done. And being in competition in the alcohol department really wasn't a priority.

Carl was busy making arrangements for his pilot to take them back to Botswana the following evening. He had pressing business meetings to attend and was desperate to arrange a slot that could get them out before it was too dark.

"Why are you looking so stressed, my friend?" Strillian enquired as he passed Carl who was sitting on the sofa sweating, looking like he had the world's problems on his shoulders. "We have a grand dinner this evening. Lots of wine, women, and fun. We'll start around seven thirty p.m. Dinner is arranged for eight thirty, and then the party begins. Dress is casual. And the show? Well, the show, my friend, will blow your mind. Don't worry about tomorrow. Enjoy the now; it only comes once." And for a moment, Carl relaxed and smiled. Strillian's words touched a chord and rang true. He did always seem to put himself under pressure and miss out on enjoying the moment. Perhaps it was time to try and change—certainly for this evening, anyway. The party sounded wild.

Richard was almost ready to leave his cabin. He had to admit it was absolutely fabulous. The sun was just setting over the horizon, the sky ablaze in an array of colours, from blood orange to soft lilac. His floor-to-ceiling glass panels were open, and a warm breeze softly blew into the enormous room. As he admired his surroundings, he hoped that once the deal was done, he and Karmen along with Josephine and James could enjoy this amazing yacht for a little while longer before they parted company with Antonio.

Suddenly, his phone rang, snapping him out of his thoughts. It was James. He wanted to let Richard know he was on his way to collect Carl and Antonio from their suites and suggested they meet in a few minutes by the staircase that was mid-ship on their floor.

Richard checked himself in the beautifully ornate mirror, splashed on his favourite fragrance—Dolce and Gabbana's Intense, surprisingly a woman's perfume, even though he was all man—and left his room, pressing the light switch as he went. Immediately, the lighting dimmed, and all that could be seen was the twinkling of stars. Richard felt on top of the world. His skin was bronzed, and he was ready to have a party.

The four men met by the spiral staircase mid-ship, which would lead them to the bar area two floors above. Cocktails and canapés would be served at 7:30 p.m., and since it was only 7:15 p.m., Antonio took the opportunity to speak.

"Gentlemen," he began in a hushed voice, "I believe the deal is nearly done. I assume the next time we return, this beauty will be mine." He gestured with his arms, rotating his body.

"The only thing I need now from you, Richard, is the list of gems we should use to equal the two transactions: one for the *Golden Eagle* and one for the two hundred fifty million in cash. You already know which diamonds we have decided not to trade."

"It's all ready, Antonio. I've done exactly as we discussed, put a value on each diamond. The majority are perhaps not the cream of the bunch, but as we all know, the Kasparovsky brothers aren't fools, so I've put in a few pieces that are very special, so they can act as loss leaders. You can have my spreadsheet first thing tomorrow."

"Hope we're not up too early, if you get my drift," piped up Carl.

The other three looked sadly at the little man, who suddenly felt foolish and began sweating profusely.

"Come on, Carl," said James, feeling sorry for him. "Let's get to the bar; I'm sure the party will be great."

And with a gentle slap on the back, James led the other three toward the music, which was quietly wafting down the staircase. The mood had changed, and all four men were looking forward to the evening ahead.

The bar they were in tonight was one of three. Unlike the others, which oozed modern chic, this one had an old colonial feel to it. Very gentleman's club-like. Very British. The wooden mahogany bar ran the whole length of the room. There were comfy sofas scattered around, with dim lighting from numerous lamps that stood on mahogany tables. The soft furnishings were made of rich fabrics, mainly deep reds and greens, adding to a bygone-era feel. Strillian and Mical were sitting on stools deep in conversation. They were smoking enormous cigars, and in front of them stood an incredibly handsome well-groomed bartender, who was shaking martinis in a very professional manner. The walls were adorned with murals of palms and exotic birds, much like ones you would expect to find in the West Indies.

"Gentlemen," boomed Strillian. "Come, let me introduce you to my favourite bartender, Seon.

Seon, this is Antonio and these are his colleagues, Richard and James. I believe you've met Carl previously."

"Pleasure to meet you," smiled Seon, showing a set of beautiful white teeth framed by an enormous, friendly smile. "Can I fix you a martini or maybe an old-fashioned rum punch, for which I'm famous?"

"You have to try the old fashioned, if you've never had one," Mical interrupted. "It'll blow your head off!"

"Then, Seon," replied Antonio, "I think we have no choice but to try."

"Coming right up, sir." It was clear this guy loved his job, and Antonio hoped he would remain on the payroll once the *Golden Eagle* was his.

Before long the bar was full. Albert had joined his brothers, bringing a number of beautiful-looking people with him. They were introduced as friends and business associates and were a balanced mix of males and females. There were a few outstanding-looking blondes, who were introduced as distant relatives. James, Richard, and Antonio doubted this was the case but happily mingled with everyone. Carl was running around like a headless chicken, weaving his way through people's legs, seeming to want to get to know everyone personally in advance of dinner.

Just before 8:30 p.m., after plenty of drinks and delicious canapés had been consumed, there was a drum roll. A beautiful woman, standing all of six feet five inches tall and wearing an exotic red headdress and towering red heels, entered through the bar's wide mahogany doors. She wore the tiniest red bra, just barely covering her ample breasts. A gold chain was attached and ran down past her flat stomach, connecting to a matching mini bikini bottom.

"Your hosts Strillian, Mical, and Albert would like to welcome you to a night of food, drink, and exotica. Please follow me." With that, she turned and led the way. The bikini bottom was invisible from behind. As she walked, her naked, full bottom swayed provocatively from side to side.

Carl immediately attached himself to her, leaving behind the group he had previously been talking to. His head just reached her hips, and as she moved, his whole body bounced in rhythm with her thighs.

He turned to James and Richard, giving them a wink.

As they filtered through, it became apparent how beautiful the evening was going to be. There were seven circular tables, each set for eight people. The table settings were magnificent. Everything oozed sophistication, down to the last crystal glass. White lilies were draped around the room, hanging from sheer opaque curtains that created a feeling of being inside an Arabian tent. Ice carvings depicting all sorts of birds and animals were tastefully positioned around the room, bringing an air of coolness to the warmth of the night.

Each table was to be hosted by one of the seven men involved in the deal that was taking place. The seating had been well thought out; four men and four women, hand chosen by Strillian, were put together to get to know one another over what he hoped would be a meal to remember.

The head chef, along with his team, entered the room, dressed in the whitest of whites and introduced themselves and their menu. Soon after, the room buzzed with activity as the wines were poured and the food was served. Gentle background music, jazzy and sultry, played as the evening began. The talk became louder at each table as the wine flowed, and then the music very cleverly went up a notch.

Antonio, Richard, and James were extremely comfortable being separated and looking after three other men and four remarkably beautiful women at each of their tables. Their minds were focused on the task at hand.

Carl was being his usual self, sitting lower than everyone else at his table, booming conversation at people, especially the two glamorous ladies that sat on either side of him. They laughed at every joke, funny or not. And when he slipped his hands under the table and touched their knees, there was no concern shown by either; in fact, a gentle, encouraging hand placed on his moved his fingers higher. Strillian sure knew who to put with whom, thought Carl. He was in his element. He knew the opposite sex couldn't resist his charms.

After an incredible meal, a group of seven beautiful girls entered the dining room, each dressed as provocatively as the girl who had originally called everyone to dinner. They had lean physiques with large firm breasts and tight rounded bottoms. They all wore headdresses, high-heeled shoes, and very little else. The only differences among them were the colour schemes of their tiny bikinis, headdresses, and shoes.

One girl approached each table and made straight for the host. In a seductive fashion, they leaned forward, pulled the men up, and told everyone else to follow.

Music thumped in the distance, and as they made their way along the plush carpeted floors, the girls flirted obviously with Antonio, James, and Richard. Carl had one hand planted on the naked bottom of a leggy black girl and the other on the bottom of a miniskirted Russian bombshell,

As they approached the spiral stairs, the head dressed ladies, holding on to the hands of Antonio, James, and Richard, took the lead and slowly mounted the stairs one by one with their long legs, showing their nakedness to the fullest. It was clear they had been instructed to tempt the four men. And happy to please, James followed closely behind the girl in red, Richard behind the girl in green, and Antonio following the girl in purple. Carl was panting behind the girl in yellow, still trying to hold on to the Russian girl's behind at the same time.

Strillian, Mical, and Albert followed suit, but the effect on them was less dramatic. They had seen it all a thousand times before.

Once they reached the top of the staircase, the girls led everyone into the nightclub. Tables were scattered around the enormous glass dance floor. Below, Koi Carp swam peacefully in the underwater channels that ran in all directions below everyone's feet, taking no notice of the activity above them.

Each of the seven men were taken to a separate table with seating for six. The music got louder. Stunning, partially clad women brought around vodka shots, and strobe lighting rotated around the nightclub.

In front of the tables, a stage slowly elevated from the ground. The head dressed women were wrapped around poles, still in their heels. They swayed and moved in perfect time to the music, each more erotic than the last.

The other guests were watching from their seats, some completely engrossed, others more interested in the company that surrounded their immediate table. Strillian had created a party full of beautiful women to accompany each man present, and most of the men were full of testosterone and anticipation.

Antonio, James, and Richard were no different, but they knew they had a job to do and had to keep their wits about them. So they watched and enjoyed from a distance, minds always focused on the end result.

After a while seven topless guys joined the stage, bringing with them burning flame throwers. They began to bring the flames over the bodies of the girls, who continued to dance. The guys were swallowing the flames and blowing jets of fire from their mouths as the girls limboed beneath the blaze.

When the show was over, the heat was immense. The stage retracted below ground, and the music became louder. Cold dry ice blew through the club, bringing the temperature down quickly.

People began dancing, the vodkas continued to flow, and soon enough, the dancers returned without their headdresses, still in their heels and still almost naked.

The dance floor went wild, and the party began in earnest.

By the early hours, women were wrapped around most of the men, whose shirts were undone or, in some cases, completely off. Vodka after vodka was consumed, along with bottles of the finest champagne. Music was still pumping. Antonio was cuddling a bottle with a girl on his lap. James had taken centre stage, showing off his Greek dancing skills, surrounded by semi-naked beauties who were belly dancing provocatively around the room, while Richard was swaying to the music in a world of his own.

By 4:00 a.m. just a few stragglers were lying around. The music continued playing but more quietly than before. Albert was out for the count; his brothers nowhere to be seen.

Sunlight broke, and it was clear that the evening had been one hell of a night. The women had gone; bottles and food lay around everywhere. Staff filtered in and began the cleaning process.

The last remaining party animals were assisted back to their cabins, and silence prevailed.

At two thirty the following afternoon, Antonio was woken by the telephone. He fumbled to answer it. It was Strillian, who enquired how he was feeling and jokingly jogged Antonio's memory about the evening before. Antonio began to remember the stunning woman who had danced the night away with him before he staggered back to his suite. Alone, thank God. He told Strillian he would join him in half an hour, after a shower.

Richard and James were tucking into a hearty brunch, discussing the antics of the previous night. Both felt rather tender, but they were enjoying each other's stories of what incredible fun they had had. They remembered the beautiful women who had spent the evening dancing with them and laughed when Richard showed photos of James dancing like Zorba the Greek, surrounded by semi-clad beauties. James was feeling the physical aftermath of his dancing. Besides his head, his whole body was aching.

As they chattered, Antonio joined them and ordered coffee.

"Christ, guys, how are you feeling? I feel like shit."

"Yeah, Antonio, you look awful. Did you go back to your suite alone?"

"Thank God, Richard, I did, but I tell you, what a bunch of horny women. I've never seen anything like it before. These Russians know how to throw a party."

Strillian arrived, looking fresh as a daisy. His brothers followed, not looking quite as fresh.

"Afternoon, gentlemen. I trust you're feeling recovered. May I suggest some Bloody Mary's?"

Richard, James, and Antonio declined the offer as a tray of drinks was brought in by a beautiful woman. Following behind her, running to keep up, was the little man, Carl himself. He looked exceptionally bright. He stared at Antonio, Richard, and James. "Fuck me, you look awful!"

"Thanks, Carl. How come you didn't get smashed then?" came James's response.

"Well...I was with the hostess in yellow and that sexy Russian beauty. I left you lot drinking and took them back to my suite. We had a few recreational drugs and a very, very good time." Carl gave them a little wink. "Those girls can go on forever. Your heads are hurting from vodka, but my crotch is hurting from something much more fun than booze, if you know what I mean."

The others wondered if Carl was making this up, but considering the Kasparovsky brothers' clout and the women who were there last night, they doubted it. The women were absolute stunning professionals who could make even a man like Carl feel he was desirable. Deep down, they all envied him, even though they knew they'd have regretted it today.

After everyone had finished, the men made their way through the corridors of the *Golden Eagle*, noticing there was not a sign of the previous night's party. As they passed the room where they had eaten, Richard peered in. "Where's the dining room gone? It was here, wasn't it, Strillian?"

"Yes Richard, it was. But, remember, we have an electric floor that covers the whole pool area, and then this space can be transformed into anything we choose. Last night, it was used as an exotic Arabian-themed dining room. But now, as you see, my splendid crew has returned it to the indoor swimming area. You guys want to do some laps before our final meeting?"

The men declined the offer, first due to their heads, which were still thumping, and in Carl's case, his crotch. Second, they had arranged to leave Cape Town later that afternoon to head back to Botswana. Brick was doing a fine job looking out for the girls at the camp, but the men wanted to get back to them, and as Carl had pressing meetings to attend to later that night, it seemed they needed to cut their stay short.

The seven men sat around the enormous boardroom table. Richard handed over his spreadsheets, identifying the diamonds to be used in the final deal to purchase the *Golden Eagle* and secure the $250 million cash. Attached were the certificates confirming each of the diamonds' validity.

Strillian carefully studied the information on the spreadsheets:

      Yellow intense radiant cut 125.36

      Blue vivid 25.87

      Pink brilliant 28.02

      Round brilliant cut 50.81 D Flawless

      Emerald cut 76.21 E VVS1

      Pear shape 48.67 D Flawless

      Marquise cut 37.34 D Internal flawless

      Princess cut pair of 50.81–50.85 D Flawless

      Emerald cut 100.81 D VVS1

Heart shape 85.98 D Flawless

A perfect set of twenty-eight stones 663.01 round brilliant cuts (all cut from one piece of rough) Colours ranging from D–E VVS1–VS2)

Alongside each gem, the valuations were clearly outlined.

Antonio, James, and Carl sat quietly as Richard explained the intricate details to Strillian. They understood very little and prayed the deal would go forward based on Richard's undeniable expertise. After what seemed like an age, a smile broke out on Strillian's face. He turned to Antonio. "I think we have a deal."

The relief in the room was immense. The men shook hands, then bear-hugged one another, and in typical Kasparovsky style, vodkas were ordered.

"All we need to do now," interrupted Antonio, "is to arrange for our legal representatives to be present when we come back next, to insure all loose ends are tied up and we have no complications."

"There will be no complications, my friend. The deal is done!" boomed Strillian, and with that, the men raised their glasses and toasted their futures.

"I expect to return with my lawyer in a couple of weeks. Carl, can you coordinate between the two parties and make sure when we return all the papers can be signed and sealed, there and then. I want no delays; I would like to take immediate possession of the *Golden Eagle* once the legalities have been finalised. Therefore, Strillian, I intend to bring seven very special people with me. They will remain on board for some time. Of course, Carl will be joining us but only temporarily; he has his business interests to take care of in Botswana. And I trust you and your brothers have plans to move on?"

"Absolutely, Antonio. Once we have finished with the legal side of things, and we've had a few parties to celebrate, we'll be out of your hair."

With that, the men returned to their suites, packed up their things, and said their good-byes to the Kasparovsky brothers.

Antonio gave the yacht one last look as he boarded the tender. He smiled at the uniformed crew that were speeding them away, back to the bush, back to the girls. He knew when he returned, this would all be his, including most of the staff hopefully who made everything run so efficiently. He turned to James and Richard and quietly said, "I love it and can't wait to own it." The men smiled, and they all felt an incredible sense of excitement. Their new lives were about to begin.

# Chapter Twenty-Five

On the runway, the Gulfstream jet engines fired and stood waiting for the men's arrival. Abbey and Carla waited on either side of the cabin door, looking as professional and sexy as they had previously.

The men climbed the stairs, Carl in the lead. The stewardesses smiled and subtly motioned to remind them to remove their footwear. Antonio groaned as he bent to take off his perfectly clean shoes. His head was still thumping. What a complete dick, he thought as he grappled with his laces. Carl was barefooted, embracing both women, giving each a gentle tap on the backside. James and Richard followed suit without the bottom touching, and shortly, they were all sitting in their luxurious seats, drinking champagne and looking forward to the journey ahead.

The captain came through the intercom, and in her sultry voice informed them that air-traffic control had given clearance to take off immediately. She and her co pilot, Tanya, would come and greet them once they were at their cruising altitude. The plane eased into the skies, and within minutes it levelled. Jessica came out of the cockpit, leaving Tanya in charge.

"So, my darling, how was your stay in Cape Town?" Carl enquired.

"Mr. Finkelstein, we had a wonderful time at the Cape Grace, thank you. Although I have to say, we were all a little disappointed not to be invited to join you. We hear the *Golden Eagle* is one of the most magnificent yachts in the world. We were dying to see her."

"Well, honey, you have no worries there. When my dear friend Antonio has purchased it, all you girls will be welcome. Is that not right, Antonio?"

Antonio smiled cautiously. "Sure thing. The pleasure will be all mine." Inwardly, he knew Doris wouldn't be overly keen on entertaining all Carl's beautiful employees, but he'd deal with that when the time came.

Canapés was about to be served, and as Jessica took her place back in the cockpit, she turned and looked toward Antonio and smiled. How strange, he thought, that she had barely noticed him previously, and suddenly, after hearing he was to be the new owner of the *Golden Eagle*, she was obviously flirting. He needed to keep an eye on that one.

The flight was smooth, and the men managed to get some sleep before dinner was served. Their expected landing time was in half an hour, and everyone was feeling a whole lot better than they had that morning.

The seat belt signs went on, and within moments, the plane started its descent into the Johannesburg private air strip. Once on the ground, Jessica and Tanya came out of the cockpit to say good-bye and to be briefed by Carl about what he needed from them over the coming few days. His schedule was hectic, and happily, the crew confirmed they could all be available for the journeys he needed to take. He mentioned that in a couple of weeks, all being well, this group would return to Cape Town with their wives and partners. "So Antonio can take ownership of the *Golden Eagle*," added Carl proudly.

"Perhaps then we can all come for a visit?" Jessica asked in a childlike voice, pouting her lips as she spoke.

Antonio was quick to answer, and without upsetting anyone, he made it clear that the next visit was strictly for wives and partners.

Being the true professional, Jessica immediately took the hint. "Of course, Mr. Cadiz. We totally understand. Perhaps another time."

"Perhaps," replied Antonio in a friendly fashion. With that, they said good-bye and kissed Carl. The men left the aircraft and walked toward a black limousine that was waiting for them.

"Good evening, gentlemen. I'll be running you over to your plane." The driver motioned to a tiny aircraft just a few feet from where they were. "Airport regulations. Can't risk having people walking around."

"No problem. We understand the red tape," replied Antonio, and within seconds of their getting into the limo, it came to a stop, and their bags were unloaded and reloaded onto the plane. The four men crouched to get inside the little aircraft, none of them looking forward to the short flight that was taking them back to Botswana.

The sun was setting, and as they left the city behind and flew toward the bush, they had magnificent views of the enormous ball of fire slowly slipping behind the horizon, sending out an array of wonderful colours. The skies changed from blue to pink, and before the men knew it, the aircraft came to the landing strip just as darkness fell. With a big bump, the small plane came to a stop. "Sorry about that, guys," came the pilot's voice. "We have a bit of a short runway here; you can get out whenever you're ready. Welcome back to Botswana, and have a great evening."

Meanwhile, at the lodge, Brick was busily helping Karmen, Josephine, and Doris get the evening's table laid for supper. Jason and his younger brother Joe had caught fish in the morning and springbok for those who fancied meat. Together, they had all helped make a choice of delicious salads to complement the meal. Flowers were placed along the long wooden table, and everyone was looking forward to the evening ahead. The men had been missed. Antonio had called and told Doris to expect them within the hour.

The usual driver was not there to meet the plane.

As the four men approached the car, they saw instead a handsome young driver waiting for them, looking smart and professional. He smiled and explained he had stepped in at the last minute, as Albert had suddenly been taken ill.

The bags were loaded and everyone settled down for the ride back to the lodge. They would drop Carl off en route to attend his meeting.

Stars were twinkling in abundance overhead, and sleep was not far off for any of them.

After smooth driving for a while, the car began bumping over extremely uneven ground. James, who was sitting in the passenger's seat, awoke. He knew something was wrong. He had made this journey before and had never experienced such an uncomfortable ride. He looked at the driver and noticed how nervously he was checking his rearview mirror. Pretending to be asleep, James looked in his side mirror and realised they were being followed. They were in trouble.

He took his mobile and silently texted Richard, who was sitting directly behind the driver. Richard and James had been friends for years, and each knew how the other ticked; there was an unspoken trust between them. Richard stirred as he felt his mobile vibrate. He looked down and read his message. Quietly, he replied and slipped his phone back into his pocket.

Carl was snoring, and Antonio was sleeping peacefully, his head slumped against the window. No one was moving.

Suddenly Richard coughed, loudly.

Immediately, James leaned over the driver. Richard grabbed him around the neck from behind and held him in a headlock as James undid his seat belt, opened his door, and screamed at the top of his voice, "Get the fuck out of this car!"

With that, James pushed with all his might, and Richard released his hold on the driver. James grabbed the steering wheel as the driver tumbled out of the car. The vehicle sped wildly along. Shots suddenly began firing as James scrambled into the driver's seat, just before the car went completely out of control.

"What the fuck!" Carl shouted, waving his hands wildly around his head as the car careered along.

"Antonio, call Dom. *Now!*" yelled James from the front seat, as the men ducked to avoid the bullets that were flying everywhere and the glass that was shattering all around them. "Tell him we're in big trouble; tell him to get a trace on one of our mobiles, quickly! And come and help us."

Antonio acted immediately, realizing who was in control of the situation at that moment.

James told everyone to hold on. He turned the headlights off and sped quite a way ahead of the other vehicle. Suddenly, he spun their car around without slowing.

Carl screamed; Richard and Antonio closed their eyes tightly and held on to the front seats, turning their knuckles white. Heading in the other direction, lights turned off, James took a sharp turn to the right and carried on at full speed.

After a while Antonio spoke quietly. "James, man, I think you've lost them. That was a close one. I just got a text from Dominic, and he's managed to get a lock on us. He's sending his guys out to catch those fuckers and to find us."

Within minutes James pulled off the road.

"We'll wait here, and give Dominic a chance to reach us while his guys find those madmen. Anyone get a look at them? Carl, did you recognise anyone?" asked James in a whisper.

"You must be joking. I was holding on for dear life, with my head under the back seat!"

"I think there could be a bounty on my head," interrupted Antonio. "It's happened before. I thought it was over, but perhaps I was wrong. The Brazilian government is relentless. I need to get this deal done fast, change my identity, and get us out of Botswana as soon as possible. They won't recognise me after my surgery, even if they find me."

The men had cuts and bruises covering most of the top parts of their bodies. They could smell and taste blood. They decided to stay in the dark for fear of being seen. Speaking in hushed voices, they agreed to wait to look at their injuries until Dominic found them.

Eventually, Dom called to tell Antonio he had come across the attackers by accident. He and his guys had been approached by the assailants while driving along the swamp road. The assailants had asked if anyone had seen a black people carrier with four male passengers and a driver speeding. They sounded and looked as if they were South American. Dom's guys had shot each of them in the head as they sat in their car. They rolled the vehicle into the swamp, but not before they found the driver some way away, badly injured on the side of the road. They shot him too, and put him into the car, which was now sitting at the bottom of the swamp, all of them waiting to become crocodile food.

"So it looks as if our troubles are temporarily over, but I'll need to speak with Dom and see if he can move us to a safer camp before we leave Botswana for good. I'm not sure these are the only men after me," explained Antonio. "Dom should be here within fifteen minutes to take us back to our lodge. I've phoned Doris to let her know we've been delayed, and she says they're all waiting for us, drinks on ice."

After checking themselves over and realizing their injuries were superficial, the men followed Dom, who had arrived with some much-appreciated beers. He had offered weed too, but the beers were all they wanted. They made their way slowly along the dirt roads back to camp, feeling relieved and exhausted.

Dominic and his guys smoked their spliffs in the jeep ahead, laughing about the evening's adventures, as if they'd just been out to a bar with the lads, instead of being on a killing spree.

The night stars enveloped all of them.

Antonio, Richard, and James thought only of a shower, food, and a good night's sleep close to their loved ones. Carl had cancelled his meeting and was delighted to join his friends overnight, wanting exactly the same as they did, except he couldn't give an iota about a loved one. No, he was quite happy to share a bed with himself. After all, he was exhausted and wanted to sleep, so what the hell would he need a lover for? He only understood love as a self-indulgent desire, a pastime; once fulfilled, it was over until the next need. And he had a list of women ready to keep him happy, so a good night's sleep alone sounded perfect.

As they drove into the lodge, everyone was waiting for them. Josephine, Karmen and Doris rushed to the jeep as the men climbed out. They were shocked at the blood, cuts, and bruises that covered all their faces.

Doris was first to speak. "Antonio Cadiz, what do you look like? You need a bloody good shower, but first give me a hug and a kiss. I've missed you so much."

Karmen was in Richard's arms, and Josephine was listening to James's account of the evening's events. He was enjoying relaying his heroic conduct, knowing his wife was totally in awe of the whole situation and how brave he had been. He had actually quite surprised himself. Amazing what you're capable of in an emergency, he thought.

Dom and his guys were parking the vehicles and rolling another joint, still laughing and joking.

"Excuse me. I don't mean to interrupt or anything."

Everyone turned. Carl was standing alone with his hands on his hips, face bruised, looking quite the orphan.

Brick suddenly appeared from nowhere. "You poor love, your face is black and blue. Let me clean you up." Carl looked confused as Brick's enormous frame approached him, his biceps pulsing, a smile so dazzlingly white you almost needed sunglasses.

"Forgive me, Carl," interrupted Antonio. "This is Carl; he is the man who's going to broker our deal with the Russians. Carl, let me introduce you. Doris, my partner. Karmen, Richard's wife, and Josephine, James's better half. And this is Brick, our friend and minder.

"And Brick, let me tell you now, Carl is the least gay man you will ever come across, so down, boy." Everyone laughed except Carl. The whole conversation had gone over his head. He, instead, was busily approaching each of the girls, hugging them, nestling his curly head deep into their bosoms. Brick shrugged his enormous shoulders and walked off to help with dinner.

Karmen, Josephine, and Doris smiled at one another, realizing Carl was going to be fun to have around and play with, especially if the deal with the Russians went forward. They assumed this little man would certainly be somewhere in the background, such an easy target for three women like them.

"Why don't we all shower, clean ourselves up, and meet for drinks before dinner so we can fill you in on what's taken place while we've been away. Doris, can you show Carl to the guest room? I assume you'll be leaving us tomorrow, Carl?" said Antonio.

"Needs must, Antonio. I'd love to stay around for a while with these lovely ladies, but business, diamonds, and money have to take priority." Carl turned to Doris and gave her a wink.

"Come, honey, let me show you to your room." Doris beckoned, put her arm around Carl's little shoulders, and led him away, but not before sliding her hand down to his bottom and giving it a squeeze. It was she who now turned and gave a naughty wink. Everyone giggled under their breath as Carl walked away, convinced he had another name to add to his list of willing playmates.

Over dinner, Antonio filled the girls and Brick in on the near completion of the deal with the Kasparovsky brothers. He informed them that Dominic was arranging a safer camp for them as he felt sure there was still danger from the bounty placed on his head by the Brazilian government.

"I promise it won't be for long," he added, as Doris and the other girls complained they were sick and tired of moving and sick and tired of Botswana. "Dom has told me about the place he has in mind. It's on a nature reserve and sounds beautiful. There are five suites, a pool, a Jacuzzi, and wonderful gardens. There's twenty-four-hour security, which right now is imperative, and trust me, it won't be for much longer. There is just one question for you girls. Do you all get on well with one another? Could you spend a long time together?"

"What the bloody hell is going on Antonio?" Doris asked, getting agitated. "We were only saying the other day that we feel like sisters; we've spent so much time together already, but none of us, and I mean none of us, want to be in the bush together for much longer. Is that not right, girls?" The others nodded in agreement. "So please stop with the games and tell us what you're planning."

"My love, trust me. I want this to be a surprise. Do you trust me?"

Doris melted; she knew Antonio wouldn't let any of them down if he could help it.

"Yes, Antonio, I trust you, but you better let us know soon, or else I don't know what I'll do to you. Honestly, you drive me mad."

Dinner continued, and eventually it was time for everyone to retire for the night. Carl said his good-byes as he was leaving at sunrise, and the others made their way back to their rooms. Before long, exhaustion caught up with them all. The night's chorus of crickets, frogs, and owls began, but nobody heard a thing. They were dreaming of the future. A future that was still unsure to them all—except Antonio.

As the sun rose, Carl was speeding back to the city. He had slept well, but deals needed to be done, and he knew it wouldn't be long before Antonio and his entourage would want to visit the *Golden Eagle* again to sign contracts and take ownership. So time wasn't on his side. He was, after all, a very busy man, with umpteen deals on the go and umpteen women to keep satisfied.

Dominic was having coffee with Antonio, discussing the nature reserve that was available to rent immediately. The move could happen today; all Antonio had to do was get the girls onside and pack up and go. He knew he had to move all of them quickly so they would be safe until it was time to leave Botswana forever, put his plans into action, and begin their new lives.

The morning sun was warming up, even though it was only 7:00 a.m. When Dominic left, Antonio took a shower before he met up with the others.

At breakfast, as everyone tucked into the delicious spread laid on by Jason and Joe, Antonio spoke. "Guys, Dom has found a beautiful lodge. It's set within a large nature reserve and has security second to none. After yesterday's fiasco, I've decided it's necessary for us to move. There are too many potential dangers surrounding us, and as we're so near to our goals, I don't want anything to stop us. We're nearly there.

I realise you're fed up with the constant moving and in particular with Botswana, but I promise this will be the last time we have to pack up and go—that is, until we leave

Africa for good. This brings me to my next point. How do I put this?"

"Antonio," interrupted Doris. "You're never lost for words, my darling."

"Look," continued Antonio, "we've all been through a lot together. I feel a bond has been created among the six of us."

Brick gave a small cough.

"Oh, I'm sorry, Brick. Of course, the seven of us. You know it goes without saying you're always included. You're like my brother."

Brick wiped away a crocodile tear. Even though he knew Antonio would never forget him, it was wonderful that the whole table knew how close he and Antonio were. Brick loved feeling important and wanted, and he loved other people knowing it too.

"How would you feel," continued Antonio, "if the seven of us carried on our journey into the next stage together? The *Golden Eagle* is far too big for Doris, Brick, and me alone, even if Carl occasionally comes to join us. There's so much space, and I personally would miss you all. The yacht has ten luxurious suites; every possible thing a person could ever need is on board. The crew and staff are incredible, and I would be delighted if we could carry on spending time together.

Richard has mentioned to me that his London apartment is being rented on a long-term basis. I understand that James and Josephine are doing the same with their home. Doris and I absolutely can't return to Brazil. We are fundamentally homeless.

Think about it. We could travel the world together, visit amazing places, and enjoy the fruits of our labour. What do you say?"

For a moment, there was silence. Then Karmen spoke. "Oh, Antonio, we'd absolutely love it! We've been discussing this idea for weeks, planning among ourselves while you've been away to see if we could make it happen, and now you've done it for us! Oh my God. It's wonderful news! Doris, Josephine, can you believe it? How many times have we talked about sailing away into the sunset together with a fortune in our pockets?"

Antonio looked at Doris. She smiled, and he knew the idea sat well with her.

"I promise you all, I will finalise the purchase of the *Golden Eagle* as quickly as possible. In the meantime, ladies, can you go and pack so we can head off to our new camp later this morning, Dominic will be ready to take us as soon as our rooms have been cleared."

Never before had Antonio seen such immediate movement. The girls rushed off with Brick following closely behind. They skipped, laughed, and hugged one another all at the same time. It was as if Christmas had arrived ten times in one day.

"What do you think of the name *Golden Eagle*?" was all he could hear as they disappeared into one another's rooms. He turned to Richard and James. "I think our ladies are happy."

The three men smiled at one another. Everything was coming together, and they all felt good.

Later that morning, all packed up, the group took one last look at the place they'd called home for some time. The women had forged close bonds with one another and with Brick, but none was sad to be leaving. Luckily, Jason and Joe were joining them to help with food preparation at the new camp, so no immediate good-byes needed to be said, and energies were high. They all knew the time was getting near to leave Botswana completely.

Brick started loading the cases onto the two four-by-four jeeps that were waiting to take them to the nature reserve, some hour and a half drive away from where they were. Dominic was high as a kite as usual, reggae music blasting from the speakers in his vehicle. "Hey, Brick man, make sure the right cases go into the right jeeps. Easier to unload the other end."

"Since when did you become my boss, you little fuck?"

"Chop-chop, man, we haven't got all day," Dom teased.

"I'll chop you in a minute," came Brick's response.

"Oooh, bitchy boy! Tell you what Bro, Dom will give you a hand; you're looking like you need help. I hear you're not exercising as much as you used to. What you need is a fine woman to get that body moving."

With that Brick threw a small holdall in his direction. Luckily for Dom, it missed, and both men began to chuckle. In spite of their obvious differences, they had become quite fond of each other. At arm's length, of course!

# Chapter Twenty-Six

Once on the road, the tunes were turned down, but each jeep still vibrated with music. The sun was high, and the heat was soaring. Luckily, the movement of the vehicles allowed for a little air to pass through, keeping things bearable.

Soon enough they approached a gated turnoff in the road. After a few formalities, they were allowed to continue. As they carried on along the never-ending driveway, it became apparent how secure this lodge was. They passed five checkpoints, each with two uniformed security guards, before they arrived at the main entrance. At each stop, a guard made a thorough check of all the documents held by Dom and a visual examination of each passenger. The jeeps were checked with the aid of vicious-looking Alsatian dogs, and only then could they move on.

"Bloody hell," exclaimed Josephine. "Talk about security."

Once at the main entrance, they were greeted by four armed rangers and a team of local women, all of whom rushed forward to take their luggage. Incredibly, the women placed the bags on top of their heads and walked off expertly, taking the cases to the rooms that had been allocated to the Cadiz party.

"Good God, look at that Karmen," exclaimed Josephine. "How the hell can they balance all that on the top of their heads? I tried once with a book and lasted about a minute."

"Darling, when I was a girl, my sisters had me do exactly that, and I actually made it once around the room. Mind you, my book was a tiny paperback."

"Oh, you two, you're so funny. I'm going to love spending more time with you. You know, I never had close people around me, nor any siblings. You're like the family I never had," added Doris.

"Ah, Doris, that is so sweet. 'Course we'll be like your family, won't we, Karmen?"

"Absolutely! We girls are gonna have the time of our lives. We've done the kid bit and the grandma bit, in my case. May I add, I did start very, very young. Now it's time for us."

"To us!" cheered Josephine.

No one noticed, but Doris was listening to none of them. She was in a world of her own.

Once settled into their luxurious suites, unpacking done, they met for lunch. Jason and Joe were in their element; working in such an upmarket camp gave them hope for better things for themselves. If Karmen, Josephine, and Doris had their way, they'd organise it for the brothers to get full-time employment here. After all, their skills were vast, their ambition immense, and with a few thousand dollars or so behind them, they could be anything they wanted to be here in Botswana.

At lunch Antonio was seated at the head of the table. He cleared his throat and spoke.

"First, I would like to thank Dominic and his team. Dom, if it wasn't for you, we probably wouldn't be alive today. If it wasn't for you, we certainly wouldn't be here on this incredible private nature reserve with the security we desperately need right now. Our history together knows no bounds. And recently, you have come to my rescue more than once. I remember Doris and I having to leave the *Dream of the Seas*—what an experience that was. Do you remember how scared we were, darling, when we launched ourselves into the dark waters onto Dom's speedboat?"

"Sure do, baby," came Doris's reply. "Not convinced I could do that again in a hurry."

"Well, Dom, the time is coming for the seven of us to move on." Antonio motioned to the people sitting around the lunch table. "I'm indebted to you, and you know I will be looking after you well."

"Never doubted it, man," replied Dom.

"Moving on. I'll be speaking to Carl within the next day or so. He's arranging for all of us to fly down to Cape Town to view the *Golden Eagle*. I assume, Doris, you're happy with the name."

"Er, what do you think, sisters?"

"I think it should do nicely; don't you, Josephine?"

"I guess it'll do, Karmen."

"OK, so I have the female vote. Thank God for that. Now, my intention is to employ the entire crew. They know the yacht well and seem to run a tight ship, excuse the pun. I've come across a number of special people, one in particular, a charming young bartender called Seon—you'll all love him—and Doris, I'd like you to meet everyone. After all, this will be your home for quite a while. You need to use your female intuition to make sure we're surrounded by the right people."

"With me, Karmen, Josephine, and Brick, I don't think we can go wrong," said Doris.

"Excuse me," Josephine added hesitantly. "Where are we heading to, Antonio? What if the crew doesn't want to stay? I hate to throw a spanner in the works, but are we sure everything's going to be OK? Oh, I don't know. Are we going to be safe? I've always been a bit of a worrier, I mean, if we get sick, do we have a medical team to look after us, and do we have exit strategies? Sorry, girls, I feel like I've let you down. But once we're on the yacht, won't you want to know, God forbid, that we'll all be safe in an emergency?"

"Josephine's one hundred percent right. We never know what the future holds. Are you sure, my darling, you know what you're doing? Floating around the world's oceans alone is quite a daunting thought. It's important to me too, to know that we have a professional team around us, just in case," said Doris.

"Doris, where's your spirit of adventure? Where's the girl who threw caution to the wind and told me I was a bore?"

"I know, Antonio. I'm being stupid. Perhaps I'm coming down with something. Forget what I said. Of course everything will be fine."

"Listen, girls," interrupted Karmen. "Let me tell you something. Life is an unusual journey. We joined Antonio from the start, no questions asked. Who knew where it was leading? Who actually cared? Let's just enjoy the ride; I'm sure our men will take care of us. Safe is comfortable. Safe is predictable. Is that what we signed up for in the beginning? I don't think so. So Josephine, darling, stop thinking. Enjoy! You get one shot in this life. Have fun. And, Doris, please don't change and turn into a granny. It won't suit you."

"Josephine, Doris, the *Golden Eagle* has a team of nurses and doctors and even a general surgeon constantly on call. There is a helipad, a helicopter, and twenty-first century satellite communications. We will be constantly in touch with the outside world. My sweet girls, there is absolutely nothing for either of you to worry about. James, man, let your lady know she's safe. She's having a moment. Come on; she needs you to let her know it'll be OK." Antonio spoke with authority.

James and Josephine went to their room. It was important that he convince her there was nothing to worry about; after all, the last few months hadn't exactly been a walk in the park. Josephine just needed assurance, and James knew exactly what to do to make her feel better. After all, they had been married for thirty-one years.

Antonio's phone rang. It was Carl. Antonio excused himself and left the others to finish their lunch. Carl informed Antonio that the Kasparovsky brothers had retained a lawyer that he had recommended. His name was Felix Simpson, an expat, originally from Scotland. He had worked on many a deal with Carl and was a brilliant lawyer. He would be present at the next meeting, ready to finalise all the details of the intricate negotiations that were due to take place. Antonio confirmed that his lawyer was lined up too, so there was nothing stopping them from making a date to finalise everything.

"Let me make myself clear, Carl. I will not produce any gems until the legalities have been completed properly. All the paperwork has to be signed, sealed, and ratified by both lawyers."

"No worries, Antonio, the brothers expect nothing less than absolute professionalism. When will you be ready to meet? Strillian is asking if you would all like to visit the *Golden Eagle* to have one last look and perhaps at the same time have both lawyers present to sign the final paperwork. Of course, only if you think it's appropriate."

"Sounds good to me, Carl. I want this yacht as quickly as possible. I've got many plans to put into practice, and I need to be able to leave Africa sooner rather than later. Are your planes available over the next few days to take the seven of us down to Cape Town?"

"Buddy, I'll make sure they are. I'm clearing my diary as we speak. It's not often a deal like this presents itself. I'll call you later and confirm, but I reckon Wednesday would work. Sound OK?"

"Absolutely. Let me know." With that, the phone went dead.

The heat was unbearable. Antonio found Doris sleeping soundly on top of their bed. The room was elegantly furnished and incredibly cool. Dominic had done a fine job. This lodge was immaculate. Perhaps once the heat of the day had passed, they could explore their surroundings. Antonio lay down next to Doris's naked body. She was so beautiful. He followed the line of her frame with his eyes. He wasn't sure, but she seemed to be looking more curvaceous than he remembered. He liked it and smiled. Soon enough, he became tired. He closed his eyes and dropped off knowing they were safe.

That afternoon at dusk, after saying farewell to Dominic, the seven friends, along with two armed rangers took a long stroll through the reserve. Animals collected freely around water holes, birds busied themselves settling down for the approaching night, and the evening's bouquet from the exotic bushes set everyone's senses on fire. As darkness fell, the black sky became a backdrop to millions of stars. The friends stood silently, looking up into the heavens. Whatever their individual beliefs were, there was no doubt that at that moment, they all knew there was something much bigger in the universe than just themselves.

Brick sniffled.

"Oh, my darling, you're not crying, are you?" Josephine asked.

"Well, it is beautiful, isn't it?" came Brick's response as he wiped a tear from his cheek.

"Oh God, guys, I think it's time for a drink and dinner," muttered Richard.

"Do you know something, Richard? You're intolerable," moaned Karmen. "Have you no heart?"

"You really love me, don't you?"

"I guess I do, you pain in the arse."

The friends made their way back in the warmth of the night and sat around the beautiful bar overlooking land that stretched for miles. Giraffes and elephants moved slowly, silhouetted across the horizon.

Antonio informed everyone that they were hopefully leaving to go to Cape Town on Wednesday to view the *Golden Eagle* and sign the final documents for her purchase. He told them about the lawyer he had retained. "He's an old friend from my boarding-school days back in England. Knew him then as Rolo. An absolute genius. He now uses his full name, Roland Briggs. One of the finest lawyers I've known. He'll leave nothing to chance, so we'll be completely safe in his hands."

By the time everyone retired, there was a positive vibe flowing through all their veins.

The girls couldn't wait to see the yacht, and with only a couple of days to go, their excitement was palpable. They hoped they could get some sleep; they had to be up early the next day to catch some sun before it got too hot. They had to look their best, after all, to meet all the crew who would be looking after them soon.

At 6:00 a.m. Carl called Antonio.

"What the fuck, Carl? It's still nighttime."

"I've been up since five thirty, my friend. If you want to be in top form, you have to exercise every morning for at least thirty minutes. How do you think I remain so virile and at the top of the business game?"

"Carl, it's too fucking early. Just text me the info, and I'll make sure I rally the troops. I'm going back to sleep." With that, Antonio turned his phone off.

"Who was that, darling?" yawned Doris, stretching her long, lean body like a cat rolling in the sun.

"Carl. He'll die of a heart attack if he doesn't slow down. Apparently, we're going off to meet the Russians soon and see our yacht. Now turn over. I'm feeling horny."

Doris began purring. God, she turns me on, thought Antonio. He knew she was the woman he wanted. They would travel the world together; nothing was going to interrupt the fun they shared.

# Chapter Twenty-Seven

Two days later Carl was leaving the Cape Grace Hotel, where he had just finished a breakfast meeting with the new Minister for Equal Opportunities, Clifford Ossanger—a young South-African man who had great ambitions for both himself and the next generation of African youth. Carl knew he needed these up-and-coming young black politicians on his side if he wanted to continue dealing in diamonds with little disturbance.

They had agreed that Carl would set up a training school within his business to give one hundred school leavers from Langa township a chance to rise through the ranks and perhaps even reach management levels over the next five years. By Carl's reckoning, either way he was a winner: cheap labour to begin with and, if there was any potential among the school leavers, it made more sense to employ them than import from abroad, which tended to cost a fortune.

He had invited Clifford and his young wife to join him for dinner the following week at one of the newest, trendiest restaurants in Cape Town. To get a table, you had to be somebody. Carl assumed Clifford wouldn't be particularly impressed, but knowing young women the way he did, he was banking that the new Mrs. Ossanger would be extremely keen.

Just time to walk over to the jetty and wait for Antonio to arrive, Carl thought. The sun was warm, and the little man had a spring in his step. How he loved his life!

The *Golden Eagle* had sent a tender over well ahead of time, so as Carl reached the V&A Waterfront, the sleek boat was waiting, glistening in the sunlight.

"Morning, Mr. Finkelstein. What a lovely day," the crew members greeted him in unison. They had known Carl for a long time; he was, after all, a regular visitor.

"Sure is lads. What time are the guests due to arrive?"

"Expecting them any minute now, sir."

As anticipated, in no time at all, a large people carrier drove toward Carl and the waiting tender. All seven passengers exited the vehicle, and their luggage was expertly removed as Carl greeted everyone.

"Carl, darling, we loved the plane. We were saying we could get used to travelling like that. Would've preferred a handsome pilot and a male crew, but beggars can't be choosers." Karmen planted a big kiss on Carl's cheek.

"Yeah, Carl," added Josephine. "Pretty fabulous."

"Girls, you only have to ask, and Uncle Carl will deliver."

The women giggled as they were helped onto the tender. They were certainly going to enjoy playing with Mr. Finkelstein.

As they left the harbour behind and headed out to open waters, it became clear how enormous the *Golden Eagle* was.

"Wow, it's spectacular!" As Doris spoke, she kept her eyes glued on the yacht.

Josephine, Karmen, and Brick said nothing. They just sat with their mouths and eyes open.

"If you don't close your mouth, Karmen, you'll catch a fly," teased Richard.

"Shut up, you!" came her answer.

Richard began chuckling to himself. He knew that Karmen loved it, and if Karmen loved something, Richard was always happy.

James sat quietly holding Josephine's hand. He whispered, "Told you it was out of this world." Josephine squeezed his hand; she didn't need to speak.

The Kasparovsky brothers were waiting to greet their guests, looking suave and professional, as usual. "Welcome back, gentlemen. Ladies, it's an honour to meet you."

Everyone was introduced, and Strillian took the lead, escorting them up to a lounge area where champagne and canapés were being served. It was noticeable to all the men that the waitresses serving were dressed in full white crew uniforms – gone were the leggy, sexy hostesses from their previous visits. Strillian sure knew what was and what wasn't appropriate. Both Richard and James felt a little relieved, if they were to be honest. Carl, on the other hand, was looking slightly disappointed.

Strillian gave a welcome toast, asking the guests to treat the yacht as if it was their own. Antonio smiled, inwardly hoping it would be his sooner rather than later.

Once the drinks were finished and canapés eaten, the three couples were taken to their suites. James, Richard, and Antonio couldn't wait to see the reaction of the girls. It was as if the men were visiting the yacht for the first time too, in their excitement to watch their loved ones' faces.

Carl and Brick stayed behind. Strillian had insisted that they share a frozen vodka or two with the brothers. Brick was slightly disappointed. He wanted to go and check out his suite with the others, but being a gentleman, he agreed to stay behind.

This time the drinks were brought in by two extremely gorgeous women. Carl recognised the taller girl from before. God, she was something! he thought. The little man perked up, rubbing his hands with glee. Brick, however, felt slightly hot under the collar, as she flirted obviously with him.

"And you think Strillian would forget his two single male guests on this trip? Never. I want everyone to have a good time. Nostrovia!"

With that, they downed the vodkas. Brick was feeling very ill at ease as he followed suit. He needed to talk to Josephine and Karmen; they'd be able to advise him what to do. He really was feeling out of his depth.

The two lawyers were due to arrive the following day at lunchtime, so Antonio, Richard, and James knew they had plenty of time to chill out and relax. Strillian had informed them that the evening would begin at 7:00 p.m. in the Oak Bar.

"If my memory serves me right, Doris, that's where Seon, the bartender I told you about, works. I can't wait for you to meet him. I know you'll love him," said Antonio.

Doris was in the bathroom, changing, getting ready to go and relax on the top deck. As she walked out, Antonio did a double take. "Wow, you look amazing. That bikini is something else! Is it my imagination, or have your boobs grown? I like them! Come, give me a kiss."

"Not now, darling, I'm covered in suntan oil. Be patient, my love, I promise we'll have fun together tonight."

"As long as you promise. By the way, what have the others said about the yacht?"

"They think they've died and gone to heaven. They're so excited at the thought of travelling around the world with us. They're even planning new wardrobes, and you know what? I may be joining them because I'm noticing that I seem to be growing a little in all the right places."

With that, Doris cupped her breasts provocatively, smiled, and made her way out of the suite to get some afternoon sun on the top deck.

Antonio smiled. He couldn't wish for a more exceptional woman. Doris loved him deeply; she looked incredible and still excited him like no one else had ever done. There was a side to her character that walked very close to the edge without falling off, and he liked that. It was fun yet safe. Both those things made Antonio tick, and he felt like the luckiest man alive. He wanted no one else to share his intimate world. Sure, the others were going to travel and share the yacht with them, but they were only friends; they stood outside from his inner world. It was just him and Doris. Just the two of them. Nothing was ever going to change that.

Antonio left his suite on a high and made his way to the pool. The wave machine was a fabulous way to exercise, and Antonio wanted to energise himself before he too went to the top deck and got some rest in the sun. He wondered if Brick would be in the gym. After all, Brick's body was his temple, and if Antonio knew his friend well, he would be pumping iron. Too many weeks in Botswana had taken their toll on everyone's fitness levels, especially Brick's.

The gym was empty, so Antonio continued through to the Olympic-size pool. Palms of all shapes and sizes enveloped the area, and as Antonio entered the warm water, he could have been bathing in the Caribbean. The only difference was that once he turned the wave machine on, he had to work hard.

Up on the top deck, the others, excluding Carl and Brick, were enjoying the peace. Each sun lounger was enormous and equipped with state-of-the-art features. Fine perfumed mist sprayed from attached headrests that acted as shade from the sun, if wanted. In the arms of each bed, a high-tech audio system was easily accessible, including TV and movie channels. It was simply amazing. Fruit skewers were offered along with the finest champagne, and everyone settled back comfortably to enjoy the afternoon sunshine.

Antonio had returned from his swim and was stretching his lean tanned body on his sun lounger. It wasn't long before he was snoring gently.

"Ah, look at my handsome man—sleeping like a baby," Doris crowed like a proud mother, smiling happily.

"Go get your phone, Doris, so we can video him. I can do a running commentary," giggled Richard in a whisper. "We can show it to him later."

Doris sneaked off quietly, returning with her mobile all ready to go.

"This is the great Antonio Cadiz, the macho man from Brazil. He professes not to sleep; he's too busy to sleep, always planning his next strategy. He never, ever snores." With that, Richard zoomed in on Antonio, who was blowing bubbles from the side of his mouth as the snoring became louder and louder. Doris and Richard giggled like teenagers.

Suddenly Antonio took a sharp intake of breath, snored very loudly and woke himself up.

"What's going on?" he questioned, still half-asleep.

"Nothing, my love," came Doris's reply. She felt rather guilty but took pleasure in Richard's obvious enjoyment of the situation.

"You haven't been videoing me asleep, have you?"

"As if we'd do that. Surely you trust us not to be so stupid as to try and catch you dribbling while sleeping and snoring."

"Doris, give me your mobile, or so help me God, I'll get it and throw it in the sea."

"You'll have to catch me first!" And with that, Doris began running around the deck, giggling. Antonio chased after her.

"I'll never show anyone, honey, promise. Come on, sweetheart, it'll be our little secret. Me and Richard, we're the only ones who know you snore and dribble."

Antonio managed to catch up with her. He grabbed the phone and deleted the footage.

"Antonio Cadiz, you're a bad sport. Next time, I'm gonna tape you, and you won't even know. And as your punishment for being such a party pooper, my offer of fun tonight is off."

With that, Doris skipped away, heading back to her cabin. She turned and winked at Antonio, and he knew she was playing with him, as only Doris knew how.

"Richard, if you ever try that again, I swear, I'll break your balls."

"Come on, man, we were just having a laugh. After all, if we're going to live on board together for the foreseeable future, we need to understand each other's ways. Tell you what. If you think I'm bad, wait till you get to know James better. He's a real joker."

Antonio smiled; yet inwardly, he wondered how things were going to pan out. After all, once the *Golden Eagle* left Cape Town and headed off, there would be days and days with only the seven of them together, twenty-four seven. Had he made a mistake? he wondered.

With that thought in mind, he made his way back to his suite to get ready for the evening.

Doris looked stunning. Her gold chiffon gown fell provocatively around her body, showing off all her curves and contours beautifully.

Together, they made their way to the Oak Bar. Once all the friends were gathered, Antonio introduced Seon to the girls. He was an immediate hit.

"It's a pleasure to meet you, ladies. I've heard a lot about you."

"Hope it's all good," teased Josephine.

As the drinks were flowing, Carl came running in, looking flustered.

"What an afternoon we've had! Has Brick shown up yet?" Carl looked totally wrecked. He was sweating profusely and sniffing constantly as he spoke to Antonio.

"No, Carl. Thinking about it, he hasn't been around all day. When was the last time you saw him?"

"Well, this afternoon I left him with a beautiful girl, who, may I add, was throwing herself at him. I had to leave and take care of some very exciting business, if you know what

I mean." With that, Carl gave a creepy wink and using his hands, created the shape of a female form, leaving no one in any doubt as to what he'd been up to all day.

Karmen, Josephine, and Doris threw each other concerned looks.

"I'm going to give Brick a call, just to make sure he's OK. Seon, can I use your phone to call through to the Amber suite?" asked Karmen.

"Sure thing, Mrs. Zimmerman." Seon dialled the number and passed the receiver to Karmen.

Josephine and Doris stood close by and listened intently as Karmen spoke. They could tell it wasn't Brick she was speaking to, and looking at her face, they knew something wasn't quite right. When she put the receiver down, they all looked at her, waiting.

"Well, you won't believe this." Karmen paused, getting ready to spill the beans. "I just spoke to some woman who said Brick was asleep in bed. She said they had spent the whole afternoon with each other, and they'd had an amazing time together. She was leaving him to sleep off his hangover and would put a note by his bedside to tell him we'd called. She sounded like a real minx to me."

"I can't believe it." Josephine sounded dumbstruck. "Brick with a woman?"

"Sounds fishy to me," added Doris. "Mind you, hearing about the Kasparovsky brothers, it wouldn't surprise me if they set him up somehow. Let him sleep. I'm sure he'll be

OK. We've got a party to get to. If he needs us, he'll see the note and call."

The women made their way over to the guys. Doris put her arms around Antonio and gave him a gentle kiss on his cheek. Antonio looked at her and smiled. She was simply stunning, more beautiful than he remembered. Something had changed. She was glowing, and he loved what he was seeing.

"You've never looked more radiant than you do tonight, my love," he whispered to her quietly. Doris stared into his eyes and melted.

"Hello, you two love birds," interrupted Strillian. "I've been watching you. My God, you make such a handsome couple."

Antonio and Doris smiled. "We've been discussing how wonderful your yacht is. Everything oozes class and sophistication. We just love it all," Doris enthused.

"Well, let's hope by tomorrow, she's yours. When we built her, we told the designer to spare no expense. Everything was of the finest quality. Then we had a falling-out with our Russian designers, and the *Golden Eagle* was completed by the Versace family. The Italian influences are stunning, don't you think? Although it ended up costing double our budget, it sure was worth it. Look what we eventually got."

Strillian motioned with his arms before continuing. "Back in those days, we never thought money would be a concern. The more we spent, the more we took from the country, but then economics changed. Things became different. Money was harder to come by; those carefree days changed. Sad, really, but let's stop this talk. The party is about to begin. Tomorrow's another day; now it's time to have fun. Come, I want the two of you to greet our guests. We've got lots of interesting people arriving, and our senior crew are coming too. Even though you'll be meeting them all tomorrow formally, I thought it would be nice for you to be introduced in a casual way tonight."

Antonio and Doris stood at the entrance to the dining area with the Kasparovsky brothers. They made a fine, glamorous couple, greeting the guests one by one, taking time to have a chat with each person. When Josephine, James, Karmen, and Richard made their way through, the handshakes and conversation were very tongue in cheek. James and Richard were in high spirits and made silly banter, causing everyone to laugh. Antonio felt slightly awkward, but he realised his friends were extremely entertaining and suddenly decided it was going to be great fun having these two guys around.

Carl followed with a six-foot-tall redhead on his arm. She was striking, and he took great pleasure in introducing her to Antonio and Doris.

Then it was time to meet the captain and his senior officers. They all looked extremely smart, and as they paid their respects to Doris and Antonio, it was obvious they had an idea that the couple would be their new bosses shortly.

Time was spent chatting with each and every one of them, and there was even enough time for Antonio to joke with them about who was taking care of the bridge in their absence. "You have nothing to worry about," the ship's engineer jested. "We're securely anchored, and I promise the yacht's going nowhere."

"Thank goodness for that," said Doris, laughing. "I feel much more comfortable. Please go through, join the guests inside, and have a wonderful evening. I look forward to meeting you along with all the other crew members tomorrow. It's been a pleasure talking to you."

"The pleasure's all mine." And with that, Simon, the ship's engineer, walked through the large doors and entered the dining room, thinking what a pleasure it would be to work for someone as elegant and beautiful as Mrs. Cadiz. It would make such a nice change after years of having to stomach the Russian brothers and their often crass and cheap ways of carrying on. He had always known money didn't bring class, and he felt excited at the prospect of things changing.

Suddenly, a voice was heard, quieting the chatter in the dining room. "Ladies and gentlemen, would you please stand and welcome your hosts for this evening?"

Strillian ushered Doris and Antonio to take the lead. They entered the room followed by the three brothers. There was loud applause as they walked through the room, the loudest coming from the table where Richard and James were sitting. Carl, being Carl, was overenthusiastic as usual and began whistling and clapping his little arms wildly above his wiry mop of black hair. His companion, who had obviously indulged in the same stimulating substance, leaped up and down, not quite knowing what the excitement was about. Her bosoms bounced in unison with each jump, almost knocking Carl off his feet.

Strillian took the microphone. "Good evening, everyone. On behalf of my brothers and I, we would like to welcome you on board. There are two very important guests here with us tonight—no, let me rephrase: friends." Strillian motioned to Doris and Antonio, who were standing by his side. "These two handsome people are here to hopefully become the new owners of the *Golden Eagle*. Please welcome Antonio and Doris Cadiz."

There were a few gasps from those unsuspecting guests, but clapping soon took over. Strillian raised his hands to quiet everyone.

"My friends, the deal is not finalised, but if all goes according to plan, these two fine people will be taking ownership of this magnificent yacht very shortly. Please, Antonio, come and say a few words."

Cheering bounced around the room. Karmen, Josephine, James, and Richard were ecstatic, feeling a mixture of relief that their journey together was almost coming to a wonderful conclusion and pride that their dear friends were being so well received.

"Thank you to our hosts, the Kasparovsky brothers, and to those of you who have welcomed Doris and I with such enthusiasm. As Strillian said, the deal is not yet done, but I hope we will be hosting all of you on board our yacht in the not-too-distant future."

"Hear, hear!" screamed Carl.

"By the way, I would like to set the record straight. Doris and I are not Mr. and Mrs. Cadiz. Not yet, anyway."

There was a wave of laughter.

"So while standing here before everyone, I thought it would be an appropriate time to ask."

The room went silent; all that could be heard was the intake of breath. Doris stood still, her mouth slightly open and eyes wide in disbelief.

"Doris…"

"Down on one knee, man!" screamed Carl. His companion began to sob.

Antonio sank down. Doris moved nearer to him.

"Doris Anne, will you make me the happiest man in the world and agree to be my wife?"

You could hear a pin drop as Antonio opened a box that held a most magnificent diamond.

The sobs from Karmen and Richard's table were getting louder and louder. Carl thrust tissues at the woman who sat crumbling beside him.

"Antonio Francesco Cadiz, it would be my honour to marry you."

With that Antonio stood, placed the ring on her elegant finger, and took her in his arms. The room went wild, the music began, and Antonio and Doris fell into each other's arms.

"What a bloody start to an evening," Josephine whispered to Karmen.

"Unbelievable," came Karmen's response. And then she added, "I do wish someone would remove that babbling woman sitting next to Carl. She's giving me a headache."

Both of them began to laugh.

At that moment Antonio and Doris came over to sit with their friends. The evening was just about to begin, in earnest.

Drinks were served and the lights dimmed. A fragrant mist swirled around the room; music indicated that something was about to happen. The mist cleared; the area where Antonio had proposed was now elevated. Standing on this platform was a group of male South-African dancers, each one lit by an individual spotlight. Their muscular bodies glistened as the music began to grow in intensity. They wore white loincloths and nothing else, except for white feathered tribal boots covered in exquisite coloured beads.

As the music got louder, their bodies began swaying in rhythm. Slowly, the beat increased, and the men began jumping, moving in all directions, and slapping their feet loudly, causing the beads to ricochet against one another, creating sounds that enhanced the music. It was electrifying.

In the distance a drum beat was heard, quietly at first, repetitive and mesmerizing, completely in tune with the sounds created by the dancers and the music. As the drums became louder, a group of men walked onto the stage. They were dressed in white, bodies moving as if they *were* the music. They drummed calmly at first, and then increased the pace until the beat rang out wildly. They danced enthusiastically, always keeping the rhythm.

The momentum continued, until eventually a crescendo was reached, and all became silent. The dining room exploded with cheering and clapping. The entertainers took their bows.

Once the room became quieter, Strillian spoke. "Ladies and gentlemen, please welcome your chef for this evening, Mr. Claude Constantine."

The head chef was applauded and confidently took the stage. He explained the menu expertly, giving vegetarian options to those who didn't eat meat, and everyone settled down to enjoy their meal.

Carl was sitting alone. He had had no choice but to escort his companion back to the suite, much to his dismay. The drugs, booze, and emotion had proved too much for her.

He was furious. If he had his way, he would have found a room below in the staff quarters and put her there to sleep it off. After all, he had his eye on a lovely young waitress who seemed to be falling under his spell, and the thought of giving that up and going back to the suite to find Carol (if that was her name; he couldn't remember) crashed out in his bed repulsed him.

Maybe with a bit of luck, she might have pulled herself together by the time he got back, and he could get a little more action. With that thought he perked up a bit.

The food was exquisite, everyone was getting on famously, and after the desserts had been served, the show continued.

A large South-African woman took centre stage.

There was silence as she took a breath and let out her first sound, a deep, throaty, soulful cry that echoed hauntingly around the room. She stared out at her audience, her frame ablaze with overhead lighting. She wore traditional attire, full of colour, with a matching headdress. She was adorned in heavy gold jewellery.

Her song was in Afrikaans. Few understood the words, but all felt the powerful emotion behind the verse. It sounded full of pain, suffering, survival, and hope.

The applause was immense.

She then introduced herself, giving a short explanation of what she had just sung.

Her name was Mama Umbo, she had been singing since before she could walk, and most of her songs were representative of the years of inequality she had witnessed throughout her life. She explained that she was politically motivated and hoped her music and words would one day make a small difference to the people of the world.

She gave a quick description of each song she was about to sing so everyone had an understanding. After about half an hour, tears were in the eyes of most who listened. Everyone was mesmerised; her tone was absolutely fantastic. There was no accompanying music, just her God-given voice.

When she finished, the lights went out, and the room sat in dark silence. She had touched a chord deep in everyone's soul. Even Carl was quiet for a moment, until he could bear it no longer. He began cheering and clapping. Everyone took his lead, and the room erupted.

Mama Umbo stood before her audience, tears streaming down her face. She felt the love that surrounded her and bowed one last time, before the spotlight was turned off.

The energy in the room was high as dance music began playing. Slowly, people left their tables, made their way to the dance floor, and began moving to the thumping beat of the music. Strobe lighting turned the event into a club scene within minutes. A female DJ appeared, playing all the latest mixes.

Carl rushed in between Josephine, Karmen, and Doris, his arms high in the air, waving madly like someone greeting a relative at the airport after years of separation. He then began throwing some shakes, arms reaching toward the ceiling, hips gyrating in all directions. He looked like a madman, freed from an asylum only minutes earlier.

The girls circled him and began rubbing their bodies up and down his little frame, dancing around him provocatively.

"Oh, Mr. Diamond Dealer, you sure know how to move," chortled Karmen.

Josephine threw her chiffon scarf around his neck, pulling him closer to her. "Come dance with me, Carl!"

"Calm down, ladies. I love you all." And with that, he began spinning on the spot, his arms stretched out by his sides.

"Christ, Karmen, if he carries on like that he'll take off."

"Or fall over."

"Or die of a heart attack; he's as high as a kite," added Doris.

Luckily, the track ended, and Carl slowed down. He was sweating profusely and staggered back to the table, where he dampened a serviette and dabbed at his face and neck, unbuttoning his collar simultaneously.

"Are you all right, Carl?" asked Richard.

"Is the Pope Catholic?" came Carl's response. "Let's have some of those frozen vodkas. I need to cool down."

James, Richard, and Antonio had been deep in conversation but decided to pay a little more attention to Carl, just in case. The three women continued dancing together, getting lost among all the other people. By the time they returned, the Kasparovskys had joined their table, and it appeared the guys were participating in a vodka-shot competition.

"Ladies, please." Ever the gentlemen, the brothers stood to let them sit down. Strillian arranged for more chairs to be brought, along with more vodka, and the competition began again in earnest.

James, Richard, and Antonio, not wanting to offend their hosts, appeared to be keeping up, but in reality, they were quietly throwing away every other glass. They needed to have their wits about them. These Russians had some innate ability not to be affected in the slightest. Carl seemed to be having a second wind and matched the brothers glass for glass.

"Ladies, will you join us?" Strillian asked.

"We'll stick to our long drinks, thanks. Vodka and Slimline," replied Josephine.

"Large, not too much ice, tall glasses, and straws. Thanks," added Karmen, smiling at Strillian. She certainly was a woman who knew what she wanted.

"Actually, Karmen," interrupted Doris, "I'd like still water. Thanks."

Josephine and Karmen threw each other a glance. They each knew what the other was thinking, but it was a conversation to be had tomorrow.

"Excuse me, everyone." Mical stood up. "We thought we'd have a little fun tonight. We've arranged for some limbo dancers to come on board to show us their incredible ability. Anyone prepared to join in? Strillian, what about you?"

"As long as Antonio joins me."

"I will," screamed Carl. "But only if one of these beautiful ladies accompanies me."

The lights went out, and the music commenced. A group of lean, athletic men and women began the show. It was unimaginable that a human frame could contort itself in so many ways. Lower and lower the limbo pole went. Lower and lower the dancers went too. Eventually, there seemed only an inch of air left between the pole and the floor.

"Impossible!" Josephine mouthed to James.

The drums rolled, and a young man began his approach. His legs bent before him, his body following, almost flat, only inches from the ground. As the audience gasped, he cleared the pole and leaped into the air, landing on his feet and then taking a bow.

Throughout the room, you could hear cheers and shouts of appreciation.

Suddenly, to everyone's amazement, the pole was set on fire, and the young man prepared to repeat the performance. Silence prevailed. The drumroll quietly beat in the background. The intensity of expectation was palpable.

"I hope they won't want us to do that," Josephine whispered to Karmen.

"I'm doing nothing of the sort," came Karmen's response.

"Me neither," added Doris.

"Shit, that leaves me, then. You're both party poopers."

As she spoke, the young man hovered inches from the floor. With beads of sweat running from his chest, flames touching his skin, he inched his way under the pole. He made one last move and managed, just, to clear his head and get to his feet.

Everyone stood and applauded. The noise was deafening.

"And now…" The young man spoke with a strong South African accent. "I would like some volunteers to come and join us."

"Here, over here!" Carl stood waving his hands in the air. "We'll do it. Which one of you beauties is joining me?"

"I pulled the short straw, unfortunately," joked Josephine. Inwardly, she was petrified at the prospect of having to limbo in front of all these people. But she always gave things a go. Thank God she'd had a couple of drinks, she thought.

James gave her an encouraging smile as she and Carl walked hand in hand toward the stage. Strillian and Antonio followed closely behind. A few other people joined from various tables, and the competition began.

The pole was thankfully not on fire, and its height was acceptable to begin with. After a while, participants slowly left the stage one by one, having either knocked the pole over or decided they weren't prepared to go any lower. Eventually, the only people left were Antonio, Strillian, Carl, and Josephine.

It came as a complete surprise to everyone when the pole was set alight.

"Bloody hell, are they sure about this?" Karmen sounded genuinely concerned.

"Cue my exit," said Strillian as he took a bow and left the stage to loud applause, mostly coming from where his brothers were sitting.

Antonio, Josephine, and Carl managed to avoid the flames. They received cheers and whistles.

"I reckon it's easier for Carl, 'cause he's so short, don't you think?" asked Karmen, eyes focused on the stage.

"I think you're right. Hope Antonio quits while he's ahead. He's at least twice as tall as Carl." Doris sounded a little worried.

The pole was once again lowered. Antonio raised his hands to indicate it was over for him. Whistles and clapping surged through the room as he returned to the table.

"And now, ladies and gentlemen, our last two remaining competitors. Make some noise for Carl and Josephine!"

Carl went first; he kept his hands close by his sides and lowered himself. Everyone began clapping. Unfortunately for him, he lost his balance and collapsed in a heap on the floor.

The room went wild as he returned to his table waving his arms, looking as if he was a presidential candidate who had just won his seat. He began shaking hands with all those he passed on the way.

Next it was Josephine's turn. She took a deep breath and went for it. "Lower! Lower!" was all she heard as she felt the flames warm her torso.

"My God, James, your wife, she's so gutsy!" complimented Strillian.

"I know," replied James proudly. "She is a bit of a daredevil at times, and no doubt the vodkas are helping."

Josephine managed to negotiate the pole, just, but when asked if she would try going lower, she declined.

"Sorry, everyone. If I go lower, I'll set fire to myself."

A big cheer went up as she walked back to the others.

"What a great lady," Strillian said, joining in the applause.

The area was expertly cleared, the DJ returned, and the party continued.

By 4:00 a.m., most people had retired. It had been a memorable night. Carl was helped back to his suite by James and Richard. They laid him fully clothed on his bed next to his friend, who was fully clothed too and out like a light.

"Don't reckon they'll be up to too much," Richard said as he and James made their way back to their suites.

Antonio cuddled up to Doris. She had her back turned to him. "Are you sure you enjoyed yourself tonight, my love? You seemed slightly off, and you weren't drinking. I thought you'd be ecstatic, knowing we're getting married. Are you OK?"

There was no reply; Doris was asleep, breathing steadily. Antonio snuggled up closer, and as he put his arms around her waist, he realised how much larger she felt. He hoped she wasn't going to allow herself to get fat, especially now that they were to be man and wife. One thing he couldn't abide was women who let themselves go. As he thought about it, his eyes got heavy, and in no time, he was asleep too, Doris lying peacefully in his arms.

Karmen woke to the phone ringing. She was tired but luckily, not hung over. She stretched across Richard, who carried on snoring, to reach the phone.

"Karmen, it's Brick, I need to see you. Something terrible has happened. Can you come over?"

"Of course. Give me half an hour, OK?"

Karmen jumped out of bed and rushed into the shower. What could possibly have happened? she thought.

She left Richard to sleep and put a note on his bedside table, telling him where she'd gone.

# Chapter Twenty-Eight

Antonio and Doris were having brunch. They had a busy day ahead, and even though they had been up very late, neither of them felt bad. At noon, they were to meet all the crew, and at two o'clock, the lawyers were arriving to finalise the purchase of the *Golden Eagle* and arrange to transfer the cash funds.

"I hope Carl gets himself together in time for this afternoon's meeting. I heard he was in a bad way last night," said Antonio.

"Talk of the devil, Antonio; here he comes now."

They both turned as Carl walked in.

"Hi, you two lovebirds. How's things?" Carl sounded completely fresh and alive. "I'm starving. Just said good-bye to Carol; she apologised for disappearing last night. She looked awful this morning. Funny how a stunner like that can become an absolute horror in a matter of moments. I don't understand it; fine vodka never affects me badly or gives me a hangover."

Sure, thought Doris, remembering his inebriated state the previous evening.

"So," he continued, "the meeting is at two p.m. I'll see you there—got to go and eat and perhaps have a strong Bloody Mary." With that, Carl scurried off toward the top deck, arms flapping backward and forward.

"That man is unbelievable! How the hell does he do it?" Doris muttered.

"He sure is one crazy individual, and yet, I kind of like him. And on top of everything else, he's one hell of a businessman."

"You know, Antonio, Karmen and Josephine were talking about him last night after he left the dance floor, and they agreed Mr. Finkelstein is an annoying lovable fool."

At 11:50 a.m. Strillian came and found Antonio. He told him the lawyers were on board. Both men had apparently read through all the documents, and seemingly, there was nothing to cause any holdups. Carl and Mical were with them, going through certain formalities, and they were looking forward to getting things underway at 2:00 p.m.

"In the meantime, let's go meet your crew."

"They're not mine yet, Strillian, not until everything has been checked out thoroughly, and all the appropriate papers have been signed and lodged."

"Antonio, you sound like you don't trust me. You upset me, my friend. I was actually thinking earlier, if you gave me the gems, we could have a gentleman's agreement, and the yacht could be yours, along with the cash. We could save time and money. We'd get rid of the lawyers; they're all bloody thieves after all. You know in Russia, we always do our business based on trust."

Antonio shot Strillian one of his looks. "Do you think I was born yesterday? I trust no one. In fact, at times I don't even trust myself."

Strillian laughed, put his arm around Antonio's shoulder, and led him, along with Doris, toward the bridge.

"I like you, Antonio. You remind me of me."

Doris and Antonio walked into the enormous bridge area, where the entire crew was gathered. The captain and his officers stood in front of another twenty-five people or so. They were all dressed in their smart starched uniforms.

Antonio cast his eye around the room quickly, noting faces he recognised—the handsome guys who looked after the tenders and transferred people back and forth; Seon, the bartender; waitresses; housekeepers; the head chef and his team, along with many unknown faces. He was impressed. They all looked immaculate.

Strillian stepped forward. "Good afternoon, everyone. As you are all probably aware, my brothers and I are in the final stages of signing the *Golden Eagle* over to these lovely people, the soon-to-be Mr. and Mrs. Cadiz.

"I thought it appropriate for you all to meet them, in advance of them becoming the legal owners, which, if there are no unexpected hiccups, should be very soon. I wanted you to know who your new bosses would be, so you have a chance to decide if you want to continue serving on board this yacht and work for them.

"When the legalities have been finalised, you can let them know your intentions. I believe Mr. Cadiz would like to say a few words."

Looking smooth, debonair, and completely in control, Antonio spoke. "Hello, everyone. It's a pleasure to see you all standing here before us, looking impeccable and professional. I have spent a short time observing the running of this incredible yacht. Doris and I intend to make no changes. We have seen nothing that needs to be changed. Am I right, darling?

"Over the years, I've created many businesses and made them great successes. I've always had one policy: a good company is only as strong as the staff and team that help run it. I hope, if we become the new owners of this majestic yacht, we can gel as a family and have a happy, exciting future together. My beautiful wife-to-be has exquisite tastes, and she has had nothing but praise for the standards that surround us. You should all feel very proud of yourselves."

With that, both Antonio and Doris gave everyone a clap, trying to visually engage each member of the crew as they did. An immediate sense of pride and camaraderie rippled through the team.

"There is something you should all know," added Antonio. "We intend to be joined by five of our very dear friends, who are on board with us now. The seven of us are going on an adventure together. We've all got grown-up families, except for my minder and friend Brick, and he has no intention of starting a family at this stage of his life." A quiet giggle could be heard from the crew, just as Antonio had hoped.

"So we're all completely free, and we want to explore this enormous world and have fun together before we're too old." Another ripple of laughter could be heard. "We're going to be on board for quite a while, and we would be honoured if you would choose to remain with us. As Mr. Kasparovsky mentioned, you have time to make up your minds, but before we leave, I wonder if you'd give us an idea of how many of you will want to stay. If there aren't many of you, I may have to do some serious advertising." Everyone began to laugh. "So please, can I have a show of hands? Who thinks they'll stay?"

There wasn't one hand that remained down. Both Doris and Antonio were overwhelmed.

"Well, we're delighted. Of course, you can change your minds between now and then. I just hope this afternoon's meeting goes well between the Kasparovsky brothers and ourselves, and the *Golden Eagle* becomes ours. Otherwise, we may look to you to start a mutiny."

Everyone began laughing, and then the crew began to clap. As Doris and Antonio left, high levels of excitement vibrated around the room.

"That went well, don't you think?" said Antonio.

"Yes, very well, darling. Can I ask you a question?" replied Doris. Antonio nodded. "Would you never want to start another family?"

"Come here, my love. Let me tell you something—been there, done that. It's not all it's cracked up to be. Trust me. Kids drive you mad forever. You're what I want, and all I'll ever need." And with that, Antonio squeezed her firm bottom tightly. Doris looked at him and smiled sheepishly.

Richard read Karmen's note. It suited him for her to be busy. He was meeting James for a chat before they saw the lawyers, and knowing she was occupied meant he could get on with his day. It could, after all, prove to be a long one.

Meanwhile, Josephine received a call from Karmen; they arranged to meet for lunch. "I've got so much to tell you. Poor Brick, he's in a terrible way. Tell you all about it when I see you," said Karmen. Josephine was intrigued and continued getting ready.

The table was long and oval, made from the finest mahogany. It complemented the whole feel of the library. Carl was deep in conversation with his old colleague Felix Simpson as Strillian and his two brothers arrived. Carl introduced the men, and they took their seats.

Name cards had been laid around the table for ten so those present were strategically positioned and also reminded of names, should they forget.

Richard and James arrived at the same time as Antonio and Doris, who had their lawyer, Roland Briggs, with them.

"Good afternoon, Roland and Felix," began Antonio. "I'd like to introduce you to my future wife, Doris…"

Doris smiled.

"…my diamond expert and valuer, Richard, and my organiser and strategist, James."

The men shook hands.

"And for those who don't know him, Carl Finkelstein, probably the largest diamond dealer in South Africa."

Carl gave a wave, looking very small at the large table. Each person was handed a folder, and the lawyers began discussing in detail the pages within. It was going to be a while before things were finalised.

Meanwhile, Josephine had just arrived to meet Karmen for lunch. Karmen had their drinks ready, and the two women were desperate to talk.

"Well? Tell me everything," said Josephine eagerly.

Two hours later, Antonio and the Kasparovsky brothers were finally shaking hands. The deal had been agreed, and both parties had signed on the dotted line. The gems chosen had been identified and were in the process of being sorted and stored safely at the warehouses of Brinks Securities in Botswana. As soon as the funds were released and the documentation confirming new ownership of the *Golden Eagle* had been stamped, which were expected to take place the next day in Johannesburg, the diamonds would be handed over.

Antonio asked when the $250 million would reach his various banks. He was told that ten payments of twenty-five million dollars would hit his accounts simultaneously the moment the diamonds were passed over to Strillian. Nothing was going to go wrong; the lawyers were absolute professionals. Not a thing had been left to chance.

"And now it's time to celebrate," announced Antonio. "Go find Karmen, Josephine, and Brick."

Karmen and Josephine were deep in conversation on the top deck when a steward arrived. He told them their husbands were asking for them. Both women hoped the news was going to be good, and deep down, they believed it would be. When they got to the library, they quickly told everyone that Brick was not coming to join them. They said he was unwell and needed to rest.

Antonio was genuinely disappointed. He really wanted his friend to be there to celebrate with him. "Maybe I'll look in on him later."

"Not a good idea, Antonio." Karmen spoke with force, and immediately Antonio knew it was best to leave Brick alone. "After all," Karmen continued, "we want to celebrate. There'll be plenty of time to share this moment with Brick when he's feeling better."

The twelve people gathered in the library smiled and joked as the pink champagne began popping. They drank and ate exquisite finger food, delighted the deal was completed at last.

Strillian asked the captain and his senior officer to join them so Antonio could give them the news in person. Within minutes, they arrived. The captain shook Antonio's hand warmly.

"Mr. Cadiz, on behalf of myself and the entire crew, and I do mean the entire crew, it will be our honour and privilege to serve you and your lovely wife. We're also very much looking forward to welcoming and taking care of your guests. Everyone here is extremely excited to join you on your journey, and we assure you of our dedication at all times. We'll make sure this will be a most memorable adventure for you."

Antonio was touched. "Thank you. Can you pass the news on to the entire team and tell everyone we can't wait to return."

"I will, sir. Have a safe trip back to Botswana tomorrow."

With that, the captain and his senior officer left the others to carry on celebrating. The late afternoon sun shone in the sky, and everyone chatted, drank, and ate, feeling very content and happy.

As the sun began setting, Karmen and Richard stood together, looking out over the water, thinking of the future.

James sat quietly with his arm around his wife's shoulder, not quite believing the deal had actually been done.

Carl was busy talking to the two lawyers about some business ideas he'd had and wondered if they'd be interested in getting involved.

The brothers were chatting in Russian and seemed extremely animated.

Then Antonio spoke. He apologised for interrupting. "Everyone, I want you to know that Doris and I can't wait for our journey to begin. To have you four dear friends join us—and Brick, of course—makes it all the more exciting. Every time I think of what lies ahead, I smile, probably the biggest smile I've ever smiled, except, of course, when Doris agreed to marry me. So I'd like to make a toast. Here's to all our futures."

"To all our futures," the group responded in unison.

By the time the celebrating was over, everyone was exhausted and ecstatic simultaneously. They had achieved their dream, and their journey was about to begin.

Karmen had thankfully managed to catch Doris and fill her in about Brick. "Poor love, let's hope he feels better in the morning."

"He's so embarrassed to show his face, Doris. Let Antonio know, then everyone can avoid making him feel even worse tomorrow than he already does."

With that, the two women went to their suites.

Josephine told James all about Brick and Precious. Apparently, the vodkas had been flowing late into the afternoon, and the next thing Brick knew, he was lying naked on his bed with Precious beside him. He was sick to his stomach, and when Precious woke, he asked her about the afternoon. She sensed his unease and displeasure and then tried to seduce him, taunting him when he rebuffed her. They ended up having an argument, which turned into a tussle. In the process Brick was on the receiving end of a punch. Once again, he remembered nothing more until he woke an hour later with a massive swollen eye. There was no Precious, only a note by his bedside. It said that she'd never been so insulted. That no one had ever turned her down before. And that he was a pathetic excuse for a man. She told him a woman named Karmen had phoned, who obviously didn't know what a weirdo he was.

Brick was totally devastated and didn't want to talk about it again to anyone.

"So you have to promise—not a word," Josephine added.

James agreed, although he didn't know how that would be managed in the morning, unless Brick's eye had completely healed, which he doubted very much.

The next morning, Carl was in a flap. He wanted to make sure they got to the airport on time. His pilot had told him there was only one slot free that morning, and if they didn't make that, they couldn't leave until much later that afternoon. He had to be back in Botswana for a meeting, and missing it was not an option.

"Antonio, please hurry up. Get everyone together; we have to go."

"Carl, chill out, will you? The way you're carrying on, you won't live to get to the airport. Look at you. You're sweating and so stressed out. Just calm down."

Soon enough, they were all in the car, about to make their way to the airport. Brick was quiet; he had a large hat and dark sunglasses on. He looked like a pimp. The guys kept glancing at him but managed to keep quiet. Inwardly, they felt like laughing, but they didn't dare. The women would berate them. Everyone had said their temporary good-byes to the Kasparovsky brothers, and Carl was feeling less stressed as they sped off to catch their flight.

That evening back in Botswana, the mood was high. Everyone was busy making their own plans, all wondering where they may be heading, what their first stop would be, and which cabin was for whom. The chatter around the campfire was nonstop.

"Can you all shut the fuck up? My head is spinning," snapped Antonio.

Everyone went deathly silent.

Antonio was feeling the pressure of taking responsibility for them all. It seemed they were only thinking about trivial things: which cabin they would have, where the first port of call was going to be, and how long they were going to be at sea for. He, on the other hand, had a lot more on his mind.

"Antonio, are you OK? You really blew a gasket just then," said Doris.

"Sorry. Doris, there's something important I need to talk to you about."

"I need to speak to you too, Antonio. I've been waiting for the right time."

"Well, what is it?"

"No, you go first."

"OK. Before we set off on the *Golden Eagle*, I've decided we've got to change our identities. I've been recommended a plastic surgeon who is coming here tomorrow to discuss all our options. He's supposed to be a miracle worker, and once we've changed our look, we can arrange new passports and disappear from the face of the earth."

"I've always fancied a smaller nose and higher cheekbones." Doris sounded excited.

"Now, darling, what's on your mind?"

"Antonio, I'm pregnant—almost three months. I'm so sorry, I know this is the last thing you want, and I've been so worried to break the news to you." She began crying.

Antonio was numb, a thousand thoughts rushing through his mind.

"I'm sorry; I've ruined everything, haven't I?"

"Come here. Give me a hug. Darling, I'm thrilled. Even though I said a family was the last thing I wanted, I'm over the moon. We'll make wonderful parents, and with twenty-four people looking after us, we'll never be short of babysitters. Does anyone else know?"

"No. I've been bursting to tell someone, but I wanted to know what you thought first."

"Well, now you can spread the news. I hope your condition won't interfere with any surgery."

"Antonio, I'm only pregnant. Just be cool about it, and everything will be fine."

With that, the two of them embraced. Antonio held her close. "I love you," he said. "I know everything is going to be fine. I'll make sure of that. I'll never let you down, Doris."

The next day, the plastic surgeon arrived as arranged. He was a very interesting, suave-looking guy, sporting a good suntan. His hair was sandy, there wasn't a line or blemish on his face, and his jawline and nose were just perfect. He was dressed in a very sharply cut royal-blue suit and had a wonderful positive energy about him. He introduced himself as Mark Gardener, an old friend of Carl's and a world-renowned plastic surgeon.

Antonio took him into his office where they talked privately. Mark listened intently as Antonio explained how he wanted to totally change the way he and Doris looked. He discussed needing passports once the new identities had been created and his intentions to travel the world as soon as the transformations had taken place. Mark sat taking notes, missing nothing that Antonio said.

Once he'd finished, Mark spoke. "Carl mentioned that this needed to happen quickly. So I've brought my computer with me. Its software is the most advanced available in the field of plastic surgery. This is how it works. First, we take profile pictures of you and Doris. Then we scan your facial images into the computer and see the various options that are possible. It takes about thirty minutes to have a hundred or so potential new looks."

At that moment, Doris arrived.

"Darling, this is Mark Gardener, the plastic surgeon I was telling you about."

"It's a pleasure to meet you, Mark."

"The pleasure's all mine, Doris. I've been explaining to Antonio that when you're both ready, we can take photographs of the two of you, feed them into the computer, and within half an hour have more than a hundred varieties of new faces to choose from. Then we can sit down together and carefully, jointly create the perfect new you."

"Wow, that sounds amazing. I'm ready to begin whenever you are, Mark. Antonio, I can't wait to choose a new me and a new you!"

"Mark, she's like a kid in a sweet shop. That's what I love about her. So come on then. I think we're both ready; let's get this show on the road." Antonio sounded as excited as Doris.

With that, Mark began to set things up. Doris and Antonio had photographs taken from all angles. After thirty minutes, the three of them sat closely around the table, looking at the computer screen.

"As you can see, I move the mouse around your face, Antonio, choosing different noses and chins. I can make your eyes and ears smaller or larger. Jaw lines can be squared, like this, or rounded like this. Teeth can completely change your mouth and smile. In fact, a whole new face. See what I mean?"

Mark created a number of new Antonios in minutes. Both Doris and Antonio were amazed at the transformations. They appeared on the screen so quickly, each different, but still Antonio, if you looked closely.

"Let me show Doris how she could look. And then we can take things step by step to create the perfect new you. You have to trust my expertise, though. There are faces that may look amazing, but surgically creating them could prove too complicated. If you leave me awhile—let's say an hour—I'll find half a dozen of the best combinations, and then we can choose together. What do you say?"

Antonio and Doris looked at each other, but it was Antonio who spoke. "We have to create new identities for ourselves. We have no choice, and I trust you, Mark. You come highly recommended. We'll leave you, and in an hour, we can decide on the final face for each of us. What about costs?"

Mark explained clearly that his terms were nonnegotiable. It would come to $250,000 per person, including all surgical procedures and new profiles, national insurance numbers, bank accounts, driver's licences, credit cards, passports, and birth and marriage certificates, where applicable. There were no hidden extras. Payment terms were fifty percent up front, nonrefundable once the face had been chosen, and then twenty-five percent after the surgery was completed.

"The last twenty-five percent must be paid six months later. How does that sound?" Mark asked.

"Sounds good to me, but tell me, whose identity do we get?"

"There are plenty of people who go missing around the world. There are plane crashes, bodies that will never be recovered. Mafia hits, where people will never go home again. I have connections. You need not worry yourself; that's my problem. But rest assured the job will be done, and you'll be sailing off into the sunset looking fantastic. Carl can vouch for me. Now go, have a drink, and come back in an hour. Leave me to work."

As they walked to the door, Doris turned to Mark. "There's one thing you need to know—I'm pregnant, almost three months. Will this make any difference to me having the surgery?"

"We'll have to move quickly, and I'll choose the least invasive procedures to get the best results, but no, there's nothing for you to worry about, Doris. Pregnant women have surgery all the time."

An hour later, the three were sitting together looking at the final choices. "Antonio, what do you think?"

"Wow, even I think I look good. Will I really look like that? Doris, what do you think?"

"I love it, darling; you look years younger and so handsome. It's like I'm getting a new man. And now, Mark, show me the final me. I know I've chosen the eyes, nose, chin, and so on, but I want to see them all together."

"Voilà. Do you like?"

Doris examined her profile. She looked so different but so beautiful. "My God, I'm amazing. Antonio, what do you think?" Antonio whistled, and she knew he liked what he saw.

"So Mark, take me through what you'll be doing to me. I'm not squeamish, so tell me all."

Mark explained he would initially be breaking her cheekbones, then raising them. Her eyelids would be lifted, improving the shape, giving a wider, rounder eye and socket. Her chin would be rebuilt, giving it a softer look. Her nose, which at the moment was rather thin, would be rounded slightly at the end. Finally, a small gap would be created between her front teeth, which would give her smile – in an otherwise perfect mouth – a more interesting look.

"Oh, and a little bit of collagen will do wonders to plump those lips. Last of all, I'll transplant hair to the front of your hairline to reduce the size of your forehead and give you the flowing locks you see before you."

"And I thought you said you weren't going to do too much to me!"

"Doris, rest assured this is not a lot in the big scheme. You should see some of my other clients."

"I love how I look, Mark. Antonio, what do you think? Would you still love me if I changed?"

"Doris, darling, I love you, not your looks. But wow, if you looked like that, I'd be the envy of every man on this planet. You will look magnificent."

With that, Doris smiled and held her stomach. "I just felt our baby kick for the first time. I think he's going to be a footballer."

"And what a beautiful mother he'll have," came Antonio's response.

Before Mark left, they all agreed the surgery would take place the following week in a small private clinic in Cape Town. The agreed fifty percent down payment, $250,000, was to be transferred immediately into his bank account.

Mark took blood samples from both of them to check their potential healing power, but he assumed it would be about eight weeks, and then two weeks later, photographs would be taken to match their new identities.

At Antonio's request a fully qualified nurse would accompany them on the *Golden Eagle* for about six months, just in case. Costs for this, being the only extra, would be discussed nearer the time.

Finally, the meeting was over. Hands were shaken, dates were booked, and Mark was driven back to the airport by Brick. Antonio and Doris sat quietly, thinking about what lay ahead. They were excited and scared. Antonio eventually spoke. "Doris, I'm going to talk to the others and let them know our plans. While we're recovering, they can start getting the yacht prepared, so when we're ready to go, we won't have to waste any time. I want to leave South Africa with you, our crew, and our friends as quickly as possible. I can't wait to begin the next chapter of our lives. The world is our oyster."

Doris smiled; Antonio always managed to make her feel safe. She laid her head on his shoulders. What were the coming weeks going to be like, and the next year? She wondered. So many thoughts raced through her mind. She closed her eyes, quietly listening to the steady beat of Antonio's heart. Her unborn child kicked gently.

"Antonio, let me tell them about the baby," she whispered.

# Chapter Twenty-Nine

As soon as Doris approached Josephine and Karmen and told them she had something to discuss, they both smiled quickly at each other. They had talked a while ago and had put two and two together.

So they were completely unsurprised when Doris told them she was expecting. Of course, they didn't let on; they were both too nice to do that. But when they were told of the surgery that was to take place within a week or so, both sat with their mouths wide open. It sounded too ridiculous to be true. New faces, new identities, a baby on the way, plus all of them travelling the world together on the *Golden Eagle*. How could this be occurring within the next couple of months?

"Wow, Doris, it's mind blowing. How's Antonio reacting to everything?"

"Actually, Josephine, he's taking it all in his stride. It's me who's freaking out. The surgery is a real concern, but we have no choice. We have to become new people so we can live our futures in peace. We can't keep looking over our shoulders worrying all the time, especially now we're having a baby."

The women continued chatting. There was a lot to talk about.

Meanwhile, in another part of the camp, Antonio was filling James and Richard in on the entire goings-on. Brick was nursing his eye in his tent and wasn't present. Antonio would speak to him the next day.

Everyone was giving Brick a wide berth, and thankfully, the swelling and bruising were becoming less obvious.

"So Richard, James," Antonio continued, "I want you to begin getting the *Golden Eagle* ready for our departure while Doris and I have our surgery. It will take approximately eight weeks for the healing to take place; then we'll be ready to have our new IDs created. So I guess we're looking at ten weeks until we'll be leaving South Africa for good. By then Doris will be almost six months pregnant."

"Bloody hell, Antonio. It's a lot to take in, buddy. How are you feeling about fatherhood?"

"To be honest with you, Richard, at first I was horrified. I've been there, done that before, when I was younger. But once I got my head in gear, I began to look quite forward to the idea. After all, there's going to be plenty of help on the yacht, so it shouldn't be too hard. Only problem is, when I told Doris I hoped it was going to be a boy, she said if it wasn't, we could try again. At that point I had to put my foot down. I'm too old for a football team. This is going to be an only child for sure."

# Chapter Thirty

Three months later, Barbara was sitting in Mark's recliner, waiting to be examined. "Well, Mr. and Mrs. Garcia, how have you been enjoying your life as a married couple, and more importantly, how do you like your new faces? I have to say, you both look amazingly well and at least ten years younger. Barbara, come let me take a closer look at you." He examined her closely under his illuminated magnifying mirror, the light making her blink.

"You've healed wonderfully. How do you like the new you?"

"It's strange getting used to my name. My friends still forget and call me Doris, but it's happening less and less as the days go by, thank goodness. I'm constantly reminding them to eradicate Doris from their minds. My face, on the other hand, takes me by surprise every time I look at it, but Mark, I have to say, I love it. I feel so beautiful and young. Antonio—oops, I mean Charles—can't take his eyes off me. He says it's like having a new woman without all the hassle."

"Well, I think you're ready to go, Barbara. You've passed the worrying time for healing. How are things coming along with the baby? I must say you've put on very little weight hardly anywhere, although your stomach's enormous. Are you sure you're only six months pregnant? Or are you having triplets?"

"Just had my scan and no, just one baby and yes, only six months, but they did say he or she is one hell of a size."

"Well, you look after yourself and that little—or should I say large—one. Now, Charles, let's make sure you're not going to be the person to hold everything up."

After a thorough check, Mark confirmed, much to everyone's pleasure, there was no reason to delay. Both his patients were in fine health and ready to begin their new lives.

"Mark, we can't thank you enough. You've done an amazing job. We love the way we look. Our new identities are perfect. The yacht has been registered to a company in the Bahamas, and Mr. and Mrs. Garcia are both directors of that company. So Antonio and Doris no longer exist, and it's all down to you. We are homeward bound."

"Charles, it's been my pleasure, and my work hasn't come cheap. I'm pleased I've been of help."

"By the way, Barbara and I were sorry to hear about your divorce, and we wondered if you might consider joining us on our travels. We could use a top doctor on board. It could also give you a chance to get away from your troubles. What do you think?"

"Sounds tempting. My ex has been the bitch from hell over these past few months. She's squeezed and squeezed until there's not a lot left. The kids, although grown and living alone, have taken her side. She's spun them all sorts of lies. And you know what? Worst of all, it was she who had an affair. With the decorator, of all people. Said she was lonely, that I worked too hard. What a bitch. I could kill her. No,

Charles, I can't take off and go travelling around the world. I need to earn some serious money. I have clients booked; I can't let them down, plus I need the dough. She's taken me to the cleaners. I'd be constantly flying to and from different hospitals around the world to earn a living. It wouldn't work, even if I wanted to join you. But thanks for the offer."

"You do know we have a fully equipped hospital on board? We have a very decent GP and a team of three nurses who work permanently here. An experienced doctor of your standing and a surgeon to boot would be a wonderful addition. You could even fly your patients in as we approach different parts of the world. You could get your secretary to do the bookings in advance, and then your clients could experience luxurious recovery time on board the *Golden Eagle*. Think about it. You could charge a fortune for all that added luxury and attention."

"Oh, Mark, do think about it," pleaded Barbara. "I have an incredible midwife joining me, but I'd feel so much more comfortable if you could be around when I have the baby. It's going to be born on board, which scares me, and I'm toying with the idea of a water birth, which scares me even more. What do you think?"

"Do you know something? I may just take you up on your offer. Knowing I could continue my work and start a new life at the same time is certainly tempting, and as far as a water birth goes, Barbara, if you have the right midwife, you'll be just fine. Can I have a little while to think about it and let you know?"

"Absolutely, but we're due to leave in three days, so don't take too long to make your decision. I think it's just what you need to kick-start a new life for yourself, and Barbara's told me the midwife is a stunner and a divorcee," said Charles.

With that, Charles gave Mark a slap on the back and a friendly wink. Barbara kissed him good-bye, whispering, "Please try and come Mark. It would mean so much to me."

Then the two of them left the clinic and walked toward Brick and the waiting car.

"How'd it go, boss? Get the all clear?" enquired Brick.

"Sure did, my friend. We'll be ready to leave here in three days."

"And guess what, Brick?" added Barbara. "Mark Gardener may be joining us."

"You mean him, the plastic surgeon?" Brick pointed his thumb over his shoulder, motioning to where they'd just come from.

"Yes, Brick. Him." Barbara chuckled to herself. Brick was such a character, she thought.

"Do you think he could do some work on me?"

"What do you fancy? A nose job?"

"No, I'd like bum implants and a hair transplant." Brick was deadly serious, and Charles and Barbara smiled happily at each other.

"If he comes with us, Brick, you can have whatever you want. Promise. But my baby takes priority, OK?"

"Sure thing, ma'am."

The rest of the journey back to the yacht was silent. Brick dreamed of the new Brick, full headed with a tight bottom. Barbara prayed Mark would accept their offer, and Charles looked forward to starting his new life with his wife, his friends, and the new addition that would be with them in about three months. It couldn't get much better than this, he thought to himself.

# Chapter Thirty-One

Charles received a call from the navigation deck as he sat relaxing with his wife and friends. Dusk was slowly fading, and stars were becoming visible in the darkening sky.

"Excuse my interrupting you, sir, but I wondered if it would be possible to run through the route that my senior navigations officer has suggested for tomorrow."

"Sure thing, Roger. I can pop up in, let's say, half an hour. How does that sound?"

"Perfect. See you then, sir."

"Roger, please call me Charles. I'd feel much more comfortable if we were on first-name terms."

"Of course, sir—I mean Charles. See you at nine."

The group of friends began returning to their individual suites to get showered and ready. Dinner was to be served at 9:30 p.m. On the top deck, staff were in the process of setting the table. It was to be alfresco dining, and a lot of extra effort was going into creating a perfect setting for the first evening's meal. All the stops were being pulled out.

Below in the kitchen, the chef and his team were busy creating an absolute feast of culinary delights. Everything had to be perfect for the new owners of the *Golden Eagle*. Tonight would set the standard that Mr. and Mrs. Garcia would come to expect of their crew. It had to be impeccable.

As Charles was leaving his suite to meet with Roger, he walked into the spacious bathroom area. Barbara was putting the finishing touches on her make up. She looked a little pale.

"How are you feeling, sweetheart?" He lovingly put his arms around her waist and gently stroked her enormous belly.

"I have to say I seem to be feeling a lot less sick, but I still have an absolute mad hunger for red meat. The rarer the better. I don't understand it, Charles. It's freaking me out a bit."

"Darling, that's how your body's reacting to the pregnancy. You have a strong, beautiful baby growing inside you, and it obviously needs all the vitamins it can get. So relax and stop worrying. You'll probably be a vegetarian again as soon as it's born. I'll meet you on the top deck in twenty minutes or so. Get yourself ready, and promise me you'll stop thinking too much about the changes that are occurring in you. Everything's going to be fine."

With that, Charles kissed his wife's head and left the suite. He was extremely concerned about her. There was something not quite right, and it was worrying him, but he couldn't let Barbara know how he felt. He needed to keep her as calm as possible, for her well-being and for the safety of his unborn child.

Barbara was looking at herself in the large mirror as Charles left. God, this baby was draining her, she thought. She looked so pale, her eyes were sunken, and her hair was thinning. How she wished the pregnancy was over. She hated every minute. Suddenly, the baby kicked violently. Her breath left her body for a moment. It's almost as if this child is reading my mind, thought Barbara as another strong kick came. It knows how unhappy I'm feeling, and it's punishing me for my thoughts. Tears welled in her eyes as she applied her lipstick and began to dress for dinner.

Charles agreed to the route that the yacht was to take the next day. The captain and navigations officer confirmed that the weather conditions were favourable, supplies were on board, and there was nothing to stop them from heading out of Cape Town and making their way up toward Dubai. Roger confirmed that they would stay in Dubai for a few days. Fuel would be replenished and fresh supplies brought in while everyone relaxed.

"It'll give you and your guests time to explore a little. Stretch your legs, so to speak. We have an Arab-speaking member of staff who has spent many years travelling through the UAE. He's more than happy to be your guide, show you around. The ladies may like to visit the gold souks. Some of the best jewellery in the world, all tax free, so bargains galore. We'll then take in a few neighbouring Arab nations before continuing on to the next leg of our journey. Does that sound all right to you, Charles?"

"Sounds wonderful, Captain. I leave everything in your capable hands."

"By the way, Charles, it's Roger, remember?"

"Apologies. Roger, do feel free to join us for a nightcap after dinner tonight. In fact, I insist you do."

"Yes, sir!" Roger saluted jestingly, and they both began to laugh. A friendship was being created. With that, the two men shook hands, and Charles made his way to dinner.

The top deck had been transformed; it looked beautiful. Trees covered in fairy lights twinkled everywhere. It looked like the magical forest on the set of *A Midsummer Night's Dream*. Behind soft, sheer gauze, butterflies of differing sizes and colours fluttered elegantly back and forth.

Under one of the larger trees, a woman sat playing the harp. She was dressed from head to toe in white glittering lace. Everything was exquisite.

As Charles walked toward the others, who were chatting softly among themselves, Richard grabbed him by the arm and pulled him sharply into an alcove, putting his finger to his lips to indicate quiet.

"We need to talk, Charles. Barbara's been acting very strange. We're all really worried about her. I'm not one to tell tales, but she's been raiding the fridges in the kitchen. The chef mentioned it to Karmen. Apparently, four enormous rib eyes are missing, and yesterday the sous chef actually saw her eating one, tearing at it with her teeth, using her bare hands. And buddy, it was completely raw! She didn't know she was being watched.

"Charles, there's something else. Early this morning, James cut his finger, a paper cut of all things. As you know, he takes blood-thinning medication, and boy, did he bleed. Wads of cotton wool were thrown in the dustbin before he was bandaged up, and…and I really don't know how to tell you this, but out of the corner of his eye, he saw Barbara go to the bin, take the dripping cotton wool out, and then he watched as she began sucking wildly at it. James said she seemed in a frenzy, completely oblivious to the fact that he was there. Apparently, blood was dripping from her mouth by the time she'd finished. Charles, it can't be normal, can it?"

"Richard, she's expecting. I'm sure there's some logical answer. Tomorrow, Mark Gardener arrives. He's an amazing doctor, and he'll sort things out. Perhaps she's just terribly deficient in iron. Look, thanks for giving me the heads-up, but please tell the others to calm down. Everything's going to be fine. Now come, let's eat." With that, Charles placed his arm around his friend, and the two men walked toward the others. Inside, Charles was terrified. Something was very, very wrong.

Dinner was wonderful, although no one dared look at Barbara as she ploughed through her raw and rare meat courses. Conversation flowed among the others as always, but Barbara seemed only interested in her food.

Later that night, as everyone returned to their suites, they could hear raised voices. It was Barbara and Charles. No one knew what they were saying, but the noise grew until the shouting ricocheted around the yacht.

Fortunately, the content of the argument was inaudible.

Karmen, Richard, James, and Josephine knew their dream journey was suddenly turning a little sour. They hoped it would be sorted and sorted quickly, but somehow, they weren't feeling particularly confident.

Roger made his way back to his quarters after visiting all three bars on board, looking for Charles. Funny, he thought, Charles forgetting he'd invited me for a nightcap. Oh well. He had an early start, so it probably wasn't a bad thing. He had stopped for a brief chat with Seon and had two of his famous old-fashioned rums, so bed was rather enticing.

The next morning, Mark Gardener arrived on board. He was ushered through to the middle deck where breakfast was being served in a very casual fashion. His luggage was being unpacked in his suite, so he was feeling relaxed and settled already. He was delighted to be offered a nice strong cup of coffee by Karmen, who greeted him warmly.

"Mark, how lovely to meet you. I'm Karmen; this is my husband, Richard; and these two lovely people are James and Josephine. We've heard so much about you, and we're all delighted you were able to join us on our exciting journey. Always nice to have a doctor around, but a plastic surgeon—well, that's fantastic. We must have a chat once we're at sea."

"It'll be a pleasure, Karmen." And looking toward the others, he added, "It's lovely to meet you all."

"Feel free to help yourself to breakfast. There's a wonderful spread inside, and of course, if you fancy anything cooked, just ask," added Josephine, smiling warmly.

Suddenly, Charles appeared, looking fresh and rested. "Good morning, Mark. Welcome aboard, my friend. Have you been introduced?"

"I certainly have, and I'm already feeling the stresses of my old life leaving me. It's wonderful to be here, Charles."

"The pleasure's all mine. Mark, once you've eaten, I'd like to have a quiet word with you about Barbara. She's been out of sorts for a while, and I'm a little concerned."

"Absolutely. I'm not a big breakfast eater, so I'll be ready in a few minutes. Just let me grab another coffee and some fruit."

Everyone else quickly glanced at one another, not making eye contact with Charles. They all hoped Mark could help get Barbara back to her old self again.

Just as the two men left the middle deck, Brick came rushing in. "I hear he's here! Where's he gone? They told me he was with you having breakfast."

"Calm down, Brick. What's up?" asked James.

"You know the doc who's joining us? Well, he's no ordinary doctor." Brick lowered his voice, looked around, and added proudly, "He's a plastic surgeon. The one who fixed the bosses. Mrs. Garcia said I could get implants for my bottom and have my cheekbones enhanced. I wanted to talk to him."

"Well, Brick." Karmen spoke gently and kindly. "That sounds wonderful, but I really think there are other priorities that must be addressed before you, or any of us, approach him for ourselves. Like Mrs. Garcia and her baby."

"Oh, I know, Karmen. We agreed that the baby must come first. I just got overly excited; I've never met a plastic surgeon before. Is he extremely handsome?"

"He's absolutely gorgeous, Brick; just up your alley," teased James.

"Yeah, Brick, just the kind you'd go for. Very sophisticated, greying slightly around the temples," added Richard, giggling.

"Shut up, you two. Stop being mean. Brick, he's lovely but not for you, sweetie. Mind you, once you've had your surgery, the world will be your oyster."

"Thanks, Josephine. You're so kind. And you two, you should grow up!" Brick threw James and Richard a death stare as he tossed his head in the air and wiggled back inside.

"Don't you just love him?" Karmen looked at her friends, and they all began to laugh.

"Let's just hope," added Josephine, "that poor old Barbara can be fixed as easily as having a bit of plastic surgery."

Everyone agreed, and they went on eating their breakfast.

"So Charles, tell me, what's been going on with Barbara?" asked Mark.

"Well, Mark, she's been acting very, very strange. It all began a couple of months ago. First of all, from being an absolute vegetarian, she started to eat red meat. Then the meat got rarer and rarer and lots of it. Then one night at the camp in Botswana, she began vomiting. I thought she was going to die, Mark. Remember when I called you?"

Mark nodded his head.

"She was white, her eyes were sunken, and she looked almost inhuman. The vomit was projectile, and she was dripping with sweat. Her body was so frail, and yet her stomach was so enormous. When she appeared completely better the next day, and you'd put my mind at rest, I kind of put it in the back of my mind. The baby was moving and obviously very alive.

"Then recently, it's gotten worse. She's now eating meat completely raw. She's stealing steaks from the kitchen, and the other evening, she was tearing into a rib eye with her bare hands standing by the refrigerator. She didn't even bother to close the door before she ripped into it.

"A few days ago, James cut his finger. It bled a lot, and he saw her retrieve the sodden wads of cotton and suck the blood out of them. She didn't even notice that he was looking at her. Mark, she seems obsessed, and I'm scared. Scared for her and scared for our child."

"Charles, we have talked previously about Barbara's past and her involvement with the CIA. I remember you telling me there were a number of hormone trials and implants that were tested on her when she first joined the agency. Were these removed? Did she go through a detoxification programme?"

"To be honest with you, Mark, when I first met Barbara, she was…well, what can I say? A complete freak of nature. From early on as a kid, she was experimented on by the

CIA, making her one of their top agents. So much new technology was pumped into her that she was almost superhuman. I know very little, really, except there were pellets implanted in her. They gave her incredible hearing and sight capabilities. She was incredibly sexy and seductive yet callous and cruel. She was stronger than any man and so agile, as quick as lightning. She was beyond belief, and I just fell under her spell.

"Then we became lovers. I saw a sensitive, caring side to her that touched me. She had vulnerability, and I wanted to look after her, keep her safe. I asked very few questions. She had escaped the grip of the CIA by then and was happy to just be with me. We've been incredibly happy ever since. Her superhuman powers seemed to fade away; she became normal, and to be honest, I forgot all about her past. She was just my amazing Barbara, who then became my beautiful wife, falling pregnant and giving me a chance of fatherhood again at my age. Then these strange things began to happen, and here we are. I know little else."

"OK, do you think she'll have any idea what drugs her body was subjected to and whether the implanted pellets were ever removed?"

"To be truthful, Mark, I want to avoid any discussions with her about the past. She's extraordinarily touchy. We had a blazing row last night, and I want her to relax. Questioning her will only add to her stress levels. Can you do some in-depth blood tests and some scans and try and ascertain what's going on with her?"

"'Course I can, Charles. Barbara will think nothing of it. She's pregnant, and I'm her doctor, so leave it to me. I will give her an internal examination to make sure the baby is happy and in position. Then I have a dear paediatrician friend based at the world-famous Al Husain hospital in Dubai. I'll put a call in to him now, and when we arrive in a few days, he can do all the tests immediately.

"We'll be there for a while, according to the captain, so there's no rush. Just relax and leave Barbara and the baby to me. I'm sure we'll find out your baby is just fine—extremely large for its gestation period but otherwise perfectly healthy. The scans will tell us if there are any devices still inside Barbara, and the bloods will show any hormone issues other than the ones that are common in pregnancy. Then we'll know what we're dealing with. But remember, the baby is kicking and moving; that shows it has a strong heartbeat and is very much alive."

The two men left each other, Charles feeling somewhat calmer but Mark full of concerns. Something wasn't quite right, and he needed to try and get to the bottom of it, the quicker the better.

After receiving a call in her suite where she had been napping, Barbara walked into Mark's office. It was an inviting space that made her feel comfortable. It was attached to a small hospital, which was far more clinical and threatening.

"Thanks for popping down, Barbara. Thought it'd be a good idea to check your general condition before we set off. Find out how you're feeling physically and emotionally. Then if it's all right with you, I'd like to give you a little internal examination. How does that sound?"

Barbara nodded. She felt exhausted, as usual, but decided to be honest with Mark. After all, he was a doctor and hopefully he could make her feel better. After an hour's conversation and her internal examination, Mark smiled at her.

"Right. Barbara, everything seems pretty OK. I'm slightly concerned at the size of your baby and wondered if we could do some blood tests now, rather than waiting until we get to Dubai. I can get them sent over to my colleague at the Al Husain hospital, so we will have the results before we get there."

"You're scaring me, Mark."

"Don't be silly. I'm just being extra careful. You are, after all, hosting me on your wonderful yacht. I owe it to you to be vigilant. Now, you'll feel a little prick. All done. I'll get it off right away. And Barbara, relax. Stress is no good for mum or baby."

With that, Mark gave her a warm smile and walked her out of his office.

"Thanks, Mark. I feel much better knowing you're around." Barbara gave him a kiss on the cheek and walked back to her suite. She felt happier than she had for ages.

Mark sat at his desk, rubbing his temples. Things were worse than expected. Although he couldn't confirm it, from his initial examination, this child's head was oversize. Oversize for even a full-term baby. Barbara's eating habits, emotional state, and frailty all led him to believe there was a big problem. But until he had her blood results and could get her scanned in a state-of-the-art neonatal department, he felt he had no choice but to keep his worries to himself.

Upsetting Charles and Barbara now would serve no purpose, and what if he was mistaken? He needed a drink.

Two hours later, the *Golden Eagle* was ready to leave Cape Town. Roger had phoned through to Charles to ask if he wanted him to announce their departure through the Tannoy System. Charles liked the idea, and as he sat on the top deck, arms around Barbara, who looked the happiest he'd seen in ages, the announcement came through.

"Ladies and gentlemen, this is your captain. I'd like to inform you that we'll be lifting our anchors in the next thirty minutes and making our way towards Dubai. Your in-suite TVs will give you minute-by-minute information on our route. Dinner will be served at nine thirty in the main dining room this evening, and a small gaming room will allow those of you who wish to gamble to do so. The weather conditions for this evening and through the night are wonderful. Entertainment will be provided by the famous jazz artist Dizzy Gillespie Junior. So please have a fabulous first evening at sea. Relax and enjoy the journey."

Karmen, Josephine, Richard, James, and Brick raised their glasses. "Here's to us and to our dear friends Charles and Barbara."

Barbara snuggled closer to her husband. "I love you," she whispered.

Just as she spoke, the child inside her kicked out, and Charles could actually feel the force against his side.

"Gosh, that's a strong baby. I love you too, my darling. Here's to our future and our journey." With that, he gently kissed his wife on the lips.

Early the next morning, while Barbara slept peacefully, Charles sat outside their lounge area watching the sunrise. It was a beautiful sight. The yacht cut through the still waters, making little sound. He'd ordered coffee, croissants, and fresh orange juice, which had been brought to their suite only a few minutes earlier, and he was happily eating and drinking, enjoying the tranquillity, observing a flock of large birds swooping playfully over the ocean. Suddenly, his mind wandered, and he began to think about Barbara and the baby. Reaching for the phone, he pressed the button to connect him to the hospital below deck. It was manned twenty-four hours a day, so someone should be there. It rang; he waited and waited. He found himself getting more annoyed as no one answered. Surely there couldn't be an operation in progress at bloody seven thirty in the morning, he thought to himself. Just as he was about to hang up and make his way down there to find out what the hell was going on, someone answered.

"At last!" he snapped. "Why has it taken so long to answer the bloody phone? This could've been an emergency."

"Excuse me, who is this? And please, would you mind not being so rude?"

"My dear, this is Charles Garcia, the man who pays the salaries around here."

"Oh, hello, Mr. Garcia. I'm Caroline Peters, the midwife who you pay to take care of your wife. I'm afraid my job description didn't include being a receptionist, as I recall. The nursing team is having their early-morning meeting with the two doctors, and I just happened to walk in, so I apologise if I kept you waiting too long." Her voice was huskily gentle with a lovely southern Irish lilt to it, but it was clear she was no pushover.

"I'm sorry for my abruptness, Nurse Peters. Is Dr. Mark Gardener around to have a word with?" Charles definitely didn't want to upset Caroline at this crucial time. He needed her throughout this pregnancy and beyond; she was, after all, to be the baby's nanny once it was born.

"Please forgive me," he added.

"Mr. Garcia, apology accepted, and if I'm not mistaken, the doctor just walked in." Caroline looked toward Mark. She knew the other doctor, Steve Phillips, so this, she guessed, had to be Mark Gardener. She smiled at the handsome man who walked elegantly toward her, handed him the receiver, and said in her husky voice, "Mr. Garcia for you, Mark." She walked slowly out of the room.

"Hello, Charles, what can I do for you?"

"How did it go with Barbara? How are they both doing?"

"We had a good chat, Charles; she got a lot off her chest. I'm afraid I'm not at liberty to discuss our conversation with you, but I assure you Barbara felt a lot calmer after our lengthy talk. I gave her an examination and her bloods are on their way to the hospital in Dubai as we speak. Results will be with me by tomorrow, hopefully, and I'll have a clearer picture of what's going on. Then we can talk further. Is that OK?"

"Sure, Mark. I'm just a bit on edge at the moment. Can you smooth things over with Nurse Peters, explain the situation to her? I'm afraid I was rather short with her this morning."

"Of course. Now go take care of your wife and baby; that's an order."

Charles thanked him and put down the phone. He'd go and take some coffee to Barbara, he thought, and wake her up gently.

Mark hoped and prayed that the news, when it came, wouldn't be too bad. He wasn't looking forward to having a conversation with Charles if it was. He then went to find Caroline Peters. She was in the hospital area keeping busy.

"Miss Peters, let me introduce myself properly. I'm Doctor Mark Gardener, but please call me Mark. I'm here to care for Barbara throughout her pregnancy." He reached out to take her hand, and as he did, he stared straight into her eyes. She was gorgeous. "Unfortunately, it appears the pregnancy is somewhat complicated. Perhaps we can discuss this confidentially later?"

"Of course we can, Mark, and call me Caroline." She blushed as she spoke, looking away from his stare, which made her all the more attractive to him.

"I love your accent; it's from the South, isn't it?"

"Yes, born and bred in Dublin. I've been a midwife for the last fifteen years. I accepted this job to try and have a little more excitement and still do the work I love, you know, before life passes me by. Being in the local maternity ward back home day after day, mainly in the rain, was getting to me. When this offer came my way, a chance to see the world was just too good to refuse. I'm staying on to care for the baby once it arrives as well, so I feel extremely lucky."

Mark loved the way she spoke and the way she looked.

"Talking about the baby, there's a lot to discuss. Why don't we open a bottle of wine together tonight, perhaps in my quarters? We can relax, go through Barbara's history, and get to know each other a little better. After all, we're both caring for the same person, so we need to work closely."

"Sounds good to me, and seeing as neither of us is going anywhere soon, it'll be nice to make a friend. Some after-work company, so to speak. How will I get hold of you? This is a very large boat."

"Take my mobile number," he replied, handing her a business card. "Call me around eight p.m., and I'll come and escort you from your cabin. Maybe we can have a cocktail at the bar before we go to mine. Seon, the bartender, makes a mean old-fashioned rum punch, I've been told."

"That sounds grand, Mark. I'll call you later." And with that, Caroline left.

Mark stood watching as she closed the door behind her. He couldn't believe his luck. He punched the air as he let out a long whistle. Wow, what a beauty, he thought; his life was definitely going to change now that he'd met Caroline Peters.

# Chapter Thirty-Two

The journey to Mina Rashid, the port of Dubai, was going to take ten days. It was a total of 4,754 nautical miles. Weather conditions were good, and everyone settled down comfortably, wanting to relax and enjoy the trip.

Barbara was tired most of the time; she stayed in her cabin for days resting and continued to crave raw meat. Everyone hoped by the time they arrived in Dubai, she would be feeling a whole lot better. They had all noticed that with Mark and Caroline close by and the team of medics at hand, a calmness had come over her. Even Charles began to relax a little. So luckily, the journey was calm and peaceful. The friends ate and drank together and felt happy to know Barbara was being cared for in her cabin by professionals. Rest was after all what was needed, and Barbara was getting a lot of that. The child was moving and growing, so things weren't too bad, thought Charles. He prayed he was right in his assumptions and put on a brave face, trying to be ever the optimist.

Barbara's blood results had come in from the obstetrics department of the Al Husain hospital a few days ago. Mark had discussed them with Caroline at length, and as he sat at his desk rubbing his temples, he continued to read and reread the paperwork that sat in front of him. His colleague Dr. Ahmed Ali was in no doubt that the baby was a boy, and he was showing signs of being affected by albinism. Further tests were needed, and he recommended admitting Barbara as soon as they arrived in Dubai. Rest was imperative for mother and child, and quite blatantly, he stated that any other issues they might find after a thorough scan with his far-superior equipment would be unrectifiable at this late stage of the pregnancy. If the baby's head size was confirmed to be completely out of proportion, as Mark suspected, then nothing could be done except to identify the cause and then ascertain the effect it would have on the child's prognosis. It made for grim reading.

Mark took a deep breath as he heard Caroline greeting Charles in the reception area outside his office. He would not mention any of the "possible" facts until they were known one hundred percent, but he knew he had no choice but to relay clearly and calmly the facts that were absolute.

Charles immediately knew it was not good news; Mark's face was like an open book. Caroline closed the door quietly behind her as she left the two men to have the conversation. She felt terrible for them both: Mark for having to be the bearer of the awful news and Charles for having to hear how his unborn child had an awful condition that affected such a small percentage of the population. She prayed that all the other possible problems she and Mark had discussed over the past few evenings in Mark's cabin would be proved unfounded and that this was all Barbara and Charles would have to face.

"Please, Charles, sit down."

Charles slowly lowered his body into the chair opposite Mark and waited silently for Mark to continue.

"First, I would like to inform you that you are almost one hundred percent going to have a son."

There was silence. Charles was motionless, and Mark knew he had to continue.

"Barbara's blood results show quite conclusively that your son has a condition known as albinism. This is a very rare condition that affects the colour of the skin. It shows itself quite obviously in those suffering with it: white hair, very light blue eyes, colourless pink skin tones. It's due to a lack of pigmentation in the blood that feeds the skin and could potentially explain Barbara's craving for red meat. Somehow, she may be feeling his condition through their shared blood supply, and the desire for excessive iron is a way that her body is trying to help her son.

"There is, however, nothing that can be done to change the situation. For many sufferers the pigmentation never improves; for a small percentage, the melanin production can increase during childhood, and the albino effect is less extreme. In these cases, sunlight exposure can cause freckles and moles, so skin cancers are an issue. In many cases vision can be seriously affected. There are often rapid involuntary back-and-forth movements of the eyes that weaken the sight rapidly, often leading to partial blindness. I wish the news could have been better for you, Charles. I really do."

Charles sat, lost for words. His world felt as if it was spiralling out of control. He caught his breath.

"What about the size of the baby, the head size you mentioned, that appeared too big? Is that no longer a concern?" His eyes pleaded desperately, wanting Mark to give him some good news.

"Until the scans have been completed, we really don't know what other issues there may be. My advice to you as a doctor and a friend is to digest what we do know and decide whether to share it with Barbara now or wait until we have the whole picture. With luck, Charles, everything else will be fine. And Charles, if this is all we are dealing with, rest assured these children live long and fulfilling lives. At the moment Barbara and your son need to remain calm and rested."

Charles felt numb; he stood, thanked Mark, and silently left the room.

Minutes later, Caroline walked into the office. She stood behind Mark and began massaging his shoulders. Mark closed his eyes and remembered the previous few evenings they had shared. After professional conversations about Barbara and her unborn child, they had continued talking, late into the night, drinking wine and getting to know each other. She excited him and made him feel alive again. He needed to have her next to him tonight. He needed to lose himself and forget about everything. Slowly, he pulled her toward him; she responded passionately. God, she makes me feel good, thought Mark.

Charles walked into his suite; he'd been for a swim and cleared his head a little, and he bravely smiled at his wife, who was lying on the enormous sofa watching an old Bette Davis movie and eating a steak sandwich. She looked beautiful, if a little pale and tired.

"Darling, how are you feeling?"

Barbara shushed him. Joan Crawford was shouting at Bette Davis, and Charles felt a surge of love for his wife as she watched intently. She looked like a child seeing a Christmas tree full of presents for the first time. Barbara pressed the pause button and turned to him, her eyes sunken and dark.

"Wow, Charles, have you ever watched this? *What Ever Happened to Baby Jane?* It's so exciting."

"Yes, my love, shall I tell you the ending?"

"Don't you dare!" With that, Barbara playfully threw her serviette in his direction.

"You're looking relaxed," said Charles.

"I'm not too bad, just so very tired. To be honest with you, being here, watching movies, eating like a horse and sleeping whenever I want is really suiting me. How are the others? I know Josephine and Karmen have wanted to see me, but I just haven't had the energy. Tell them I'll be fine soon and I miss them."

"Darling, as long as you're happy, they're happy. You know those two; they only want what's best for you. Trust me, they're having a great time. Cocktails from noon till dusk and then dinner and drinks until bedtime. They're unbelievable. So don't feel guilty. Listen, my darling; I have some news for you. I've just been with Mark, and guess what?"

Barbara's eyes widened. Charles saw her fear. Tears welled in his eyes. "We're going to have a baby boy. You, my love, are giving me a son and heir to continue our family name."

Barbara began to cry. Charles took her in his arms; her body relaxed into him. He couldn't tell her anything else, not now. He cried quietly and prayed nothing worse was going to confront them. If this was all they had to deal with, they would manage; they would give their son all the love in the world. He prayed silently to himself for the first time in years.

Later that afternoon, on the top deck, James, Josephine, Karmen, Richard, and Brick were sunning themselves. A cool breeze was blowing, taking the intensity out of the sun's heat. Lunch had been light—lobster with a selection of scrumptious salads. Tonight, they were being treated to an Indian evening, which included entertainment as well as foods from both the north and south of the country.

"I can't wait for dinner," muttered James. "I really fancy a curry."

"Me too. A nice chicken tikka would go down a treat," chuckled Richard. Neither man opened his eyes as they thought of their stomachs yet again.

"I did an hour on the cross-trainer this morning," Richard whispered as he yawned and stretched.

"You bloody liar, Richard; it was more like ten minutes," quipped Karmen.

"Do you know something? Karmen's got ears like a radar. Even when she sleeps, she listens. I watch her at night. I think she's a witch."

The friends began to laugh, and still none of them opened their eyes.

Charles had left Barbara sleeping. He'd tell Mark later how much he hadn't shared with her, Once the scans were done, they could talk. Please God, he'd only have to break this one bad piece of news to her; they'd be strong together, and everything would work out. They'd be fine, he reassured himself.

As he sat quietly outside the library, relaxing in a large wicker chair, drinking a gin and tonic, watching the yacht silently cutting through the crystal-clear waters, his phone buzzed. He looked down and saw a message from the captain's deck. Roger was asking if he was free to come up. There was something bothering them. The navigations officer had picked up signals and needed to discuss them with Charles. Drink in hand, Charles stood and made his way up to the bridge.

"Afternoon, gentlemen. What's going on?"

"Look, Charles, this boat has been following us for the last few days. It keeps about three nautical miles away, but our equipment and telescopes are picking it up. If you look through this lens, we can zoom in. See? We've identified five males aboard."

"Why haven't you mentioned this before?"

"We told both Richard and James the minute we saw it. We made an executive decision not to bother you. You've had a lot on your plate recently, and as long as the boat stayed at a distance, we didn't want to give you more to worry about. But we noticed one man holding a gun this morning and decided we had to inform you."

"Keep a close eye on them. Report to me if you notice anything else or if they get closer."

"Yes, sir."

Charles prayed his past wasn't catching up with him again. He left the bridge deep in thought.

Later that afternoon, he caught up with Richard and James to discuss the situation. They told him everything was under control. Brick had been advised, and the three of them were keeping a close eye on developments.

"How's Barbara? We're all worried about her. The girls are desperate to see her."

"She's doing fine, Richard," lied Charles. "Once we get to Dubai, they'll do further tests. By the way, it's a boy."

"Congratulations!" said James and Richard in unison. "Send her our love and don't worry. We'll let you know as soon as we think we have any trouble regarding the boat that's out there," added James.

With four days left until they arrived at the port of Mina Rashid, Charles hoped Barbara remained comfortable. He tried to push the information about his son to the back of his mind. He'd wait until all the tests had been completed before he'd allow himself to think about any of it. He trusted his friends to be vigilant regarding the suspect boat and made his way back to his suite to see how Barbara was doing. As he walked in, he saw his wife lying sound asleep on the bed. She looked so incredibly frail. He lay next to her and cried silently.

Meanwhile, as Karmen, Richard, Josephine, and James were getting themselves ready for the evening's activities, Caroline was finishing up in the hospital office. Very little had happened. Barbara was resting, Josephine had made a visit earlier to get some painkillers for a toothache, and it was nearly time to close up shop. As long as all hospital staff were available twenty-four hours a day, contactable by their pagers, there was no need to stay later than 5:00 p.m.

Just as Caroline switched off the hospital lights, her phone buzzed. She answered.

"Hello, stranger. I thought you forgot about me."

"How could I do that?" Her voice purred like a kitten.

Mark felt himself becoming aroused; he couldn't wait to explore her body. He'd held back long enough. "I'm waiting here in my suite for you."

"I've got a few things to do first; can you give me an hour?"

"Caroline, you know I'm in charge. I'm ordering you to put your pager on and come here right now."

"I love it when men are domineering," came her reply.

Minutes later, she stood outside Mark's suite, her white nurse's uniform slightly unbuttoned, her breasts visible beneath a lace bra. She'd lifted her skirt teasingly to show the tops of her stockings. Before leaving the hospital, she'd changed her flats and was wearing a pair of stilettos.

Mark opened the door. She knew exactly what to expect. He stood before her, wearing a silk dressing gown, open, showing his nakedness. They both had the same thing in mind. An open bottle of chilled chardonnay sat in an ice bucket, candles flickered in the breeze, and music played gently.

After filling two glasses, Mark turned to her. "Miss Peters, I want to show you my bedroom."

"Dr. Gardener, I can't wait to see it."

"Did anyone ever tell you you're sex on legs?"

"Do you know what? I think they have." With that, Caroline unbuttoned her uniform completely and let it fall provocatively to the floor. She walked toward the bedroom, flicking her auburn hair away from her face.

Mark watched as her body moved. Wearing only her bra, panties, and stockings, she looked incredible. Nothing like his ex, who'd wear nightdresses that covered her from head to toe. She lay down on the oversize bed and smiled. Mark took a slow mouthful of wine and savoured it. As he watched her, he felt young again.

# Chapter Thirty-Three

The seagulls woke Charles with a start. The sun was hot and rising in the morning sky, casting hazy movement above the level of the water. Barbara was breathing deeply, so he quietly crept out of bed and sat on his terrace. He saw Dubai rising majestically in the distance. It looked as if they would be arriving within the next hour or so. He felt thankful that they'd made it here without any major incidents. Soon enough, Barbara would undergo all the scans necessary, and he'd know what they were dealing with. Neither Richard nor James had mentioned the boat again, so he assumed their visitors were still waiting at a distance. Hopefully, it was a big mix-up, and there was nothing at all to worry about.

As Charles was ordering breakfast in the lounge area, Barbara walked in looking bleary eyed and exhausted.

"Hello, my darling. Do you feel better this morning? You slept for almost twelve hours."

"No, I don't," snapped Barbara. "Charles, I'm getting really bad cramps. Something's wrong; I know it. Last night, when I went to the loo, I'm sure I saw blood in the water. Although I might have been mistaken. I just don't know anything anymore. I'm so tired all the time. If I don't feel better in a while, you can call Mark and Caroline. Right now, I just want to lie down. Please just let me rest. I promise I'll let you know if I get worse."

"Honey, let me call them, just to be on the safe side. We're arriving in Dubai soon, and they can decide whether it's time for you to check into the hospital. The Al Husain has one of the best maternity units in the world."

"No, Charles, I just need to go back to bed and sleep. Please leave me alone."

"OK, go lie down, but call Mark or me if things don't improve. I'll be close by."

Within minutes, Charles was in Mark's office, and they were making arrangements to transfer Barbara to the hospital. Roger confirmed their exact arrival time. An ambulance would be waiting to take her on the short journey to the Al Husain hospital to meet Dr. Ahmed Ali. He suggested that Barbara be given a mild sedative, so the journey would be less stressful for her and the baby. Caroline went to the suite and gently administered the medication. Barbara made no fuss. She was so very tired, and within minutes her sleep became even deeper. Nothing would wake her for a while.

Charles told the others where he, Barbara, Mark, and Caroline were off to but shared nothing else with them. He'd decided that until he had definite answers to everything, he would say very little. Karmen and Josephine suspected things weren't good but knew there was nothing they could do, so they continued with their plans: a day off the yacht, lunch at the Royal Mirage Hotel, and an early evening visit to the souk. Brick was joining them. They had befriended Mohmand, a very handsome young Jordanian purser who spoke fluent Arabic, and he, on the captain's say-so, was to be their guide for the day.

James and Richard were delighted to be alone for a few hours and willingly passed over the credit cards.

"Are you sure you don't want to join us, darling?" Josephine asked, genuinely wanting James to come, but when he said he had calls to make and Brick shouted out to her, "Come on, sweetie, we're going! We'll have so much fun without them, and think of all the lovely things we can buy," she kissed James and ran after Karmen and Brick, rather excited to just be with her two friends.

Captain Roger and his team were on full alert for anything or anyone who seemed suspicious as well as to track the boat that still remained three nautical miles away. Without any guests on board, the entire crew set about their daily rituals, all hoping the boss and his wife would return from the hospital with good news. Everyone was excited at the thought of a child joining the yacht, especially the young female crew members who longed to get a share of babysitting duties. They knew Barbara was having a tough time, but they assumed she'd be fine, especially now that she was near a proper hospital.

Dr. Ali walked into his room, where Charles, Mark, and Caroline sat patiently waiting.

"Ahmed, so nice to see you again." Mark approached his friend, and the two men hugged. "Please let me introduce you. This is Charles, Barbara's husband, and this is Caroline, a registered midwife and fully trained nurse, who is working directly with the patient."

"Nice to meet you both. It's a shame the circumstances couldn't have been better. I have all the results here, ready to discuss with you. Barbara's resting and comfortable. Please take a seat. Perhaps you'd care for some coffee before we go through this information?"

Dr. Ali called his secretary and ordered coffee and sandwiches; he assumed everyone was probably starving. It had been several hours since their arrival, and no one had eaten a thing. "Now let me see."

Charles sat rigidly as Dr. Ali gathered all his paperwork and put it in order.

"Let me start from the beginning. I'm afraid to say it's not good news." He stared directly at Charles as he spoke. "Along with the pretty conclusive evidence that your son is suffering from albinism—I believe Mark has explained this to you?"

Charles nodded, fearing what was coming next.

"We have also identified a heart murmur. While we were monitoring his heart, we observed on a number of occasions that his heart stopped beating for a few seconds. With further tests we were able to confirm your child has a small hole in his heart. This can be rectified, but he will need immediate surgery once he's been delivered."

Tears began to well in Charles's eyes. Hearing someone refer to his unborn child as "he" made it all seem so real.

Dr. Ali continued, still looking directly at Charles.

"We have also been able to confirm, as Mark suspected, that your son's head is disproportionate to his body. This is caused by excessive fluid in and around the brain. It occurs mostly due to the overproduction of the cerebral spinal fluid that either doesn't absorb properly or builds up due to a blockage that stops it from flowing away. The term for this condition is hydrocephalus. Until your son is born, we can't determine to what extent his brain has been affected, but there is little doubt in my mind there will be some degree of damage. The swelling is too large for it not to have affected his brain.

"I'm sorry to give you this news, Charles. My advice? Take Barbara back to the yacht and keep her calm and rested. Speak to her when the time is right, so she's aware of the situation; trust me, she needs to have all the facts. Mark and Caroline can look after her, now that we know what's wrong. When she reaches thirty-seven and a half weeks, which is ten days from now, I want to bring her in, do a C-section, and then immediately operate on the baby's heart. After that, our specialist neurology team can determine to what extent his brain has been affected, and we can move on from there. Do you have any questions?"

"Will my son lead some form of a normal life? Please, Doctor, give me your honest opinion." Charles sounded desperate.

"Charles, I can't answer that question. I wish I could. At this stage I'm worried about the birth and the heart operation. We need to take things one step at a time."

Charles sat in silence. Fuck it, he thought to himself. Life should be good. Now that I have money and all it brings, I should be able to enjoy everything. My poor wife, my poor unborn child, they're being punished—punished for my sins. My past is coming back to haunt me. I'm cursed. He put his head in his hands and sobbed.

Dr. Ali motioned to Mark and Caroline, and the three of them quietly left Charles to digest all he had been told.

"Poor, poor Barbara and Charles," Caroline whispered when they were alone. "Mark, we need to get her back to the yacht, settle her into her own bed. I'm going to spoil her, look after her for the next ten days. I hope you can help Charles get his head right so he can break the news to her gently. They're going to need all our support to get through this, and I'll certainly have my work cut out once the baby arrives."

Mark gave her a warm smile; she was such an incredible woman—so kind and caring, he thought.

"I'm going to talk to Charles; you go and see Barbara. Say nothing. I'll come and find you shortly, and we'll get back to the yacht before it gets dark."

When Mark returned to Dr. Ali's room, Charles had pulled himself together slightly. The two men talked for a while, going over the facts. Charles understood he needed to be strong for Barbara. Mark had made that perfectly clear to him, and Charles knew what he needed to do to help his wife cope with what lay ahead.

"I won't say anything to her, Mark, not tonight. I promise, though, I'll talk to her within the next couple of days."

"Good man. In my experience, people always cope better when they have all the facts at hand, even if breaking the news is probably the hardest thing we have to do."

The two men walked together, Mark with his arm around Charles's shoulder. They were silent.

Back on board the *Golden Eagle*, Caroline was settling Barbara. She'd had a good meal and was lying comfortably in bed, watching a movie.

"Caroline, when will we have the results from all the testing they did earlier?"

"Within the next couple of days. Until then, you rest; we need to have you strong. As you know, in ten days, Dr. Ali wants you in. He's decided that rather than wait any longer, the baby will be delivered by C-section. At thirty-seven and a half weeks, there are no worries about the baby being brought into this world too early. Of course, if it happens before then, we're all ready. But if I were you, I'd take it easy and hope nothing happens within the next ten days. A caesarean section is a lot less traumatic for both mother and baby, and once baby is with us, you can rest. You'll need a couple of weeks to fully recover. I'll take care of the little one."

"Bless you. What would I do without you, Caroline?"

"Don't be daft; that's what I'm here for. Now rest. I'm going to have my supper. I'll be back in an hour to check on you. If you need me, just call my pager. All your vitals are fine, so I'm happy."

With that, Caroline left the suite. She hated the fact Barbara was unaware of her son's condition. Hopefully, Charles would tell her everything in the morning. With a bit of luck, the heart operation would be straightforward. After all, in the majority of cases she knew of, the results of the surgery were good. As far as the hydrocephalus was concerned, the damage to his brain might be minimal, and with help and therapy, the baby could live a near-normal life. She prayed everything would be positive, although deep down, she realised there were so many problems affecting this poor little boy. He certainly had a battle on his hands, and her heart broke for Barbara.

Charles had decided to break the news to his friends. After all, they had been through good times and shit times together, he figured. Now, as he and Barbara were facing the hardest thing in their lives, he wanted his friends to know exactly what was going on. After discussing things with Mark, he agreed they would tell everyone this evening at dinner, and then in the morning at breakfast, both he and Mark would very gently tell Barbara what the diagnosis was.

Karmen, Josephine, Richard, James, and Brick sat silently as Charles spoke calmly to them. They knew things had certainly not been right throughout Barbara's pregnancy, but hearing Charles list the problems his son was facing was too much to bear. Mark gave medical explanations when necessary. Tears welled in everyone's eyes. Josephine's and Karmen's hearts were breaking for their friends, and Brick began to sob.

"You know what?" Charles poured himself a large brandy, raising his voice slightly. "I feel like my past has come back to haunt me. I've been a real shit for many years, and now it's payback time. I'm being punished for all the wrong I've done, and my poor Barbara and my unborn son are being punished too. It's not fucking right." With that, he finished his drink in one gulp and began to cry.

"Charles, man, don't beat yourself up." Brick's voice was shaky. "You've been an absolute gentleman, at least to your friends."

Charles managed a little smile; Brick sure knew how to lighten a situation.

"What a fucking journey. This was supposed to be fun and exciting, and look, I'm being cursed for all my wrongdoings. Maybe you guys should continue, go ahead, and I'll stay behind with Barbara and wait until the baby's born. And then, depending, we can catch you up later."

"That's out of the question, Charles. We started this journey together; we'll continue the same way, united. Don't you all agree?" Richard looked toward the others.

There was no doubt in anyone's mind.

"You're the best friends a man could have. I'm so, so terribly sorry things are not working out like I planned."

"Listen, Charles, stop it!" Karmen took everyone by surprise. "Right now, we need to be strong for Barbara. Maybe things will be better than you expect. We need some positive thinking."

"She's right," added Josephine. "Come here, Charles."

With that everyone came together and hugged.

"Here's to positive thinking!" said Charles, feeling a surge of strength. "Let's open a bottle or two of the finest champagne the Kasparovsky brothers left in the wine cellar. We'll toast to life, and together we'll overcome whatever is thrown at us."

The next morning, Charles woke at 6:00 a.m. The sun was streaming into the suite. He'd gotten his thoughts together the previous evening with the help of his friends. He felt much more positive and relaxed. They would cope.

Barbara was sleeping peacefully. As he watched her breathe, he realised how much he loved her. Slowly, she stirred, as if she knew he was looking down at her. She opened one eye. "Why are you up so early?"

"I couldn't sleep."

"Oh." And with that, her eyes closed again. "Charles," she continued without opening them, "I have a strange feeling in my tummy, and the baby hasn't moved in ages."

"Darling, try and rest. It's too early to wake; get another couple of hours of sleep. I'm going for a swim, and then we'll have breakfast, and we can talk about how you're feeling and everything else. OK?"

"OK."

With that, Charles quietly left the bedroom and got changed to take his early-morning swim. He knew breakfast was going to be the hardest time of his entire life. He needed to be strong. For the first time in ages, his mind wandered back to when he was Antonio Cadiz, the man who could take on the world.

He quietly crept out of the suite, making sure nothing was going to disturb Barbara.

# Chapter Thirty-Four

There was no pain. She felt sick, violently sick. Her body was heavy, lifeless. She was sweating, and she felt as if she just wanted to curl up and die. Everything seemed outside her control. Without realising how, she took herself to the enormous bathroom. Sitting on the toilet, her bowels emptied. There was no substance to it. Water escaped from her back passage, gushing. Sweat was dripping from every pore in her body. Her hair and nightwear were drenched. She took deep breaths, not knowing why; it seemed like someone else had taken control of her, trying to keep a sense of normality, of life, within her.

She felt the vomit rise from deep down in her stomach. She retched and threw up all over the floor. She couldn't stop herself. For what seemed like an eternity, she expelled every ounce of liquid that made up her being. She had no pain that she remembered, just an overwhelming sense of weakness. Once the violent emptying had finished, she was aware that she needed to clean herself desperately, but there was no energy left inside her. She lay on the bathroom floor, her breathing laboured.

When Charles returned, he took one look at his wife and knew it was bad, very bad.

Barbara opened her eyes; she had an oxygen mask on. Tubes were connected to her body, making it hard for her to move. "Where am I?"

"You're in the Al Husain hospital."

"The baby! Where's my baby?"

"Please lie still, Barbara. You need to remain calm."

With that, more medication was added to the tube that went directly into Barbara's main artery. Within seconds, her eyes fluttered, and she was out for the count...

Back on board, the captain and his navigation officer were keeping a close watch on the small boat that was circling some five miles outside the port. With their sophisticated telescopic system, it was possible to see the same five men who'd previously been on their tail. They weren't getting any nearer but were constantly hovering, keeping the *Golden Eagle* in their sights.

Knowing Charles was at the hospital with a lot on his mind and not knowing when he might return, Roger decided to call Richard and James to the bridge so he could make them aware of the potential problems coming their way. After a long chat, they decided that being in port was probably safest. Less chance of being attacked or hijacked. When Charles returned, they could decide their next move.

"After all," Richard said to James as they walked back to meet Brick for lunch, "the likelihood of this being trouble from the past, now that Charles and Barbara have nothing to link them to their old selves, is pretty slim. Perhaps we're dealing with a few petty chancers. See an expensive yacht and hope there are some rich pickings to be had."

"Yeah, you're probably right, Richard. Any news from Charles as to how Barbara's getting on?"

"Not a word. I thought Mark might have called if there were serious problems or Charles if the baby had come, but I guess they're all too busy. Let's just keep vigilant here, and I'm sure we'll hear soon enough."

Back in the hospital, Charles paced. The waiting was killing him. Suddenly, the door opened, and Mark stood with Dr. Ali by his side. Their faces were solemn.

"How's Barbara?"

"Charles, Barbara should be fine. She's been through a lot and needs to rest."

"Thank God!" Charles buckled with relief as he found the sofa and let out a whimper. He slowly looked up, eyes pleading. "And my son?"

"Charles, I'm sorry to tell you, my dear friend, your son was stillborn."

"There was nothing we could do, Mr. Garcia, nothing at all," added Dr. Ali quietly. His head lowered. "He had so many complications, and he couldn't fight any longer."

Charles began to sob. "He was to be my son and heir. Oh, my poor child."

"Charles, listen to me." Mark came and sat by his friend. He motioned to Dr. Ali, who took the opportunity to leave the room quietly. "Your son would never have lived a normal life. Charles, look at me. He had too many problems. He would have been severely brain damaged, and he would have been a real burden to both you and Barbara. He would have entered this world fighting a losing battle. It was God's will to take him. You wouldn't have wanted to watch him suffer for his entire life, would you?"

"Does Barbara know? Will she come through this tragedy, or will there be long-term complications?"

"It's early, but she's a tough lady, and with rest I see no reason why she won't be back to her old self very soon. She's lost a lot of blood. If it wasn't for Dr. Ali, I'm not sure she would be with us, but he was incredible. Remember, even the healthiest of pregnancies needs recovery time after a C-section, so be patient, my friend. This was far from an easy pregnancy or delivery. Barbara needs your strength, not your pity. She's aware that her son was stillborn, but she's sedated at the moment and is drifting in and out. We feel she's better off like this for a couple of days, so her body can begin to heal."

"Can I see her?"

"Give her a couple of hours, Charles. Go, have a nap yourself. Perhaps get a bite. You've got a long road ahead, and trust me, Barbara needs you. She's lost the baby who was growing inside her for nine months, and although he was your son too, your pain is not comparable to hers. There are so many more things she'll have to face. She'll need medication to stop her breasts from becoming engorged as her milk starts to flow. This is a painful daily reminder and takes a while to stop. Remember, she knows and you know your child has gone, but Barbara's body has no idea. It will act as if she's given birth, and it'll be a roller coaster of emotions for her. She has no control over any of it. She'll need every ounce of your support and love. Now go, rest, and be there, strong and every bit the man she'll need you to be."

Two hours later, Charles sat by Barbara's bedside. She looked so beautiful lying asleep with the hospital sheets and blankets cocooning her. The machinery checking her vital statistics let out a quiet rhythmic sound that gave a feeling of safety, and Charles closed his eyes. He smiled softly and hoped Barbara would wake and agree on their son's name.

Earlier, Mark had encouraged Charles to say good-bye to his son, and Charles trusted his friend to know what was best. But nothing readied him for the pain he felt when he saw how disfigured and strange the baby looked. His head was twice the size of his body. His skin was white as porcelain, almost translucent. Everything about him looked terribly wrong, and as Charles slowly walked away, tears falling from his eyes, he knew Mark had been right. What had happened was for the best. His son was in the care of a far more capable father now, he thought. One who would keep him safe. Nothing would be a problem; his son would be with all the other angels of the world, past and present. His tears subsided. Charles's heart felt free.

"Hello, darling."

Charles woke and looked down at Barbara.

"I'm so sorry," said Barbara.

"About what?"

"Losing our baby." Tears slowly trickled down Barbara's cheeks.

Charles gently wiped them away, bent toward her, and kissed her softly. "Darling, the most important thing to me is that you're going to be well."

"I do love you Charles; you know that, don't you?"

Before he had a chance to answer, she drifted off to sleep, with still more tears following the tracks of the previous ones. Charles gently wiped them away and closed his eyes once again.

After about fifteen minutes, Barbara began to stir. She smiled up at Charles, pleased to see him still there.

"In answer to your question," began Charles, "yes, I know you love me, and, my beautiful wife, I love you more than you'll ever know. Darling, I've been thinking. I would like to give our son a name. Something that will never allow us to forget him. What do you think?"

"Oh, Charles, I'd love that…I saw him, you know? He was…very peaceful. I knew he was…asleep. Dr. Ali explained all the problems he faced, and I know he is better off where he is now. What name were you thinking of?"

"Gabriel."

"Like the Angel Gabriel? That's nice. Yes, I like that. My little angel. My little boy, Gabriel. I like that name very, very much."

With that Barbara drifted off again, and this time, Charles wiped away his own tears.

# Chapter Thirty-Five

Within ten days Barbara was improving and ready to return to the yacht. She and Charles had had a small burial service for Gabriel the week before. The only person besides themselves present was the hospital chaplain, a kind, gentle man who made the service truly special.

As they said their good-byes to all the staff who had looked after them so well, Charles held Barbara's hand tightly. "Are you ready to go home?"

"Yes, Charles, I am. You know, darling, we must look to the future. I thought I was going to die ten days ago, and here I am with the man I love, friends waiting for me on the yacht, and a whole world to see. We've been given a second chance. Our son is at peace, and we must look forward."

Charles stared deeply into his wife's eyes and smiled. What an amazing woman, he thought. "I love you, darling; now let's get out of here."

As they walked through the enormous revolving doors of the hospital, he teasingly pinched her bottom, which he had to admit was already getting back to its sexy self. Barbara yelped and turning to him, gave him a gentle slap on his arm, all the while smiling and giggling. Charles winked at her lovingly.

Karmen and Josephine were overjoyed to have Barbara back and had to admit she was looking wonderful. After a short moment of condolence talk, Barbara let her two friends know, in no uncertain terms, that the past was the past, and she only wanted to look ahead. She wanted to have a wonderful journey and share all the excitement and fun she intended to have with her friends. "Now, let's go choose what we're wearing tonight for supper. I feel like getting really dressed up."

That evening, while they were having dinner, Charles announced they would be sailing later that night, making their way through the Gulf of Oman, heading for Muscat. The journey of approximately 376 nautical miles would take them a day and a half. Once there, they'd stay until they decided to leave, and then they'd make their way out to the Arabian Sea and head to a very small island called Socotra, in Yemen. It would take about three and a half days to reach the island's Hajhir Mountains, and there they could relax and decide on their next destination.

It all sounded extremely exotic and spontaneous. Everyone felt young at heart, anticipating what lay ahead.

"So friends, as you can see, Barbara is well and looking beautiful, as are all the ladies. And Brick, I have to say, what an incredible shirt. I love the colours. Now, our journey begins in earnest. So let's make a toast—to all our futures."

"To all our futures," came the reply.

The next day, Charles was first to wake. He stepped outside onto the veranda and breathed in the fresh morning sea air. He was amazed by how calm and peaceful the ocean was. The yacht silently cut through the deep-blue water. Flying fish leaped in and out of the sea as if they were playing chase with the boat. It was magical. As he stared out, he suddenly felt Barbara creep up behind him.

"Morning, my darling. Isn't this beautiful?" she purred.

"You startled me. How are you feeling, sweetheart?"

"So much better. My scars are healing, and my tummy's almost back to normal. My waistline is returning, and Caroline is really happy with me, so I'm feeling wonderful. Maybe in a week or so, we can get our love life back to normal. What do you think, Charles?"

"That thought has crossed my mind on a number of occasions. You just let me know when you feel ready, and I'll willingly assist."

Just at that moment, the phone in the suite rang.

"Who can that be so early in the morning?" asked Charles.

"Well, if you answer it, you'll know." Sometimes she could be so curt, he thought. Barbara walked into the bathroom, blew him a kiss, and began running herself a bath.

Minutes later, Charles came in. Barbara was soaking in masses of bubbles. She looked so content. He told her he was off to see the captain and would meet her on the sundeck in about an hour. As he bent down to kiss her, he couldn't resist putting a handful of bubbles on the tip of her nose. "See you later, my love."

"Bye, darling. I may go and get breakfast with Josephine and Karmen, if they're around, so I'll find you on the top deck afterward."

"Morning, Roger. What's the problem?"

"Look over here Charles. Our radar screen shows we're still being followed by our friends. We changed course through the night, backtracking on ourselves just to be sure, but there's no doubt about it. These guys are on our tail. Also, we observed what we believe to be a drone hovering above us for more than an hour at around two o'clock this morning. If our suspicions are right, it could indicate that the ship is being spied on and photographed. This could potentially be a very dangerous situation for our yacht, her passengers, and the crew. Do you have any idea why this could be happening or who these people could be?"

Charles looked incredibly agitated and stressed. His mind reeled. "Roger, come to my private office in an hour. We need to have a talk. I've got a feeling this could become extremely serious. I'm going to ask Richard, James, and Brick to join us. We need to find out who the fuck these guys are and soon. They're not tailing us for fun. We need to be one step ahead in case they're planning an attack."

"Right you are, Charles. I'll finish charting our route and join you in an hour."

With that, Charles left the bridge, praying that his worst fears were not being realised. Christ, he thought. Just as things appear to be getting back on track, I have to deal with another major fucking crisis.

An hour later, the five men sat around the lounge area of Charles's private office. Coffee and sandwiches were laid out. Charles started by telling everyone how well Barbara was doing. "Losing the baby's taken a lot out of us, but we're strong, and life goes on. Barbara's started to boss me around and dominate me again, so things are almost back to normal."

They all laughed.

"That's women for you," chuckled Brick quietly.

"And you're such a bloody expert," Richard replied.

"Moving on, gentlemen, please." Charles regained everyone's attention. He told them about the potential problems they faced after the navigation-tracking system picked up their pursuers. He filled them in on the drone and what that implied, and then he turned directly to Roger.

"Roger, I haven't been completely honest with you. I'm not whiter than white. In my past life, I had trouble with the Brazilian Mafia and the Brazilian government over drug deals. I believe there were a number of government officials who were corrupted by the Mafia, and they built up a vendetta against me. The Mafia wanted control; they wanted me out of the picture so they could run all operations themselves. Then rumours began to spread, wrongly, that I imported inferior-quality drugs and sold at the highest prices. I may have done some bad things in my time, but I only sold the finest to those who would otherwise buy crap elsewhere.

"Anyway, as the stories spread, the Brazilian government tried to freeze my worldwide assets. I got wind of what was going on through a contact, and in a nutshell, I withdrew all my funds. I was then introduced to a consortium of diamond dealers. Over a period of time, I bought some of the finest diamonds the world had to offer. They were smuggled out of South Africa, and both the Mafia and the government of Brazil were after me.

"As you know, I underwent extensive plastic surgery and my whole identity was erased. I guess you could say I became a fugitive on the run. It now seems that maybe I wasn't home and dry like I thought I was. Roger, if you think it's too risky, you can resign. It would leave us in the shit, but you have the right to walk away now. If you choose to stay, you'll be rewarded generously."

"Charles, I love this yacht, and I love working with you. I must tell you, I haven't been completely honest either. I did my research on Antonio Cadiz before I left the Kasparovsky brothers and before I agreed to join your team. I knew you were on the run from South America and that the Brazilian government had a warrant out for your arrest. After years of working with the Kasparovsky family, I figured you were a darn sight cleaner than ever they were, so please don't explain yourself anymore. Count me in, and we'll sail out of this mess together."

"Roger, you have no idea how relieved I am that you'll remain in charge of this vessel. I owe you so much. As the others can attest to, I'm a man of my word, and I will look after you."

Everyone in the room acknowledged Charles's comments.

"Together," Charles continued, "we can overcome whatever lies ahead. We make a good team. Each and every person in this room has something valuable to bring to the table, and I have no doubt that jointly we'll achieve all our dreams. But for now, let's move on to more important issues. What action should we take? Should we just ignore the situation and wait for our friends to make the first move? I believe James has some ideas, so let's have a rest, and we'll continue shortly."

The five men stood, shook hands, and stretched. They knew there was a unity among them, and as they broke for coffee and a bite to eat, they felt sure they'd eventually make the right decisions. It was going to be a long afternoon.

# Chapter Thirty-Six

James spent a while outlining his thoughts on the best way to handle things. Everyone had a suggestion to add, and often the conversation became heated. After what seemed an age, they finally finished. They agreed they would continue making their way to Muscat, enjoy the journey, and beef up security to keep watch twenty-four seven on the boat that was tracking them. Charles would pay the staff overtime at a rate that would ensure total dedication, making sure there were never fewer than four guards on watch.

Brick had suggested making contact with Dominic back in Botswana to see if he would be able to provide them with firearms, in case things got nasty. "He owes me a favour, boss, so I'm sure he'll come through with the goods. We just need to be careful with how and when he can get them delivered."

Charles was impressed, and Brick left to put the call in to Dominic. He loved feeling important, and he especially loved pleasing his boss.

Before they returned to their cabins, Charles told everyone that what they had discussed had to remain among the five of them. "The women must not know about any of this. We don't need them to start panicking. Roger, you keep a close eye on the situation, and let us know if there are any changes."

"OK, will do. For your information, Charles, we're on course to dock in Muscat at around eight thirty a.m. I absolutely feel that while we're in port, we'll be safe. So let's really try and enjoy our time. See you all later at dinner."

The evening was perfect: a light breeze, the calmest of seas, and a thousand stars penetrating deep into the endless void of blackness.

"Just look at that." Karmen gazed toward the sky. "I've never seen so many stars. It's magical. Kind of makes you feel so small and insignificant, don't you think?"

The whole group spent a while in silence, just watching, all feeling a spirituality that the moment had brought.

Suddenly, Brick sauntered in. He seemed pleased with himself, and an air of importance oozed from his every pore. "What's all the silence about, guys? It's like a funeral. Someone died?"

"Shut up, you big drama queen. We're actually admiring the beauty of the universe. Not that you'd know much about that. Too shallow and interested in chucking a whole bottle of Tom Ford over yourself."

"Oooh, Richard, takes one to know one, darling. Got out of bed on the wrong side, did we?"

"Stop being so pedantic. You know what—?"

"Richard!" Karmen interrupted. "Why do you always have to ruin things? Honestly, grow up!"

"I don't believe this. Now it's my fault. Nothing to do with him." Richard threw Brick daggers, and Brick, in his campest way, smiled and turned to Karmen, saying under his breath, "Sweetie, I don't know how you put up with him."

"Come on, guys, stop bitching. Dinner's almost ready. Let's enjoy this wonderful evening. Brick, shake hands with Richard."

"I will, Barbara, but only if he goes first."

Karmen kicked Richard under the table.

"Oh, for God's sake. All right, Brick, my hand's extended first. Happy?"

With that, Brick stood and walked toward Richard, wiggling his bum, lips pursed. He took Richard's hand and then leaned in for the two-cheek kiss.

"Oh, bloody hell, Brick, you always have to take it to that extra level!"

"Love you too, Richard."

Everyone giggled, finding the dynamics between the two men hilarious. It was almost as if they had their own little sideshow going on.

The meal was, as usual, spectacular. Conversation flowed easily among them, and it was well past midnight when they decided to call it a night.

"After all, we're arriving in the exotic capital of Oman tomorrow, so we need our beauty sleep. I'm so excited!" said Josephine, who was first to stand and leave the table. The others followed soon after.

As they filtered out into the corridor, Brick grabbed Charles by the arm, whispering, "Boss, I've got some news regarding my conversation with Dom. Can we talk privately?"

"Do you have any idea what time it is? Can't this wait till the morning? Have you had too much to drink or taken something stronger?"

"Boss, this is going to make the hairs on your hands stand up. We need to be somewhere secure, somewhere that no one else can hear. This is for your ears and your ears only."

"I hope you're not wasting my time. Meet me in, say, ten minutes in my office? I'll let Barbara know I'll be busy for a while."

Brick pranced off. He loved being the bearer of important news, and even though he knew his boss wasn't going to like some of what had to be said, the mere fact that it was coming from him made him feel special and needed.

As Charles walked in, Brick was pacing around the room, his energy palpable.

"OK, Brick, let's have it."

"Well, I've spoken to Dom; he can supply us with an array of weapons. He needs fifty thousand dollars up front, to be transferred into his account tomorrow. He told me you have those details."

Charles nodded.

"He's going to provide us with a supply of pepper spray, stun and machine guns, coshes, and a couple of Uzi automatics."

"Well, that's a result, Brick, but did you need to keep me up to tell me this? You seem to be handling everything so well. Surely, this could have waited till morning."

Brick continued to pace.

"For fuck's sake, can you stop walking around like a headless chicken? You're making me dizzy, and I'm bloody tired."

"Sorry, boss. I'll sit down, but I'm afraid what I'm going to tell you isn't good. In fact, it's very bad."

Brick began to relay the conversation he'd had with Dominic, leaving nothing out. Charles sat silently, slowly digesting all he was being told. It did make for very, very bad and worrying news.

By the time Brick had finished, Charles's head was reeling.

"I'll arrange a meeting first thing at seven a.m., and we'll fill Richard, James, and Roger in with all that's happened. Thanks for your professionalism, Brick. We need to get some shut-eye; we've only got five hours, so see you back here then. Make contact with the others as soon as you wake up. They need to be aware of what's going on before we arrive in Muscat. Good night, Brick."

Charles got into bed, his mind in a spin. Barbara was breathing peacefully. He cursed Brick for not having waited until the morning to tell him what Dominic had said, but he knew in his heart that he'd have to face the situation head on, whenever he'd found out. So one night's interrupted sleep wasn't going to make much difference now.

Brick was wired. Having broken such important news to the boss made him feel powerful and important. He knew Charles, armed with knowledge, would be able to deal with the situation. After all, his boss had single-handedly killed more men than most had had hot dinners. He had broken the toughest street gangs in the roughest parts of Rio and survived it all. This would be sorted, and it would all be OK because he had informed his boss. He had arranged for the weapons to be delivered, and Charles would forever be grateful. He felt good.

There was, perhaps, one other thing that was making him feel extra good, one thing that he hadn't shared with Charles. After all, this was private, nothing to do with business—well, not that kind of business anyway. Dom had given him a number, the number of a gay Arab friend. A really handsome young man looking for fun and maybe even a relationship. The thought of this waiting in Muscat made Brick feel really, really good.

At 5.30 a.m. Charles was running on the treadmill, his thoughts becoming clearer. It was amazing how he found exercise and solitude the perfect recipe for working out difficult situations. He had numerous conversations with himself at these times and normally came up with the right solutions.

He began sweating profusely as he ramped up the speed, and by the time he showered, he felt ready to meet with his friends. Barbara was still snoring; he wondered how she managed to sleep so well. He concluded she must have a very clear mind.

At 7:00 a.m. on the dot, all five men had assembled in Charles's office. Charles gave Brick the opportunity to relay the information, but Brick chose to let Charles do the speaking. He was, after all, a far better orator, and Brick did waffle at times.

There was absolute silence as Charles told everyone about the weapons that were being delivered within the next few hours. He told them that $50,000 had been transferred to Dominic and that Brick would be informed how and when the arms would get onto the yacht as soon as they were docked in Muscat.

All eyes turned to Brick, who smiled proudly. He loved seeing their surprise and disbelief that he, the drama queen, had been so actively busy working with the boss, unbeknown to them. Then Charles cleared his throat, in a way that made everyone stop focusing on Brick.

He began.

"It has come to light that both the Brazilian government and the Brazilian Mafia—I assume there's little distinction between the two—have information that Barbara and I underwent surgery to change our identities. They're aware that we're alive and kicking, and I believe they've got people out looking for us. Probably amateurs, looking to earn a buck or two. There's a bounty on my head, but that's payable only when I'm dead. So until they can determine where I am, they'll use second-rate guys to try and track us. It's therefore become clear to me that this small boat on our tail is more than likely manned by greedy lowlifes with little expertise among the lot of them. We'll shortly have a stash of weapons to deal with them, should they make a move. In the meantime, I suggest we carry on as usual, making no mention of any of this to the women.

"A drone has been sighted and captured. I've looked closely at the CCTV footage and forwarded the images to a friend of mine who works in the espionage department of the Israeli government, and it is, as I suspected, a cheap version of the real deal. The sort of thing people have at weddings. So once again, I'm not overly worried. But there is one thing that's been playing on my mind. How did the Brazilians find out about my identity change? I suspect we may have an informer on board. So I want Brick to do some sniffing around."

"We'll help too," added James.

Brick shot James a look that could have killed; he wanted to continue handling the project for his boss by himself. Charles took little notice.

"Great, the more ears and eyes the better. I believe while we're in Muscat, we'll be safe. The worry is when we're in no-man's-land, on the open waters. But by the time we leave, we'll have plenty of weapons to protect ourselves with. Let's keep our itinerary to just the five of us. Nobody knows our plans outside this room, so if anything leaks, it must be one of us."

Suddenly, the room became deathly quiet. Everyone looked at each other, fear radiating in all four sets of eyes. Charles scrutinised them all in turn, using his observation skills and previous training to the fullest, trying to see if anyone showed any signs of guilt.

"Guys, I'm not saying one of you here is a traitor, not at all, but be aware. Until we've found the culprit or culprits, trust no one. Our lives depend on finding the spy in our midst. The Brazilians are looking for me. They know a lot but not everything, so the quicker we kill off the scumbag who's passing info, the better. This fugitive on the run intends to be around for a long time yet, so go enjoy your day. We'll be reaching Muscat within the next half hour or so."

Silently, the men left the office. All had a hell of a lot on their minds.

Charles returned to his suite. Barbara was showering. He walked onto his enormous terrace. In the distance he saw land with an array of exotic-looking buildings sprawling before him. Muscat, the capital of Oman, a place he'd longed to visit but had never managed to, not yet. Now he was very nearly there. His imagination conjured up vivid stories that could only have come from the mystical nations of Arabia.

As his mind was being transported back to bygone eras full of mystery and intrigue, he suddenly saw movement coming from the sea. He snapped out of his daydream and focused his eyes. There by the side of the yacht was a pod of dolphins leaping high into the sky. There had to be at least twenty of them, all different sizes, each trying to outdo the other, showing off their acrobatic talents. The sea was the richest blue he'd ever seen. Charles took an intake of air and suddenly became incredibly emotional. What a lucky man he was to be privileged to see such beautiful things in an otherwise cruel, sad world. He went to get Barbara, hoping the dolphins would escort them to their next destination.

As they stood in each other's arms, the dolphins jumped and danced for them, chattering loudly. Muscat drew closer and closer. The hypnotic sound of morning prayers wafted across the calm seas. Barbara squeezed herself tightly into her husband. Charles stroked her hair and prayed everything would turn out all right. Something told him it would, and he smiled as his yacht silently headed toward the bustling, beautiful port that lay ahead.

# Chapter Thirty-Seven

"Good morning, ladies and gentlemen." Roger's voice rang out over the Tannoy System. "Your captain here. As you may have noticed, we have arrived at the port of Muscat. It's a glorious day outside; temperatures are due to reach forty-two degrees, so make sure you use your sunscreen.

"Before we can disembark, we have to go through a few formalities with the Omani authorities, so please be patient. As soon as our paperwork has been cleared by customs, you'll be free to leave the ship. Have a wonderful day."

As the yacht slowly pulled into the busy harbour, a customs tender ran alongside, directing the captain into the appropriate mooring space. It was a magnificent sight to behold as Roger manoeuvred the yacht into a space that appeared to be far too small for such a large boat. But soon enough, they were neatly positioned between two other luxurious yachts of similar size.

Three customs officers dressed smartly in pure white uniforms and sporting lots of impressive gold regalia came up the gangplank to clear the yacht for customs purposes. Brick caught sight of them, and as he approached, one of the men spoke, obviously assuming he was on his way to disembark.

"Can you remain here, sir, until we have checked that all the paperwork is in order?" He spoke very quietly but with absolute authority.

Under his breath Brick replied, "I'd like you to check me out, big boy."

Luckily his comments were unheard, and the officers began looking though the piles of paper that the captain had ready for them. After a short while, they turned to Roger and asked if there was anything on board that should be declared, such as weapons, drugs, livestock, et cetera. Once they received a negative answer, they stamped the papers and duly left the ship, wishing everyone on board a pleasant stay in Muscat.

Brick headed to his suite. His step was light, and he was whistling happily to himself as he imagined what might lie ahead. He couldn't wait to meet up with the handsome young blind date that Dom had arranged for him. As long as the photograph didn't lie, he was going to be in the company of one gorgeous hottie. Brick had decided on his outfit the night before, so all he needed to do now was shower, moisturise, jump into a cab, and head to Old Town Muscat to meet his date in Bar Jazeer, a notorious undercover gay hangout.

Roger had finished briefing his security team. They agreed that every delivery had to be checked by hand while they were in port, just to make sure there were no sudden surprises from the men who were still watching and waiting out at sea. Any delivery persons were to be thoroughly searched before they were allowed to board. "Better safe than sorry. Now, all of you get to your stations; contact me here if there's anything suspicious to report."

"Aye-aye, Captain." The security team spoke in unison as they left the bridge.

"Charles, let me put some factor fifty on you, darling. It's going to be blistering hot out there, and I don't want you to burn. What's on our agenda today? I'd mentioned perhaps going and doing a spot of shopping with Karmen and Josephine last night, but you know what? I'd rather it be just the two of us. It's our first day somewhere other than Dubai, and that place doesn't hold the best of memories for us."

"Of course, my love, I couldn't agree with you more." Charles felt a pang of guilt. He hadn't even thought about how Barbara was feeling. God, he loved that woman. She was so special, he thought. "We can spend the day checking things out by ourselves, and then you can go off with the girls when you've gotten your bearings. After all, we're here for a few days, so there's no rush."

Barbara smiled at her husband. "What would I do without you? You're always so smart. I love you, darling."

Charles called James and Josephine's suite and told them not to wait. "You four go off and explore. We want to have a day alone. We'll see you tonight for dinner."

"Fed up with us already, Charles?" James chuckled, and it was quite clear that he wasn't the slightest bit bothered. "Sure, mate, see you tonight. I'll tell Richard and Karmen. Be careful out there in this heat."

As Barbara and Charles were walking through the main reception area to leave the yacht, Brick passed them, seemingly in a hurry.

"Looking smart. Where are you rushing off to?"

"Well, Charles, I want to make sure the captain's beefed up security before I leave, and then I'm meeting up with a gorgeous young man. A blind date that Dominic arranged for me. I can't wait."

"Well, have fun, and don't do anything I wouldn't do." Charles winked jokingly at Brick. He then put his arms around his wife and led her down the gangplank.

"Be safe, Brick. Don't get too carried away until you get to know this guy a bit better," she shouted as she followed her husband onto the dock.

"I'll be fine, darling. Stop mothering me. Have fun!" Brick waved them off. He had no time to waste. They were, after all, only in Muscat for a few days, so if this guy was as handsome as he appeared, safety measures were the last thing on his mind.

Charles was busy negotiating a ride from a local tour guide who spoke English well enough to be understood, while Barbara took in the hustle and bustle that surrounded her. It was hectic and hot, everyone looking to make a dollar or two, and she prayed Charles would hurry up. Other tour guides kept approaching her, flashing their ID cards under her nose to prove they were legal and gibbering away in broken English. The majority of them were wizened beyond their years—probably from the scorching sun—and she noticed that most of them had rotting teeth. She began to feel uncomfortable.

"Barbara, come meet Abdul. He's going to show us around."

"It's an honour to meet such a beautiful woman. Please let me walk you to my luxury air-conditioned people carrier. She is the pride and joy of our family. My brothers and uncles and cousins all make a living from this car, and it will be my pleasure to show you and your kind husband the best places that Muscat has to offer."

Once inside the vehicle, Barbara noticed it was immaculate and wonderfully cool, so she relaxed. Then Abdul spoke again, as fast as the last time. Barbara smiled at him but grimaced inwardly; this man was going to drive her bonkers with his incessant chatting. Why did Charles choose him, she wondered?

Abdul continued. "We are a humble, hardworking family. All our immediate relations earn their living from this car and four others. We have many, many women to feed. I'm about to have my seventh grandchild any day now. All granddaughters so far; hopefully, this time I will receive a grandson, inshallah. We need more boys to be born. Boys become men, and men can work and bring riches to the family. Now, where shall I take you?

"I think it should be the Sultan Qaboos Grand Palace, a magnificent palace. My mother, bless her soul, would go many times there and sit for hours, praying to be blessed with sons. I will show you the cloister area, so beautiful. Then we will go to the Mutrah Souk. You will find the finest silk carpets, all handmade. My brother will make deals for you beyond anything you have dreamed. He has the largest stall in the souk. From there we shall go to my favourite restaurant. I hope you will be happy to remove your shoes; it's custom there. The food is the best in the whole of Muscat, traditional and delicious. My uncle buys all the finest ingredients, direct from his brother's farm. You will love it. The meat is so fresh and served on steaming platters of hot fragrant rice. After you have eaten, the children of the family will dance for you. You will see three of my daughters and one of my wives. They all wear traditional clothing, and it is a sight to behold. Would this agenda be to your liking?"

Charles was getting agitated with Abdul too, so Barbara spoke on his behalf. "That would be absolutely great, Abdul. But can we listen to some music and quietly watch the sights as you drive us around? Thank you."

Charles smiled at Barbara; she always seemed to know the right thing to say and do. "Thank you," he mouthed to her. Their journey continued in silence.

As Brick began to descend the gangplank, Roger called to him. "There's a large container just arrived for you. Security checked it, and it's a collection of fine South African wines. The sender was a Dominic Uzabi. A friend of yours? Must have a few quid. The collection sounds superb." Roger winked.

"Great. I've been waiting for that to arrive; can you take me to it?"

"Sure can. It's down in the storage bay."

As Brick followed the captain to the storage area, his first thought was of the chaos that would have occurred if security had found the container's real contents. Then he worried about the professionalism of the security team for not having found the real contents. Then he thought how cool Dominic was for arranging things so well, even when he spent most of his life stoned out of his head.

And then, finally, his mind turned to Khalid, who would be waiting for him in less than an hour. He had to text him right away and explain why he had to cancel today's meeting—well, not truthfully why, just a few small untruths. Hopefully, they could meet up tomorrow. He had important things to do right now, and he had to put his boss and fellow passengers first.

The two men walked into the storage area, and Roger switched the overhead lighting on. "There you go, Brick. One massive container of wine. Your friend sure must like you. By the way, I managed to get security out of here as soon as they opened the container. They were happy to let me do the checking. After all, I am the captain."

"Yeah, I was wondering how come they hadn't checked things more thoroughly. But now I know. Shall we try and get to the real contents while everyone's off the yacht?"

Together, Roger and Brick removed six dozen bottles of wrapped wines—a mixture of cabernet sauvignon, merlot, pinot noir, chardonnay, and shiraz cabernet. The floor was covered with the bottles, and as they removed the last few, they could see wooden slats. Both men knew the weapons would be underneath. Brick pulled at them, and finally the merchandise below was visible. Four Uzi submachine guns, hand grenades, coshes, knives of varying sizes, handguns, rounds of ammunition, ropes, and a selection of plastic ties.

As Brick handled the ropes and ties, his mind wandered to Khalid. He imagined what he would like to do if he had these beauties with him when they got together. He became aroused and had to immediately snap his mind into a different place.

Roger had gone to fetch empty water-ski holdalls so they could store the weapons. He came back carrying ten.

"Shit, Brick, these are heavy. I didn't know how many we'd need. But my guess is at least six, and when they're full, they'll weigh a ton. We need to transfer them tonight when it's dark. I'll get security to watch elsewhere so we can complete the job. I reckon it'll take us a good couple of hours. Are you fit enough for the job?"

"Actually, I had a hot date this evening, but for you, Captain, anything. I've always liked a man in uniform. And, in answer to your question, you'll never see a fitter person than me."

"Great. So after everyone's finished supper and I've sorted the security team, we'll transfer these to a safe place. There's a lockable area in the hull of the ship, adjacent to the engine room. I'm the only one with a key. These weapons will be secure there."

The two men transferred the weapons into the ski holdalls, keeping machine guns with machine guns, knives with knives, until the job was completed. They ended up with a total of eight enormous bags.

"So, Brick, see you tonight after supper, and we'll get started on moving these."

"OK, Captain, see you tonight. By the way, I love your uniform. It's a real turn-on."

Roger chuckled to himself as Brick turned, wiggled his hips, and walked out of the storage area. Roger continued to tidy up the wines and make sure everything was in order before he turned out the lights and locked the door securely.

Charles and Barbara were the first to arrive back on board. They were totally exhausted, and as they climbed the gangplank onto the yacht, they panted, dripping with perspiration but full of themselves. The day had turned out to be a great success, and once Abdul had stopped talking, he'd proven that his knowledge and suggestions were second to none. He would definitely be their guide while they were in Muscat, and the others had to visit his uncle's fabulous restaurant, they agreed.

Karmen, Richard, Josephine, and James arrived an hour or so later, looking as shattered as Charles and Barbara had.

"Nothing a nice long bath won't sort out. Come on, Richard, let's get a move on. Dinner's in two hours," said Karmen.

"I don't know where she gets her energy and positivity from," Richard whispered to James proudly.

"Don't knock it, Richard. You could be married to a miserable can't-be-bothered type."

"Yeah, I know. See you at dinner, James."


Later that evening, as they were having their coffee, the conversation was rife with everyone's experiences of the day. It appeared they'd all fallen in love with heady Muscat and agreed they'd have to venture into town one evening and enjoy the night life. Just before they retired for the evening, Richard noticed that Brick was no longer at the table.

"Where's Brick gone? Heard he had a hot blind date earlier."

"Oh, yeah, he excused himself," replied James. "Said he had a bit of a pain in his back and needed to get to bed."

"Sure he did," said Richard sarcastically.

"Right! Time to go to bed Richard. I can't take you anywhere." Everyone laughed as Karmen led the way back to the cabins.

Meanwhile, Brick and Roger were moving the weapons, ski bag by ski bag. It was a long, laborious task. After two hours, the last bag was put safely away. The two men collapsed in a heap on the floor, exhausted and sweating.

"Well, Brick, that went well. No hiccups. We make a good team. Let's go get a Scotch and soda. I think we deserve it."

"I prefer bourbon and Coke with ice and lemon."

"You've got it, big guy. Let's go to the bar. I'm sure Seon's gone to bed by now, but we can help ourselves. We have no rush as there is nothing to get up for tomorrow."

"Speak for yourself, Captain. I'm hoping to go on a big date."

A friendship had been forged between the two men; each had a new respect for the other. They locked the door leading to the hull of the ship and walked away together, slowly, toward the bar.

# Chapter Thirty-Eight

The next morning, breakfast was served on the top deck. The views of Muscat were spectacular: modern mixed with old. The sun rose behind the city, casting an array of colours as different parts of buildings were lit by the sun's rays.

"Morning, guys. Bet you all slept well last night," said James who was in fine spirits. He'd had a wonderful sleep. Josephine and the girls had eaten breakfast earlier and were shopping; Abdul was taking care of them. "Top of the morning, Brick. What's wrong with you?" asked James.

"My back's killing me."

"That'll teach you to mess around with a young, cool dude," he joked.

"For your information, James, I never saw him. While you were all enjoying yourselves, I was working."

Charles entered the breakfast area just at the right moment. Brick was about to lose his cool. "You OK, Brick?"

"No, Charles, actually, my back's killing me."

"Why don't you go and see Caroline? She'll give you a good massage." Turning to the others, Charles continued, "Roger informed me this morning that while we were out and about yesterday, Dominic's consignment arrived. The container held a collection of fine South African wines, and hidden below was a large stash of modern weaponry and enough ammunition to not only defend ourselves from those little shits who have been tracking us but also to take on much bigger fish. He and Brick emptied the container and transferred everything, working well into the night. Now our arsenal is stored in a safe place adjacent to the engine room. So this, my friends, is the reason for Brick's aching back."

"Gosh, Brick, sorry for winding you up." James was genuinely upset.

"Yeah, man," added Richard. "We really appreciate what you've done. Sorry."

Both men went up to Brick and gave him a little hug.

"Don't you two try and get around me. The wine is mine. If you play your cards right, I might let you have a taste. I'm off for a massage," said Brick.

"I suggest we all meet tonight, once the women are sleeping and the majority of the staff have retired for the night. Roger will divert the attention of our security staff, and we can all have a turn at holding, using, and understanding the weapons we're in charge of. There's only one thing concerning me," said Charles.

James and Richard looked at Charles and waited for him to continue.

"Roger is the only one with a key to the area where the weapons are stored, so we need to decide where to put it. If we do get attacked, we don't want to be running around looking for him, and we don't want extra keys floating around in case one gets lost. But I'm sure we'll come up with some ideas."

"Perhaps we could have a few hiding places and work out a rotation system, so we move it around regularly," suggested James.

"Not a bad idea, not bad at all, James…so let's agree to meet around midnight. Roger and Brick will join us, and we'll get to play with our toys. I've got some work to catch up on, but perhaps we can have a cocktail or two before lunch?"

"That sounds good, Charles. Richard and I are going to relax by the pool. The women are out for lunch with Abdul. They won't be back till much later, so cocktails sound great. No one to nag us and an afternoon siesta to be had. Can't get much better than that."

The three men walked off, feeling relaxed and happy; the day ahead was theirs and theirs alone.

Once dinner was finished, the women all retired for the night, leaving the guys to have brandies. They'd all had a wonderful long day and were absolutely shattered, so the men didn't have to make up any excuses to stay behind. But there wasn't going to be any brandy drinking. Each man needed his wits about him. They were going to be handling lethal weapons, and no mistakes could be made.

After three hours of loading and unloading machine guns, learning how to pull pins from grenades, deciding which knives were best for what, and practising the best ways to kill someone quickly and silently, they all felt confident in their ability to use the weapons they had in their possession. Dominic's instructions were informative; he'd left nothing to chance.

"Well, guys, job well done. I think we all deserve a stiff drink, but before we go to the bar, let's all take a turn at locking and unlocking the door. We don't want to fumble in an emergency."

"Quite right, Charles. The lock can be a bit tricky. I've got the knack of it by now, but no one else has ever opened it." Roger showed them how to turn the key, and after a little practice, all the men knew what they were doing. The key was put in its first hiding place, known only by the five of them, and then they began making their way to the bar for a well-deserved drink.

Suddenly, a deafening high-pitched hum came from the terrace outside the bar.

"What the fuck is that noise above us?" Charles sounded furious.

Roger, followed by the other four, rushed outside to investigate. Floating above them was a drone, hovering a few feet above their heads.

"Those scum shit people are spying on us. Look, they're taking photos. See the lights flashing? Guys, act normally, be cool. Just lads about to have drinks together."

"Boss, shall I go get an Uzi while you're acting normally and come back and shoot the motherfucker down?"

"No, Brick. Keep calm. Roger, stroll out casually, get hold of our communications officer. Tell him to work out how we can get in touch with those bastards."

Within minutes the drone left. It headed in the direction of the boat that had been watching them for weeks. An hour later, the men received a call in the bar to say that a line of communication had been opened. They all rushed to the navigation deck.

"Sir, we can now speak to our bounty hunters, if that's who they are."

"Right, let's speak to these bastards."

After a couple of minutes, the message had been written:

> *This is the Golden Eagle. We know you've been tracking us for weeks. Why are you spying on us with a drone?*

Charles pressed the send button. "Let's see what they've got to say for themselves. It's a waiting game now."

# Chapter Thirty-Nine

"Charles!" Roger yelled. "We've got a reply."

"What does it say?"

"Just waiting for Pete from IT to make sure nothing's going to corrupt our network system. No viruses to cause us any problems, and then we can see what these bastards have to say for themselves."

Charles was agitated. He wanted answers, and he wanted them now. It seemed an eternity before he was reading the reply:

> *Golden Eagle, your owner knows what we want...him. Give us Antonio Cadiz, and nobody will get hurt.*
>
> *We are only interested in receiving the bounty that's on his head. The bounty being offered by the Brazilian authorities.*
>
> *They want his return so he can face trial for drug offences and tax evasion and are willing to pay highly.*

> *We have no interest in anyone else. Maybe you'd be tempted to hand him over for a cut?*
>
> *If you don't listen to our demands, we'll have to use force, things will get nasty, and we promise that.*
>
> *You have twenty-four hours to decide whether all your lives, including those of your beautiful women friends, are worth the sacrifice of harbouring a wanted criminal.*
>
> *And before we leave you to make this decision, let us assure you, the men will be killed first, the women second. But only after we've finished having fun with them.*
>
> *You'll all be dead, and we'll get our man anyway, so be smart. Hand your boss over.*

Charles was shaking; his eyes were bulging wildly, and his face was red with rage. "Those fucking bastards—who the fuck do they think they are? How have they traced me?

"There's someone here on the inside leaking information. Someone is betraying me to pieces of shit like these scum chancers. I swear I'll kill the person responsible for this with my own bare hands.

"Find Brick, Richard, and James. I want to meet them in the library in fifteen minutes. And tell them to read this before they get there."

Roger had never seen anyone in such a rage. He stood dumbfounded as Charles threw the paper in his direction and stormed out. Once alone, Roger read the message and immediately contacted the other three men and told them to get to the library straightaway. There was no time to waste.

Within twenty minutes, everyone was focusing their attention on their boss. They'd all read the reply and waited anxiously to know what was to be done.

Charles had digested the information and felt more in control of his emotions. Nevertheless, his anger was palpable.

"There are two scenarios here." Charles was pacing the room like a caged tiger. "One, we have an informant in our midst, someone close enough to know the journey I've travelled to change my identity, someone who's contacted these scumbags and told them everything. Someone who knows these bastards are a small-time gang who want to earn a quick buck and want me out of the picture.

"Or they're just a bunch of fucking idiots who know nothing about me and are taking a shot in the dark. They've heard of a bounty on a man called Antonio Cadiz, and our yacht and lifestyle fit the picture, and they're hoping they will earn some dough.

"Right now, I can't decide which of the two options is more likely. But if it's the first one and someone is trying to destroy me, this is what I'll do. I will kill them with my bare hands, mark my words. But as long as these people have no evidence of who I am, I think we can call their bluff and get them off our backs."

Charles was looking aged and tired. He slumped into a chair, and his mind continued to race, trying to work out what was really going on.

James interrupted the silence. "Boss, the first thing we do is not panic. Let's show them we're strong, calm, and in control. Perhaps we should let them know we're prepared to take them on—let them know we've got enough gun power on board and their threats are making us laugh."

"I don't agree," interrupted Richard. "I don't think we should show our hand. Let's play it cool to begin with. Let's deny any knowledge of ever hearing of or knowing an Antonio Cadiz. See what they have to say. That way, we may find out if we have to worry about there being a grass among us."

"Boss," Brick chimed in, "let me get my hands on them. We can bring all the weapons up from below. Leave Muscat at dusk. They'll follow us, and then we can blow their fucking boat out of the water, and I can personally drag the bastards on board and rip them limb from limb and feed them to the sharks. That'll sort all our problems out."

"Shut up, Brick," said Richard and James at the same time.

"Why are you both such a pair of bitches? Anything I say, you jump down my throat. I've had enough of you two." And with that Brick sat down, crossed his legs, and sulked.

"I agree with Richard." Charles spoke quietly. "We'll tell them there's no Antonio Cadiz on board. We've never heard of the man. We are a group of close friends having an extended holiday together, now that all our families have grown and flown the nest. We'll tell them to do their homework like good little boys. And if they continue with their nonsense, we may have to retaliate by getting in touch with the authorities and report harassment. We won't mention weapons. We'll leave them guessing. Throw the ball back to them. We'll remain here in port and wait for their response.

"That way we will, as Richard said, perhaps know a little more about whether we have an informer among us or not. Nothing is to be discussed with anyone. I mean *anyone*. Roger doesn't let Pete have any more access to any of our communications. It's just the five of us who know anything about any of this. Do I make myself clear?"

All four men nodded and muttered their agreement. Brick was quieter than the others, still in a sulk.

"And Brick, grow the fuck up." Charles threw him a look as he left the library.

"How bloody dare he!" Brick whined.

"Shut up, Brick," James, Richard, and Roger all shouted simultaneously, trying hard not to laugh.

With that, Brick stood and wiggled his tight bottom from side to side as he made his way out the open door. "I doubt I'll see you tonight at dinner. I'm busy this evening. I'm meeting up with some true friends. Not like you lot. I actually think I hate you—well, not you, Roger, just those two."

James and Richard smiled at each other. They were very fond of Brick, even if he drove them both insane.

"Well, guys, I'm off to send our response. See you in the bar around eight thirty. By the way, I think we're doing the right thing."

All three men left the library and headed in different directions.

As he sipped a brandy on his veranda, Charles received confirmation from Roger that the message had been sent. He hoped it would do the trick, but in his heart, he knew this problem was not over. It was only just starting.

# Chapter Forty

Fourteen days passed without a word from the bounty hunters.

Karmen and Josephine were becoming extremely bored. They'd exhausted all the shops in Muscat, those that were worth looking at anyway, and with nothing else of interest to see on land, sitting on deck in the searing heat was becoming tiresome.

The men were getting edgy, and each day that passed with no communication from the enemy found them feeling more and more concerned. Charles knew it was time to move. Everyone needed a new location and a new adventure. But he didn't want the adventure to include the gang of men who two weeks ago had threatened their lives.

A decision had to be made.

As the sun was rising, Charles made his way to the navigation deck. "Morning, Roger. Still no news from our friends?"

"Not a word. I've been testing all the communication lines, and everything is working properly. Perhaps they've decided to pick some other potential money-earning scheme and leave us alone."

"I've been thinking, Roger; it's time for us to move on. However, I don't mind admitting I'm worried. While we're in port, there's a safety element. As soon as we hit the open seas, I wonder if our friends will try something."

"But surely, Charles, they would have responded to us if they'd known about you. Let us know they knew the truth and then tried to negotiate, don't you think?

"And by the way, the port authorities are losing their patience with the continual changes in our schedule. They want confirmation of our departure date, and I keep putting them off. They're becoming very difficult, so leaving would be a great idea."

"OK. Prepare a route, and let's think about sailing out of here by tomorrow."

Later that afternoon, as everyone lay under umbrellas, seeking shade from the immense heat that wouldn't die down until at least 8:00 p.m., Charles approached the others.

"Hi, guys. I've got some good news for you all. We're leaving Muscat first thing in the morning."

There was a big sigh of relief from everyone.

Karmen muttered under her breath, just a little louder than she'd intended, "Thank God for that. We're all turning brain dead."

"I know, Karmen. We've certainly stayed far too long, and I apologise. A number of business issues made it impossible for me to leave before now, but we're ready to go, to seek pastures new. Roger can take over and explain the intended route."

"Sure thing, Charles. We're leaving at dawn, heading for Bahrain and Qatar, travelling along the Arabian Gulf. It shouldn't take longer than three days for us to cover the five hundred thirty-two nautical miles. The weather conditions will remain similar to those we've experienced recently, but there'll be pleasant sea breezes to keep us all slightly cooler than of late.

"When we arrive at our destination, I think you'll find a lot of new and exciting things to occupy your time. So ladies and gentlemen, I bid you farewell as I begin preparing the *Golden Eagle* to leave Muscat first thing in the morning. Looking forward to seeing you all tonight at dinner."

"You won't be seeing me. I'll have to say my good-byes to Khalid if we're leaving tomorrow." Brick spoke with sadness.

"Oh, you poor darling, I know the two of you have been getting on so well. I did say to be careful and protect your heart. It's always so hard saying good-bye." Josephine was genuinely upset for Brick.

The others were not much interested in Brick's love life and quietly walked away, leaving the two friends talking.

"I know, Josephine. I'm truly heartbroken. I knew this time would come, but I was blocking it out of my mind. We seriously had something special. You know what? He actually gave me an Arabic name, a name he'd have called his son if ever he had one. Imagine that. He called me Jalal. And I named him Rob in memory of my brother, who was my best friend and who died far too early. Khalid was so proud when I gave that name to him; he really is extremely soppy, you know…

"…We would talk for hours and hours, and even though I fancied him like mad, we never so much as held hands. We just shared our memories, good and bad, and our dreams for the future, and now we've got to say good-bye to each other."

Josephine couldn't reply out loud; she just walked over to Brick and hugged him, whispering in his ear, "Say good-bye to Rob from me. Tell him if you loved him, I would have loved him too. Be strong, my darling. At least you've had someone special in your life, even if it's only been for a very short while. Some people never get that in a whole lifetime."

Brick wiped away a tear and spoke quietly. "I know you're right, Josephine. Rob will be forever in here." He touched his heart gently, turned around, and walked away, his hips wiggling from side to side as they always did. Josephine knew Brick would be fine. He was a romantic beyond imagination, but he was also a survivor.

Before supper that evening, Charles, James, Richard, and Brick were having drinks at the bar. Seon was mixing his famous old-fashioned rum punches for them, looking as smart and dapper as ever and throwing his cocktail shaker into the air like a juggler. The ladies were still getting ready, so there was a chance for the guys to speak privately. They took their drinks from Seon and found a cozy table on the deck, where the cool night air blew in from outside. The lighting came from individual lamps scattered around the room, and a warm glow shimmered throughout the bar area. Quiet jazz was playing in the background through the Sonos system, and Charles spoke in hushed tones.

"I'm somewhat concerned that hearing nothing from our friends doesn't necessarily mean they've gone away. I hope they have, but they may be sitting and waiting for us to move on. And seeing as we're heading off tomorrow, we need to be alert at all times. We'll have to speak with the security team and make sure Roger puts his oldest and most trusted men in charge of each group, just in case one of the security guys is an informant or even worse, working with the bounty hunters from the inside. You never know anything for sure.

"They'll need to increase their hours while we're at sea and be on lookout day and night. We can't take our eyes off the ball. We'll issue firearms to the head of each security group, and we need to make sure our stockpile of weapons are loaded and ready to be used at a moment's notice. We're still the only people who are able to get access to them, so no heavy drinking. We need to be prepared for any eventuality. That includes you too, Brick. I know you're saying your good-byes this evening, but take it slow."

Brick smiled, acknowledging Charles's concern. He had absolutely no intention of partying; he was going to say good-bye to someone who had touched his heart like no one else. And who knew? Maybe one day he and Rob would meet again, in this life or the next, he hoped.

"I pray to God," Charles continued, "that I'm just being overly cautious, and those bastards have gone away once and for all."

All four men looked at one another with serious faces. They knew they had their work cut out for them. They finished their drinks in silence.

The following morning, the *Golden Eagle* silently left its mooring and headed out toward the big, wide ocean and the unknown. Security was in place, as Charles had requested. Each group had an armed, trusted leader who kept a close watch on his team. There was never a moment when the *Golden Eagle* wasn't being patrolled.

Karmen and Josephine were busy comparing websites, looking for places of interest to visit, the best restaurants to eat in, and of course, the best boutiques to shop in. They'd been at sea for a few hours now and dazzling blueness surrounded them.

"Bahrain looks pretty amazing, don't you think?"

"Sure does, Karmen, but you know what? I'm just pleased to be here on the top deck sunbathing with a breeze and not feeling as if I'm being burned to death in that stifling port of Muscat. God, that stay was far too long. Fancy a cocktail?"

"What's the time?" asked Karmen.

Josephine checked her watch. "I make it just gone twelve thirty."

"Well then, I reckon a cocktail is quite appropriate. It's passed midday, after all. Shall we get one for Barbara? She said she'd be here twelvish."

The two women chuckled; they really loved each other's company.

James and Richard were playing backgammon, but unlike their wives, they were sitting in the shade. Both of them were playing very tactically. Each man was extremely competitive; neither could bear to lose to the other.

Brick was swimming laps. He felt positive he'd see Khalid again, and until that time, they'd agreed to text and FaceTime each other. Things could be worse, he reckoned. He'd make sure to keep his body looking good for their next meeting. And now he had someone to dream about, someone who loved him, and that made him smile.

All in all, the atmosphere on the *Golden Eagle* couldn't have been more relaxed.

# Chapter Forty-One

"Make sure you keep our boat out of sight," Domingo ordered as he passed by Rodriguez, his right-hand man. "Our prize is waiting out there. I smell the money, and I don't want any fuck-ups."

"Aye-aye, Captain," replied Rodriguez.

As he spoke to his boss, he held his cigarette tightly between his nicotine-stained teeth, showing two large gold incisors on either side of his mouth. Inwardly, he was thinking it might be hard to keep the seventy-five-footer with a small tender on the back out of sight, but he knew better than to say anything to his boss. The man was crazy, and Rodriguez just wanted his share of any cash that was to be had. So he'd learned to keep his mouth shut over the years and hope for the best. Sometimes things worked, and money came his way; other times nothing came, and he'd revert to pickpocketing and mugging to feed his addictions to drink, drugs, and gambling. Life had never been easy for Rodriguez.

Domingo was a hefty Brazilian. He looked as if he hadn't bathed or showered for weeks. He was always either smoking a big fat cigar or sucking on one, so the end was always soggy. He drank constantly, his favourite drink being very, very, strong doctored brandy, made by a lowlife he knew back in Brazil who owed him money. He knew he was never going to be repaid, so he took case after case of the poison instead. His filthy shirts were always half-undone; otherwise, the buttons would pop open as the threadbare material stretched itself over his enormous belly. He was actually a relatively wealthy man—he had to be to own his own boat—but years of self-abuse had caused him to lose all interest in his appearance. He had four other down-and-outs from the slums of São Paulo working alongside Rodriguez. All of them were rough and ruthless. Just how Domingo liked them.

The one person besides Domingo with half a brain was his son Juan. A decent education had equipped him relatively well, and technology was his passion. He was the person who manned the drone. But as the saying goes, the apple hadn't fallen far from the tree, and Juan was very quickly following in his father's vile and slovenly footsteps.

The only thing any of them had in mind was the capture of Antonio Cadiz. Then they'd be wealthy and have lifestyles like the extremely rich men they'd read and dreamed about.

Back on the *Golden Eagle*, Roger was picking up sound waves. There was another vessel in the vicinity. The ocean was often full of traffic, but ships always maintained communication, even if the distance between them meant they could not be seen. This craft was remaining silent, but it was definitely out there somewhere.

Roger called Charles to the navigation deck, and after a long conversation, Charles left and met with Brick, Richard, and James.

He told them the time had come.

"I fear the worst, my friends. We have three nights ahead of us before we reach land. Roger has confirmed an unseen, noncommunicating vessel. We can only assume the worst.

"We need to get our weapons out now, before dusk, so we can be as prepared as possible. I suggest I tell Barbara everything, so she can diplomatically tell the girls what may happen. They need to be prepared for the severity of what could lie ahead, the dangers we all face. I think it may cause less panic if they get the information from another woman—perhaps while we're preparing to bring the weapons out of the storage area. What do you think?"

The other three nodded their approval, all of them feeling fear pulsing through their veins.

"Fuck, James," whispered Richard. "Karmen's gonna kill me when she hears this news."

"Yeah, mate, Josephine, too. We're really in the shit, but we've got no choice. We've got to get the weapons out and take these guys on, unless it's some false alarm."

"I bloody well hope it is, for all our sakes."

Charles walked slowly toward the hull of the *Golden Eagle*. He'd arranged to meet the others there in twenty minutes; Roger's top security men were joining them there too.

The weapons had to be at hand.

Charles was muttering to himself, as he often did when he was facing massive problems. "Why, why, just as we start to have a nice life, do these bastards have to come along and ruin everything? What the fuck have I done to deserve all this?"

He passed the lounge area and looked out of the enormous glass windows. The sea glistened electric blue; hundreds of flying fish danced out of the water. Life just isn't fair, he thought.

# Chapter Forty-Two

Domingo was lying in his hammock, sucking wildly on his unlit cigar, muttering nonsense to himself. A stranger would have thought him a crazy man. I've got it, he suddenly thought. He began to bellow and shout to get everyone's attention. He stumbled to his feet, wrapping the hammock around his fat, sweaty body in the process. Staggering, he got his footing, smoothed down his hair and lit his cigar. Somehow, being under the influence of alcohol made him think more clearly. He always seemed to have his best ideas when he was paralytic.

His feeble team collected around him, looking as if they too had been drinking the day away. Domingo loved being the centre of attention, and with these lowlifes around him, he felt powerful, like God. He pulled his sagging, stained trousers up by the belt, puffed on his cigar, and began his masterpiece speech. They'd all heard it a hundred times before, but they listened, not saying a word, as usual.

He told them how lucky they were to have been chosen by him; how lucky they were to be on this mission. And when it was over, life would never be the same for any of them again.

Blah, blah, blah, they thought. They just wanted the money.

Then Juan, who occasionally dared to ask a question, spoke. "So what is the plan, then, Dad? We need a plan, you know."

"Don't be fucking rude to me, you little bastard. I taught you respect, when that whore of a mother of yours left us…Rodriguez, pour me some moonshine, and I'll tell the lot of you the plan. They don't call me 'the Man' for nothing. I've got a plan, oh yeah, and you lot better not fuck it up, or I'll kill you—even you, my boy. You're all gonna be stinking rich, but only if you follow what I'm going to tell you exactly."

They listened. The plan sounded remarkably convincing, much to their surprise.

"The night after tomorrow, under the cover of darkness, wearing black diving suits equipped with ultraviolet lights—you'll have to check, just in case some aren't working—the five of you will leave in the tender, taking machine guns, grenades, poisonous smoke bombs, ropes, and pepper spray. The poison wears off after about twelve hours in most cases, so it doesn't do any long-term damage—just puts people to sleep. Miguel created those beauties for my last mission.

"The two best swimmers—you'll have to decide which two you are—will dive into the water and swim up to the *Golden Eagle*. My contact is in communication with their contact, and they'll drop ropes on either side of the ship. The ropes should be in position for your arrival. If this plan fails for whatever reason, each man will approach from opposite sides of the yacht and throw his own hooked ropes onto the lower decks. You've all seen the yacht's layout from the drone's photographs, so it should be easy.

"At the same time, the other three will start throwing grenades and poisonous smoke bombs. The gas rises and hopefully will knock everyone out pretty quickly. Then you'll all get on, wearing your gas masks, and find Antonio Cadiz. Remember, he's not to be hurt in any way. I don't much care about anyone else. The informant on board will be wearing a gas mask, and we've been given strict instructions to leave that person alone. If you mess up with this clear instruction, I've been told we won't get the money, even if we get Antonio Cadiz. Here's a photograph of the man we are looking for. Remember his face.

"You will remove him from the *Golden Eagle*, or once you're on board and everyone's out for the count, we can decide if we hijack the whole bloody yacht. I'll be in radio contact with my boy at all times. So, son, has your father got a plan, or has he got a plan?"

"Sounds like a plan to me, Dad."

"Boss," Rodriguez asked quietly, "how much do we make? How much is the bounty?"

"Nosy fucker, aren't you? Two-point-five million, if you must know. You lot get fifty percent to split. So fuck off, and do the math."

Everyone's eyes lit up. They were going to be rich; their lives would be made for ever.

"Get some shut-eye; we've got a busy day tomorrow." As Domingo spoke, he walked away from them, smiling to himself. What a bunch of fucking idiots, he thought. The bounty was five million dollars, and he was on to make a nice $3.75 million for doing nothing much. As long as no one fucked up, of course.

Darkness had come, and still Charles hadn't said anything to Barbara about the situation. They all had dinner and acted quite normally. The women were totally unaware of anything. As they retired for the night, James caught sight of Brick sitting quietly by himself.

"Josephine, do you mind if I go and have a word with him? He looks really out of sorts."

"No, go. He's probably missing Khalid, poor love. I'll see you back in the suite."

"Are you all right, Brick? You look like you've got the world's problems on your shoulders. Love life getting you down? Or are you worrying about what might be ahead? We've got your back, you know. Talk to me."

"James, this needs to be between us. Will you promise me?"

"'Course I will. Come on, spit it out."

"Well, you know the boss thinks there's a spy on board?"

"Yes."

"There is, and I know who it is. It's Barbara!"

"Are you sure?"

"Yes. Charles asked me to get some papers from his suite. He told me they were on his bedside table. I went in and heard water running in the bathroom. Barbara must have been having a shower. I was going to leave, and then I heard an e-mail coming through on her phone. It pinged. It was on her side of the bed, and I took a look. It wasn't locked. I read it."

"What did it say?"

"It said, 'The time is getting nearer for us to complete our assignment. Cannot wait to start our life together again in the CIA.'"

James sat still, staring at Brick. He had gone into a trancelike state, his mouth open in disbelief. He couldn't digest what he was being told. Even though he knew Brick was telling the truth, it was inconceivable that Barbara could be a traitor.

"Are you sure you read the message properly? You're not playing a practical joke on me, are you, Brick? Please say you are."

"Would I joke about something as serious as this? What the hell am I going to do, James?"

"You've got to tell Charles straightaway. He's going to go absolutely mad, but he needs to know what's happened, and he needs to know now."

"They're probably in bed, asleep. Can't it wait till morning?"

"No, Brick, he could be telling Barbara about everything as we speak. Remember, he was going to let her break the news to Josephine and Karmen, and up until dinner this evening, I know he hadn't said a thing. You've got to get hold of him now."

"Fuck, this is going to cause a total eruption. Can't imagine what he'll do to her. It doesn't bear thinking about."

James walked with Brick into the bar and watched as he picked up the house phone and called Charles's suite. It was obvious by the conversation that Charles was furious to have been disturbed. But Brick held his ground and insisted his boss come to meet him immediately.

"Shit, he was seriously pissed off with me; will you stay here, James, while I tell him? I'm afraid of what he might do, and if he loses it, we might need to restrain him."

"Yeah, but I'm not looking forward to this one little bit."

Charles appeared, looking furious. He was wearing a silk dressing gown, his hair was ruffled, and it was obvious he'd been in bed. "This better be fucking good, Brick. You interrupted me and Barbara just at the wrong moment. What the fuck's he doing here?" Charles was staring directly at James.

"Boss, sit down. Be prepared for the shock of your life. I don't quite know how to tell you, but—"

"Stop pissing me off. You're worrying me. Just get to the point. Tell me what's going on. That's a fucking order!" Charles's voice was raised, and his face was reddening.

"The other evening, you sent me to your suite to collect some documents."

"Yes, I remember. I haven't got Alzheimer's. So what about it?"

"Well, boss, while I was there, I heard Barbara's phone receive a message. She was showering in the bathroom, and I know I shouldn't have. I don't know what came over me, honestly, I don't, but I took it upon myself to read the message."

"You're bloody right, you shouldn't have. How dare you? Is this what you dragged me up here for? To alleviate your guilt?"

"Charles, give Brick a chance to tell you what he read," interrupted James.

"Go on then, tell me! What did you read on my wife's phone, while she was showering and you were creeping around my bedroom?" Charles was getting angry and inwardly scared of what he was about to hear.

"It said, 'The time is getting nearer for us to complete our assignment. Cannot wait to start our life together again in the CIA.' So boss, it looks like we've found our informer. I'm so sorry."

Charles remained silent. His temper was rising. The blood was rushing to his head, and his face was turning redder by the second. He stood, steadying himself on the back of the chair. "I'll kill her with my bare hands if this is true. The bitch, how could she betray me like this?" His voice was low, and he growled like a wild animal. "Get out of my sight, the pair of you. I want to be alone." He screamed again, this time even louder. "Get out of here now!"

Charles had a few straight whiskeys, and when he felt more in control, he called Barbara. She answered the phone, purring as she often did. "Hello, lover boy. I'm getting lonely here all by myself. Are you coming back to bed? What did Brick want?"

"I'll tell you all about it, darling. I'll be back in a few minutes. Get yourself up, and let's have a drink together. There's no rush, is there? We've nothing pressing to get up for tomorrow. Only another long day at sea, so let's enjoy tonight."

Christ, Barbara cursed under her breath. She hated this charade. Charles's demands on her made her sick to her stomach. She couldn't wait to get this over and done with and start her life again with Judith.

How he had never realised that she found men absolutely repulsive was beyond her. She figured she must be a very convincing liar.

Once Antonio Cadiz was back in Brazil, convicted and imprisoned, she would have all the money in the world and a job she adored, working alongside her partner, the love of her life. As she applied her lipstick and sprayed her body with perfume, she heard Charles come in. One last look in the mirror, and Barbara was ready. She sauntered into the living room, wearing only a tiny black lace negligee.

"I've missed you, Charles. Come over here; I'll open a bottle of champagne."

Charles sat down and watched his wife pour the champagne. She was bending over provocatively, showing the firmness of her bottom.

"Is there a problem, Charles?" She sounded concerned.

"Why should there be a problem?"

"I'm just sensing something, that's all. Maybe I'm mistaken. Here, take this glass." She sat herself down next to him. "Cheers, my love."

Charles didn't respond to her.

"There is a problem, isn't there? I've known you for so long now. Come on, darling, tell me."

Charles stared at her and under his breath said, "You're my problem." He grabbed her hair tightly and pulled her head backward. The glass fell out of her hand, smashing into a hundred little pieces. "Why have you been leading me up the garden path?"

With that, the first blow hit her face. She screamed out in fear and pain. Charles knew the suite was soundproofed, so nobody outside could hear a thing.

As the blood began to trickle down her face, she screamed out. "You've gone crazy. Please, Charles—"

"You think I've gone crazy, do you?" With that, he smashed her in the face again. "Now tell me the truth. What is going on with you and the CIA? Who are you in cahoots with?"

"Nothing's going on, I swear, Charles. On Gabriel's life."

"You're a fucking liar, and Gabriel's already dead. Now tell me the truth."

Charles threw another blow, this time to her body. Barbara fell to the floor, sobbing, blood pouring from her mouth and nose.

"Tell me what's going on, if you want to live to see another day. Speak to me." He grabbed her by the arm and stared straight at her. She stared back, her eyes beginning to swell as fear pulsated through her body.

"There's nothing to tell you. You've got everything wrong. Please calm down."

"I know you've been informing someone about our movements and keeping them updated. You're a fucking liar. Who is it that can't wait for you to start your lives together in the CIA? Answer me, you whore!" Charles was shaking with rage as he shook Barbara violently.

"Please stop...please, Charles...I love you." Barbara realised Charles knew she'd been double-crossing him and was desperately trying to stall him to give herself time to think.

"OK, you want to play games with me, do you?" He grabbed her by the arm, her body bouncing around like a rag doll. Blood smeared along the marble floor as he dragged her into the bathroom. He started to run the bath with cold water.

"What are you doing, Charles?" Her voice was weak and quiet.

"Tell me the truth, you bitch, or you will suffer."

The bath was filling up quickly.

"Charles, you've got it all wrong."

"Even now, you still lie to my face. You whore!"

He dragged her to the overflowing bath and forced her head below the surface. As she began to choke, Charles held her head down with all his might. The icy blood-tinged water turned a deeper red by the second. Barbara tried to bring herself up, but Charles held her head under until he felt her begin to give up the fight. Only then did he bring her up for air. She gasped as if it were her last breath, but amazingly, her breathing regulated into sharp intakes of air.

"Now tell me the truth, or I swear I'll kill you."

Barbara knew it was over. She admitted she was working for the CIA. She'd had time to decide what else to add and told him quietly that she was being blackmailed and her life had been threatened if she didn't do as she was told. "I had no choice, Charles. Please believe me."

"You're a liar, Barbara. You've ruined my life. I put my trust in you, I loved you, and you double-crossed me. You fucking bitch. You whore." He threw her to the floor, her body landing in a heap. His head was reeling. "I hate you for what you've done. You've killed me. I loved you, you nasty, evil cow."

He kicked her in the stomach with all his strength as she lay on the floor. Barbara yelled in pain, and with shallow gasps whispered, "I didn't mean it to end like this."

Then her eyes stared up at him, piercing blue against her bloodied face. She drew a breath and drifted away, still staring at him.

"Barbara, speak to me. Don't play games with me. Speak to me!"

She said nothing, just continued to stare at him without blinking. "Barbara? Barbara don't you…don't you dare die on me!"

But she was already dead and gone. Charles crumbled to the floor; he hadn't meant to kill her. Tears welled up in his eyes, and he found himself sobbing uncontrollably.

Once the tears stopped, he panicked. He looked down at her lifeless body. What am I going to do now? he wondered. He tried to give her mouth-to-mouth resuscitation, pressing firmly on her chest, willing her to come back to life, but soon enough he realised it was futile. There was no pulse; there was no life. Barbara was gone.

He grabbed the phone by his bedside in a complete state of shock and called Mark on the emergency medical line that was available twenty-four hours a day.

Mark answered on the third ring, sounding very groggy.

"I need you to come to my suite, Mark. It's an emergency. Hurry. I think I've accidentally killed Barbara." As he spoke he was trembling. His words were interrupted by sobs and tears. He threw the receiver down and sat motionless on his bed, looking at the blood that seemed to be everywhere.

Mark jumped up and rushed to get dressed.

"What's going on?" Caroline spoke quietly, her eyes still closed.

"It's an emergency. Go back to sleep. I can deal with it." With that, Mark left his cabin and rushed to the lift.

"Christ, Charles, what's been going on here?"

Charles didn't answer. Head slumped, he walked toward the bathroom. Mark followed him in silence. He bent down and examined Barbara. Then he gently closed her eyes and turned to Charles.

"She's had a massive heart attack, Charles. I'm sorry, but there's nothing we can do. She's gone. Charles, tell me, why is there so much blood everywhere? Barbara's covered in bruises. What the hell happened here?"

Charles stared blankly and managed to answer, "We had an argument, and things got out of hand. I didn't mean to kill her—I swear I didn't. You do believe me, Mark, don't you?"

"Listen, Charles, we need to get her out of here, get her down to the mortuary in the hospital area. But first, we need to clean up. We've got to get rid of the blood on the floor. I'll clean Barbara and the bathroom. You clean yourself and the rest of the suite. Does anyone know what's gone on here tonight besides the two of us?"

Charles shook his head.

"Good, let's keep it that way. Barbara has had a sudden heart attack. Nothing more needs to be discussed. Now get yourself together. We've got work to do."

"Mark, thank you. I'll make sure there's a big bonus for you once this is over."

"Charles, make sure this stays between us and the four walls, OK? Otherwise, I could be struck off by the medical board."

"You have my word."

Within an hour the suite was back to normal, and Charles had showered and changed his clothes. He looked awful and pale, but that was to be expected.

Mark had cleaned Barbara's body, and it lay covered on the floor of the bathroom. Then he called Caroline, told her of the tragic events, and asked her to bring a trolley from the hospital as soon as she could.

The two men were sitting in the lounge, each holding an extra-large brandy in their hands, saying very little, when Caroline arrived, looking extremely tired and extremely upset. She walked over to Charles and put a comforting arm around him.

"I'm so very sorry, Charles. I don't know what to say." Her Irish lilt was soft and full of emotion. "Does anyone else know what's happened?"

Mark interrupted. "No, no one knows for the moment except us. Charles wants to be the one to break the bad news, but he's not ready yet. I've given him a sedative to relax him, and in a few hours, when the others have woken, he'll be able to tell them. In the meantime, I'm going to get Barbara on the trolley, and then I can take her down to the hospital mortuary."

"Can I see her?"

"No. Just remember her as she was when she was alive. Keep Charles company until he falls asleep, and I'll see you back in the cabin."

Caroline nodded quietly and turned her attention to Charles. He was slumped in his chair; the sedative along with the trauma had kicked in. Soon enough he was fast asleep, breathing heavily. She walked over to him, kissed him gently on the head, and left the suite quietly.

Meanwhile, Mark secured Barbara's body onto the trolley. As he wheeled her past Charles, he wondered what the hell had really happened here tonight. The thought of it sent shivers down his spine. Perhaps it was for the best that he never knew. After all, he didn't want to lose respect for his boss, and if he knew the truth…well, Mark didn't know how he'd feel, and that thought scared the life out of him.

Charles woke after three hours. His body was stiff and aching from having slept in such an awkward position. It took a couple of minutes for the memories to flood back. He felt the bile rise in his throat as he remembered Barbara's last words.

He had killed his wife. He was a wife murderer. Had she deserved this? To be beaten to death? She said she loved him. Did she? His head was all over the place. Was she being blackmailed? Why hadn't she shared this with him if it was true? Who had texted her? A lover from before? A lover she couldn't wait to be with?

No, it was clear she was double-crossing him, he thought. She was the person passing on information. That's why they were being followed. She had deserved to die.

"I must be strong. Work out a story for everyone," he said to himself. "I've been in more difficult situations than this in my life."

Then the sadness and remorse flooded back into his mind. God, I miss her already, he thought. She was the love of my life, but did she love me? Why did she have to ruin everything? Tears were rolling down his cheeks. He rushed into the bathroom; there wasn't a trace of her anywhere. He caught sight of himself in the mirror. He looked dreadful. This was his punishment for murdering his wife.

He ripped his clean clothes off and stepped into the shower. He turned it to cold and let the icy water pour over him. It was freezing and unbearable, but he remained there, rubbing his body violently with a rough sponge. He wanted to cleanse himself, to wipe away all memories of the past few hours.

When he'd finished, his body was red and raw. He stepped out of the shower and immediately smelled Barbara's perfume. Am I losing my mind? he wondered. He rushed to the bathroom shelf, gathered every bottle of fragrance she possessed, and threw all of them in the bin. He needed to arrange for the cleaners to remove her things. Everything of hers had to go. He had to get rid of anything that reminded him of her.

Afterwards, he phoned Mark. He told him that his head was feeling extremely heavy, and his mind seemed to be playing tricks on him. Mark said he'd come to his suite right away. When he arrived, they talked for a while, first as friends, then as doctor and patient. They had very strong coffee, and Mark gave Charles some prescription pills.

"Take them as prescribed over the next few weeks. They'll help you get through this; you'll feel much better, able to cope. Have you spoken to the others yet?"

Charles told Mark he hadn't been able to face them, and Mark suggested he begin the pills immediately. Charles did as he was told, and within half an hour, he started to feel a whole lot better.

"What have you done with Barbara's body? Have you written a death certificate?"

"She's being kept in cold storage until we get to our next port of call. Don't concern yourself about any of this; just leave everything to me. As far as the death certificate goes, yes, Barbara died of a sudden, massive heart attack. There are indications that heart problems ran in her family, so it's not too surprising that she died prematurely."

Charles felt the weight release from his body. He wasn't sure if hearing how in control of everything Mark was made him feel like this or if it was the pills. But whichever one it was, he didn't really care. All he knew was he suddenly felt as though he could cope with everything and move forward.

"I must go and speak to the others and give them the sad, tragic news."

"That's my man. You're going to get through this; just wait and see." With that, Mark patted Charles on the back, delighted to see him take control, and left him to go and find his friends.

Charles wandered up to the top deck to breathe in fresh air. He hoped he wouldn't meet anyone for a while, but unfortunately, within seconds, he heard Karmen and Josephine calling to him. He composed himself and turned to face them.

"Charles, what's wrong? You look absolutely awful." Josephine had never learned the art of being diplomatic.

"Girls, something tragic has happened." His head slumped downward, and Karmen took him by the arm and led him to the sun loungers where they all took a seat.

Charles took a deep breath and blurted out the sad news. "Barbara had a massive heart attack."

"Is she all right?" Karmen grabbed Josephine's hand as she spoke.

"No…I'm afraid she's not. She passed away. It was so sudden. One minute I was discussing a problem with her, and the next she was gasping for breath and holding her arm. I…" Charles began to sob.

"I tried to resuscitate her, but it was too late. She died…oh my God, my Barbara's dead!" With that, Charles put his head in his hands and cried like a baby.

Karmen and Josephine began to tremble, and their tears fell. They each put an arm around Charles, and the three of them sat hugging, saying nothing.

After a while, Karmen managed to squeeze some words out between her sobs.

"Did you get hold of Mark, Charles?"

"Of course I did. After trying to breathe life into her, I called him. He was there in minutes. There was nothing anyone could have done…absolutely nothing."

"Oh, my poor, poor darling friend. When did it happen, Charles?"

"Late last night. Then Mark sedated me. I was in a state. This morning, Mark told me Barbara was carrying a gene. It showed a history of heart disease in her family. He said under the circumstances, she was a time bomb waiting to go off. There was nothing I could have done to save her. You two are the first I've told. I need to find the others; where are they?"

"Brick and James are having breakfast; Richard is taking a swim. Do you want us to come with you?"

"No, I'd rather see them by myself. You don't mind, do you?"

"Of course not." Karmen smiled sadly at Charles. She felt devastated for him.

"We all love you, Charles," added Josephine as he stood to leave. "Keep strong; we're here if you need us."

Charles found Brick and James tucking into a hearty breakfast. They looked toward him as he approached. They had wondered what the outcome of last night's fiasco had been. Both men agreed there had been no choice but to tell him about Barbara, and as he neared, they thought there must have been one hell of an argument. Charles looked like death warmed over.

"Hey, boss, you OK? What went down last night?"

"After you told me about Barbara, I went back to the suite. I questioned her. I was calm, but firm…she said nothing, just went pale and stared at me…she started to tremble and collapsed in a heap on the floor…she looked like she was having a fit, holding on to her arm…I bent down; she had no pulse…I tried to resuscitate her, but she wasn't coming around. I called Mark immediately; he came with the crash equipment, but…" His words caught in his throat as he began to sob. "She was dead…a sudden massive heart attack. Barbara's gone."

There was silence; neither Brick nor James could believe what they were hearing. Then, very quietly, Brick spoke. "Boss, tell us the truth. It'll stay with the three of us. What really happened?"

"I give you my word. That's exactly what happened. Ask Doctor Mark and Nurse Caroline; they'll confirm everything I've just told you. I need to go now and find Richard. We'll speak later."

With that, Charles walked away, leaving Brick and James staring, their mouths wide open, in a complete state of shock. This was not what they'd expected to hear.

# Chapter Forty-Three

As the afternoon drew to a close, everyone had time to digest the fact that Barbara was gone.

Charles asked Josephine, Karmen, Caroline, and Roger to keep it to themselves and mention Barbara's death to no one else. He said he couldn't bear to keep repeating the tragic story; it was too emotionally draining for him. All of them completely understood and gave their word it would go no further. After all, it really was none of anyone else's business.

When Charles told Richard about Brick finding Barbara's mobile, he explained the circumstances with a heavy heart. Many tears fell, and Richard was in complete shock as he listened. He couldn't believe that Barbara was the person who had betrayed them all. Charles explained how Barbara was working for the CIA and feeding information through to someone known only as J. And that person was, in turn, relaying the information to the boat that had been tracking them for weeks.

When it came to discussing the fact that it seemed clear Barbara and J were very probably lovers, Charles broke down. Richard's heart broke for his friend's pain, and to think Barbara then died of a sudden massive heart attack was too much to imagine.

Mark corroborated everything Charles said to everyone, so Charles felt there was no suspicion hanging over his head.

Brick still wasn't completely convinced but kept his thoughts to himself.

Charles was feeling a whole lot better, although his mind still played games with him. He questioned Barbara's motives and still couldn't believe she was totally evil and had never loved him at all. However, Mark's pills were making such a difference. They were taking the edge off everything. He wondered if he should up the dosage; they were really changing his ability to cope, and his mood was so much better in such a short time.

He sat in his suite checking Barbara's mobile. Luckily, he remembered her pin, four-zero-three-one-five. He thought back to when she explained why she had decided on that number. It brought an immense sadness to him when he remembered how she'd laughed when she told him.

"Darling, this is why I chose four-zero-three-one-five. It's my name. See, *D* is the fourth letter of the alphabet, zero is *O*, *R* is the third letter of my name, *I* is like one, and *S* is the fifth letter of my name. Get it? Four-zero-three-one-five."

She had been so excited, just like a child, and he remembered her logic was lost on him. But he had never forgotten her PIN. As he scrolled through her messages, trying to find something to assure him he'd done the right thing, the phone beeped. He felt a surge of excitement race through his veins as he opened the message.

He stared at the words: *Surprised I've not heard from you. Any news? There's only two nights till you arrive into port.*

*Do we delay? All's ready this end. Waiting on your say-so.
J x.*

He took the phone with him and rushed to find the others. As he expected, they were on the top deck: the guys playing backgammon in the shade while Karmen and Josephine sunned themselves nearby, listening to their music, lost in their thoughts and memories of Barbara.

The breeze was cool, but the sun was hot.

He approached the men quietly and told them to take a look at the message. The phone was passed around. Brick was triumphant. At last there was no doubt that he'd been right in assuming Barbara was double-crossing them all, and the guilt he felt about telling Charles vanished. He did, however, believe she hadn't deserved to die. But perhaps it really was a sudden heart attack, he thought. He hoped so, with every fibre of his body.

"Are you going to reply?" whispered James.

"Of course I am," replied Charles. "This is our trump card. Whoever this person is, they have no idea that Barbara's gone. We continue communicating with them, feed them some shit, and find out what the fuck's going on in their minds. Remember, they know Barbara as Doris, so we mustn't forget that when we reply. I guess she uses D, seeing as her contact uses J.

"It seems Barbara's being asked if the attack should take place in the next forty-eight hours or if it should wait until we leave Bahrain. They're obviously in no rush. I'm leaning toward getting it over and done with as soon as possible—

taking these bastards on now that we have the upper hand. What do you think?"

"Shit!" Richard sounded fearful. "What a question. I don't want it to happen at all."

"But Richard, it's gonna happen at some point anyway," interrupted Brick. "Surely it's better if we orchestrate it ourselves rather than wait and possibly be taken by surprise."

"I agree with Brick," added James.

"Pleased to hear it, guys." Charles sounded very upbeat. "May I recommend we reply and try to create a situation whereby we have them attack us tomorrow, when we'll be ready and waiting? It'll give us tonight and tomorrow to get our weapons ready and take every precaution we need to keep us all safe."

Reluctantly, they all nodded their heads in agreement.

"I want the women to be kept hidden," Charles continued. "Things could get messy. There's an empty area next to the life-jacket storeroom. I think they should go there. It's got a large steel door and is completely impenetrable from the outside. It's small, but it will do. I'll get Roger to show it to them later this afternoon. He can make it comfortable enough so they can stay hidden until this is all over. He won't alarm them too much. I've decided he should tell them he's received information that pirates may be working in the area, looking for money and jewellery, and if they hear an alarm, they should immediately go and hide there."

"God, Charles, you've thought of everything. I'm impressed," said James.

Charles smiled and thought, I think the pills are helping me more than I know. Everything seems so simple; I may just up the dose after all.

"What are you going to reply, boss?" Brick's adrenaline was pumping.

"Simply this, 'Tomorrow night is perfect. Any instructions? D x.' It needs to be clear and precise."

Once he got everyone's approval, the message was sent.

# Chapter Forty-Four

Domingo was sweating; it was a hot, humid day. He lay in his hammock, chewing the butt of his cigar, reading the instructions that had just come in from J. He'd never asked what this person's name was. He couldn't care less. He just knew that a number of jobs had been passed to him over the years, and those that worked out were always paid in full. J had never knocked him.

As he swigged from the bottle by his side, he shouted for Rodriguez. Minutes later, the dishevelled man staggered sleepily toward him.

"You lazy bastard, have you been sleeping the day away again? We've got work to do. It's happening tomorrow night. My contact just informed me. Its actions go! We send the tender out after midnight, and at around three a.m., we hit the *Golden Eagle*. You got everything sorted? Equipment, diving gear, weapons, smoke bombs? Not forgotten anything?" He reached for the bottle and took an enormous gulp.

"All under control, boss. Don't you think you should lay off the booze now that we're on our way?"

"Fuck off, you little piece of shit. I do my best work when I've had a drink. Now piss off, and get your team together. I don't want any cock-ups. Make sure the boys study the deck plans Juan photographed from the drone. I don't want anyone getting lost.

"Tell them to study the face of Antonio Cadiz. I don't want any mistakes. He's the one we want. And remind them the person on board with the gas mask is the informer. They're not to be harmed in any way at all, or else there's no money for any of us. And if that happens, you won't need money 'cause I'll fucking kill the lot of you. You'll all be dead. Got that?"

Rodriguez grunted and walked away, thinking he couldn't wait to get the job done, get away from this arrogant bum, and start a new life. He'd really taken as much of Domingo as was physically possible.

Barbara's phone pinged. Charles grabbed it and read, *Here we go! The time has come at last. Secure the ropes either side of the vessel, exactly as we discussed. Have your gas mask ready, wear it, you'll be taken to safety. My men will identify you when they see the mask. Attack confirmed for 3:00 a.m. on the 23rd. See you when it's all over. J x.*

Charles rushed through the ship, found Roger, and checked that the girls had been shown their hiding place. He was pleased to be told everything was in order.

"Karmen and Josephine complained it was too small." Roger smiled as he told Charles. "But Caroline lightened the situation by telling them she'd stock it with champagne and picky bits. They know what to do as soon as they hear the alarm. They believe it has to do with a possible threat of piracy and are taking all their jewellery with them. They're relatively calm."

"Thank God for that. What about the weapons? Are they ready to go?"

"All loaded, laid out, and ready. Brick did most of the moving. Richard, James, and myself made sure everything's in working order and easy to get to. The guys are in the bar having a beer as we speak."

"Great. Listen carefully Roger. At three a.m. the day after tomorrow, we're going to be attacked. I'm under the impression gas could be used. Make sure we've got enough gas masks for everyone. Get each of them marked with phosphorescent paint. I need them to be visible in the dark. Get your men ready; we need as many hands as possible. I'm going to the bar to find Brick and the others. No dinner tonight. We'll take our food in our suites; we need to be rested and ready. See you in the morning."

"Aye-aye, sir."

Charles walked into the bar and sat down with the three men.

"You heard anything, boss?

"Sure have Brick. J's bitten. It's happening at three a.m. the day after tomorrow."

He passed the mobile around. Each man read the message.

"What's with the gas masks and ropes?" Richard looked at Charles waiting for an answer.

"I believe they're planning to use gas, along with God knows what other weapons, and Barbara was to use the mask to escape and to be identified. What a bitch!

"Anyway, we have masks enough for us all, so we're ahead of the game. Barbara's been instructed to secure two ropes on either side of the yacht. We're going to do the same. That way, as they approach, they won't be suspicious, and as they climb aboard, we'll be waiting for the bastards.

"We need rest. Take your meals in your suite tonight. Roger has spoken to the girls, so they know what they're doing. They're calm, but you spend the evening settling them. OK?"

"Are you going to reply to J?" All three men looked at Charles when James asked the question.

"No. The message sent to Barbara wasn't waiting for a reply. It was an instruction. I don't think we'll hear anything else until after the attack takes place. We just need to be ready for these bastards. I'm tired. I'm going to my suite; there's a lot to get ready for. See you in the morning."

With that, Charles left the others ordering more drinks. They were confused, nervous, and sick to their stomachs at what lay ahead.

Charles collapsed on his sofa. His suite was cool; the sea breeze blew softly through the sheer curtains that were drawn. He removed the pills from his pocket and took a double dose; they went down easily with the brandy he'd poured himself.

He closed his eyes. Christ, what a couple of days, he thought. Somehow, though, he felt he'd cope well. The battle was about to begin, and he was ready to take these bastards on.

Warmth swirled through his veins. He felt good—very, very good indeed.

# Chapter Forty-Five

His sleep was fitful. Barbara spoke to him. She taunted him, telling him she'd never loved him. She laughed at him. Then she cried and asked why he'd killed her. She spoke through her tears, proclaiming her love, talking about Gabriel, her pain and sadness, and the wonderful life they were all about to have together.

Charles held her close and sobbed, asking her forgiveness. She snuggled into him; he felt happy, calm, and peaceful…

Suddenly, she pushed him aside, and then she was having sex with someone else. His face was covered. His body was naked. She straddled him, screaming, "J…J…J…" over and over again, staring directly into Charles's eyes, laughing and mocking him…

By the time morning came, Charles welcomed the daylight. He was exhausted, and the stress inside was too much to bear. He went to the bathroom and stared at his reflection. He looked exhausted. His eyes were sunken; his skin was sallow.

He took a cold shower and remembered what was ahead. He needed to get a grip. Today was the day. He needed to get this show on the road. He took a couple of his pills and within minutes felt more in control. It was going to be a very long day, and tonight, he would need all his energy and expertise.

On the positive side, once it was over, this episode of his life could be laid to rest, and he could continue living without a care in the world.

An hour later, Charles was ready, feeling euphoric. He left his cabin and took long strides along the carpeted corridors, greeting the chambermaids and cleaners as he passed. When he reached the top deck, he bumped into Caroline.

"Morning, Caroline."

"Morning, boss."

"Caroline, I know Roger mentioned to you that we may potentially have a problem with a gang of pirates operating in these waters. Are you clear about what to do to keep yourself and the women safe if this happens?"

"Sure thing, boss. Don't worry about the ladies. I've got everything covered." Her voice purred, her Irish lilt deep and warm. She wondered why Charles seemed so happy, considering he'd only recently lost his wife, but she pushed this thought to the back of her mind. He was, after all, paying her wages, and to her that was more important than anything.

As he walked away from her, he could still smell her pungent perfume. For the first time, he noticed how attractive Caroline was. She is one hell of a sexy lady, he thought, and he found himself turning around to take a second look. Her long, lean legs were visible as her short medical coat swung open.

Caroline felt his eyes bore into her. She liked the feeling, and as she walked away, she gently swayed her hips in a provocative fashion, smiling to herself.

Within minutes Charles was seated with James, Richard, Brick, and Roger in the lounge area of the top deck. All eyes were focused on him. He looked through the enormous glass windows that surrounded the room and began to speak.

"Hi, everyone. As you know, today is the day we sort the men out from the boys. Tonight could be a very challenging night. James, as you've been coordinating all the plans, I think it makes sense that you take us through the procedures, so we're all one hundred percent sure of everything."

James took a deep breath and began. "OK. Just before midnight, we'll lower the ropes at the stern and the bow of the ship. No one will know we've done this. Roger told all the crew members, except his trusted right-hand security men, who'll be armed and working alongside us, that he received information about a likely pirate attack, and everyone's to be on full alert from midnight onward. All navigation officers are to be on duty, not the skeleton staff that normally cover during nighttime sailing.

"They'll be looking for anything out of the ordinary, focusing on underwater activities as well as monitoring the seas. If they see anything suspicious, they'll sound the alarm. We'll take our positions, and the girls will go to their hiding place immediately. Caroline is fully au fait with her responsibility for their well-being.

"We're expecting our attackers to use gas to try and knock us out, so we'll be prepared. We must have our gas masks at the ready. Roger, am I right in saying there are enough gas masks for everyone?"

"Yes, every person will have one. Thankfully, Dominic made sure the assignment of weapons included everything we could possibly need. Each mask has been painted with phosphorescent paint, so we can distinguish our team from the attackers."

"Great. Once the ropes have been lowered, we'll give everyone their masks. We'll put the women's in their hiding place in advance. Caroline knows what she's doing; she'll keep them calm. When our attackers approach the ropes, we'll be aware of them coming. We must use the element of surprise and disarm them as soon as they board.

"Remember, we're not sure how many are coming, so we need to act quickly. Apprehend them, cuff them, and silence them before the next man climbs aboard. That is, of course, if there are others. We're not completely sure how many are coming first, so we have to make sure we're fast, on our toes.

"Once we've got them, we need to use force to ascertain how they're going to alert their colleagues that they've taken control of the ship. We don't want to waste any time, in case we make the others suspicious that something's wrong. We want every last one of these bastards. If we have to kill a few to get one of them to speak, so be it. This isn't a game. It's a matter of life and death, and we need to be prepared. Ready to use whatever force is necessary. We've all had enough practice with knives and guns. Tonight, my friends, we must put our training into action." James paused. "I think that's about it, Charles. Has anyone got any questions?"

They looked at one another, the realization of what lay ahead etched on their faces. They all shook their heads and thought 'Shit, this is really happening.'

Once the men dispersed, Charles approached Roger. "Roger, can I have a quiet word?"

"'Course, boss. What can I do for you?"

"Let's go to my suite. We can be sure no one will bother us there."

They entered through the enormous oak doors. Charles walked straight to the bar and poured a large Scotch and soda for each of them. "Roger, I want you to do me a favour." As he handed the glass over, Charles looked directly into the captain's eyes. "I want you to get Barbara's body out of the morgue. Bring her on deck, put her somewhere she won't be seen for a while, and shoot her."

The captain took a gulp of his drink and said nothing for a moment. "Boss, that's one hell of an ask. How can you speak so calmly about such a thing?"

"I realise what I'm asking is really hard, Roger, but remember, she's already dead. So you won't be killing her or anything as awful as that."

"But why, Charles? Why do you want me to do this? It doesn't make any sense."

"Roger." Charles spoke far too calmly for the captain's liking. "There are gonna be a number of fatalities, and it would save a lot of explaining if the authorities thought she was just another victim of our attackers. Can't you see how much easier it would be? Imagine having to explain why she's in the morgue. It could get very complicated. Too many extra questions to answer."

"But surely it'll be obvious she's been dead for some time. Rigor mortis must have set in by now."

"That, my friend, is where you're wrong. Dr. Gardener assures me that putting a body immediately into cold storage stops rigor mortis, and once she's thawed a little, she'll be like new."

Roger couldn't believe the sick and unemotional way his boss was speaking about his own wife. Charles watched the captain digest what had just been said, and after a couple of minutes, he spoke again, his voice lowered and calm.

"Well, Captain, what do you say? I need an answer; we've got no time to waste. I will, of course, reward you very well. And remember, Roger, she's already dead. Please don't forget that."

Roger finished his drink in one gulp, the alcohol stinging his throat. His mind was working overtime.

"Charles," he said quietly, "I'm really not at all happy about this. I'm a skipper, not a murderer. But considering Barbara's already dead, and I'm committed to you, I'll do as you ask. But remember, I'm really going above and beyond the call of duty here."

"Good man. Make the relevant arrangements with Mark later this afternoon, and have everything looking as natural as possible, if you get my drift. Another thing you have to do is make contact with the marine police after the attack's taken place. Send out a mayday and tell them we've been ambushed by pirates. That way, with a bit of luck, they might arrest the whole bloody lot of these bastards—those who are still alive, that is.

"If we do our job right, by the time the police get to us, we can have concealed our weapons and gas masks and look as if we've been brilliant at dealing with our attackers. Those who survive can be arrested for piracy, and the rest can be taken off my ship by the police and forgotten about. Let's just pray we all come through this unscathed and none of us have to be taken off in body bags.

"Now you need to go and get everything prepared. I've taken up enough of your time. And thank you from the bottom of my heart; you're a good man as well as a good captain."

Roger left the suite feeling sick to his stomach.

Charles walked calmly into the bathroom, took a couple of pills, and splashed his face with water. He'd take a rest before nightfall. It was definitely going to be one hell of an evening, he thought to himself.

# Chapter Forty-Six

Nightfall came quickly. Everything started to happen. It was like a military operation—lots of action and very little talking.

The ropes were secured at either end of the yacht. All gas masks were handed out. Automatic weapons, gas bombs, coshes, knives, plastic ties, and rags to be used as blindfolds were given to those responsible for defending the *Golden Eagle* and protecting Charles. Everyone was dressed in black with gas masks resting on the tops of their heads, each equipped with a light so they could see in the dark.

Charles was on edge. Roger kept in touch with him from the bridge at regular intervals, updating him with any developments. The navigation team watched its radar screens constantly, waiting for the first move to be made.

# Chapter Forty-Seven

"Domingo, when are we going to strike?"

"Rodriguez, stay calm, man. When I say the time's right, you'll be the first to know." Domingo took a long drag on his chewed, soggy cigar and let the smoke bellow into Rodriguez's face.

Coughing and spluttering, Rodriguez turned away. "Mark my words, you're gonna kill yourself with that crap you smoke."

"Shut your face, arsehole. What do you know, you creep?" Domingo grabbed his half-empty bottle and took a large gulp of the cheap brandy inside.

"Dad," Juan shouted from the other side of the boat. "Everything's ready and in place, whenever you give the say-so."

"I'm not deaf. Stop fucking shouting." Another swig, and Domingo began to cough violently.

"Dad, cut the brandy out; we need you to be fully alert." Juan was standing over his drunken father by now.

"Don't get like that bit of rubbish over there, son." Domingo pointed in the direction of Rodriguez, as he slumped into his favourite chair.

Juan knew exactly how to handle his father. He moved nearer and put his arm around his dad's shoulder. "Dad, listen to me. We need you; you're the only one who can organise this operation. Without you, we'll all be lost. So you need to cut the drink out, just until this assignment is completed."

"Son, don't worry. You follow me, and life will be good. And for you, I'll cut down on the booze, but only till this job's done. And I'm only cutting down. Now get off my back. I'm no fucking woman, so don't treat me like one."

At 2:30 a.m., Domingo lifted himself heavily out of his chair. He walked slowly along the deck toward the divers who were chilling out lazily under the stars. They needed rest before they sprang into action tonight. The men chosen to begin the attack were strong swimmers and keen divers with lean bodies—perfect for the job ahead.

"Boys, listen to me. You screw this up, and I'll make sure you never walk again, forget about fucking swimming. I'll kick you so hard, your balls will come out of your mouths!" Domingo began laughing hysterically. This, one of his favourite sayings, always cracked him up. "Do I make myself clear, lads?"

"Sure thing, boss," came their reply. "Everything is in order. We'll set the flares off as soon as we've boarded the yacht and secured our positions."

"Right. Then get your diving gear on and head off at three a.m. precisely. As soon as we see the flares, we'll follow. Don't let me down. Now piss off!"

At 3:00 a.m., a large cloud sailed silently across the otherwise star-filled sky, and under the cover of darkness, with only the glow of a burning cigar, an enormous splash could be heard as the divers' bodies hit the water and disappeared into the night.

Domingo smiled as his thoughts drifted away. This time next week, he'd be off living the life of Riley, drinking and sleeping in a hammock, an attentive Thai woman at his service in more ways than one. He was just about ready to realise his dream, and everyone else, including Juan, could fuck off! He reached for his bottle and finished the contents in one gulp.

"Captain, something's appeared on our monitors—two shapes moving in unison. Could be dolphins or sharks; can't quite make them out yet. They're some distance away. Hold on...I'm almost positive they're two divers...yes, I can see oxygen tanks. Look there, sir."

Roger rushed over, stood next to his navigation officer, and stared at the monitors. Yes, this was it, as clear as daylight. The enemy was approaching.

Roger calmly picked up the direct line to Charles, and the two men spoke in hushed tones. When the conversation ended, Roger turned to his crew on the bridge and gave the orders.

"Turn our engines down to an idling speed; we want these guys to board us quickly. We're ready to take them on.

Sound the alarm in five minutes. We need the women to get to their hiding place and everyone else to take their positions. The time has come, gentlemen."

The bridge became a hive of activity, everyone doing something different, all completely focused on the job at hand. Minutes later, the alarm rang loud and clear throughout the vessel. Three short bursts of the horn, signalling for everyone to take their positions.

The divers became clearer on the monitor as they neared.

"Why have they stopped?" a young officer asked Roger.

He examined the screen and confirmed that the divers were removing their oxygen cylinders and readying themselves to board the yacht.

Roger nodded at Charles, who was now on the bridge. It was time to set the wheels in motion.

"Gentlemen, let's get into position quickly. The enemy will be climbing the ropes shortly, and we need to be fully ready. Good luck to us all."

With that, Charles turned, left the bridge, and made his way down to his suite. He would remain there until his friends contacted him.

Brick was at the front of the yacht with two hidden crew members. His heart raced as he waited silently for the attacker to climb aboard. Sure enough, within minutes, he heard movement, and a slight man in a wetsuit nimbly swung his legs onto the deck. Brick stood squarely in front of him, twice his size and standing at least a foot taller.

Suddenly, Brick noticed he was holding a grenade in his hand.

"Stand back! I pulled the pin!" shouted the attacker.

Brick froze for an instant.

"Stand back if you don't want to be blown apart. Stand back!" The man was screaming in broken English, but his message was loud and clear.

Brick stepped back as the assailant moved forward.

In the darkness Brick could make out the two crew members silently coming up behind the man who held the grenade in one hand and a large knife in the other. One of the crew members leaped forward and coshed the man over the head with such force that the attacker stumbled.

The other crew member tried to grab the grenade, but the man was holding on too tight. As he stumbled, his arms high in the air, trying to regain his balance, Brick sprang into action. He grabbed him, keeping his eye on the grenade, and in a burst of strength and anger, lifted him high above his head and threw him overboard so fiercely that he spun through the air before landing in the sea. As he hit the black water, the grenade exploded.

Brick shook violently as he walked to the railing. He turned on the light of his gas mask and saw immediately that the waters around the yacht had turned crimson red. Bits of arms, legs, and other body parts were floating to the surface of the bloodied sea. As he stared in amazement, stunned by the lucky escape they'd just had, the other crew members came and stood by his side. They were silent too, and as they all stared into the ocean, they saw sharks circling, ready to have a very good meal.

Meanwhile, at the stern of the yacht, things were going more to plan. Richard and James stayed out of sight, disappearing into the darkness, dressed in their black clothing, balaclavas hiding their faces. They were completely invisible to the naked eye.

As the assailant climbed the rope and began to lever himself onto the deck, James surprised him. With a quick move, he had the lean stranger in a stranglehold before either of his feet had a chance to touch the floor. Richard wrestled him to the ground, and within minutes, they had plastic ties around both his arms and legs. He was trussed up like a helpless chicken, his eyes darting around wildly as Richard put gaffer's tape over his mouth to silence him. Then they blindfolded him. They looked at each other, amazed at how easily they'd managed to overpower their attacker.

Brick came running toward them, panting breathlessly as he spoke. "How's everything on your end? Looks like you've managed to deal with things well. Unlike me—my guy's dead and being eaten by sharks as we speak."

He filled Richard and James in as his breathing returned to normal. As they listened, they noticed their man wriggling, trying hard to undo the plastic ties around his wrists.

"Let's get him to the stern. I left the other two crew members there; we need to interrogate him quickly. I'll get hold of Charles."

Soon enough, they had their guy tied to a chair. His blindfold was removed, and his eyes moved quickly from left to right as he tried to see the shapes in front of him. Fear radiated from his every pore. All five men stood before him in a threatening fashion. Richard ripped the tape from his mouth and started to question him.

"I speak no English. Please, I don't understand!" the man wailed.

Brick moved forward and grabbed his hair so forcefully that his head snapped backward and looked as if it would break from his body. He held a razor-sharp knife to the man's throat and slowly began to run the blade along his outstretched neck. Blood started to trickle from the line Brick was carving. The man began to tremble.

"Now you listen to me, you piece of shit; I'll continue to run this blade around your neck, going deeper and deeper until your fucking head falls on the floor. Do. You. Understand. English. Now?"

With that, Brick cut deeper and harder into the man's throat.

"Stop! Stop! I can speak a little English. Please stop!"

Brick took the knife away and motioned to Richard to get some rags to stem the flow of blood from the man's neck.

"Right. Now, before we get you seen by our doctor, you need to answer one very easy question. Do you understand me?"

The man nodded his head wildly. He seemed delighted to hear a doctor would be called.

"Yes, I understand."

"Good. Now, how were you and your friend going to let the rest of your team know that you'd accomplished your part of the job, and what was that job?"

"Once we got on board, we were to use gas canisters to knock you out. We had grenades in our waterproof bags to use in emergencies." The man motioned to a large bag lying in the corner of the deck. "Then we were to set off flares, let them know things were done, and they would come on their boat with more gas to knock everyone else out. We only wanted to get one man. We did not want to hurt anyone—I promise. Just one man was wanted."

"How many more men are coming? And who is the man you want?"

"There are fourteen more men. We all come aboard at different times. My friend and me first. We are best divers, so we swim furthest. The rest follow. The man we want is called Antonio Cadiz."

# Chapter Forty-Eight

Domingo, still chewing the end of his dirty, rotten cigar, was very calm and deep in thought. Perhaps the drink had taken its toll at long last. Rodriguez, on the other hand, felt deep down in his bones that something was wrong. He felt uneasy.

Juan sat by his father, who was still sitting in his favourite chair. "Dad, they should have made contact with us by now, don't you think? And I swear I heard an explosion. I'm worried."

"Son, you think and worry too much. Be like your old dad. Don't worry about a thing. All that worry will kill you."

With that, Domingo went into one of his coughing fits, spitting phlegm inches from where they sat.

Suddenly, two flares hit the sky, equidistantly apart, just as it had been planned. Both ends of the yacht had been secured!

"You see, son, you worry for no reason. Guys, let's get the boat ready. We're on our way to being very rich!"

# Chapter Forty-Nine

James picked up the nearest phone and called Charles. "We've got someone here you might want to meet. Everything's under control. Brick had a hiccup, but nothing for you to worry about. The flares have been set off. We're anticipating the rest of them turning up within the next thirty minutes or so. Fourteen more of them are coming, boss."

"Thanks, James. I'm on my way."

Within minutes, Charles arrived. He was dressed like everyone else, head to toe in black. He walked silently around the frail-looking Brazilian, who sat trembling on a chair, hands and legs tied. The blood was still trickling from his neck, making him look very pale and drained.

Richard filled Charles in on the entire goings-on; Charles listened silently, not taking his eyes off the captured man.

"So you and your friends wanted to take me hostage, did you? Hefty reward, I assume. Thanks for telling my men all about your plans. I bet the fourteen others who are on their way will be delighted to know you're a grass."

Charles spoke calmly and quietly. The Brazilian looked confused. His words sounded menacing, but his tone didn't. Charles began to circle the man.

"What am I to do with you? Perhaps we need to get the doctor to look at that neck of yours. Or shall we let you slowly bleed to death? Or better still, shall we wait for your friends to arrive and tell them you grassed them up under the first bit of pressure? What do you think I should do, Richard? James? Brick, any ideas?"

No one answered. Everyone seemed confused by Charles's reaction to the man sitting before him.

Charles continued to walk slowly around the Brazilian, and just as he faced him for the umpteenth time, he pulled a semiautomatic rifle from the inside pocket of his black jacket. He calmly lifted the weapon and sprayed a round of bullets directly into the body and head of the frightened man. The Brazilian wriggled wildly as the bullets penetrated him, and then he slumped forward and moved no more.

James, Richard, and Brick were glued to the floor where they stood. They had never seen such a cold and callous side to Charles. They were absolutely stunned.

"OK, men; get his body off the ship. I expect it won't be long now till the others arrive. We all ready to take them on?"

"Sure thing, boss," came the rather guarded reply.

Charles walked off, leaving the three men staring blankly at one another. Brick broke the silence.

"What the fuck just happened there? Man, I knew he could be mean, but that just took the biscuit. Never saw it coming…I'll get rid of the body, and then we need to get ready quickly. They'll be here soon."

\*\*\*

Domingo and Rodriguez gathered up all the weapons they had and placed them in accessible areas on the boat. Their motors were running at full throttle as they sped toward their target.

\*\*\*

Meanwhile, Roger had one job left to do before everyone had to be on full alert, ready for the approaching enemy. This job bothered him more than any other. He had been fond of Barbara, and what lay ahead made him feel sick to his stomach.

He made his way down to the morgue where Dr. Mark Gardener was waiting for him.

"I've got her ready for you. I think deck three is an ideal place; she can be hidden by the lifeboats until the time is right for her to be found. I don't envy you, Roger. If Charles had asked me to do this, I don't know what I'd have done."

"Guess that's the way you can judge the loyalty of your captain. And I am a loyal man…anyway, Mark, there's little time. Can you bring her to me? I'll use the staff lift. Everyone's in their positions, so I won't be seen."

Within moments, Roger was in the lift, standing by the covered body of Barbara. He had an overwhelming urge to take a look at her, and as he removed the crisp white sheet to show her face, he was taken aback. She looked beautiful. She was as he remembered her; the freezing and embalming oils had kept her perfectly preserved.

Once on deck three, Roger lifted Barbara's fully clothed body from the gurney. She was very light and very cold. He gently placed her behind a lifeboat, and using the pillow she'd been lying on, covered her face. He lifted the pistol and with shaking hands pulled the trigger. He did the same to her body, keeping his eyes away from her at all times. Then he silently walked away, taking the gurney back to the morgue.

It was only after he'd done all this that his body began to react. He shook violently and threw up, emptying all the contents of his stomach. Then he staggered back toward the bridge. He had a ship to run and a boss to take care of. This had to be his priority now. He reminded himself that Barbara had gone a long time ago.

Within minutes of Roger's arriving at the helm feeling rather unwell, the chief navigator called out to his captain.

"Our attackers are about one nautical mile away; I've been tracking their approach. But sir, there appears to be another unidentified vessel gaining on them."

Roger immediately got onto his loudspeaker.

"Mayday, Mayday! Take your positions!"

He looked closely at the surveillance screen. It appeared the vessel steaming toward them was sporting a Brazilian flag.

"Keep a close eye on them; see if you can find out who the boat's registered to. It looks as if it could be a government flag, but whatever it is, it's certainly not friendly at the speed it's travelling toward us…or them."

Inside their hiding place, Karmen was beginning to panic. She felt as if the small space around them was closing in on her. Josephine was scared, but claustrophobia wasn't her problem. The only calm person was Caroline.

"Karmen, stop panicking. You're making me nervous. Caroline, have you got something to give her to take the edge off?"

"You know what, Josephine? I should have been more prepared, but I didn't think to bring my medical bag, and I should have."

Caroline put her arms around both women and held them tight.

"It'll be all right. I promise. We've got to stay quiet and calm. We can do this, girls."

Very slowly, both Karmen and Josephine relaxed. They stopped thinking about what was going on above them and allowed Caroline to take care of them.

# Chapter Fifty

Domingo was standing at the helm of his boat as it sped toward its target. The wind was blowing through his matted hair, and he chewed violently on his unlit cigar, feeling slightly concerned that the divers hadn't made radio contact with him as agreed. But they had set off the flares, and being the laid-back drunk he was, he assumed it was nothing more than bad satellite connections.

As the *Golden Eagle* came into view, he gave the signal to cut the engines. He didn't want to arrive in advance of his bosses.

"Son, can you see the other boat anywhere around us?"

"Yeah, Pa, they're making their way toward us as we speak. I've been in contact with them, and they're ready to take transfer of AC as soon as we have him in our possession."

Silently, Domingo and his crew edged closer and closer to the *Golden Eagle* as it idled in the dark waters. His men had done a fine job so far. The gas had worked, rendering the night crew useless and allowing them to take over the bridge and stop the yacht's engines. And now it was stage two. He loved it when his plans materialised.

When they were near enough for the next team of divers to go and assist their colleagues, Domingo signalled that it was time. All six men took their instructions and dived into the ice-cold sea. They swam under water until they reached the ropes that hung on either end of the yacht just as planned, ready and waiting for them to climb aboard and finish the job.

One by one, they removed their guns, gas canisters, gas masks, and radios from their plastic containers and nimbly began to climb.

Domingo, Juan, Rodriguez, and five other crew members remained on board, waiting for the next stage of the operation to play out. Then the final part of the job would come. The end was nearly in sight.

# Chapter Fifty-One

Charles locked himself inside his cabin. Soon enough, blood would be flowing; he hoped for all their sakes it wasn't theirs. He decided to open the safe and take a look at his magnificent collection of diamonds. He hadn't seen them in a while, and he needed to look and touch them. They were, after all, what everything had been about.

He poured himself a large Scotch and took half a pill. He'd been reducing his intake gradually, as he knew he needed his mind to be clearer than it had been in recent weeks. He needed his wits about him. He removed the trays of diamonds and placed them on the dining-room table. Their immense sparkle lit up his eyes.

Hello, my precious belongings, he thought. You're all I've got left. Everyone's looking for me, wanting my head. My wife and child are dead. I have nothing. But while I have you, I can always buy a new, safe life.

One by one, he cleaned each stone, using the special cleaning cloth that had been a gift from his great friend, the famous diamond dealer Carl Finkelstein.

He wondered where he was and what he was up to. Knowing Carl, he was probably with a gorgeous, leggy black girl—or two—having the time of his life. Charles smiled to himself as he thought of his friend and the wonderful times they'd shared. Maybe once this was all over, they'd meet up again. He truly hoped so.

As he rubbed the gems, removing oily finger marks, they glistened, throwing out rainbows of colour. He was just returning the last diamond gently to its tray when he heard a louder-than-usual bang on the door to his suite. He pressed the security monitor and saw a tall man dressed from head to toe in black pacing furiously outside his cabin.

Why the fuck hadn't he been informed that the attackers had boarded the yacht? he wondered impatiently.

He rushed to the dining-room table and stacked his collection of diamond trays one on top of the other, too high to put back inside the safe.

The banging was getting louder and harder. The assailant was on the verge of breaking down the door.

Where the fuck was everybody? Charles thought to himself wildly.

He had little time before this imposter would be through the door. So instead of placing the diamonds back inside the large safe with many dials to turn, he rushed to his bedroom and put the trays in the large space below his bed. He knew time wasn't on his side.

Charles crept to the front door and waited until the intruder had his back turned. Holding a heavy bronze statue in his hand, he quietly opened the door and dived, smashing the man with all his strength. One massive blow to the back of the skull did the trick.

The man stumbled, dropping his weapon to the floor. His hands immediately rose to hold either side of his injured head. Charles grabbed him and dragged him inside, kicking the door shut as he did so.

Blood began to pour through the balaclava that covered the man's face.

"Who are you?" shouted Charles as he ripped the balaclava from the man's head. Blood gushed everywhere. The man stared, bewildered, as he lay on the floor.

"I speak very little English. Please leave me alone."

Charles picked him up by the scruff of his neck, nearly choking him in the process. "Who sent you? If you don't answer me, I'll kill you, right here and now. Do you understand? Speak to me. Speak!" Charles was raging. His eyes bulged like a madman's.

"I work on this yacht. For five years. I'm a steward. I clean. My brother asked me to help him. I'm Brazilian, and we help our families whenever they ask. Please don't hurt me anymore."

"Who's your brother? What are you helping him with?"

"He told me that the owner of this yacht was going to be worth millions of dollars. He is a bad man, my brother. Me, I'm a good man, but I said I would help him. He is my family. I have to help. He and his friends are coming to get you. He paid me one thousand dollars, and once they take you away, I'd get another thousand. I just had to catch you off guard and tie you up, ready for them. Please let me go. I will disappear. You never see me again. Please."

Charles knew he was wasting his time on this man who lay coiled, pathetically, bleeding all over his beautiful white carpet. He walked calmly to the sideboard, opened a drawer and removed a revolver, then looked the man straight in the eye and spoke.

"When you play games for money, it gets dangerous."

Charles pulled the trigger and shot the intruder directly between the eyes.

At such close range, the man's head exploded like an overripe watermelon smashed with a hammer. Blood and brains splattered everywhere.

"No one messes with Antonio Cadiz. No one!" Charles screamed in anger at the dead body as he picked up the in-house phone.

"James, get to my cabin right away!" There was no asking politely. This was an order.

Minutes later, James arrived. "Charles, what's the problem?"

"Don't have one anymore. Come and see for yourself."

James stared in disbelief. "What the fuck happened? Who is he?"

"He was a piece of shit who's been working on my yacht for five fucking years, that's who he is, and he's in cahoots with the gang of people about to attack us. One of them apparently was his brother. James, get the body out of here and get the walls and carpets cleaned. We need to find out if there are any more spies working for me. I thought I had a great security team. Seems I was badly fucking mistaken."

"I'll get everything sorted, trust me. But Charles, right now, we've got bigger things to worry about. We need to get ourselves ready. It won't be long till the others come. We have to be totally prepared for our attackers."

The two men walked through the damaged door. Charles made sure he locked it, and they went to get themselves ready for the action that lay ahead.

# Chapter Fifty-Two

Three divers climbed nimbly up the ropes that hung securely at either end of the yacht. They were dressed completely in black; in the darkness it was hard to see them, but the navigation team had picked the six men up on the CCTV monitors.

"OK, men, let's go and take these bastards down!" Charles was ready to lead his team – also dressed in black, gas masks on their heads, guns loaded and knives at the ready – to the bow of the lower deck.

Mark took his group to the other end of the same deck. They knew exactly where the enemy was hiding.

Charles's and Mark's men moved quickly, quietly, and lightly. They needed the assailants to believe that the first two attackers had used their gas effectively and that most of the people on board were down for the count.

Meanwhile, Domingo received the message that the six divers had boarded the silent yacht, and everything was ready for his last few men to board. He gave the signal for Juan to go full speed ahead toward the *Golden Eagle*.

Within minutes their boat pulled up alongside the yacht.

Rodriguez threw a rope expertly, and its hook caught the bottom-deck railings perfectly, just as planned. The last five men, who were agile but not divers, scrambled up, one after the other, like a group of chimpanzees.

Charles, James, Richard, and Brick, along with five burly security-staff members, inched their way along the silent deck, weapons adorning their bodies, ready for action.

Suddenly, Charles stopped, raising his hand to let the others know something was amiss.

A thick grey smoke began to swirl toward them.

"Gas masks! Now!" he ordered, as quietly as possible.

At the other end of the yacht in complete silence, Mark and his eight men were crawling along the floor, gas masks on, inching their way through the toxic fumes.

Suddenly, shots were being fired from all directions, lighting up the darkness. Bullets ricocheted from wall to wall.

Both ends of the yacht were under attack.

Richard saw two assailants just in front of him with their masks on and firearms raised. "James, cover me." His voice was muffled by the gas mask, but James heard him and nodded.

Richard crawled along the floor like a cat looking for its prey. He held his automatic weapon in front of him and fired randomly, as soon as he saw movement.

Bodies fell to the ground as smoke surrounded them all.

Mark and his team could see their own men clearly by the fluorescent paint that lit up their gas masks. So any movements shrouded in darkness were absolute targets. Gunfire came from everywhere.

Meanwhile, on the bridge, Roger and the navigation team watched the cameras closely. They saw a man wearing a fluorescent gas mask fall. It was obvious that men were being killed and one of theirs had definitely been hit.

"Christ, how long till the marine police get here? I called them as soon as the attack began, just as Charles instructed me," said Roger.

"Sir, just received a message. The authorities are on their way. They've called for reinforcements. Should be here within minutes.

"They also said another vessel is circling us in the distance. They managed to put a trace on them, and it seems to be a ship owned by a known Brazilian drug-smuggling gang."

"Shit. Let's pray the police get here before everyone's killed. It's bedlam down on the lower deck. Just hope it's their men rather than ours taking all those bullets."

On the lower deck, from close behind them in the darkness and smoke, shouts came.

"Don't move, or you're dead men. Drop your weapons and slowly put your hands in the air. Now!"

Charles, Richard, and James heard the reloading of guns and cautiously did as they were told. A couple of shots were fired above their heads as they turned around, holding their hands high in the air, gas masks covering their faces.

There before them, wearing their gas masks too, as the poisonous fumes swirled around them all, they saw their assailants. Anyone watching could have mistaken it for a comedy sketch. But it was deadly serious.

"Which one of you is Antonio Cadiz?" The man who spoke waved his revolver at each person standing before him.

"There's nobody by that name aboard this yacht. You've got it completely wrong. You need to look elsewhere. We're just a group of friends travelling together in our retirement. Now get off this vessel." Charles spoke calmly but with immense authority.

"You! You, man, are a comedian. Now keep your hands in the air, or I'll shoot your fucking brains out."

The person speaking was clearly the leader of the group. In Brazilian, he gave orders to the other men. Suddenly, Charles, Richard, and James were having their hands tied. They were violently pushed along the lower deck by the men who had absolute control over them, and they all felt immense fear. Richard wondered where Brick and the rest of the group had gone. James prayed they weren't dead.

As they passed a stairwell, shots were fired. A couple of the assailants were hit and fell screaming. But the other attackers fired back, and the three men found themselves being forced up to the deck above.

Within minutes, they were flung into a cabin, guns aimed at their heads. And because their hands were tied, they couldn't do anything about anything. They were prey, vulnerable, scared, and helpless.

Once inside the cabin, the leader gave the order to remove the balaclavas and masks covering the three men's faces. "Now I can see who you are." He spoke decent English, though with a strong Brazilian accent. "Don't play games with me. Which one of you is Antonio Cadiz?"

He was staring at a photograph, scrutinizing the faces before him.

"Speak. I'm running out of patience. I'll shoot all of you if you don't tell me."

Richard spoke up, his voice quivering. "We don't know an Antonio Cadiz."

The leader gave him an ice-cold stare. Pulling out a gun, he pointed at Richard's head and fired. The shot missed by an inch and hit the wall behind where the three men were standing. He walked up and down, studying their faces for a few moments and then stopped, staring directly into Charles's eyes.

"You are Antonio Cadiz. You've had surgery, but it's you. I see your eyes. Now answer me, or I'll shoot your two friends in the head and kill them both. Tell me!" He was waving his gun around like a crazed man.

Charles thought for a moment. He couldn't put Richard's and James's life at risk, but he realised the man before him wasn't sure if he was Antonio Cadiz or not. And it would be no good for him and his gang to take the wrong person. There'd be no reward for any of them if they got it wrong. Knowing the authorities were on their way, he spoke slowly and purposefully, trying to buy time.

"OK, I'm your man. Just let my friends go, and I'll do as you say. Where are you taking me?"

"Now that's better," came the reply. "At last, we talk the same language. You come with us off this vessel; there is a large reward on your head. No one is interested in your friends. So come now, and they'll be fine. You sure you're the famous Cadiz?"

"Quite sure. When your bosses fingerprint me, they'll know you've done a good job, got the right man. Now please, let my friends leave the cabin."

James and Richard stared as Charles walked forward to go with the group of men, who were all pointing their weapons at his head.

Suddenly, the seas were ablaze with powerful spotlights.

Speedboats with automatic weapons perched on their bows came from all directions. Flashing blue lights surrounded the yacht. Commands were shouted through loudspeakers.

The assailants saw and heard the commotion and began to panic, grabbing Richard and James and pushing them out of the cabin, along with Charles, who hoped his captain had managed to get the authorities to them in time.

As the Brazilians shouted instructions to one another, they forced the three men up to the next deck.

Brick was patiently waiting inside a storage cupboard, his gas mask removed and his Uzi automatic weapon fully loaded, with the catch unlocked, ready for action. He'd seen the men coming from the deck below and taken cover.

Just as they passed, he made his move. Opening the cupboard door carefully, gun raised, he shouted at the top of his voice. "Stop right there. Put your hands in the air." He jumped toward the group, taking a roll along the corridor in true commando style, landing firmly on his strong legs, only feet away from the assailants.

They in turn grabbed Charles, James and Richard.

It was a stalemate.

James and Richard had their hands tied and guns aimed at their temples. They stood staring at Brick, his automatic weapon pointing in their direction. Charles was in a headlock, the leader of the group looking straight at the enormous man standing before him.

"Put your weapon down now, or these three will be executed right here, right now!" As he spoke he twisted his arm tighter around Charles's throat, causing him to wince in pain, as his legs buckled beneath him.

Brick stood his ground, his muscles flexing. He felt powerful, strong. Adrenaline pumped through his veins.

"I've got an automatic weapon in my hands, and I don't care who I kill. I'll put a round of lead in your head, along with your mates. You'll all be dead in seconds, and I don't give a fuck! Now let him go."

"You think I'm frightened, Mr. Tight Ass?"

"My name is Brick, shithead. Don't play fucking games with me."

Beads of sweat were forming on the Brazilian's brow. Brick stared into the eyes of the man who stood before him and knew he had the upper hand. He was in control, and he loved the feeling.

He gave James and Richard a reassuring look that spoke volumes. Having been friends for quite a while now, it was easy to understand his message. They were all on the same page, ready and waiting…

Charles was getting weaker; the force around his neck and throat was making it hard for him to breathe.

"Let him go, or I'll shoot him, and then you'll have a dead man on your hands, who'll prove useless to you. A dead man's worth nothing; surely you know that." Brick stared directly into the Brazilian's eyes, not flinching as he spoke, aiming his weapon at Charles.

Slowly the assailant released his grip, and Charles collapsed onto the deck like a rag doll, coughing and spluttering.

In an instant, Brick darted away and made his move, firing a round of bullets from his automatic weapon into the bodies of those surrounding him.

James and Richard had taken cover while protecting Charles, who still lay on the floor.

One by one the attackers dropped, like flies being swatted.

Brick quickly untied James's hands, and James released Richard's. They dragged Charles into a corner, far away from any more shooting.

It was obvious that Brick had received expert training, and his agile, fit body moved with lightning speed. Minutes later, there was silence.

Charles was slowly coming back to the land of the living, dazed and blurry eyed.

"Christ, that was close." He spoke to Richard quietly, his voice hoarse and croaky.

Brick was walking around the deck, weapon held out in front of him, turning quickly from left to right, kicking the bodies that lay scattered around to make sure they were all dead. After a while, it was clear. No man who had been shot had any life left in him.

James and Richard leaned over the side of the yacht, staring out across the sea, trying to register what had just happened.

More blue lights came into view. Reinforcements were arriving. Some of the speeding vessels went off in other directions, and the men could see the marine police were circling and surrounding two smaller boats.

Charles and Brick walked over to where Richard and James stood.

"Let's hope Mark and his guys have been as lucky as we were," said Charles. "I can't hear anything coming from the stern, so with a bit of luck, it's over for them too. Brick's disposed of any possessions that could identify these guys. It won't be long till the police board, so we should go and find the others, see what's happened. We need to take our weapons, just in case we come across any more of these bastards who are still alive. And Brick, thank you. You saved our lives."

"All in a day's work, boss," came Brick's reply.

The four men made their way slowly along the deck as blue flashing lights and loudspeakers interrupted the silence and darkness that had overtaken the *Golden Eagle*.

The girls were huddled together, frightened to say a word. The shooting and noise above had stopped. There was silence.

Josephine was the first to speak, whispering, "Should we leave here and go see what's happened?"

"What if the pirates have taken over the yacht? It could be a trap to draw us out. I think we should wait. What do you think?" Karmen looked pleadingly at Caroline, hoping she'd agree.

"Let me go and investigate. If there are any pirates up there, I'll be seen as a member of staff in my nurse's uniform, and you never know, I might be needed. I can find out what's happened to everyone. I'll come back and let you know what's going on. You two stay here, and I'll be back soon. OK?"

They nodded their approval, and Caroline opened the heavy door very slowly and carefully, making sure she made no noise to attract any attention. She had no idea who was on board and needed to be extremely careful. After inching her way along for a while, Caroline neared the lower decks, leaving the bow of the yacht behind. She was darting in and out of little alcoves, wishing she had a torch, as everything was in total darkness.

Eventually she came to one of the staircases at the stern of the yacht that led to the decks above. She began walking very carefully up the stairs, trying hard not to stumble.

As she moved, she waved her hands in front of her to make sure she didn't bump into anything. Her feet hit a large object that was blocking her way. She bent down to see what it was, and as her eyes strained in the darkness and her hands investigated, she realised it was a body, limp and lifeless. Feeling for a pulse in the neck of the victim, she confirmed to herself that this person's life was over.

Caroline's hand touched another object lying nearby. She picked it up. It was a flashlight. She fumbled to get it to work. She held the light over the body, her heart racing wildly. She looked into the face of the stranger who lay before her and shuddered as she saw a gaping hole right in the centre of his forehead. Blood had seeped completely from his body, indicating the presence of other gunshot wounds. The white soft carpets that surrounded her had turned a deep crimson. Bile rose in her throat as she climbed over the dead man, making her way upward.

With the flashlight stretched out in front of her, Caroline made quick progress. Soon she was opening the door that led out to the deck. A few dim lights were on, so she put the light away and continued to creep quietly, keeping herself as close to the walls as possible. She heard no noise, but as she turned the corner, she saw carnage.

Bodies were lying all over the deck, pools of blood staining the wooden floors.

Caroline began to tremble as she passed corpse after corpse, eyes wide, staring back at her in horror. It was as if they had seen their death coming in their final seconds, taking one last breath.

So far, the faces she looked at were strangers to her. Then she found herself staring at Seon the barman, a bottle of five-year-old whiskey lying by his side. She gasped, then gently closed his eyes, and moved on in silence.

Some people were known to her—a couple of the security guards and some of the housekeeping men—but more were unknown.

There was no doubt in her mind. The battle that had taken place here was well and truly over.

Suddenly, she heard some voices, speaking quietly, coming toward her. She dropped to the floor, and as she did, she found herself staring into the face of her beloved Mark. He lay right by her side.

She gasped. "Oh no, no! Oh my God, please tell me no! Mark!" She screamed out loud as she buried her face into the bloodied chest that lay lifeless.

"Caroline, Caroline…Oh no. Not Mark." Charles came running to her side, putting his arms gently around her heaving body.

"You three go and see if any of our men have made it. Remove documents from the others. It won't be long before the marine police are here."

Richard, James, and Brick stood staring down at the doctor.

"Now! Go! We don't have much time. I'm here with Caroline."

# Chapter Fifty-Three

"Put your hands up!" The Bahrain police had now begun to board Domingo's vessel, dressed in white suits with lots of gold regalia and holding submachine guns in their hands.

Instructions were blaring out in English from loudspeakers on the ships that surrounded the craft.

Rodriguez and Juan remained still, arms in the air. They knew they were outnumbered. The game was over.

"Are you the owner of this boat?" The policeman had only a gun strapped to his waist band. He was surrounded by others holding guns high in the air to protect him.

"No, he isn't. I am." Domingo sauntered over with a swagger, cigar hanging loosely from his lips, brandy bottle in hand. "What do you want from us? Why are you boarding my vessel?"

"Sir, we've impounded another craft one nautical mile from here. We've been tracking it for some time. It's a known drug-smuggling vessel, registered to the Brazilian Mafia. We've been listening in on your communications with this ship. Does "J" register with you? A code name, we assume. As we speak, the Bahrain and Qatar authorities are making a search of that vessel, and we wish to search this boat now for drug smuggling, along with possible piracy."

Domingo began to get aggressive. "I'm no fucking drug smuggler. Now get off my ship!" He swigged from his bottle, wiping the excess from his mouth on the back of his filthy shirt sleeve. "I've never been involved in trafficking drugs. Now, all of you, fuck off!"

"Dad, calm down."

"Fuck off, boy!" Domingo was raging, his bottle swinging in all directions.

"Sir, I suggest you stop being so aggressive—"

Before the policeman had a chance to finish his sentence, Domingo had smashed the bottle and lunged toward him, grinding the glass into his face. Bullets rang out in unison. Domingo wriggled and fell in a heap.

The policeman screamed as blood poured from his once-handsome face. His uniform turned from white to red in seconds; his colleagues rushed for towels to try and stop the bleeding.

Juan and Rodriguez stood, shaking, holding their hands high in the air.

Everyone on the Brazilian vessel had been arrested. There had been no casualties. Drugs had been seized, and everyone on board knew they'd probably die in a Bahraini prison.

Judith had been identified as J, the person keeping in contact with Domingo and his motley crew. The Bahraini police were dumbfounded that she was a woman and assumed it was all about drugs. There was no connection whatsoever to an attempted abduction.

That's how it had to remain. Any more indictments against them would lead to a death sentence for sure.

No one had any idea that "J" had worked and was still working for the CIA. She had been double-crossing them and the Brazilian Mafia for years. Neither organization had a clue.

This was to have been her last money-making scheme, and then she and Doris were to go home. Home to the safety of the United States, home to the safety of the CIA, with enough money to last a lifetime.

But that was all over now. Judith accepted that her good fortune had run out and prayed Doris would survive without her.

Back on board the *Golden Eagle*, crew members were coming out of their hiding places. All the attackers had died, but only a handful of Charles's men had perished in the battle.

Caroline was given a Valium, and she slept fitfully.

Karmen and Josephine were reunited with Richard and James.

The carnage that had occurred was clear for all to see. The Bahrain and Qatar authorities had boarded the *Golden*

*Eagle* with military efficiency, each officer carrying a weapon, but it was clear they'd arrived too late.

They were amazed that these untrained civilians had managed to disarm and kill the pirates by themselves, with no assistance from the marine police. One officer said it was remarkable that they had lost so few of their own in the process.

Captain Roger Cookson allowed the authorities to search the yacht and identify all the remaining crew and registered guests. The pirates were removed, and those bodies belonging to the yacht were taken to the ship's morgue, including that of Barbara Garcia, the wife of the registered owner Charles Garcia.

The authorities completely understood that the owner of the *Golden Eagle* was in terrible shock.

"Please pass on our sincere condolences to your boss. We will, of course, need to speak with him. Maybe tomorrow? Would that be suitable, Captain?

"Once we've left and taken the corpses with us, you can arrange for this beautiful yacht to be cleaned up. On behalf of the Bahrain and Qatar governments, we wish to thank you for the magnificent way you've all handled this dreadful situation, and we are saddened that it had to happen in our waters."

The two men shook hands and agreed there would be a meeting the following day.

# Chapter Fifty-Four

Charles had showered, and as he removed his diamonds from under the bed, he smiled to himself.

He really couldn't have wished for things to have gone better. No one suspected a thing, and besides a few employees losing their lives, it really had worked out quite well.

Shame about Mark Gardener, he thought. He wasn't a bad man—a fool but not a bad person. He hadn't deserved to die.

Charles knew he had to move on and stop thinking of the people who had died. He had to begin his new life. Tomorrow, after meeting with the authorities, he would speak to Carl Finkelstein and make his plans.

He wondered how Caroline was doing. She was such a strong woman; even after she found out that Mark had intended to return to his ex-wife and family, she hadn't flinched. She carried on with her duties on board and was genuinely distressed by Mark's death, even though she had felt betrayed by him.

Mark had no idea she had read the messages that had been passing between him and his ex for a number of weeks.

Caroline was the ultimate professional, in every sense of the word.

She hadn't mentioned a thing to anyone else, except Charles, in a moment of weakness, and he had kept the secret to himself. He decided Mark was an absolute idiot to have even contemplated leaving her to go back to his old life.

But once Caroline knew of his betrayal, there was no doubt in her mind that Mark was not the man for her. She had been biding her time before she told him. But now it didn't matter. His life was over. Charles would inform his family of their loss in the morning. Hopefully, after a good night's sleep, Caroline would be feeling better and stronger.

Charles poured himself a drink, put his trays of diamonds into the safe, and stepped out onto his balcony. His silver-grey hair blew in the evening's gentle breeze. He pulled his white terrycloth robe tightly around himself and felt a warmth flood through his veins as he drank his whiskey.

He looked out at the calm, peaceful waters. A thousand stars twinkled majestically in the immense darkness that encased him and his yacht. He realised how small he was in comparison to the universe that he inhabited. Caroline appeared before him; he heard her throaty voice, and he smiled. She made him smile.

The next morning, the seas were glistening as the sun beat down on the still waters.

On the top deck, James and Richard were finishing their coffee. Charles walked in and joined them. No one said a word as they stood looking out at the crystal-clear waters, all of them thinking of the last twenty-four hours. It seemed unreal that so much chaos had occurred; so many lives lost and now…quiet.

Charles broke the silence.

"Look at this fantastic view. It's paradise. Who could believe what happened yesterday was even real?"

"Sometimes, Charles, things just happen. They're out of our control. We've come through it, we've survived, and that's all that matters."

"I know, Richard, you're right. You two, you're like my brothers. I love you both."

Charles turned to James and Richard, and the three men hugged one another. As they did, they felt the stress of the previous night's chaos seep away. They all felt immensely emotional and just managed to keep their tears at bay.

Charles composed himself.

"Guys, I've been making some decisions. I've spoken to the captain, and he's contacted the designers of this yacht. They've agreed to come down tomorrow. They're in their private jet. I'm not sure yet of their ETA, but they'll take a helicopter from the airport and land here on our helipad sometime in the afternoon. They're going to assess the damage and then arrange to bring the *Golden Eagle* back to its former state. I've told Roger there's to be no expense spared. Everything's to be pristine and beautiful. They may add a few modern twists while they're at it. I want this yacht to be cleansed of the blood and horror that has taken place. It'll take time and money, but I have both."

"Are you overseeing the project, Charles?"

"I was coming to that, James. I've decided I need to get away for a while. I need to get off—take a break. I want you two and your dear wives to stay on board and treat the *Golden Eagle* like your home. Enjoy the yacht, enjoy the staff, enjoy yourselves. The captain is arranging a permanent docking space in deep enough waters so the works can take place. I'd like you to be in charge of the project, along with Brick.

"You'll have use of the helicopter and the jet whenever you need a break, and when I return rested, I want our voyage to continue. No more looking over my shoulder, no more blood and death. Just fun and joy. My friends, life is far too short for anything else. Please speak to the girls and see if they'll agree to my proposal. That is, of course, if you two are happy with my suggestion."

James and Richard looked at each other and smiled. It seemed like a pretty good offer to them.

"I'll take that as a yes. You just need to convince your wives. Tell them the bodies in the morgue will be removed and taken to their respective families to do what is right for them. I'm dealing with Barbara. So the yacht will be free of anything to remind anyone of the goings-on. It will be a new beginning.

"Now, gents, I've got a meeting with the marine police in an hour. I'd like you to be present, so can you go and fill Josephine and Karmen in on our conversation, and join me in the library in, let's say, forty-five minutes?"

"Sure thing, Charles. We'll be there, and by the way, I'm sure the girls will be happy to stay on board."

"Hope so, James."

With that, the men went off in different directions. Charles had a sudden spring in his step and looked far more relaxed than he had in days.

Captain Roger stood at the top of the gangway, smart and professional, as was his way, awaiting the marine authorities' arrival. As arranged, dead on the hour, blue flashing lights appeared, and one by one, a team of equally smart men boarded the *Golden Eagle*. Pleasantries were passed, and the men made their way to the library.

Charles was waiting.

"Good morning, gentlemen. Welcome aboard my yacht. I'm saddened it couldn't have been under more pleasant circumstances. Please may I introduce you to my very good friends James and Richard. These men, along with my bodyguard, Brick, who can't be with us today due to injuries that are thankfully superficial, were by my side throughout the horrific experiences of the evening before last. I know you've met my captain, and he's informed me of the conversation you had yesterday. Please, gentlemen, be seated."

The tallest man began to speak. He had an air of authority about him.

"Mr. Garcia, once again, the Bahrain and Oman governments send their sincere condolences to you and your family and friends for the losses and suffering you've experienced while in our waters. If there's anything we can do to help, please, we are at your service."

"Thank you." Charles's voice was low and sombre; he waited for the conversation to continue, keeping his head down, playing the victim.

"We unfortunately do need to take a statement from you, today. We understand your distress at this time, but it's necessary for us to fill out all the paperwork and allow you and your fellow passengers to move on with your plans. As I mentioned, you have our governments' full and comprehensive support with anything, anything at all."

Once again, Charles answered quietly. "Thank you."

"Now, Mr. Garcia, when you're ready, can you please detail the circumstances leading up to and during the attack? Please, sir, take your time."

Charles began to stroll around the room as he did when he was concentrating.

"We had been monitoring a small vessel for a number of days. It seemed to be following us. The captain and the navigation team had their eyes on things, and I was kept informed. We were all aware that the waters can be rather dangerous for a lone super yacht in certain parts of the world. But I had full faith in my crew. On the evening in question, we noted that the small boat was making significant ground. We were in no hurry, so our speed was negligible. I was told that we were being approached by underwater divers, both fore and aft. My head security man, Brick, is a trained commando officer, and he, along with other security personnel on board, went into action. Our female passengers were sent to the safety of the bow, and within a short space of time, we were all ready for the imminent attack. We didn't know who or why, but I assumed it was piracy, and I believe I was right.

"Once the attack began, we were ready. We took their weapons as they climbed aboard. As they kept coming, we were ready for them. They were very well equipped, and we had no choice but to turn their weapons on them. It was horrific. James, Richard, and I, never having been exposed to such things, worked on impulse and adrenaline. I'm still in disbelief that we survived, but as you know…" Charles placed his hands to his face. His voice faltered as he began to cry.

Richard rushed to his side.

"I'm so, so sorry to push you, Mr. Garcia, but we need you to finish."

Charles turned to Richard and spoke quietly. "Thanks, my friend, I'm OK." He took a deep breath and continued.

"I lost my beloved wife, Barbara; my dear friend Dr. Mark Gardener, the chief medic on board; and a number of very special employees. I know my captain has given you all their names, and you've identified their bodies.

"But through it all, we prevailed. We beat those pirates, those evil men who work in your waters and in waters around this sad world. You must, I beseech you, make sure you continue to get rid of these people, continue the fight. Make my wife's death have some meaning…"

With that, Charles broke down. There was silence. After a while, Charles regained his composure and spoke quietly.

"What can you tell me about these people? You've obviously been questioning those who survived for the last thirty-six hours."

"We have, indeed, and you're right. The smaller boat was a known gang of pirates, working alone at times and with others at other times. Family, most of them, apparently. All crew members of the second boat are now in custody, awaiting trial. They are part of a Brazilian-mafia drug cartel.

"It appears there was a relationship between the pirates and a member of the Brazilian gang known to us only as J. We intercepted coded messages between them for a number of days."

Charles tried to hide his interest.

"J? And what did this J say to the contact on the pirate ship?"

"Unfortunately, we were unable to make sense of what was said at the time, but now that we have her in custody, she says nothing. She is obviously part of the drug cartel. She will never leave prison in Bahrain, so we are prepared to leave it at that. Although I have to say given my experience, I could not believe such a beautiful woman could have been so involved in such badness."

Charles was trying to digest what he was hearing. Doris in love and waiting to get back to the CIA with J, a beautiful woman, working at the same time for the Brazilian Mafia? It made no sense.

"Mr. Garcia, are you all right?"

"Yes, yes, I'm fine. Everything is so overwhelming. When the pirates boarded the yacht, they asked for a man by the name of Antonio Cadiz. A very Brazilian name, I thought at the time. They said he owned the *Golden Eagle* and that if we passed him over, no one would be hurt. We told them I owned the yacht and had no idea who they were talking about. Then things got out of hand. I can only assume it was a question of mistaken identity."

"Yes. We agree with your theory, and there are no survivors from the pirate ship to question. The Brazilians have all been arrested and will remain in prison for life, if they're not executed. I believe the case will be closed. All we need to do now is take statements from your crew, and then we'll leave you in peace. Am I right in saying you'll be remaining here for some time while repairs are being made to your vessel?"

"Yes, that's right. There's a lot of damage that needs to be dealt with, and I thought some upgrading might as well take place at the same time."

"Well, sir, there are two things…first, it will be my government's pleasure to waive any port-authority charges to you for as long as necessary. And if we need to revisit you for any reason, will you be staying on board?"

"That's extremely generous, and thank you. No, I won't be remaining with my friends on the yacht. I need to get away for a while. I need time, time to get over things, but I'm always contactable. If there's anything you need, just speak to my captain."

"Will do, Mr. Garcia. You take care."

The two men shook hands, and the room emptied.

Charles was left standing, James and Richard were sitting, and no one spoke until Richard began to laugh.

"Charles, you were fantastic. I had no idea you could act so well. Bloody brilliant!"

Smiling from ear to ear, Charles replied, "Well, boys, we all have hidden talents, don't we?"

He winked at them and walked out of the library.

Caroline had awoken. She felt groggy but calmer. Was it night or day? she wondered. She had no idea.

Her mind turned to Mark, his eyes staring up at her, gas mask by his side. Thinking about the horrors of that evening, she remembered most of the dead had no masks on. She remembered frightened faces, lifeless, just staring, fear etched deep into their soulless eyes. Perhaps the gas that was used had faded into the night air, and breathing had becoming hard and laboured inside the restriction of the masks. She realised she'd never know the answer. It was over. Done.

She'd never see Mark again, nor would his family. As much as his deceit had crushed her, made her cry silently for nights, he hadn't deserved to die. She had all intentions of telling him that she'd known about his plans for some time but kept putting it off. She couldn't bear the thought of the fight that would have followed, once she allowed her anger toward him to be unleashed. He had betrayed her, and once betrayed, Caroline could never go back. But that didn't matter anymore. It was over. Life had changed; things had changed. She had to move on.

Back in his suite, Charles was calling Carl Finkelstein.

"Finkelstein, you son of a gun, how are you?"

"Charles, my old mate, I'd recognise that voice anywhere." Carl's voice was shrill with excitement, making his South African accent stronger than ever.

The two men chatted, filling each other in on the latest events in their lives. Carl was quiet as Charles told him about Barbara, the attack, and his future plans.

"And I thought my life was exciting. I've got nothing on you, my friend. Biggest thing for me is Shanika. You remember her? The six-foot-tall stunner, massive tits?"

All Carl's women rolled into one, so Charles had no idea who he was talking about.

"Well, she only made me a father again. Twice over. I couldn't fucking believe it. Fucking twins. And at my age. Thank God, I've got money. I put her in an apartment, got her a nanny. She's set for life. They're quite cute really. Two little girls. Maybe you'll see them when you get here."

"Yeah, that'll be great." Charles couldn't think of anything worse, but he didn't want to upset his friend.

"So, Carl, you'll fix me up with your contact? I need to shift a few million dollars' worth of my least favourite diamonds, just to clear a few out. The rest, well, we can talk about them later. I've for sure got plenty of them. And as you know, a number of them are so exquisite we need to really source the buyers well. Could take plenty of time. But you know what, my friend? I'm in no rush."

Once the conversation was over, Charles felt relaxed. He poured himself a large whiskey, took a pill, and crashed out on top of the bed. Life was good.

The next morning, Charles was up bright and early, in top form. He sat on his balcony, having his usual cappuccino with half a pill, washed down with freshly squeezed orange juice. He was definitely cutting down. The rest of the diamonds were packed safely in his small wheelie case and grip bag. He was planning to break the habit of taking the magic pills slowly while he was away. Mark had told him these drugs needed to be weaned out of the system over time. And time he had.

All families of the deceased had been contacted and arrangements made for the bodies to be returned to them. Large amounts of money had been given to them all in recompense for their dreadful losses. Charles felt exonerated.

As far as Barbara was concerned, he would have sent her to her lover J in prison were it not potentially suspicious. He'd even thought of chucking her to the sharks, but instead, she was sent to Carl, supposedly a long-lost uncle, and he was arranging a quick cremation, well in advance of Charles's arrival. Charles was taking his time before he ended up in Cape Town.

With suitcase in hand and a very large grip bag for his diamond collection under his arm, he was ready to go. He'd buy all the things he needed, as and when. He was free. Free for the first time in years.

"Roger, lower the tender. I'm ready to go. Keep in touch. You can send one of the guys to collect it from the dock later. I want to go alone."

"Aye-aye, sir."

"How many times, Roger? How many times?"

"You take care, Charles. I'll be keeping my eyes on everything here, so go and enjoy."

"Will do, my friend."

Charles placed his suitcase in the bench on the left-hand side of the tender, and it was slowly lowered and landed on the water with a splash. Charles took one look behind him, smiled, and jumped confidently into the tender, his grip bag close by his side.

He started the engine.

Suddenly a voice shouted from above. "Room for one more?"

Charles looked up. There was Caroline, smiling the sweetest of smiles. God, she is beautiful, thought Charles.

"Can you jump?" he asked.

"Is the Pope Catholic?" Her sultry Irish voice got him every time.

She jumped, and he caught her in his arms. They both fell backward onto the padded benches.

Her body was lying on top of his as their eyes locked and their lips met. They kissed. The excitement was unbearable for both.

Suddenly, Charles's mobile rang.

"Shit!" Charles fumbled to get it from the pocket of his jeans. Caroline looked at him, eyes twinkling naughtily.

"What?" Charles was stressed.

"Charles, it's only me. Just wanted to tell you the girls have said yes. They're delighted to stay on board."

"That's great, James, really great. Listen, I'm busy, can't talk. Something very important has just popped up!!!"

He winked suggestively at Caroline. She grinned back.

"Have to go."

He looked deeply into her blue eyes as he hung up and threw the mobile to one side.

"Now, where were we before we were so rudely interrupted?"

*The End*